MW01388022

AUNT BECK

# AUNT BECK

BY ROLAND D. MULLINS

OLD SEVENTY CREEK PRESS 2016
ALBANY, KENTUCKY

***To the grandchildren and those yet to come***

Aden, Silas, Celia, Lydia, Clara & Corey

OLD SEVENTY CREEK



**2016 OLD SEVENTY CREEK FIRST EDITION**
PRINTED IN THE UNITED STATES OF AMERICA



PUBLISHED IN THE UNITED STATES BY OLD
SEVENTY CREEK PRESS
RUDY THOMAS, PUBLISHER
P. O. BOX 204 ALBANY, KENTUCKY 42602

**ISBN-13: 978-0692654194**

**ISBN-10: 0692654194**

**COVER ART BY ROSEMARY MATHIEU**

What others have said about *Aunt Beck:*

*Aunt Beck plunges readers into slices of the muddled, funny, sad, brave lives of modern Appalachia's drug culture. With wonderful eloquence, all the characters speak Southern Country Appalachian ... noble and base, smart and addled, brave and cowardly, honest and criminally inclined. Gradually, readers come to rejoice in their hard-won successes, grieve their frequent failures, and come to respect their infinitely human selves. Dickensian with more grit... a wealth of characters*

Henry Bourne, M. D. Professor Emeritus, UCSF
Author of **Paths to Innovation** and **Follow the Money,**
Bourne & Vermillion

*An uncompromising look at the drug problem in Southern Appalachia ... both those who are addicted and those who are called to treat. .. The characterization, especially of the addicts, is fresh and revealing; and the dialect is genuine Eastern Kentucky.*

Jim Broaddus
Professor, Indiana State University (R)
Author, Publications on **Faerie Queene,**
University North Carolina Press

*Not since john Fox, Jr. has an author conveyed such a deep understanding and profound respect for the people of Appalachia, both those who are addicted and those who are called to treat. Mullins expertly explores the stressors of life in isolated communities ... a clear-eyed and empirically-qualified approach to explaining the roots of despair ... a testament to long years of experience and living among those he clearly has the highest regard for. If one has even the most passing interest in Appalachia, in the personalities who inhabit this unique area or in addressing substance abuse anywhere, this book is an invaluable addition to your body of knowledge.*

Captain (Sir) Roger Coldiron, USN
Naval Attache to Denmark (R)

*Aunt Beck explores the tragic consequences of drug abuse and its devastating effect on families throughout Eastern Kentucky. Mullins articulates a hopeful vision by which those who have become slaves to drugs can return to productive lives.*

Honorable Joseph Lambert, Chief Justice,
Kentucky State Supreme Court (R)

Author's note: all characters and/or incidents reported in this book are fictitious; resemblance to any person or to any incident or any location is purely coincidental. However, the picture presented is as accurate as historical experiences and study permit.

# ACKNOWLEGEMENTS

It is not an easy task to thank all who have contributed to the writing of this book—as the number may be legion. My thanks to Rudy Thomas, able editor and publisher for the Old Seventy Creek Press; to my wife Nancy for her patient listening to each chapter as I read to her late into the night, and for her editorial comments; to Carrie Mullins who insisted that it be sent to press; to Bob Amburgey for his reading and commenting and keeping the computer tuned as I wrote; to Dr. Callie Shaffer, and Michael Shaffer who read the manuscript, and encouraged me; to Dr. R. Dyche Mullins who supported the effort and so enjoyed the colloquial phrases that he was long familiar with, and to his wife Jenna Phillips for her support; to Cecil and Ann Hampton for reading and commenting on two of the chapters; to the Kentucky Community Behavioral Health programs that allowed me to serve as CEO and board member for fifty years and the hundreds of training events provided; to the people of Rockcastle County for eighteen years of service, experience, training as Mayor and County Judge-executive; to friends encountered while farming; to all the authors that have meant so much—the Holy Scriptures, Cato, Nabokov, Dostoevsky, Tolstoy, Steinbeck, Harding, Elliot, Cervantes, Stribling, Faulkner and Berry to name but a few; to Hindman Settlement School for providing the atmosphere at their summer writers workshops; and, to my mother Hattie whose avid reading had such an influence on my adult behavior.

# CONTENTS

CHAPTER PAGE

1. THE FINAL CALL 11
2. DEIDRA AND FREDDIE 27
3. REHAB AND BOUNCY LEGGS 33
4. KEITH AND THE TREATMENT TEAM 45
5. OLD MAN BIRDWISTLE 50
6. AMANDA IS LONESOME 56
7. THE CUMBERLAND GAP AND ANN 62
8. HARLAN 78
9. AUNT BECK 86
10. THE BOYS GET BUSTED 97
11. LA PEARL OBSERVES 105
12. EXAMINING RIDDLES 110
13. NEW ENGLANDER IN MIDDLESBORO 116
14. OLD CARL'S SOCIAL SECURITY 124
15. HAMMOCKVILLE 131
16. BECK'S FAMILY BUSINESS 137
17. DEIDRA REPORTS AND ALMOST SHOCKS THE COUNSELOR 142
18. OUR BEST AND ONLY DOCTOR IS OUT OF CONTROL 153
19. AMANDA RUNS AWAY 162
20. AL AWAKENS TO NEW TREATMENT, NEW GOALS 173
21. BECK TAKES ON THE COURTS 180
22. THAD'S INTRODUCTION 188
23. ESCAPING WITH BOUNCY LEGGS 195
24. THE PARTY 206
25. THE LOBBISTS 213
26. THE BOARD MEETING—A CONFLICT OF INTEREST 223
27. FREDDIE GETS A RIDE 227
28. CITY HOSTS BECK'S SALES MEETING 239
29. RENFRO VALLEY WITH ANN, KEITH & AL 248
30. A SECRET PLACE 255

31. DEIDRA'S COMING OUT 261
32. RIDERS UP 268
33. THE CONFESSION
IN DR ANN'S EMERGENCY ROOM 271
34. THE FLORIDA SUNSHINE 275
35. AND ONE MORE MAKES THREE 281
36. THE PRESIDENT SPEAKS 286
37. CARL IS BREAKING BAD 291
38. TWIN MATURITY 309
39. OLD CARL'S KIN 325
40. AMANDA TAKES A TURN
FOR THE WORSE 337
41. FREDDIE AND BUDDY 352

EPILOGUE 373
ABOUT THE AUTHOR 375

## CHAPTER 1

# The Final Call

"Hello." When the phone rang, Beck was peeling shrimp at the sink and thinking—big waters, boat, cruise in that sequence; then about her and Sis taking a cruise, that is, if they could talk somebody into managing their wheel chairs. They could even get matching outfits, possibly a perm.

"Hid'dy, Beck." The voice sounded familiar. It wasn't someone from down at the church or the TV cable man that Beck had waited for all morning. Finally, Beck conjured up the identity, maybe. "Hello. Carl? Is that you? You don't sound like yourself." It had been some time since Beck had talked to Carl. Maybe something is working on him was her first thought. He's a right smart older than my eighty years. Anything could be wrong with him.

"Yeah, it's me, Beck. I've got some powerfully bad news for you and Amanda's mammy." In their phone discussions over the years they had spoken in lowered voices about Amanda, wondering where she was, if she was still alive. Nobody had talked to her since that day a decade ago when she disappeared in Florida, leaving ten year old Freddie Jr. with Beck and her mother; so Beck was wondering why Carl mentioned mother, daughter, and bad news in the same breath.

"What is it, Carl? You ain't heard from Amanda have you?"

"I'm afeerd I have, Beck, and it ain't good. They buried her last year somewhere around Knoxville, Tennessee."

"Buried her? How'd you find this out?" The impact of death hadn't fully struck Beck.

"That ain't all neither. She's here now." With that statement Beck was sure something was wrong with Carl. Poor old feller has lost out completely, she quickly decided. "Carl, listen to me now." Beck raised her voice in case louder speech could penetrate the fog the old fellow was in. "Amanda can't be buried in Tennessee and be there in Kentucky at the same time."

"They dug her up, I reckon." Still wondering about Carl's mental state, she ignored the comment and changed hands and ears with the phone.

"Can I speak to her? Put her on the phone." Beck decided that Amanda might be at Carl or Freddie's.

"She can't talk, Beck. She's dead." Carl wanted to explain but was having trouble getting to the starting point.

"Amanda died sometime back, in Knoxville. The county or somebody buried her 'cause they didn't know nothin' about her or us, or where she was from. It took nearly a year for somebody there to track her here. All they found on her was a picture of her and Freddie, Jr—back when he was a baby. She had wrote his name and age on the back. They brought her body in yesterday mornin'. She's down at Morgan's Funeral home right now. Me and Freddie went to Knoxville ahead the ambulance and identified her. That weren't easy neither."

"Oh, Carl, poor thang died right by herself, no family to care. I could a done so much for that girl." Beck began to wail and dropped the phone, but after gaining control, took up the receiver. "She never did have a lick of sense, you know. We did the best we knowed how with her. How's Freddie taking it, and the boy? Well, he ain't much of a boy now, twenty past, I guess."

"They hate it, I reckon. It's a sad thang. I'd better hang up. Just thought you all'd want to know."

"Carl, I don't know if we can come up or not. Can't neither of us drive now you know; can't walk nowhere but across the room."

"Well, you can just do what you can do. Sometimes thangs just can't be holped." Carl stood from his cane bottom chair as he said this, stretching his left leg, fighting a cramp.

"Bye, Beck. Tell your sister I hated to pass such news." Beck laid her head back in her easy chair, wiped her eyes and hollered her sister in from the den where she had been watching her soaps.

"Sis, I've got some bad news." She hesitated then reached out and took her sister's hand. "Amanda's gone."

"I know that, Beck. She's been gone for years. We ain't heerd hardly a word since she left young Freddie here."

"No, Sis, I mean she is gone, passed on."

"You don't say!" As it finally sank in, Sis's head dropped, her hands covering her face. In her wheel chair and there alone with her only kin, she began crying, her shoulders shaking. "Oh, no, my baby, my only baby is dead, I ain't seen her in years, couldn't offer her a little comfort."

"Now, Sis, you'll have to get hold of yourself. Let me help you back to the den and get you something to drink. Gettin' all tore up won't do, you with your heart ailment." The two rolled and wrestled Sis back in front of the TV. After a glass of tea, they sat silent, each thinking her own thoughts.

"Do you remember that little stuffed toy hound she carried everwhere she went that summer? She must have been about four." Amanda's mother was remembering the child, not the Amanda who had abandoned them, the Amanda with a blue streak in her hair and a ring in her belly button.

"Yes, she had pigtails that summer. I'd braid her hair and put that little red shorts outfit on her. She was so good about staying clean. Never give us a minute's trouble back then." Beck was thinking about the years before Amanda turned twelve: after that she was mostly out of control, disregarding both Beck's and Sis's quarrelling at her not to do this or that. She appeared to have no internal anchor. "She bobbed and floated between bad fixes". That's the way Carl had described her behavior.

"Sis, you go back to watching your programs. I've got some studying to do." The remembrances of Amanda's early childhood began to cast an entirely different light on what Beck thought she and Sis must do, and as always with Beck, a plan emerged.

"Hello, Pastor. This is Sister Beck. We've had a mighty bad family thang to come up." Beck needed help to carry out the plan she'd settled on.

"Yes, Sister Beck. Is there anything I can do? What's the problem?" Beck seldom asked for anything, maybe transportation for a shopping trip or someone to move a piece of furniture. Pastor John was always quick to respond to these requests.

"Yes. You can help us. I need a van and driver to drive Sis and me up to Kentucky. My niece, Amanda, you know, you've had her on your prayer list for years, has passed away."

"Oh, I'm so sorry, Sister Beck, so sorry."

"Of course, we're neither one able to drive and we can't get around well enough to fly or take a bus."

"Well. Yes, I know." Pastor didn't know if this was something the church could do. "Sister, this is a little out of the ordinary. I probably ought to consult the trustee committee."

"It is out of the ordinary. That big contribution I made to the parsonage campaign last year was a little out of the ordinary too." Beck was in no mood for hem-hawing. Pastor John hung up after assuring Beck that he would take care of the situation even if he had to drive them himself. On the day of departure the sisters were comfortably seated in the large church van, the seats laid back for comfort, the rear seats removed and an air mattress installed allowing the two to alternate taking naps. This was not a portable throne for two ladies of a royal court, borne along by carriers, but an equally proud sight, at least in the minds of the two. Carl and Freddie had been notified of their arrival time and arrangements made with the funeral home allowing a delay for the service to accommodate these far flung family members. The sisters' talk on the trip ranged from considering their move down to Florida, the hardships encountered on that trip, to how good it'd be to see the old home place and Old Carl. "It's untellin' what we'll run into at home. That sorry Freddie ain't likely kept it like we left it." Beck was seeing the mess, the trashing as she spoke.

"Beck, I wonder who Freddie Jr. favors?" Sis had begun to think about Amanda's daddy.

"You know well as I do, they's more than one possibility." Such talk continued all day and a great part of the night, but always circled back to Amanda—mostly the toddler and child. Little was mentioned about her later years, all the bad luck she encountered. Their luck had been pretty good. Amanda's hadn't, they decided.

At the funeral home the following day, Beck and Sis were wheeled into the room off the sanctuary to where the body was. Both were ambulatory, but only for short distances. A closed coffin was necessary; however, the two requested a viewing. Sis peered over the edge at the body and sank back heavily in her wheel chair, not knowing for sure if that was Amanda she had viewed. She was kept from sliding onto the floor by the accompanying parlor staff.

Beck looked, then laid her head over on the casket and began a near scream. It had been at least a decade since Amanda slipped away from them. Her looks weren't changed just by the year internment. "Now, now, Beck, we've got to hold up for Sis and Freddie, Jr." Carl's hand was on her shoulder. His other hand gripped the new cane Freddie had bought him down at the Rite Aid drug store—

just for the funeral. He'd been using a tobacco stick, with no rubber tip that was much too long for comfort. Nothing Carl said seemed to stem the outburst. Carl wondered if she was crying for loss of the gal or because of the part she might have played early on in the making of the poor thing. Arrangements had been made to have the service the following day.

Beck and Sis spent the night with the two Freddies in the old home place. Both surveyed the grounds on arrival and mentioned events associated with the old well, the cellar, the front porch which sported new steps and a ramp for the elderly sisters. Each room was examined, closets opened and inspected by Beck. "Look here, Sis. You remember this little bonnet. We got it for her on her third birthday." The bonnet, pink with roses around the brim, hung among Amanda's clothes still there. Low rider jeans, short tops with straps, lacy around the bottom, were hanging just as she had left them.

That evening Kentucky Fried Chicken was served in the kitchen. Neighbors had provided amply for the gathering. Beck suddenly glared at Freddie, "What went with Mammy's good kitchen table?" This question, not the first of its kind, was asked not so much for information as to establish that things weren't just right. Actually, Beck was surprised: central heat and air, new windows, and carpet had been added; the leaning stone chimney now torn down. She was sure Carl had orchestrated these improvements. In her mind she heard him. "The place'll likely fall to Jr. and you ain't payin no rent. Look on it as a invesment," he'd have said. Freddie explained that the old table was worn considerably, that one of the legs kept falling off, and that he had moved it to the smokehouse when he got the new one. This explanation took several starts and stops with some probing in between.

After dinner the family sat around the table long into the night. Amanda's mother cried and repeated several times: "I didn't get to tell the little thang goodbye. The last thang I said to her was 'don't stay up too late'." That was the night before she left them in Florida.

"Now, Sis, it can't be helped. We did the best we could by her and you know it." Beck thought more than she said at this time. Not that she felt guilty, but things could have been different around them. Changing the tone, she took on the slightest sly grin and rolled her eyes at Freddie, Jr. "I advised ya mammy to watch that boy. He'll break ever thang on the place before he gets married." Freddie Jr. reddened and looked down at his hands in his lap. Beck considered he might look a little like Freddie, couldn't tell though. It might just be the uniform shirt with his name over the pocket.

"She left for the drug store the last time I seen her." Freddie had more to say, but he needed time. The night before she and Louie left, Amanda had gone out. Freddie was asleep when she returned and she was asleep when he left for work the next morning. The talk wore down and one by one the group left the table for other parts of the house, leaving only Carl and Beck, drinking coffee.

They were quiet for a few minutes. Then Beck said quietly, "Why don't you and me get married?" Beck was giving Carl an uncommonly kind look, he thought. It took him a minute to realize what she'd said.

"Why, Beck, you know better than that. We're kin." Carl grinned. He didn't know if she was kidding or if the old lady was slipping. "Besides we're way too old for any such undertaking."

"Pshaw, I weren't planning to have no children." Somebody to talk to besides Sis appealed to Beck, especially since she couldn't go and come like she'd always done. "Actually, best I know we're only about fifth cousins. The Hawkinses, the Crowleyes, the Rutherford's, nearly ever body we knowed married their fourth or fifth cousins. Weren't nobody else. Fifth ain't close kin." Noting she might be serious, Carl tried a different tack. "I'm on a cane. You're in a wheelchair mostly. We'd be a pretty lookin' sight rollin' into Sarasota, on our honeymoon, in a church bus." With that Beck laughed her big laugh and began tugging at the table in an attempt to rise.

The funeral arrangements were simple. The old people were not up to a big show and not many people were there. A large spray of red roses adorned the closed casket; pictures of Amanda as a baby, a toddler, a teenager, some including the twins and Freddie, had been placed on a table nearby. Freddie stood at one end of the casket and Freddie Jr. at the other, as greeters. Both looked shy, like they were too much on display in their two piece suits and clip-on ties, maybe a first for both. Mr. Keith, the old rehab counselor, stood by Freddie. He had come to support Freddie, whom he considered one of his successes, and because Freddie called and requested it. Dr. Ann was there with Keith. The two planned to go on to Lexington to see a University of Kentucky basketball game that evening. They were accompanied by Dr. Al and Deidra, now Al's assistant. Both were old friends of Dr. Ann. Having gone through rehab with him, Deidra also considered Freddie a friend, even though they had been out of contact for years. Carl sat with Beck and Sis. Seeing Beck, anyone who had been present in the court room at her last public appearance in town, might note she was still in a wheelchair, but communicative and not drooling. Ann leaned close and asked Deidra, "Who is the elderly lady in the wheel chair with the wild eyes?"

"I think that's Amanda's aunt." Ann filed this in her mind. Part of her objective today was to gather information.

"Carl, ain't Louie coming?" Beck happened to remember Carl's nephew.

"No, Beck. He's in a nursing home in Scott County." Louie had survived the trash bin episode, but had been left incapacitated. Carl and Freddie had visited him once, but he hadn't known them. "In bad shape, I don't expect he'll ever get any better." Carl said this and looked at his cane standing between his knees, clasped in both hands.

"What about the twins?" Beck was looking all around seeing who was present, and thinking how people had either changed or else were strangers.

"You heard about Earl, I reckon." Carl's lips were tight. He still felt bad about Earl's downfall.

"Yeah, we use to watch him preach on TV; Ain't seen him for some time though."

"Earl plumb lost out. His big preaching's over. He's back down at Willow Grove, reopened the old building." Several congregations had failed since he left there several years ago. "I thought you might've heerd that. Jerald, he ain't been seed in ages. Last account I had, Earl had gone to Mexico to see if he could get some word about him." Beck shook her head, and then continued to survey the crowd. "Who is the fat, bald man in the wheel chair across from us?"

"Buddy Mustang." Carl reported this with considerable disgust in his voice, Beck thought. "I'd a never made Buddy out of him. Who is them people two rows behind us?" Beck had spotted Ann, Al, and Deidra.

"They's friends of Freddie. Two of 'em is doctors."

"That fidgety one, keeps pulling at her dress tail and rummaging in her pocketbook, is she a doctor? The one all buttoned up to her chin; looks like that blouse would smoother her."

"No, she was in rehab with Freddie."

"You don't say. Did Amanda know about her?"

"They weren't nothin between her and Freddie, if that's what you're gettin at. She's some kind of medicine expert now."

Compliments of Beck, a funeral dinner for the family and the few close friends who attended the service, was served at the city convention center, the same location where Beck had had her last training session for her couriers. Carl suspected that she wanted to show the townspeople how little odds she asked the authorities by having the dinner at that location. As people finished eating, Dr. Ann set to work, moving politely among the guests, offering condolences and talking at length with select members. "Was Amanda's daddy a big man?" she asked Amanda's mother, hoping to open discussion that might provide insight into the lineage.

Her mother embarrassed by the question and the presence of the questioner, "Naw, not too big, about like

Mr. Keith over there." What kind of question was that anyway?

"Uncle Carl, how well did you know Amanda's dad?" Again, Ann was probing.

"Not the best. He come and went, leaving Sis expectin' the baby. His people come in here early, sometime after the big war, settled over on the ridge."

The somber gathering required Ann to hold a straight face over the 'come and went' comment. "You mean World War II?"

"No, Lincoln's war; they's from Pike County. Said his granddaddy rode in here on the coupling pole of the wagon, dressed like a girl; had to get away, secret like from bad doings back home. Amanda's granddaddy was waylaid here in the county and killed in his tobacco patch. Old timers said they never knowed who done it. Some thought it had to do with the trouble back in Pike."

"Oh, you mean the Civil War."

"Weren't nothing civil about it, that is, if I know civil." Carl leaned forward in his chair, one hand on his knee, the other grasping his cane, his head down as though trying to think of something or else organize his thoughts. "I'll tell you one thang I remember about Amanda's daddy." A big smile spread across his face revealing both plates of his false teeth. He'd catch me or anybody, for that matter, down around the court house or the store talking with two or three others and come up and pull on my sleeve or bump my arm and motion for me to step aside, maybe around the edge of the building or behind a tree as though he had a big secret. He might just be wantin' to know what time it was or if I had any baccer."

Ann smiled, "What do you think was going on in his mind?"

"Don't know. There weren't nary bit of harm in him though."

Dr. Ann's questioning, listening, and mental noting continued. She was determined to acquire as much data as possible in every community possible. Deidra assembled and collated the material during evenings when the two met for long hours in Ann's condo. Years ago, Ann had determined that something must be done about the slide her mountain people were on, riding addiction ever downward. Poverty, family constellation, trauma, genetics—all were blamed by experts. A thread or threads, when unraveled, she was sure, held the answer to prevention. She was determined to untangle the knot.

Quarterly meetings were held with a group that Ann had brought together to study and interpret findings. Her data was to include Amanda's toxicology records, that is, providing the funeral director had necessary information for her to trace them back to Knoxville. Al had smiled a smile that said, not likely, when she originally presented him with the group's make-up and work plan. "I'm going to assemble a team—psychiatrist, geneticist, psychologist, sociologist, internal medicine specialist, and economist to look into the problem," she had stated emphatically.

"Economist! What in the world are you thinking?" Al had made the proclamation, yet at the same time he was considering Ann's logical nature, her fostering of big ideas on those around her and generally succeeding in any quest.

"Did you read Gladwell's, *Outliers?* An economist explained *the hidden advantages of star athletes*, why not the disadvantages of the addicted?"

Al responded, "No, but I bet I'm about to get a report." This is what he enjoyed about the amazing woman. He was challenged during every encounter and had no doubt as to the efficacy of her plan of attack. That had been four years ago; the team had met quarterly, the answer though was still hidden among the tangled complexities of life.

The funeral over, Freddie and son Jr. returned to work. Beck and Sis decided to stay a few days. Beck wanted to gather the news. Carl alternated spending his morning at the shop, his afternoons with Beck and Sis, each napping between stories. Early on, Beck again raised the issue of marriage, the second time in three days. "You've already seen me naked," she said, referring to a childhood event at the swimming hole.

Carl pursed his lips as though to whistle and made a blowing sound that came out close to "*swuupp*," looked at the ground, grimaced mockingly, and shook his old head. The church van driver camped on the porches, in the kitchen, visited with Freddie at the shop and waited.

---

**(Author's note)The week of Amanda's funeral, her home town's weekly newspaper featured the grand jury indictment report—twelve were indicted—ten for illicit drug trafficking; eight of the ten for Oxycodone, one of whom was also trafficking in Alprazolam; two for morphine; one unstated; Two indictments were for other charges—assault and fleeing and evading police. In a second stor, two were arrested but not yet indicted for heroin trafficking, and a third for impersonating a nurse. A*
*The police department spokesman in the same town (pop. approximately 3,000) reported confiscating/destroying 35 active meth labs during the current year, and destroying 30 more inactive labs containing enough ingredients for a conviction.*

On the evening of Amanda's funeral, Ann, Keith, Deidra and Al stopped for dinner after the game. In an upscale second story restaurant, as they sat around the table, their discussion as usual ranged far. Significant game plays had to be dealt with first. "Did you ever see such passing? That point guard will be in the first round draft, I guarantee." Keith's adrenaline was still pumping.

Deidra broke in. "It could just as easily have been me, if not for you three and Doctor Lee."

Realizing from her shaky voice and welling eyes that Deidra was hung up back at the afternoon funeral service, Ann passed her a tissue and with some firmness said, "Cherk-up. You're tough. You'd have found some other three if we hadn't been there." Turning to face Al and Keith, Ann continued, "You know, Old Carl touches me. I think it's because something in him represents memories of my Appalachia."

Keith, ever ready to discuss his people asked, "How's that?"

"I don't know how to express it exactly. Maybe his honest approach to life, his love of the land, his seeming willingness to give the best of himself to Freddie and that family."

Al offered, "You mean he reminds you of your grandfather or some old Uncle?"

"Could be."

Al didn't give Ann a chance to further explain. "My father told me a tale the morning I was to leave for Iraq the first time. He said his father related a tale to him about his father, my great grandfather. He said he was preparing to go pick blackberries, dreading the snakes, chiggers, briars, and whatever else might be lurking in the near woods. And that my great-great grandfather recognizing his fear told of going into the briar patch as a boy and snatching the family's dinner dessert from among the bruin. It made him feel tough, strong—best feeling in the world for a boy."

"Brown bear?" Deidra interjected.

"No, I think he was using bruin in a more generic sense just meaning bear. The story stayed with me, especially during the tour there in the fiery-hot desert. I guess maybe Father saw my fear as he stood watching me pack my things. Anyway, that's my Madison County Appalachia."

---

*On the street below their window view the three could have observed a staggering man traveling south, and passing a staggering man going north on the sidewalk; while across the same street, in a darkened doorway, a girl sat staring, a hypodermic in her left hand...not a bad neighborhood, just a bad scene.*

## CHAPTER 2

### **Deidra & Freddie**

Deidra's Journal:
Mr. Keith, I trust this writing, though not my own, will be acceptable. I got it in San Diego, I think. That's where I did part of a rehab program. I've been derailed and stuck most of my life; from here in the Kentucky hills to Las Vegas, to San Diego, then to Florida, and to the faded points in between. In this place, with you and the group, my vision clears a little. The road to some place is visible, at least for a short distance. A life story follows:

*WHERE'S GRANDMA*

*Anonymous*

*My life, once disrupted, has never been the same*

*The original intent has been progressively lost with each successive detour.*

*I've been tossed into and out of sexuality's trash bin only to move on through passages better kept secret, but always I stumbled on.*

*Attempts to recapture some direction have come in increments, increments awash in life's rains and hardly recognizable.*

*As the journey continues, I follow a lane forever shadowed in darkness*

*I'm captive of a new king, unseen, with no guards—merely a spirit carried by smiling compounds, promising relief or something.*

*The carnage, my accomplice, lying just off the original route, is wrought not by military might, not by philosophical bent, but by unseen molecules lacing the mind*
*Grandma's gestures pointed the way, her beckoning hand always misunderstood as corruption darkened the winding cave.*

*My direction, ever unclear as the faded light revealed only barriers.*

*Any illumination has eventually been overtaken by time and its mate—the limping gray fog.*

*If I quit the journey to perish, I leave no track, no name, if I travel on it'll be to new suffering, no gain.*
*Does nature always win? Is all laid out before the beginning, is hope a mere substitute for present shame?*

*What I'd like to do is modify reality, exit into the narrow corridor with a clearer vision from curve to curve, and beside each interruption imprint a journey marker to defy the deadened nerves.*

*Maybe then I could mount the obstacles, ride them, ride them as freedom waves*

*And search for the lighted foot log, a short-cut home to Grandma's grave.*

After reading Deidra's writing assignment, Keith considered the content. Not sure if the grandma note was her writing or something she'd been carrying around for over twenty years as she'd have him believe, he marked it for review by the treatment team. He wasn't exactly comfortable assuming someone else composed it years ago.

The lighted foot log to grandma's grave, a little scary for his level of expertise. Caution first marked most of his decisions regarding patients.

After Deidra's record, Keith proceeded with Freddie's which revealed a letter, presumably his writing assignment, but assistance in the effort was clear or else Freddie talked much more freely into a recorder than his face-to-face three word sentences. Keith smiled as he struggled in starts and stops examining the contents.

Freddie's letter…

*Dear Mommy:*

*I wish't you'd send somebody down here to git me. So far we ain't done nothin' but talk, talk, talk. Makes no sense to me, how sittin' around tellin' big tales to one another helps any thang. You got no idee what some of these people tell and expect me to believe it. I'd a called you, but they won't let me use the phone but on onest a week—reckon they think a few days with them and all your business shuts down. If you can't git nobody to come and git me, could you send a few things; surely that ain't against some rule or other. Pop, cigarettes, cookies, none are furnished. They don't give us a bite between meals neither, or at bed time. If you'd send twenty dollars, it'd be a comfort to me just to have a little spendin' money.*

*Best I can tell, they have their pets here. Some get took to town. The rest of us are expected to pick up the messes, wash dishes, dust, pick up the grounds around the outside door where ever body smokes. They call it policing. I didn't mention it, but no smokin' is allowed inside the buildin', and no goin' outside after 8:00 p.m. You know how I like a smoke before goin' to sleep. These people ain't my kind. I'm not just talkin' about the workers. Some of them are pretty nice. Mr. Keith, he asks me ever mornin' how I'm doing, if I slept o.k., if anythang's botherin' me, if he can do any favors for me. Now he is all right, but he aggravates me some, too, tryin' to enroll me in a G.E.D. course of some kind.*

*These fellers like me, you know, here cause they got troubles are mouthy always cut the fattest hog so to speak. One old gal, well she ain't so old, forty-one she says, just six years older than me, she's got a tattoo all over her front, you know, just below her neck. Don't know how far it goes down, got roses and some other kind of flowers red and green and blue, and a yeller cat's head right in the middle, its blue eyes lookin' straight at you. She favors that girl at Wendys night drive through a right smart. Can't remember her name, but expect you've seen her. Anyway, this woman's teeth are light and not eat away like some, and she is fleshy enough, not wasted lookin' like. She's got some kind of trouble though. The courts sent her. If I find out it's not for knifin' a boyfriend or somethin' like that, I'm studyin' about askin' her to eat at my table some time. That's another thang, all eatin' is done at the table with a fork, spoon, knife, and napkin. No eatin' out of a can in front of the TV—right fancy, don't you think. I tole you about settin' around and talkin', this is part of the deal.*

*One day this week, Mr. Keith spent all mornin' tellin' us how to watch out about our money: plan before spendin', save a little, keep a balance in the bank and so forth. He surely don't know that I don't have a dime to count.*

*Has anybody been looking for me? If Buddy what's his name, the boy that drives that black Mustang inquires, don't let on where I am. Me and him ain't gitten' along too good. But don't worry, I'll handle it when I git home .*

*Tell the boys over at the trailer I said hid'dy and that I hoped they got the electricity turned back on, and that I ain't sayin' nothin' to nobody. That reminds me, I wonder if Amanda's baby is sure enough mine. She was in and out over at the trailer a lot when I wasn't even there. That's another thang I'll deal with when I git back. Gather me all the news you can.*

*Until they make me write agin, Your sweetie-boy, Freddie. Bet you never thought I'd write any such long letter. Well, I didn't. I told it into a recorder ha, ha. Ms. Linda is gonna copy it for me. She's nice. Don't show it around.*

*P.S.*
*No way I'd be here if you hadn't got with that church bunch up on the mountain and started carpin' on me ever minute. Mommy, Mr. Keith told us we had to write home tonight, that is, if we had one, practicin' tellin' about ourselves.*

Freddie's letter revealed a lot. Hidden from these lines, however, was a story almost too horrific to repeat.
Dr. Lee's evaluation notes along with the social history, which Keith had already reviewed, revealed a lot more: "During Freddie's toddler years, his mother concocted a plan to support the family. The father was not in residence, and she was addicted to pain medicine, unable or unwilling to work. Certain behaviors got teachers to refer their charges for evaluation and treatment. Freddie's mother likely learned about these behaviors from friends who already knew them. It appears she began training and conditioning Freddie. As a result he was diagnosed and prescribed the drug *Ritalin* believed to qualify him for aid payments. The disaster for the boy came not because he was prescribed the wrong treatment, but that his mother

likely treated him in such a way as to get the necessary behavior. Examples include, but not limited to, slapping him when he properly responded to a request.

Freddie's mom was not ordinary. Neither was she necessarily psychotic or developmentally handicapped. Her treatment of him likely sprang from a combination of drug use, fear of an uncertain future, an absence of mothering skills, and an inability to see beyond the immediate." On reading the documents Keith was reminded of the story from India where parents crippled a child so he or she could beg on the streets. He was sure that education provided a partial solution, yet he also knew that sometimes these difficult cases show up at rehab coming from homes where the parents had taken advantage of educational opportunities, and no abusive parenting is revealed. Further, the absence of such abusive child rearing might also be found among cases from the most illiterate cultures. "A conundrum, the answer of which is beyond my training," he had emphatically pronounced to Dr. Lee when discussing the case.

Dr. Lee had grimaced and responded, "Mine too." Thus far this new group appeared to be much the same as those coming before, like sheep circling in a temporary fold; their demon's weight reflected in their carriage, the absence of direction in their eyes, the hopelessness in their smile. Health status of each, Keith read in their skin, gait, and hair. None were throwbacks for him, however—keep on keeping on, his mantra. Detoxification to rehabilitation one time or ten so long as there is breath; never give up.

---

*Dr Nora Volkow, M.D., great granddaughter of Leon Trotsky, and Director of the National Institute on Drug Abuse: "Instead of abstinence, we are devising ways of treating addiction in which the individual is trained to think that the environment in which they were consuming their drugs is no longer pleasurable."*

# CHAPTER 3

## Rehab

Freddie and the other nineteen residents filed into the conference room at eight sharp and claimed their seats. Seats were not assigned, but some were preferred and all together they formed a partial circle near the back wall. On the right beyond the chairs, a metal table bearing coffee, fresh fruit, and fiber bars stood stark against that wall. A low candle-power light blinked from the other end of the room signifying charged batteries in the emergency detector. Cheap black frames holding the mission statement and other administrative documents hung near the door. Morning meal and cleanup already finished as well as beds, floors, and outside policing looked to, this first of two daily three-hour sessions was about to begin. Mr. Keith and others he might bring in led the morning sessions. Freddie hadn't figured out just what was happening each day. It wasn't school exactly and it wasn't church, at least not like any church he'd ever heard of, nor did it resemble a family gathering. The closest thing probably was the waiting room at the doctor's office. He and Mommy used to visit for his Ritalin prescription which she later sold on the street. People gabbed about most anything there. Mr. Keith's explanation that the talk here provided residents a chance to figure things out would just have to do, but he wasn't sure he understood or agreed.

"Good morning folks" Mr. Keith broke through the circle, his personal McDonald's coffee cup precariously leading the way. His black summer weight wool slacks were fading—the result of many dry cleanings. Every black hair was in place. His red tie dangled slightly below his belt. "A few things we need to do today. First, any facility issues need to be reviewed?" Mr. Keith put his foot in a chair and balanced a notepad on his knee.

The thin girl near the coffee table spoke up. "Yes, you people are freezing me to death here. I could hang meat in my room." She clasped her arms to her bosom and shivered.

"Any other issues," Mr. Keith inquired, apparently noting her issue on his pad. The man diagonally from Freddie bounced his legs quickly—almost a quiver—on the balls of his feet. Others looked at the floor, examined their nails, rubbed a shoe toe on the back of their pant leg, yawned, and stretched, but not the woman with the flower cat tattoo. Her posture was junior high straight, backpack and purse stashed beneath her seat, pen and paper at the ready on her lap. Freddie looked at her and thought she could just as easily have been going to do something important. Then he thought maybe it wouldn't be a good idea to ask her to sit at his table during meals—might be a little too highfalutin. No one spoke up.

Mr. Keith continued, "This morning's session will be divided into two segments: First, I have some information that I'm required to pass along to you; second, we'll review the letters you were to write." Freddie's heart ratcheted up several beats at mention of the letter. "Has anyone been in a facility like this before and if so how much did it cost?" Several nodded and one reported a figure of thirty-one thousand dollars for thirty days. Mr. Keith spoke again, "Note that thirty days here cost you only six hundred and fifty dollars. Anyone know why the difference?"

"Poor service," the girl concerned about being too cold responded. Everybody laughed.

"No," Mr. Keith continued, "it's because this facility receives state and federal dollars along with insurance and other payments. Most of you don't remember the early 1970's, but it was then that President Nixon declared war on drugs. This program grew out of and is somewhat an extension from that era and is now part of the community mental health endeavor started even earlier during the Eisenhower and Kennedy years.

"Whoa, that's a long war," someone muttered. Another added, "Best I can tell we've lost it too."

"Leaders from several nations recently reached the same conclusion." Mr. Keith smiled as he said this. "Something else you might not know. One of our neighboring counties has had eighteen deaths due to prescription drugs OD in a matter of months, or that the average cost to treat a meth burn victim at $130,000 is three times higher than other burns, or that local news reports that official destruction of meth labs has increased three fold in the last year."

The man with the bouncy legs stood quickly, his chair sliding out of line, and shouted, "I don't see how in hell this lecture, if that is what you call it, is going to help me with my problem." Then he left the room, slamming the door behind him. Later Freddie would hear the receptionist explaining that he left the premise walking and carrying his duffle while the group was still in session. Bouncy Leggs was dropped from the roll.

"Maybe we should move on." Mr. Keith looked a bit perplexed, but didn't raise his voice. "Let's review your letters." The two men who slouched, with their legs outstretched and crossed at the ankles sat up, uncrossed their legs and viewed points away from the speaker; others looked down or hunted a pencil in purse or pocket.

After considerable time, Tattoo spoke, "Oh, well, I'll do it." Mr. Keith sighed and asked her to proceed.

"*Dear Ms. Virgie. I don't expect you will remember me. I was in your sophomore honors English class about twenty odd years ago, but dropped out after the first semester. You meant a lot to me, ignoring note passing, and too much eye shadow, encouraging us to create something beautiful on the page—painted in words that anyone could understand and enjoy; words that expressed our deepest feelings, or told an interesting story, or explained an unknown; words that revealed what was across the next hill. I haven't forgotten. I remember, too, how you complimented my word choices, my clean tennis shoes and wrote a special note on that first theme. It was about picking wild strawberries with Grandma. You can't find them now because of the wild turkeys, some say. Grandma is gone too.*

*Ms. Virgie, I didn't leave school because of you or because it wasn't interesting. Buck, the big center on the football team got my attention. After his injury and knee surgery during that first semester, the doctor put him on pain medicine, of course, and he moved on from that to other self-prescribed medicines which he described as making you feel so strong, like nothing could hurt or dare challenge you, like your mind expanded and quickened. Like Eve back in the Old Testament, I wanted to know more, and began experimenting. You might say I developed an Eve complex. By second semester I was so deep in nothing else mattered, including the football hero. I will not go into the next years of sleeping in cars, shoplifting, selling myself and every degrading thing imaginable.*

*After years of spiraling downward, my parents got legal papers and had me arrested. To avoid lockup, I agreed to get the GED and enroll in community college. That lasted a total of two years. It wasn't the Eve complex that time. It could have been the Adam thing though—just going along. Fact is, I can't explain what happened, except to say that a lot of friends were involved. So I waited tables, cleaned houses for THE CLEAN FIX ASSOCIATES company, did landscaping and whatever else was available. Finally a serious wreck and driving charges landed me back in court and the referral to a rehab center.*

*I might make it this time. Please don't think ill of me. Inside I want desperately to be like you or mother. I'm still me, I think. You don't have to answer this letter. It is part of our treatment program, an assignment designed to help us open up and tell our story. If you choose to, however, I'd appreciate any comments on the writing just to see if I can still tell a story… With Love and Admiration, Deidra Hammock*

Mr. Keith looked intently at the woman. Freddie couldn't tell if he was focusing on the blue-eyed cat, the flowers or what. "Thank you, Miss Hammock, or is it Mrs.?"

"It is Miss," was her quick response. Deidra pushed back in her chair and adjusted her skirt.

"You express yourself well. Now, does anyone else wish to read?" After a pause, and with no takers, Mr. Keith wondered if anyone had comments on Deidra's letter. One of the men who previously had his legs extended allowed that her story might well sum up, in general terms, the experience of the whole bunch, except, of course, Mr. Keith. The cold woman said, "I didn't have any nice teachers." When no one else spoke up, Mr. Keith declared a twenty minute break. Each grabbed coffee and went outside to smoke.

The smoke break presented an opportunity for residents to get acquainted. More likely it was utilized for each to tell his or her story, at least during the early days of rehab. Residents dispersed into knots of two, three or four throughout the garden, just beyond the exit. The garden area's beauty rose and declined, depending on current residents, as they provided the maintenance. Deidra noticed Freddie circling the various groups slowly, listening until someone looked at him. One of the men who slouched and sat with his legs crossed at the ankles during the morning session, slapped both thighs and ran at Freddie, much as he might have an unwanted stray dog. Freddie moved on. The man and his two comrades snickered.

To Deidra's right, a gathering of four—three men and a woman—were laughing loudly in response to a story. She heard the next report: "I have three brothers and three sisters. One sister is an honor student in high school, one a nurse, and one an elementary school teacher. One of my brothers is in the pen for pushing his pregnant wife out of a moving car causing her to lose her baby, and one brother has been in the pen for selling cocaine. My youngest brother is dealing in a Vegas casino after finishing law school and after getting in trouble over his use of client funds. We thought the family women were going to make it until Mom got sent up for making meth. Three grandchildren were in the house at the time." Again everyone laughed. Not mentioned was the fact that the grandchildren's classmates had to be decontaminated as did their classrooms.

As Deidra circled and mingled, the stories continued, each one virtually a repeat of the one before. Her own story wasn't the terrible exception she decided. She knew the preposterous stories were likely true. She'd heard many such reports while sitting in court awaiting her turn to answer charges.

Eventually Deidra and Freddie met and settled into conversation, that is, she conversed. He mumbled three word responses, but he smiled throughout. She told him about having had a Mazda automobile at one time.
He said, "I fixed one." Hers, she said, was a fairly complex vehicle with heated seats and lock-out overdrive. She doubted he could have repaired it, but didn't say so.

^^^

Bouncy Leggs, now an angry, addicted, dropout, hadn't always been. In college he'd been part of the drama department for a period having fun performing parody at various campus events.

"I don't know, Dick. Everybody hates me."

"Now, Bill, stop that and don't you even think about quitting. If I had it to do over, no way would I have given them that satisfaction; got rid of all those ninnies who were advising me to do what is right for the country, for my family, for me, that's what I should have done and would do if I had it to do over. Do you think I could have pardoned myself?"

"Dick, quit that beatin' yourself up. Say, was there anything to the Chinese rumor, about the girl, I mean?" This was whispered into the mouthpiece.

"All hogwash, Bill, just enemy lies. I never had a woman look at me and swoon, heck they usually turned their heads away when I walked by. I don't understand it. Always stayed clean, never talked ugly in front of any of them. For sure none of them ever showed me their tong or whatever you call it, ha, ha."

"Listen, Dick, most of that is just press. All men are about the same, women too. It ain't all it's cracked up to be."

"Bill, I know the stories must have been exaggerated. You'd be drained. Look like a pickle if half were true, but doggone these women out here. They start pulling at their blouses, adding lipstick, fluttering their eyes just at the sight of you on the news."

The actor now crying loudly into the phone and stamping his foot as the Nixon/ Clinton parody continued, "Dick, it just seems the right thing to do, quitting I mean."

"Take you a little dose of salt-peter, and stay right where you are. You've got to protect the presidency, Bill. Next time, that is after you're gone, somebody gets mad over something, they'll demand a man quit and go home—maybe just for passing gas in the mansion or leaving the toilet seat up."

Still crying, "Dick, you've helped me a lot."

"I'm not a crook you know." The voice breaks, the actor removes a tissue from the table where he's sitting and wipes first his eyes, then his nose.

"Shoot I know that, Dick. Me and some of the boys went down to Fort Knox and had a look. Best we could tell it was every bit still there."

"Ha, ha, Bill, these kind words and funnies from a man like you, well they mean a lot."

The lights go out. The performer on each end of the stage begins moving props for the next act. Reggie Coots (alias Bouncy Leggs) and the other performer move from the stage and claim seats in the audience, each taking up his now warm beer, laughing and accepting congratulations and or snickers on their performance. The bar just off campus served as a gathering place primarily for first and second year students away from home for the first time, nervous about classes, disgusted with dorm life, and needing respite provided by the unrehearsed student performances. Reggie's roommate from Pennsylvania created the act, a sort of *Saturday Night Live* parody, "The bar manager censured all the good parts out." He had reported this to the table before taking up the mock phone on stage. Reggie cared little about the plot, thinking about as much about the two presidents as he did about Chaucer's writing, required reading in his second semester English Literature class. He was there to see and be seen.

That barroom scene happened during Reggie's second and last semester. After Reggie left, the roommate changed his major from biology to theatre and stayed on.

On returning home that spring, Reggie confronted his dad. "I've had all that crap I can take. I want to get hiking, make some money, know what I mean." Reggie's dad noted the young man's talking fast and getting up and down from his chair, but attributed it to nervousness about discussing dropping out of school or to his condition, whatever it was, that made him bounce his legs so. He had tried a few years ago to break Reggie of the bouncing by first calling attention to it, then assigning the nickname.

"Look son, you going to college was your mother's idea. I paid the bills and supported it, but I know there is more to making a living than memorizing the atomic chart. So what are your plans?"

"I want to get a good job, one that pays a lot of money."

"The second part of that may take a while. For right now, go out to the parts department and tell Claudette to sign you up; report to the garage at seven sharp tomorrow. I'll see that you get a work uniform and an assignment."

"Woah. Wait. I didn't say anything about wanting to mount tires." Phillip, Reggie's dad, owned the most successful GM dealership in Southeastern Kentucky. He'd worked his way up. So could his son.

"You don't start at the top, son." Remembering the new Vet he'd presented Reggie with on his sixteenth birthday and how it had been reduced to junk by his next birthday, Phillip was leery regarding the boy's judgment. However, Reggie took the bit and plunged ahead, not happily, but steady enough to establish his dependability. After six months, Phillip allowed Reggie to join the sales crew on Fridays and Saturdays. Again aptitude and willingness were observed in the young man.

"By George, son, I think you may be ready. I'm going to move that string of cars off the back row of the lot down to our receiving area, across from the welfare office. You know where I'm talking about."

"Yeah, so?"

"Well, they're clunkers compared to our new line and one-owner trade-ins. They don't go with the others. They diminish our atmosphere, so to speak."

"What are you actually saying, Dad?"

"I'm saying that I'm setting you up son. We'll move a trailer over there for your office and you can sell these vehicles. I'll move more in as you move them out. Older trade-ins, you see."

"Who is going to buy that junk?" Reggie was more of a Vet man and didn't think too highly of a ten year old minivan.

"Now wait a minute. Those cars have several miles left in them. A lot of poor people can't afford better. Fact is, those poor fellows who get a tax return, even though they haven't paid any taxes, I've found are readymade clients. A tax refund for down payment and you've got your investment back. Eighteen percent interest on the balance and you don't have to get many payments to make some big bucks." Phillip rolled his cigar in his mouth with the thumb and forefinger of one hand, and patted Bouncy's shoulder with the other. "You'll do okay." So Bouncy Leggs was launched. By the time all the particulars were worked out, sales were becoming brisk, and cash reserves soon mounted.

"I've got ninety-two thousand dollars." Bouncy was talking to an out-of-town financier. "What I want to know is, how much can I borrow with that amount down?"

"Not enough to do what you're suggesting, I'm afraid." Money-bags was not your average banker. In fact, he wasn't a banker at all, just a man with money to hide in places where it was pretty sure to grow. "What about your old man? Will he sign?"

"Nope, I don't even want him to know what is going on." This discussion led to others, to alternate possibilities. Agreement was finally reached for Bouncy Leggs to borrow enough money to purchase twenty near-new automobiles on a floor plan. Interest nearing twenty percent APR was included in the package. Adding the better line of automobiles to the clunker lot allowed Bouncy to travel in style. So stylish was the young man that he now cruised up and down the streets in a yellow Vet. Girls all but hung onto the hood. These were not Sunday school girls, however. But Bouncy wasn't looking for Sunday school girls anyway. These girls liked cocaine, late nights in disco bars, and such.

^^^

"This is it, Reggie!" Phillip was standing over Reggie's desk with a hand full of papers, including bank overdrafts, legal notices, and threatening notes from the "money-bags." "I'm bailing you out with that shark and settling these." With that Phillip waved the papers at Reggie, brushing his nose. "But I'm also cutting you off. You are on your own." The Vet, the girls, the drugs had drained Reggie in less than a year and Reggie had drained his mother's account of the nest egg left her when her parent's estate was settled. Complications from this downfall eventually landed Bouncy in rehab for a brief stay. Phillip, being a true salesman, survived and Reggie's mom had her wine glass and bridge club to help her through.

# CHAPTER 4

## Mr. Keith and the Treatment Team

During the break Mr. Keith made his way to the staff meeting room off the women's wing. In session were three professionals—psychiatrist, psychologist, and social worker. He preferred to think of them as Goatee, M. D., Long Hair MMPI, and La Pearl (her good looks created a striking contrast to the other two). Keith had come to the counseling field after an extended tour in the air force and a stint as high school social studies teacher. Working years under the supervision of licensed clinicians while attending state mandated training programs, he had finally achieved certification as a drug abuse counselor—not a commanding resume' in the eyes of the clinically trained.

The team was in the process of reviewing social histories, medical reports, and other intake materials of the twenty recently admitted residents. Copies of the resident letters were brought in by Keith for screening. Goatee didn't put much stock in the content of these letters, while MMPI hung on every word for hidden meaning and La Pearl often leaked from her eyes as she read. Keith generally considered the writings get-acquainted documents or discussion starters. This was part of standard procedure. Following the group review, the psychologist and the social worker would follow up, producing substantial paper for the medical record. The two also spent long hours discussing the letters produced by the residents.

"Looks like you've got another challenge." La Pearl looked at Keith and smiled as she made the remark.

Keith pulled a chair to the table and sat, sat like a man suffering fatigue. Returning her smile, "They're probably no better or worse than the last." He knew the three members well: dedicated professionals, each possessing a recognized licensed body of knowledge, an advantage he would likely never achieve. Years of submitting his work to one or more of them for approval and signature, even though he was thorough and operating at a level commensurate with his training and expertise, was somehow demeaning and left him feeling marginalized. At fifty-one years old Keith lived with his mother. His wife left shortly after the Gulf War and he hadn't considered another so he had few domestic barnacles. He was free to ski on winter retreats, to fish, hike and travel during other seasons, reprieves he considered necessary for the daily grind of head to head counseling with addicts. The groups oftentimes left him feeling helpless and ungratified. Out of the current twenty enrollees, seven could be expected to celebrate a year of sobriety; possibly one to die of an accidental overdose/suicide, the remaining eight likely relapsing into old patterns. Especially vulnerable were those returning to old neighborhoods. Now and again, however, a visit, a phone call, email, or card provided him new energy. Somebody out there celebrated an extended sobriety and cared enough to report it directly to him. Oftentimes pictures accompanied these notices revealing a thriving family and wholesome activities. Psychologically, these reports served as his hole in one, the six pound bass—near ecstasy. These patient responses came from the group's final four, the winners.

Two of today's letters stood out for Keith, Deidra's and Freddie's. One revealed an individual capable of success and contribution, a person who had traversed the drug world, but could function elsewhere. While the other exemplified a personality developed in the underworld of poverty, drugs, crime, and ignorance with a need to hide.

Functioning in modern society presented too many barriers for him.

Hiding for Freddie had never been difficult. Disappear when one of the visiting men screamed at his mother. Sleep in the back seat of the visitor's car. Take advantage of his learned/trained behavioral diagnosis when confronted in public school. Later, running when the man in the black Mustang came seeking payment. About the only time the keepers of the social contract noticed or thought of his kind came because of a broken lock, a missing power drill, laptop, or cash from the money jar. Otherwise, except for Christmas baskets, the church food and clothing distribution days, or indigent contingency fund expenditures, Freddie went unnoticed. Even those making a feeble effort to do good in his behalf discussed how his kind wouldn't work, stayed high, lived like animals, made terrible decisions, and concluded by stating that something should be done about them.

None of the staff as yet knew that concomitant with Freddie's dysfunction, he had a natural ability to repair most any piece of equipment—farm or automotive, making him desirable in wide circles as a day laborer. Often, however, he couldn't be located after starting a job and receiving the first day's pay, no matter the employer's inconvenience.

Deidra, on the other hand, might have more to work with. She was intelligent, understood that something positive existed on the other side of drugs and hopelessness. Society might label her sorry; medicine—bipolar; psychology—borderline personality; social work—the latter two and deprived. Keith must be pragmatic, utilize the wisdom of all the professionals. Surely something locked inside her head just says no to success, causing her to withdraw from the fray for no apparent reason. Her parents, coping with a former honor student who is now addicted, homeless, hungry, and a prostitute, must be more than devastated. War and pillage, drought and famine, the death of a child—this loss ranks right up there among those calamities in Keith's mind. Even so, while enrolled in college, Deidra had worked for the business school department head, doing data entry, scoring student examinations, and performing general office management. She accumulated excellent evaluations, but often disagreed vehemently with college regulations. These bits were revealed to the social worker on intake.

"Doc, I'd appreciate some feedback on two of the patients—Deidra Hammock and Freddie Byrd." Keith, weighing his thoughts, hoped the treatment team really did know (and would share) techniques that he didn't. He had never taken the Hippocratic Oath to do no harm, but he instinctively practiced it as best he knew how. The intrigue often associated with individual residents kept him guessing and often stupefied. The last federal court referral, a parolee through the court in London, was sentenced to thirty days rehab. He performed every task, exhibiting exceptional behavior. This lasted twenty-eight days. On the twenty-ninth day he smoked in bed, not just tobacco, but marijuana, knowing the infraction meant dismissal and more prison time." "I just wasn't thinking," had been his response to inquiries as he sprawled nonchalant in the therapist office. His parole officer, having been called in, just shook his head and commented, "I see this more often than not." Keith understood the lure of drugs, but the apparent desire for more prison time escaped him. A review of the man's social history revealed that he had two children, had earlier been gainfully employed in sales work, and had no serious criminal back ground outside the drug trade.

"Is prison a safe place for our parolee who seemingly prefers prison to sobriety?" This was the first opportunity Keith had to question Dr. Lee about the man. "It might be," said Dr. Lee. "You're talking about a safe place in his mind, right? We know so little about what is inside the head in his case. Remember, the family, the community, and the legal system had him for twenty-seven years. We had him less than a month. Most of his behavior patterns were established in the first years of development. Then you have to consider what is done to and for him as time progresses."

"I agree, I think. But how do we know where to begin, if we're in midstream for this fellow?" Keith was thinking about various other patients whose life experiences he became aware of daily.

Dr. Lee looked over his reading glasses at Keith. "Assuming our treatment represents a logical response to life's questions as he sees it or to his previous encounters, our imprint may prove too limited to help him build necessary decision-making and coping mechanisms. Years of therapy might be necessary. To provide space and environment, so to speak, for an individual to re-program is probably all that can be expected. You and I have to address the situation presented us, do the best we know how and move on. Others need us."

Keith didn't know if the doctor was merely placating him, holding back inside information that only the doctor was capable of understanding or what. The answer left him unsatisfied. Forgetting that patient, that man or woman, was not something he chose to do. Yet, that seemed to be the doctor's only recommendation.

## CHAPTER 5

### Old Man Birdwhistle

Deidra dusted every piece of furniture, such as it was: twin maple bed, matching chest of drawers; a surfing picture on the wall above the chest, an oak desk-dresser combination with a plastic waste can beside it. The shear curtains, she hand-washed in the bathtub after running the facility vacuum over the gray, glued down carpet, being careful about the strings and frayed edges in the doorway. Her makeup and other toiletries, she aligned perfectly on the bathroom vanity. Conditions had been worse. She thought of the complex near downtown that her mother and dad had all but dragged her from. It had once been a flourishing motel before the traffic no longer passed. From that it progressed to dirty rooms rented as apartments by the week or month. Occupants came to the rural Kentucky community from Oregon, Texas, Florida, and states in between. They seemed to have no connections and disappeared after a few months. Some said it had to do with the welfare laws. Strollers passing along the sidewalk by the overused motel smelled the stale cigarette smoke, the dirty bed clothes, the old pizza packaging wafting from each room.

On the other end, she'd once been put up in Vegas, the high-end district at that, experiencing the frolic, the bright lights, the bells and whistles of casino life.

The day had gone well for her. The morning session, reading her letter to the group wasn't bad. It seemed even better during the afternoon session when others read. At least she hadn't whined about being mistreated and how it resulted in her awful behavior or that clean living and smooth sailing from here on out was sure to come of this rehab experience. Enough ups and downs in her life disproved the likelihood of that. She also remembered her last extended sobriety and the phone call that led to it. "Hello, Deidra?"

"Yes, who is this?"

"You don't know me. Your name was given to me by Ralph, a friend of mine, works down at UPS in London—says I need to get to know you."

Sounded like an old guy. "Yeah. Why?" She knew the why, but wanted to hear his line for analysis.

"I'm not from here, and don't know anyone. Ralph says you're good company, a reader and somebody with interesting qualities. I was wondering if we could get together for coffee or dinner, a movie or something." She knew Ralph and was certain he hadn't recommended her personality qualities; however, the money was gone and the big C was about worn off. Old guys were bigger spenders, maybe up to two hundred dollars a night and generally much nicer than young ones who often left a bloody lip or black eye for no understandable reason.

"Sure, I'll meet you. When and where?" Thus began a six month liaison, which other than his wrinkles, skin tags, and yellow toe nails was bearable. Against medical advice, he was on Viagra and followed its dictates. He had paid her rent, furnished food and gasoline, bought new outfits, attempting to make her feel like a lady. No longer did she have to clean houses, take the gruff from unhappy wives, or the advances from leering husbands. The cleaning hadn't been that hard. Keeping help had been a problem. Her last helper had nearly driven her batty—often in jail, hiding from social services, bringing her children to work, and a tendency to steal something from every house.

The benchmark day, however, occurred shortly after her six month anniversary with Birdwhistle. The old man's heart had run its course and he was taken back to his home county up near Louisville for burial. Deidra re-entered the workforce, this time doing landscaping around town. She had just planted and staked a blue spruce and surrounded it by blues, yellows, and other ornamentals when the attorney, the one her parents used for various civil matters, drove up and presented her with a document. Huh-oh, what now she thought as she quickly reviewed recent events. Operating on the edge, she knew there were issues, particularly regarding her drug use.

"Deidra, this is your lucky day. Old man Birdwhistle, your deceased buddy, left thirty-five hundred dollars cash money for you. Sign here." He pointed to a line on the paper he was extending. Deidra read the entire document before signing. "And by the way, it's no business of mine, but you could be doing better. This might provide just the opportunity. I know you've already been told, but you are a pretty girl with potential. The community needs you. Heck, the world needs you." Deidra looked at him as though to say, yes, I've heard that before, thank you, and leaned back to her shovel work. "Also, Deidra, death comes soon enough to us all, but earlier to some," meaning, of course, to her kind. "Thank you, Honey, and good day." The attorney returned to his automobile. Deidra was surprised.

The lawyer knew, but hadn't mentioned certain information during the document review and signing. Such an encounter should be kept solemn to his way of thinking. Facts were facts, however. The coroner had revealed certain details to him regarding to Mr. Birdwhistle's demise.

According to the coroner, with no lilt in her voice or glint in her eye, Deidra had responded to the questions relative to circumstances surrounding his death. "Mr. Birdwhistle was always attracted to the cat's wink." At this her chin dropped until her eyes focused on the tattoo, "And he would be to follow it till his lane ended. You might say he just petered out."

Thus began the longest period of sobriety since her sophomore high school semester. After experiencing phases of emotional storms—highs, punctuated by overconfidence, lows riddled with guilt, retreat, and doubt—Deidra finally settled among the books at the community college.

Between her last high and her college enrollment, however, she encountered lots of advice. Her mother encouraged church attendance, Bible study, and prayer. This led to sessions with the pastor at the large church on the corner just off Main Street. He was a short heavy-set young man with a soft unassuming presence and who appeared to forego any judgment. His eyes reflected this to Deidra. In fact, she initially found his blue eyes very attractive, but there was no evidence of interest on his part. He mostly let her do the talking and that she did, explaining how guilt haunted her, guilt for wasting her high school years, for her parent's agony, for causing numerous marital problems. She discussed her search for reasons for her self-destructive behavior, for following the wrong cue, the wrong friends. The list continued. His answer was "*Christ.*" He quoted scripture, "All have sinned and come short of the glory of God, I don't understand myself …I really want to do what is right, but I can't… there is no condemnation for those who belong to *Christ."*

Hope. There was hope in what he said and he was so serious in the quoting. He presented her with her own Bible which she carried at all times, read each day. She prayed fervent prayers. This was the Deidra who entered the community college. While many considered her religious fervor radical, others invited her to study groups, and encouraged her in the new walk.

Accompanying this enlightenment though were unexplainable, explosive outbursts over college regulations, over lectures by ignorant professors spouting theories, which she doubted they understood. The uncontrollable episodes involved throwing books, stomping out of class, breaking the office computer screen. This was followed by refusing to see friends, skipping class and work. Eventually, during one of these darker periods, a roommate suggested a solution and provided the cure. "Honey I've got something that will calm you down," she had reported. One dose, however, and the new walk, the new opportunity, the better life again ended—this time a full two years after it began. Eighteen months of accumulated college credits and excellent grades, but with no finish. The underworld welcomed her back—smiling, veneered in beauty. Like her fellow travelers, she failed to see beneath the surface.

But today was different. Deidra was determined to complete the thirty day program, skip through the treatment and training and progress on to the ninety day rehab to work experience. Maybe she'd work in the sheltered workshop an offshoot of the community mental health organization. Workers there assembled or made items for the military, other governmental units, and private community concerns. Salaries were meager, but better than fast food or most secretarial positions. Life would assuredly get better this time.

In this state of mind, she moved to the bathroom mirror to fix herself for dinner, brushing her shoulder length hair, adding just a touch of green eye shadow. Sometimes she used blue. Each accented the blue/green eyes which her mother often described as "ocean beautiful," whatever that meant. At five feet seven, one hundred and thirty to forty pounds, depending on current habits, she filled her slacks or skirts in a classy way, according to old man Birdwhistle. He also liked the slimness of her ankles, and her small high waist line. She hoped her dinner seating arrangement included someone neutral, the man Freddie might be a safe fit. Football and NASCAR were not part of her lexicon. Not only that, she had no intention of being suckered into relations with another ignorant loser.

## CHAPTER 6

### **Amanda is Lonesome**

After the day's last session, Freddie entered the room he shared with two other fellows, tired and needing a nap. The dinner had consisted of roast beef, peas, and green salad. The latter was pretty hard to swallow. The rest was fine, but didn't exactly match up to his usual meat balls eaten from the can in front of the TV. After dinner he had been anticipating some free time before the evening checker games and a little TV. He thought it was *Turtle Man* night. He felt his face get warm and red as he recalled Tattoo—he didn't remember her name—coming directly to his table at dinner, even though lots of seating was available. His words came slow, some forgotten in mid-sentence, but she didn't seem to notice. "I'm gonna fix deisels," he'd explained.

"That's good, Freddie. You'll be an independent man." Deidra hadn't been certain that the young man could achieve this goal. He had such trouble talking to her, making her skeptical of his ability. Her heart went out to him though.

Freddie jerked and reentered the present as the wall speaker buzzed and a woman's voice announced, "Freddie Byrd has a phone call. Please come to the lobby." Something wrong at home? Buddy Mustang located him? He made his way to the front lobby considering these possibilities.

"Hello, yeah, this is Freddie. Who's this?" It was a female, but not Mommy.

"Freddie, don't you even know me? Surely you ain't been gone that long. Your Mommy give me the number. I could tell she didn't want to. But Freddie Jr. in his baby seat, us both standing on the porch just looking at her, I think did the trick. Mommy says he favors you. I can't see it. Babies look like babies to me."

"Amanda, have you got something to tell me?" Freddie's thoughts began coming fast, at least for him. "Is your baby okay? Has somebody give you a message for me? Is old man Carl wanting his tractor put back together?"

"Yes, nope, and I don't know." Freddie, a bit confused, asked what in the world she was talking about.

"I's just answering your questions, Honey." Freddie, trying to get his thoughts organized, tried again.

"Why did you call?"

Amanda proceeded a bit more cautious, thinking he might hangup."Freddie, Honey, I just thought you might like to hear from somebody at home, you way off down there, not knowing anybody and all. Maybe you'd like to know how I'm doing, or the baby, or what the boys are up to over at the trailer. You're not going to believe this, but they're telling that that bunch has learned how to boil or whatever and make you know what. Money is going to flow. They're going to get the car fixed and the electricity turned back on. I hope they get the septic working, smells like an outdoor toilet. If you ask me somebody is going to wind up in jail or dead over there. Ever body up and down the road thinks they got the copper out of the air conditioner up at the Church on the Mountain." Freedie leaned against the wall and listened. "I guarantee they'll use more than they sell. Besides old man Carl won't put up with a lot of traffic through his field back to the trailer. You know how they got that stay place don't you? Old man Carl bought it several years ago for a man tending his tobacco to live in, paid thirteen hundred dollars for it. When the tobacco played out, the man left. He let it a couple of times to people he hoped would work a day now and then for the rent. Then the last one got arrested right out in the middle of his corn field. Sherriff shared his poop sheet off the computer with Carl."

"Shared his what?" Freddie heard poop but didn't connect it with anything.

"His poop sheet, his arrest record scared the daylights out of Carl. He let the thing stay empty untelling how long. Horseweeds growed highern the roof. You can't tell what color the thing is. The boys had to machete their way in the door, just a path through. The stalks still stand all around blocking the windows. They wouldn't a got it 'cept one of 'em belongs to Carl's brother."

Freddie shifted from first one foot to the other wishing all the time that Amanda hadn't mentioned the boiling, making, taking, selling, or the copper on the phone. Women just don't understand. "Amanda, why did you call? I'm busy here twenty-four seven. This ain't the easy life. I'm responsible for a right smart. Have to make my bed, set and listen to a room full of gab all day, then wash the supper dishes, no TV 'cept 7:30-9:30. How'd you like it if the screen went dark right in the middle of *Gold Rush,* or *Moonshiners?* I asked Mommy to send somebody down here to git me. You know her though, liable to forget."

"Well, if you don't want to talk to me, just say so. I thought you might want to hear about Freddie Junior's six week checkup or how I'm feeling by now." Amanda's tone shifted closer to a mad whine. "Besides how do you think my life is going, a baby to take care of, not getting to go nowhere, ever body bitching because they have to help out now and then. You're partly to blame, you know. I thought you'd be proud that I didn't take nothing the whole time till the baby come. Durn hospital nurse started right the day he come. 'Healthy babies get mother's milk,' she crowed. Then the health department nurse got in my face soon as I got home—same thing. You know how nervous I get, but I've held off, 'cept I did slip and take one of Aunt Beck's nerve pills. She bellowed for two days, complained I cost her forty dollars. Well, it was already gone. She just had to get over it. Get her calendar out and see which one of her contact's prescriptions comes up next, I say." Freddie changed the phone from one ear to the other and winced as Amanda continued her report. "That calendar looks like some kind of a social planner or maybe a board game. It's a wonder to me how she got all the names, much less keeps them all straight. They're scamming doctors in three counties. Of course, I ain't too sure some of them doctors don't just want to get scammed—return customers—you know what I mean. The doctors think they are so smart."

Again, way too much talking: "Listen Amanda, I want you to do a few things for me. Tell old man Carl it'll be around the first of the month before I can fix his tractor. He needs to get the water pump seal. See if he might consider paying me something on it. Send me the money if he does. Tell Mommy about talking to me and that I'm missing her. You might say that I'm wanting to see your baby too. Maybe she'll send somebody after me. Whatever you do don't let on where I'm at to Buddy, you know the Mustang driver. Got all that?"

"Yeah," Amanda got it but didn't like it, Freddie had always done what she wanted when she wanted it done, agreed when he was supposed to. His attitude didn't seem just exactly right tonight.

"Well, bye." Freddie hung up the phone and looked first around the phone area to see who might have heard his end of the conversation, then to the receptionist at the other end of the room, and wondered if she might a had a secret way to listen.

^^^

An outside observer might consider Freddie's phone discussion and his relationship with other residents humorous. In one of the staff training sessions, Dr. Lee had discussed the back and forth between residents that incites laughter within the group.

"Humor often grows from humanity's darkest places: *W. C Fields's* drunkenness; the great warrior *Achilles' heel*; and *Jerry Lewis'* falling down are typical. Fortunes have been made from re-telling or revealing these mishaps/unfortunate circumstances on the screen. Residents at the rehab offer prime examples, that is, of humor growing out of dark circumstances. Stories told between the residents for laughs are often tragic events. We find ourselves wondering, crying, and laughing at a resident's description of previous drunken behavior, his/her crippling accidents, or comedic fall. Life's plans are seldom written before the act. Even a big financial payoff for most people comes unexpected. The plan, the pride of the recipient, gets written after the fact. Rehab clients certainly had no previous plan to pan the gutters of life. Their reports reflect staggering, falling down, and injuries—each outside life's logical course. Life for them has moved in increments toward the bottom. Instead of being able to boast about successes that were planned, their reports often reflect being saddled with scattered thoughts. A depraved ending follows. Restated, however, their fall-downs or Achilles' heels, and so forth, are often made entertaining, a relief mechanism.

"Many of the twenty men and women in residence pin their hopes on procuring a disability diagnosis and the security of a monthly check. These attitudes condition the minds that we as the treatment team face. Our Freddie, on the other hand started out on the bottom. His focus is entirely serious. While he is here for rehab, the treatment process differs from most others.

"Educating for proper decision-making and success is no small task. Undoing the ravages of addiction compounds the problem. Undoing a lifetime of being abused is equally daunting. We have had to accept that a twenty-five to thirty percent recovery rate is the norm, and counted as success in most circles. Along with our efforts to restore each resident's health, the securing of housing and jobs are add-ons for us—beyond the bounds of treatment and education needed."

While Keith had agreed in principle with all Dr. Lee said, he still considered no case hopeless. His expectations for the Freddies encountered are much higher than the clinical team. He looks for and often finds a spirit not revealed by psychological evaluations, verbal discussions, or previous behavior. The team respects this. Dr. Lee credits him with "feeling things" that aren't apparent to many observers.

# CHAPTER 7

## The Cumberland Gap

The sun was warm for early April. The birds were making their music all around. Keith's backpack was filled with water bottles, a packaged green salad, and a ham and cheese sandwich. He felt the freedom of an early spring morning. Along the path, low bushes were producing greenery. The poplars, oak, and hickory were awakening, reaching high above the sandstone boulders scattered over the mountain. In Keith's mind Kentucky in spring is poetry, music, painting, and sculpture. No museum or opera house is necessary. He felt sorry for those searching for beauty behind walls, the replicas of beauty guarded by uniformed guides. The drive down U. S. 25, less than fifty miles, but a life away, had brought him to the Cumberland Gap, the early gateway to the west. The winding trail to the pinnacle promoted healthy breathing and heart rate. His entire body had already benefited, he thought, from the excursion.

Along the trail a fortyish woman hiked along with a teenager, likely her daughter, whose expression was less than pleasant. The mother smiled, "Beautiful morning isn't it?" Keith returned the greeting and smiled as she passed. At the peak, Keith placed his backpack on a huge sandstone boulder, spread a towel, and climbed aboard. From here he could look far, the mountain range rising and falling like a great leviathan stretching slowly toward Pineville, Kentucky, Harrogate, Tennessee, and Bristol, Virginia. The gap itself likely was changed now from the 1790's when men, women, children came through seeking a new beginning. But even today the natural contours provided a visual outline of the path followed first by the buffalo, then the American Indian, later by early European hunters. The mountain itself is now pierced with a great tunnel.

Kentucky to Tennessee traffic covers the distance in seconds instead of the day or so journey being imagined by Keith. His tranquility was suddenly disturbed as a man lumbered up the trail, smiling, and greeting him, "Mind if I join you?"

"Sure, come on up," Keith noting him to be four or more inches taller than himself, maybe six three; his eyes deep set, friendly, black as Kentucky coal (or as locals were fond of saying black gold). They differed significantly from Keith's protruding eyes—one of the residents at rehab recently described him as always having a startled look. The stranger's frame, strongly suggesting weight lifting, settled on the boulder, his legs hanging precariously over the edge.

"Been up here before?" The question presented in a quiet, friendly voice implied a desire to talk.

"Yes, I grew up over in Harrogate, came here often as a boy. As teenagers we camped, scaled the rock faces, and generally performed escapades dangerous to life and limb. When I'm up here I often think about the early twentieth century John Fox, Jr. novel that portrayed the young character reaching for a ledge, seeking a hand hold next to a huge poisonous viper." The tall visitor chuckled, then quoted the Fox line depicting the scene. Keith was impressed.

"Reaching adulthood is another of the miracles, don't you think. I guess your parents always knew when you were up here?" The visitor apparently felt at home on the mountain and comfortable with Keith.

"No, I was past thirty before they knew about such teenage escapades. We crawled into deep holes, rafted rough currents, and had many near misses. What's your story?" Keith expected the stranger to elaborate on his boyhood and was surprised when he said his reportable experiences, other than football, began in early manhood. Having grown up in Madison County, he attended nearby University of Kentucky, getting by pretty much unscathed only to march off to Iraq for two tours. "During the first tour, I drove patrol for convoys." The stranger looked down over the precipice.

"That must have been an eye opener." Keith was considering this report in light of his own war experience.

"When that armed vehicle bounced along through the dust and extreme heat or cold, I was never comfortable. You can't believe how unbearable the uniform and flak gear were. On one of these rides, our right front tire rolled over an explosive. It left the vehicle in virtual shreds. My buddy was dead in my lap."

"I'm sorry. That must have been terrible." Keith understood what was said, but could not imagine the horror.

"It was weeks before I could hear revelry. I staggered so it wasn't safe for me to navigate." The hiker's eyes looked sad. Keith thought him disconnected.

"Did you get any shrapnel?" Keith asked this, not knowing how to respond regarding the man's loss.

"No. The explosion wasn't the worst though. The empty, hopeless, useless loss haunts me to this day. It's not something you want to relate to family members around the dinner table."

"I can appreciate that." Keith had his own unmentionable horrors.

"My second duty wasn't as close up, but really not much easier. My medical training was far enough along to be of use in the medical services. The blood, the missing limbs, burns, and dysfunctional soldiers and civilians. It was bad. I have visions. They clutter my mind whether I'm awake or asleep." The man again looked down over the rock and got quiet.

Keith's counseling training conjured a lame response, so he thought at the time. "Yeah, I know something of your situation. I had the pleasure of shipping out to the Gulf War a few days out of college. I attended LMU just across the way. My experience was not close up like yours. My fighting was done on a computer screen, up above the dust, blood, and destruction. I didn't see bodies intact or otherwise, but you know, even last night I was visited by a desert scene: women wearing the long dark full body covering running, screaming through the knee deep sand toward smoldering, warped, upturned trucks and tanks, decaying body parts everywhere. I never actually saw that scene from the plane, but now it's in my mind from time to time."

The discussion ended as abruptly as it had begun. After several minutes, Al continued, "I'm doing a rotation over at your old alma mater. They've got a beautiful new medical center you know." The stranger turned and gazed over toward Harrogate maybe to clear his brain. "What's your work?"

Keith responded that after eight years in the Air Force, he'd taught high school social studies for several years before joining the local community mental health system, to work in the addiction rehab program where he'd been for the past eleven years.

The stranger extended his hand, "I'm Al. Sorry about the lapse. Your name?" Keith guessed the man was talking about the few minutes break in the conversation or maybe the failure to share names earlier. He gave his name, opened his backpack, and spread the food on the rock, and asked Al if he wanted to share.

"No. Thanks." Al removed a flask from somewhere in his clothing, took a gulp and followed it with a long swallow of bottled water. Extending the flask, "Would you care to join me?" Keith flinched, hoped it wasn't visible, and declined. Nearly half the day of one more day of sobriety had passed. He was pleased he could refuse the flask. Al swung his legs back onto the boulder and stood. Before beginning his descent, "Stop by sometime, and I'll take you around campus, even spot you to a cafeteria lunch."

"Maybe I will sometime," Keith responded, wondering if his comments had been appropriate. There are times when a person concurrently sees events and tries to forget, hoping there is another reality. Forgetting has thus far proved impossible for both men.

On the way home, Keith decided to stop in Pineville. Ann, a special friend, a regional emergency care physician stationed in Pineville, unknowingly beckoned. A verbal command sped his cell phone to action and Ann's good-friend voice came through.

"Hello, Ann speaking?"

"I was just wondering if I might stop by?"

"Who is this?" Ann knew who was calling, but her nature was to kid, to jerk him around a little. He laughed. "Where are you?"

"This is three toes Charlie from over on Black Mountain. You know, the one you put the cast on the wrong foot." Both laughed. "I'm actually about four minutes away."

"Sure, come on, but be prepared. Food is unlikely, just a snuggle place." Their relationship was casual, no long term plan necessary, little fanfare, just ready acceptance under most any circumstances. The friendship had flourished since Keith's last detoxification some eleven years before. Ann, on emergency call, had attended, then counseled and cajoled him. But that was in the past. Now hours were spent discussing literature, books on the New York best seller list, history to novels. Interests ranged. They might have gotten married. Keith's fear of the past blocked him from mentioning it, however. He sometimes wondered if she would even consider marriage. She revealed nothing of her thoughts on the subject.

At the door, Ann flashed her special smile, pushed her blond bangs from over her take command blue eyes, and mockingly inquired, "Keith, when are you ever going to enter the cruel adult world, get a place, quit aggravating your mother, learn to cook, make beds? Always out roaming the mountains, getting home at unexpected hours. I'm sure your mother would welcome a little reprieve. Do you want me to call her fabricating a rehab emergency so you can spend the night?" All was said in jest. Both knew his mother loved Ann and encouraged their friendship.

"Always the nagging doctor;" Keith smiled, leaning in and down to kiss her cheek as he answered. A day in the woods walking a damp unpaved trail, sitting on a sandstone rock usually leaves a sign, but not on Keith. His shoes were wiped clean before entering the car, his trousers brushed. Ann saw Keith just as she always did, fixed, ready to enjoin her in conversation that didn't include hospital regulations, Medicaid or Medicare documentation, or cable political news.

Ann had her way. Unlike Keith, she allowed little slack for errant behavior. Always pleasant, yet she demanded action. Grab one of the lifelines. "Cherk up," a favorite Ann term that so far as Keith knew had no dictionary definition, yet he, and everyone else who dealt with her, understood. To her, alternatives always existed for the addict, the depressed or the troubled. Once finished with detoxification, Keith had been subjected to her regimen. Included were six months of mild antidepressants, natural sleep supplements, a vitamin combination, and a special diet. This was accompanied by skiing, fishing, hunting, reading, AA, and a return to stable surroundings, even if it was home to mother.

The county health authorities had offered an enticing financial package for Ann to provide medical services for their methadone program. But no way was she going to prescribe a substitute that might well be more detrimental than the abused drug. She also refused to prescribe the antibuse drug that caused sickness when combined with alcohol. It was drugs that she was fighting. So far her prescription had worked for Keith. He continued to be thankful.

Deep into the night, as the nearby waters of the Cumberland River reflected light from the moon and stars,

Ann and Keith relaxed in a deep double recliner. Ann read from and occasionally commented on *My Own Country*, a troubling account of a foreign-born doctor's encounter with Aids diagnosis and treatment early in the outbreak. His practice was across the mountains in Tennessee, his patients from Appalachian towns familiar to them. Ann identified with the doctor's dogged pursuit and Keith with his compassion. Intense attachment, whether to person, idea, or substance sometimes comes when least sought and in unplanned encounters. Keith and Ann's Saturday night of contentment thus passed.

The Sunday morning temperatures were lower, the sky overcast as Keith made his way toward home, the pleasures of a night well spent comforting him. The fifty minute trip allowed for other thoughts too, including the work week to come. A proposal had been circulated inviting rehab staff to bring a number of residents to the city of Harlan for a big hoopla. The program included addicted mothers with new babies from the women's facility, apartment dwellers from the huge rural Harlan county complex as well as his patients. The morning program was to include a nationally prominent country music singer, originally from a hollow or two away and a football coach legend from Alabama with his story of rehab. Finally, the governor was to present one of the oversized checks designed for press coverage representing funds to be used for treatment facility expansion in the region. These personalities were meant to assure the attendance of court leaders, sports enthusiasts, and country music lovers. The afternoon session was to feature resident speakers telling personal stories; experts from Washington, D. C., and various state officials conducting small group discussions. Such conventions had little attraction for Keith as he associated them with drinking and promiscuous sex from his earlier life, but as he drove home he began to consider making the trip with his little group.

Most of Keith's residents came from modest backgrounds with limited experience outside the world of addiction. Freddie, for example, likely had never eaten at a properly set banquet or seen the governor in person. Other residents' experiences were likely similar and even for those who had seen beyond their gritty world, an orderly, goal-oriented meeting couldn't hurt. Deidra, his second consideration was smart and had had exposure to the world beyond, but needed experiences. The likelihood of seeing a mother expressing thankfulness for being taken in during her pregnancy, hearing about a healthy delivery, watching young women recently transitioning from jail to apartment living and hearing them relate their torrid stories, this eye-opening involvement might motivate. He'd participate.

Approaching his exit, Keith made the decision to attend worship services with the local Presbyterians before going home. Raised a Southern Baptist, this transition to Presbyterian had not come easily. Grandpa had told dad that the family had always been Southern Baptist. Dad told him. The Presbyterians seemed, however, to better understand his sobriety issues. AA and NA meetings were held in their recreational room twice weekly. Besides, in both congregations the statement of faith included salvation through Jesus Christ; denominational and organizational issues might be important, but surely secondary. Still, his name remained on the home church register where his dad and grandpa had attended.

^^^

Alone in her condo, after Keith left, Ann began her usual Sunday morning routine—dusting, arranging, picking up. This was generally followed by yoga exercises, a shower, and church. Ann needed order. When she got to the bookcase in the den where Keith had slept on the couch, something caught her eye, briefly irritating her sense of thing and place. The object, a photo album, was out of order. She took the album down, but before returning it to its proper place, she sat on the floor and began thumbing through it. It contained her baby picture, a picture of her parents on their wedding day, group school photos, her wedding picture—a history of Ann. Suddenly it dawned on her that Keith had taken a look. At first she was angry that he had breached her privacy. After the flash, she calmed somewhat, "I should have admitted this to him years ago." She said this aloud, and looked briefly at the wedding picture.

"You stay home, little lady, and mind the hearth. I'll make us a living." That had pretty much defined the six month ordeal. Ann and Paul met at the university during their senior year. She wanted so to attend medical school, but hardly dared hope. She was a girl. She was poor. She talked country, but her advisor introduced her to the graduate school dean who heartily recommended that she apply. However, the wedding intervened. Paul took her off to Little Rock, presented her to his parents and joined the family trucking business.

"You'll get used to these men, Honey. Work is all they know." Her mother-in-law with her hands placed on the table between them quietly made the statement. That happened the second week when Ann questioned her about the odd hours. Paul left at six and got home sometime after ten for the first several days. Paul's mother was dried up. That's the best description Ann could conjure. She had read widely, but having no one to discuss the content with, she withered around the ideas and pictures of a world beyond the house and yard.

Six months into her lonely world of marriage, Ann took the money she'd skimped and saved out of the household allowance, purchased a bus ticket to Lexington, and fled, carrying only her suit case which contained all her worldly belongings including the wedding picture—the only memento saved from the mistake—no divorce, not even goodbyes. In fact, she didn't really know the status of her marriage all these years later. Enough of that, she thought and briskly turned the pages, stopping at the picture of her parents. They sat in front of a backdrop the photographer had arranged. Father was sitting in a cane bottom chair, Mother standing slightly behind but basically beside him. Ann stood on Father's left beside his knees on which the baby perched holding a teddy bear. The picture had been taken before the accident that left her father confined to a cot in the room with the stove. He neither talked nor acknowledged anyone. His head had been bashed when the mine ceiling broke leaving two of the six-man team he supervised dead and the others with various scrapes and broken bones.

^^^

"I don't know, boys, seems to me the last holdout will likely get the best deal." Abel, Ann's father was addressing several men lounging against the rail fence or the side of the barn. They'd been waiting when he dragged the sled into the barn yard and unhooked the mule.

"I'm about done in, Abel," his nearest neighbor, Fred Claymore, spoke and spat on the ground. Others were cutting a chew, filling a pipe, or rolling a smoke as the two made this exchange relative to selling their land to the big eastern coal company. "The old woman and the younguns ain't got shoes, nor clothes neither that's fit to wear." Fred stopped and looked away across the mountain toward home.

That was the last time the men came. One by one the deputy judge purchased their holdings, holdings that had been in families for four and five generations. Abel soon followed and took a job down below leading a six man crew underground, coming out twelve hours later, the whites of their eyes looking strange in contrast to the coal dust that covered clothing and permeated every pore it reached. Until this sell-out, men came from all over the mountain seeking Abel's advice as to who to vote for, whether to buy this or that, or recommendations for treating a sick cow. All this time Ann's mother, Martha, sang at the clothes line, rocked the baby, churning the milk as she rocked, prepared dishes for the family, for sick neighbors, and church functions.

The picture that stuck in Ann's mind was a different scene, one not recorded in the album. Her mother sat at the rickety kitchen table wearing her dad's old brogans and her every day print dress. She smoothed the tablecloth over and over as she talked. "Honey, things aren't the same as they were two years ago before the accident. Your father can't work or even care for himself. Your grandmother needs my help about as bad as I need hers. This is the best for you." This best involved Ann going with the two officials to the Settlement School, there to spend the next six years vacillating between the thrill of learning, and a nearly unbearable homesickness. There was no coming back home, however. "If you're going to have a chance in life, this is a must. Don't you worry; I'm taking care of your father and little brother. We'll get along. Now, young lady, get hold of yourself." Ann wasn't wailing the day she left home, like she wanted to. She just trembled and looked at her calico cat. "When you get settled there, you get in that library and learn everything in all those books. I'm looking to see your name on a door down in the county seat one of these days." Some version of this admonishment was given Ann by her mother on each of her infrequent visits. Ann would learn later that her mother had cried after each visit. The comforting encouragement she gave Ann did little to diminish her own loneliness.

Again turning the pages, she stopped at the one with her picture from the White Coat Ceremony in medical school. Ann would never forget that first day back at the university, back from Little Rock, back from the failed marriage.

"Dean, you remember Ann." The advisor presented Ann for the second time to the dean.

"Yes, indeed, I do." The dean hadn't remembered, of course, except Ann's advisor had pleaded her case for the interview and presented him with records dating back to her elementary school days on the mountain. Inside was a copy of the letter from the sixth grade teacher recommending her to officials at the Settlement School, grade transcripts from the settlement school to junior college, and transcripts from that experience—all following her and filed now with the University. Each set of records was accompanied by letters praising her abilities, work habits, attitude, and leadership qualities.

"So Ann, what are your plans?" The Dean was looking at Ann and turning a pen between his thumb and forefinger.

"I want to be a doctor, Sir."

Chuckling at his joke which he hadn't yet made, the Dean said, "You know you'll have to attend medical school first."

"Yes." This was Ann's total response, as she looked directly at him. No smile, no nod, nothing indicated that Ann had learned anything from his comment or thought it funny. The dean scooted his bottom on the chair, straightening his bearing. Maybe this young woman was everything the records indicated. He had the uncanny feeling that she might even be capable of reading his mind. "Your records are impeccable, Ann. How, if I may ask, are your finances?"

"I have no money, if that is what you mean."
At this her adviser broke in, "Dean, I was thinking we might give her a work study placement until the next term. She can't enter now anyway."

"That's a possibility." Turning his attention to Ann, the Dean continued. "Think you could handle a placement in one of the labs?"

"Oh, yes. That would suit me fine." Ann had visited several labs during undergraduate studies and was intrigued. "I can also work as a waitress or something off campus."

"You realize that your duties might be limited to clean-up, fetching, and such," the Dean interjected as he flipped something off his tie. "Also, there is money for students willing to go to underserved areas. That might be a possibility later. Where are you hoping to practice by the way?"

"I'm going home, Sir." Ann looked at the floor as she said this. Often during her undergraduate studies, the professors had implored students to leave, get away, experience a life unavailable in their home counties, to see the world.

"Where is home?" The Dean remembered from the records that she had grown up in Appalachia, but didn't remember just where.

"Bell County, Sir;" Ann didn't know whether to be embarrassed by this admission or not as she thought about various professors who had made uncomplimentary remarks about Eastern Kentucky.

"That's perfect. You'll qualify. Ever know Dr. Ratliff down there? He was the health officer for years. He and I completed our residencies together."

"I saw him a few times at the Settlement School. He and his nurse made visits there."

"Funniest thing happened once." The Dean addressed Ann's advisor. "Don't know if I ever told you, Dr. Mundy." The Dean proceeded before Mundy could respond. "Dr. Ratliff and I were performing an appendectomy somewhere out in the state. We were doing a rotation in residency that involved serving several small hospitals." The Dean laughed and laid his pen on the pad in front of him. "Tell you the truth we had no business operating, but there was nobody else. Anyway, I had given the anesthetic and Ratliff was making the cut when this big burly patient rose up, looked around wild eyed, and made a move suggesting that he was getting off the table. No way could either or both of us have held him. But just as sudden as he sat up, he lay back. I gave him another dose of ether for good measure and the operation progressed normal as one might have hoped." The two men laughed. Ann smiled a little, but she didn't think it all that funny.

Ann was brought back to the present by the phone. "Hello, Ann. Are we still on for this morning?" It was the nurse who assisted her in the local emergency room.

"Oh, yes." Ann looked at her watch. She had lost track of time and totally forgotten her commitment. "I'll be ready in thirty minutes." They often carpooled on Sundays, first to church, then to Pine Mountain for lunch. Ann never forgot an appointment, but the morning time-travel had her off center. In fact, she prided herself in never looking back, in always having a project that demanded forward motion. Those who knew her best realized this about her. They also noted that they really didn't know anything about her past, that is, before she was Dr. Ann.

# CHAPTER 8

## Harlan

The crowd of nearly five hundred already fired up by Bonnie Comer's rendition of *Coal Miners' Woes* enthusiastically greeted the governor of Kentucky as he ran up the five stairs to the makeshift podium. "Good morning, Harlan County. Good morning, ladies and gentlemen." He was off, complimenting and recognizing the crossroads community, location of the long-term rehab apartment complex. He praised those responsible for its being there. He welcomed community leaders, elected officials, and residents. "Friends, days like this make me proud to be a Kentuckian. I told my executive assistant, 'Clear the calendar, I'm going to Harlan.' Let the yapping senators meet with their whimpering friends. I'll deal with them latter. Their opposition is toward everything that's humane. They want to deprive little children, to prevent babies from being born drug-free. I don't want to hear it today. I said I want to share the stage with Bonnie and hear her sing. She's a friend of all of us and she's from right over there on Stinking Creek." This was punctuated by an outstretched arm the forefinger pointing toward the mountains. "I'm honored, friends to be with you to sit here with Bonnie and one of the most celebrated coaches of my time, a man who can feel your hurt and appreciate your hope." Turning to the coach, "I watched and supported your teams faithfully, *Coach,* excluding those games against Kentucky universities, of course." The crowd was delighted. College sports unite across the geographical boundaries. This he knew.

Then followed a litany of accomplishments for Southeastern Kentucky under his administration; the mayor of Harlan presented the governor with city keys; the chairman of the apartment complex issued a proclamation; and three of the women from the facility spoke of their personal experiences while living there and how they received good medical care delivered by a friendly staff in a safe environment.

Then Coach began, his drawl noticeable even in Southeast Kentucky, "Folks, I'm a sinner and a drunk, saved from one eternally and fighting the other daily. God saved me, but he gave me good sense to understand that certain physical traits in some of us humans are disabling and need intervention, special attention right here on earth. It's a little like the man asking of the old preacher, 'Is it right to bale my hay on Sunday if rain's a coming'? The old preacher looked him in the eye and answered, 'Son, if the Good Lord gave you that hay, He expects you to have enough sense to get it up'." At this the crowd laughed and cheered. This man could be from around here. "I woke up in a ditch-line outside Oxford, Mississippi on June 12, 1973, my pants soiled, and pardon me, but I don't mean with clay mud, my vision blurred, my head splitting, my insides trying to get out, and didn't know where I was, or how I'd got there. That ditch line was below the road. Friends, I had reached a level spot, didn't know if it was bottom or not. Seeing anything required looking up though—let's just say that. A passing Good Samaritan took pity on a poor lost, sick and stranded soul, stopped her car, and carried me to safety. That angel even bought me a beer for comfort.

"Friends, I hate to tell you what happened next. It wasn't pretty. My lovely wife, my beautiful daughters, my church, my university, even my Lions club, everybody gave me over to the life of sot and shame. No money, no job, no friends. What in the world was I to do? Well, I'd been raised in church among loving Methodists, so it came to me to pray and that I did, asking for guidance and deliverance. I remembered a local priest who loved football. We had talked often about the week's game at a diner near his church and the university. I knew the church sponsored some kind of group, organized to help people like me. To my surprise this man, even though I was not a member of his congregation, took me in so to speak. He took me in, fed me, gave me an ear, and eventually introduced me to the world of AA. What a world!" With the world comment Coach raised his fist and made a circular motion above his head. "Men, women, young and old met there in the basement of that old Catholic Church every Monday and Saturday night. We cried, we laughed, we told stories, but most important we studied and learned the twelve steps to a sober day. Halleluiah, Praise God. I was a hold of something, in God's hand, yes, but something he had given me to fight that sickness that I knew was surely leading to an early death. Do you get the picture, friends? Do you actually see this man of lamentations standing here before you? What he was? What he became? What he can be?" At that, the crowd of rehab residents were on their feet, shouting, clapping their hands, many wiping tears, others sobbing outright.

"Good bye, God bless and carry on. Remember, don't give up on your brother. Dry him out seven times seven, if necessary. You might have heard the seven times before." The crowd gave another extended applause and slowly exited for the afternoon break.

During the afternoon seminar, young women poured out their personal stories. Deidra heard of things outside her personal experiences: A fortyish mother told of her troubled childhood home. "Mother often stayed in bed for days, bruises on her face, trembling, crying. My drunken father made unpardonable visits to my bedroom beginning when I was eight years old. Social services moved me at age twelve to live with an aunt. In that home, life was almost as bad. I was often hungry and cold."

A second woman wept as she talked into the microphone: "I gave away three babies at birth. The first I saw only one time as the nurse cleaned and wrapped him; my first little girl I nursed one time. Then came little Stella. I tended her for three days, determined to keep her. Holding her close at the hospital exit, I waited for the taxi to transport us to a dirty, rat infested apartment, but the craving overwhelmed me. Rather than subject her to my culture of shame, I had the nurse call social services. After each baby I sank deeper into despair and drugs among even more loathsome companions. I'm talking about a ten year period." Her sobbing prevented further reporting for some time. Finally she concluded, "I have no idea how the babies fared or where they are now."

Deidra learned that each of these women had been in prison and eventually was sent to the rehab/housing unit. Their behavior poor, situation pitiful, hopes slim, but at least Deidra thought: my problems don't come up to these two.

Following the afternoon seminars, the full assembly met and heard from those in rehab who discussed the future with hope. All were in AA or NA. Many had relatives in support groups.

The first to speak, a twenty-something, tall, nice-looking, well-groomed man began. "Fellow residents, I'm Ed, an addict in recovery. Sober now for six months my future looks brighter than any time in memory. NA provides a stable crutch. No, not a crutch really; it's a program designed just for me. Each day I awake desiring with all my strength to get through it without seeking or using any substance that might alter my perception of reality or dull my tools of discernment necessary to make good choices. I look forward to work and study, to fellowship with wholesome people who share my new found values. Speaking of work, my counselor back at the rehab facility assisted me in getting enrolled in the local technical college. Aptitude assessments pointed me toward mechanical training. Consequently, I was steered into studies and work in repairing mining equipment, automobiles, and auto computer replacement. The work is sometimes hard, learning all the tools and their use doesn't come naturally, neither does reading the manuals, but I have a goal, a commitment. Realizing where I was came first. Daily fighting to get to a better place comes next. Thank you for listening, and thanks to my counselor for helping me write this presentation."

Freddie perked up during this talk. The seminars meant little to him. Heck, he'd seen all that stuff before, but this working on equipment, that was something real. He knew he was good at it. Mommy and Amanda would be proud, seeing him off each morning in a blue uniform, his name printed on his shirt. Might even get a car and out run old Buddy in his Mustang. Long conversations came hard, but maybe he'd try talking to Keith about this.

That night, as the group was bused back to their rehab facility, Keith reflected on the day. Maybe the convention had been worthwhile after all. Not that any of his charges were likely to aspire to be governor, a great football coach, or singer, but a lot had been said. Someone might have been jolted by another's circumstances, a speaker's goals.

Considering these possibilities, his mind turned again to Freddie and Deidra, not that the other residents were less important. But these two stood out. Each was so different, yet he saw a similar emptiness in each, creating empathy stronger than his normal. Maybe something in his past connected with them on some level, but if so, the ability to identify it escaped him. He needed to examine their symptoms and hope. See if the void sure enough existed and if it could be filled. He hoped that each heard something today that pricked their consciousness, pointed to personal weaknesses, and hopefully inspired them. He knew the remainder of the four weeks would pass fast. Both would leave his unit, either to a ninety-day stay or be discharged.

Keith planned his presentation regarding Deidra and Freddie for coming staff meetings with Goatee, MMPI, and La Pearl. He vacillated between hilarity and guilt each time he thought of and named these learned professionals. Their nicknames in no way identified their professionalism. They had trained in examining the emptiness residents felt. That special training was needed. Of course, issues he saw and would report to these experts, they'd likely label from the Diagnostic Manual, something he wasn't trained to do. So what? Life improvement for each resident was his only goal. To him that meant their staying sober, smiling or crying when appropriate, working, serving others, developing healthy relationships, appropriately separating the light from the dark one day at a time.

It was past midnight when Keith finally locked his office files and headed for home, the trip to Harlan, the full day of speeches and seminars over. All these years, all these hours, very little pay. These negatives never consumed him, but surfaced now and then. He managed to move on, the same as one moves on when minor things rankle. If the whole is good enough, or maybe excellent, one downer like a bad song on an otherwise good CD or a bad chapter in a good book, then the whole is not rejected. The value of a thing sometimes just has to exist in the thing itself, not what the market determines. He considered his work, even though it had limited market value, it paid excellent dividends to society. It reduced health costs, and maybe lessened the burden on disability expenditures. The work force increased, so tax revenues went up. Unlike *Coach* who garnered hundreds of thousands of dollars in salary, plus hundreds more from advertisers, Keith's salary package was small, non-negotiable, and stagnant. Unless handed some largess, Keith could look forward to a small apartment or an older one bath, two bed-room house. He could purchase a car with three to five years wear and eat out at Golden Corral (the 'hog trough' as Ann laughingly called it) on Fridays. Of course, he'd never submit to the latter. He'd just eat fish and salad at home with mother. Concurrently, Keith realized that income management might be just as important as earnings. The one hundred thousand a year man might often borrow spending money from the twenty thousand a year man. He'd seen that happen. At least his pay check covered his expenditures, plus a little each month. A fair retirement was being built. Health insurance was good. He would continue to stretch each dollar earned and keep his accounts paid up. He didn't have to wear Armani or drive a Lexus. Ann earned nearly ten times his income. She didn't seem to take notice, but did keep the relationship on low dollar maintenance. They didn't travel to New York for plays or the symphony. Cultural experiences were limited to programs sponsored by the local colleges. He had never known if her choices were purposeful to match his income or if they truly matched her taste. What she did with all her money never came up. Certainly her environment gave no clue—modest furniture in a low end condo, a three year old Camry, all pluses in his estimation.

# CHAPTER 9

## Aunt Beck

Amanda awoke early, just at daybreak, even though she'd been up twice during the night with Freddie, Jr. This was the day she'd anticipated for weeks. Aunt Beck was going to Florida on what she referred to as a shopping trip. Amanda had lined Freddie's mom up to care for the baby, somewhat against her better judgment. Aunt Beck's acquiescence to her company had been much more difficult, agreeing only after several bribes. She'd agreed to wash supper dishes, and to make all the beds for a month.

This was the day of departure. Four days with no dirty diapers, no looks of disapproval from her mom for slipping over to the trailer for a visit with the boys and getting to see Tennessee, Georgia, and Florida for the first time. Including Ohio that one time, this would be five states she'd have been to. She wondered, maybe she oughtn't count Kentucky—anyway, she hadn't seen much of it.

The circle of her life generally fell within a mile or so radius of home, except those times the twins took her out into the country for creek-side parties. There they shared the joy, marijuana to Percocet, and sometimes coke. Often they splashed in the water and washed the old car being careful of fingers on the sharp rusted metal on the rocker panels and fenders. Always free for a good time, the twins' responsibility never extended to gainful employment. Meeting a drug related deadline was their major concern. Amanda had responsibilities, caring for the baby, mostly at Aunt Beck's insistence.

By eight a.m. they were in the old Impala loaded with a change of clothes, a few other necessaries, and bologna sandwiches. Aunt Beck, never in a good mood, was nearer to it than usual. The shopping trip meant money, pleasure, and livelihood. Keeping the wolf away, as Aunt Beck liked to say. It took some doing. Aunt Beck said everybody wanted something for nothing. The law was always snooping around and her personal habits ate considerable profits. Aunt Beck was maybe fifty, maybe seventy. Amanda wasn't sure. She was a woman of substantial size—height, girth, with a voice to match. Winston cigarettes were always at the ready, one usually clamped between her front teeth. She generally looked to be in the process of dressing, Amanda thought—a bra strap habitually hanging exposed, her skirt hiked in the rear, her blouse not buttoned in at least one place between chin and waist. She had lived on an embankment at the edge of town all her life. Shoppers had visited the home place for bootleg whiskey as far back, in fact, as any of the locals could remember. Beck had never handled any whiskey, too much risk in making and too much bulk to hide. Besides, only the old timers bought drink now-a-days. Emerged was a new generation of clientele. They came from homes like the trailer where the twins and Carl's nephew resided, others from the upscale homes of attorneys, judges, church deacons, and businessmen.

Her product recognized no socio-economic boundaries. It worked the same for all, attaching itself to the very being and becoming nearly impossible to resist. Like chewing gum, sugar, and tobacco, her product guaranteed recurrent sales, but with quicker, more degenerating effects.

At sixty-five miles per hour, the twelve year old Impala shook with a numbing shudder. They drove fifty-five, which suited Amanda fine. She wanted to look. Interstate 75 proved somewhat of a disappointment though, nothing but guard rails, trees, and distant buildings to view. Three times before leaving Kentucky, they exited the interstate and traveled the streets of county seat towns, to visit local churches, but not for worship. They needed help. One receptionist called a deacon. "I've got some travelers needing help," they'd heard her say into the phone, as she examined an eye lash in the mirror behind her desk. The deacon approved the purchase of their lunch at Wendy's; a second stop yielded a tank fill-up, the increase only a quarter tank. No bonanza there. On the third try, Beck's plea was a bit more polished. "I need two hundred dollars travel expenses for two homeless, hungry, needy souls. This child right here before your eyes has issues too awful to talk about in polite company." With that Beck hugged Amanda to her bosom and sighed. This produced a one hundred twenty-five dollar check, the cap per request permitted by the church secretary.

"I'm sorry, Ma'am, that I can't do more." The secretary looked genuinely concerned as she passed along the check. Not that they were broke. Aunt Beck just liked a little cushion in case of emergency, not to mention alibi potential—we're down and out, but can travel because generous people help—if they got in a scrape with the authorities.

After hours on the road, which felt more like days to Amanda, they were just south of Macon, Georgia where Aunt Beck steered the Impala into a rest area, nearly collapsing the front tires against the parking block, the worn brakes doing more slowing than stopping. After the day's fourth bathroom break, sandwiches of bologna and cheese smeared with mustard Aunt Beck had pilfered from the Wendy's stop, the two settled for the night, Amanda in front, her aunt in back. "Aunt Beck, how much money do you expect to get from this shopping trip? Will it be enough for little Freddie a play pen?"

"I don't know and no. My money comes hard. Somebody has to keep a roof over younses head. Ever last one of you'd be out in the cold if not for me." At the mention of roof Amanda pictured the old house, perched on the embankment only a few feet off the highway right of way. Approaching it from east or west, the structure appeared to have a backward leaning, the end chimney separated from the clapboard by several inches and one of the porch steps gone. If not for the Impala parked at one end and the cur tied on the porch, passing motorists might think it uninhabited.

"Did great grandpa make much money selling moonshine? Looks like that'd be all profit." Amanda raised this issue, remembering having heard that he had built the home place long before the road came by. Aunt Beck's customers often discussed about how handy the location was. A few regulars came every day, some often enough to merit credit between monthly disability checks. Of course, these requests for credit were considered but seldom extended. If granted, it depended strictly on the applicant's bloodline. Some families couldn't be trusted. Aunt Beck lost no money, except through her personal consumption, and she never counted that. A big woman required big medicine.

"I don't know. Course it couldn't have been all profit. The law had to be paid, the sugar bought. Now go to sleep. I'm wore out."

It hardly dark and Amanda, having slept two long naps on the drive, wasn't sleepy. She sat thinking, dreaming about things to come, about Freddie Jr. and the boys over at the trailer. She thought maybe Aunt Beck might buy the baby something in Florida, maybe a mobile for his baby bed. Or what if Carl made the twins move while she was gone and they settled miles away?

After long hours of twisting, turning, adjusting clothing, and loud snoring, Aunt Beck awoke. She worked her neck side to side, forward and back attempting to eliminate the soreness. "Wake up, Sleeping Beauty. We're Florida bound. Want to stop at McDonalds, get some good coffee and sausage and biscuit? Maybe I'd druther have gravy and biscuit. When we get on the road, watch for the arches." Aunt Beck appeared obliging this morning, at least for her. Amanda determined not to raise any issues that might change that.

"Aunt Beck, you remember my daddy?"

"Yeah, He weren't no account".

The conversation open, Amanda proceeded to question what the aunt knew. Moving cautiously on what seemed a neutral topic, "Did Mom and him love one another?"

"Must have. You're here, ain't you?" Amanda wanted to ask about his looks, what he did for a living, and several personal things, but fearing more rebuffs she decided against it.

To Amanda's thinking, Valdosta was surely almost there. However, the road proved long and boring. The radio was broken. The air conditioner was not working properly, even though Aunt Beck declared it was and required the windows to be closed. The hot air blew across Amanda's face. Removing clothing was impossible, since she wore no bra. Not that she'd have minded, but Auntie always mindful of legal issues might explode.

In the early evening, Aunt Beck exited the interstate and began negotiating streets left and right. Beck didn't need a GPS (not that she'd ever seen one) to reach their first stop.

Down a street defined neither by business nor residential, Aunt Beck parked near the entrance to a motel, its faded Red Roof Inn sign partially readable—Red Roof being the last motel chain operating in the building. The premises now belonged to parties far removed from the motel business, but who needed a front for other enterprises. Aunt Beck negotiated hard, and finally secured a room with one bed at thirty seven dollars, a discount of five. At least it had a TV which Amanda watched long into the night beginning with *Casablanca,* continuing through *Dancing with the Stars*, and ending with a near porn cable program, the likes of which Amanda had never experienced back in Kentucky.

The next morning, after the motel breakfast, a hard donut and coffee—through which they easily viewed the cup's bottom. "No, I wouldn't care for no more, thank you just the same," the aunt had responded to the clerk's generous offer. Beck ambled her way along a broken sidewalk to the drugstore just down the street. The front window was dirty, the inventory sparse, and it was obviously manned by one employee. This belied something other than an everyday apothecary. Behind a barred window the slight be-speckled man in a dingy white coat showing wear around the cuffs was her contact for this first rendezvous.

“How may I help you this morning, Ma’am?” The clerk or pharmacist began cleaning his glasses, first spiting on the lens and then rubbing it on his coat tail.

“Cut the pretending, Charlie. You know why I’m here.” The arrangements for the purchase had been made by her controller. The necessary patients, their MRI’s, prescriptions, and other data may have been provided by a doctor, or the pills might have come from somewhere south of the border. Beck had no knowledge of the history leading up to her purchase. She merely had her directions. That was enough. She asked no questions.

“Yes, yes, Beck, I didn’t recognize you. Welcome. I’ve got everything ready.” With that, Charlie began sliding packages onto the makeshift window sill, a slit between the bars and the lower wall. Once as he turned to the shelf at his left for more, Beck slid one into her ponderous bosom while pretending to smooth her hair with the other hand. Charlie knew the routine. With his clientele he dared not miss a move during transactions. Rather than make a scene, he merely added the price plus a little transgression fine for the attempted theft.

From somewhere on her person Beck produced and peeled off ninety-two hundred dollars, bid Charlie good day and strolled to the waiting car parked at curbside. Amanda sat looking smug, having waited fifteen minutes, as directed, before leaving the motel parking lot. This was a dangerous part of the journey. The drugs were in a local mall shopping bag furnished by Charlie. Not only were police a menace—not the locals unless a Kentucky officer operating on a tip was involved—but local users who knew of the operation often demanded consideration. Beck never came armed. She depended on her bulk for protection. After repeating a similar purchase twice more at different locations across town, the two were on I-75 North in a short time, but not before the drugs were securely stored. The packaging altered for clandestine hiding consisted of cylindrical plastic bags twelve or so inches long, four inches in diameter with a zip top. They were not filled to capacity, allowing them to take varying shapes when loaded. Crevices behind the headlamps, the door panel on the back rear door, and a tubeless spare tire carried the largess. One auto in a stream, the total number unknown, moving north and bound for the Kentucky hills contained enough temporary relief for a large portion of the population in Beck's small county. Relief was not necessarily her objective. The opposite usually proved to be the reality.

After a long day's drive, the two were nearing Valdosta again, Amanda asleep in the back seat, Beck driving and singing *I'll Fly Away*. She had been very religious in her early days before taking over the business after the death of her dad. In fact, Amanda's mom related that Beck had been known to "shout her hair down" as she and others danced their way through snake handling exercises. This happened over in Bell County. Amanda didn't condemn her though. People should worship as their heart leads. Freddie, in one of his more talkative moods, had once declared that, "Beck'd still be religious if making a living hadn't got in the way. She'd put that above the Lord." Amanda thought that Freddie's talk that day might be what made her want to have his baby.

The car crawled along the freeway, easily passed by every vehicle going north or at least followed by none. Even so, blue lights, brought to Beck's attention by a siren, moved perilously close behind and in their lane. Beck, never having encountered such, had to think a bit before deciding to pull to the shoulder. By this time her mind cleared and, ever mindful of the cargo, she directed Amanda to get the pale pink towel from under the passenger seat and wrap her head, completely covering her hair and one eye. The officer came along side and asked for her driver's license. After examining it for some time, he passed it back and said he'd noticed her swerve back down the road and asked was she drinking. "Heavens no, officer, I've been driving all day trying to get this sick child home," Beck drew a deep sigh. "I took her to Florida for treatment and am terribly worried about her. The little thang may never get better." Having said this Beck wiped her nose on sleeve. At that, the officer looked more carefully into the back seat. The sight was unnerving for him as he, too, had a teenage daughter. Amanda, her head completely wrapped, one eye looking pitifully at him, smiled faintly and then moaned.

"Lost all her hair has she?" The officer addressed Beck who said she couldn't bring herself to discuss it. The circumstances and hope were too slim. "Be careful. The worry obviously impaired your driving. Wish I could be of some help. People have no idea what we run into out here. Bless you and the girl." With that Beck wiped her eyes, then her nose again on the sleeve of her blouse, and drove on toward Kentucky.

The trip was uneventful until the next day as they climbed upward a few miles north of Lafollette, Tennessee past the great rocks with layers pointing up and down, not sideways as they were deposited eons ago. The car got hot. Beck wouldn't have noticed except a passing motorist observing the steam coming from the front grill blew his car horn and pointed, finally getting the message to her. She knew enough mechanics to realize the car should be stopped and shut off. With the hood raised she stood on the shoulder peering, at what she wasn't sure. Steam was coming from a hose attached to some part of the engine. A trucker seeing her plight stopped. At first, she thought he looked like someone with hanky-panky on his mind. Beck was ready. Instead he quickly diagnosed the problem. A hose had burst. This he wrapped in duct tape. After several minutes he added the remains from his gallon of drinking water to the radiator overflow tank.

"Drive slow. Stop if the heat gage registers over on hot and let the engine cool. You can make it the next twenty or so miles to Jellico. Stop at the Marathon Station just off the exit ramp and ask the service man—Abe, if possible—to replace the hose and coolant. Don't let him work on anything else or charge you more than fifteen or twenty dollars." Beck's attempt to pay was refused. She thought maybe a little romp with such a nice fellow might actually be nice. She bowed and profusely thanked him, then followed the slow moving semi back onto the roadway.

Home looked good that night. Amanda went straight to bed, deciding to get the baby early next morning. Beck reviewed her new inventory, divided some of it into allotments for various couriers, and then counted her expected earnings. Life was in order.

Florida shopping for Beck, stressful as it was, had an unknown dimension completely beyond her purview. The pharmacy was a working cog in the "pill mill" in Kentucky drug interdiction parlance. What began as a drug leak in Florida became a veritable flood as it passed through the narrow Eastern Kentucky valleys. Coupled with meth labs, the coke from the west and the heroine from the north, local couriers were well stocked.

Beck's MO: deliver the goods from Florida; monitor the courier distribution and receipts; maintain her personal clients (calendar contacts supplemented this Florida inventory). She never met or knew the regional contact(s) that arranged the Florida connection. Rumor was that the network covered several counties. Small time operators like Buddy Mustang worked outside the organization, but offered little competition. Her monthly take was substantial. For cover, Beck drove the rickety Impala. The family collected food subsidy, visited the charity distribution centers, and utilized Medicaid, and at least one member, Amanda's mom Sis, collected disability. Existence of the strong box, known only to Beck, was never mentioned or suspected, as Amanda and Sis gave little thought to financial matters.

# CHAPTER 10

## The Boys Get Busted

Amanda decided she'd better call Freddie. He'd want to know the news. After an anxious day of looking out across the road and the corn field at the trailer nearly a quarter mile away, Amanda realized the action had played out. The boys at the trailer had finally met UNITE (Acronym for Unlawful Narcotics Investigation, Treatment, and Education). For all she knew somebody had called the drug tip line, likely old man Carl. Earlier that day two SUV's rolled along the dirt tracts through Carl's cornfield carrying two sheriff deputies, a city police officer, and two state troopers, the latter serving as local interdiction task force members. Knocking before ramming the door, entry had been swift. Meth cooking, mixing, straining, and drying were taking place among the clutter of overflowing ash trays, pop cans, pizza boxes, and assorted items of clothing. Open boxes crammed with tools, iphones, and lap-tops sat here and there on the floor. Officers, trying to hold their breath and touching nothing, did a quick visual, then backed out the door, ordering the boys to follow.

One of the twins, Jerald, bolted through a back exit, refusing to respond to halt commands. A deputy later reported, "He run like a coyote" through the waist high corn, crossing the field which encircled the trailer to the back fence. He cleared the would-be obstacle in a magnum, meth-enhanced jump, but fell immediately into the drainage ditch a few feet away where he lay for some time, the wind knocked out of him. The younger of the troopers followed just steps behind. While still in the ditch, the twin was tossed a collar made from the policeman's belt and ordered to tighten it around his neck and attach it with the dangling Velcro, which the officer ripped from his flak jacket, to a stick he had selected from the ditch line. The two men traipsing back through the corn reminded Amanda of a wild man capture from a movie scene, or maybe a man leading a two legged donkey. She knew the collar and stick allowed the officer to avoid contact with the poisons. Amanda couldn't keep from giggling. "I'm telling you the truth, from where I was Jerald looked like a two legged donkey being led through the field." This she laughingly repeated several times to anyone in her presence.

The twins, Jerald and Earl and their friend, Louie, were made to sit among the horse weeds in front of the trailer door, locking their own cuffs, Jerald removing his collar. From the SUV that had hauled no passengers, the Officers unloaded piles of tarp, tent poles, buckets, and cans of cleaner—Amanda didn't know what kind exactly—decontamination paraphernalia, she guessed. She'd seen pictures of meth cleanup printed in the local paper from time to time. They then spent hours hauling water from Carl's outside spigot to wash down the boys, the officers, and any gear involved. After stringing yellow police tape around the parameter and posting warnings of dangerous chemicals, the two SUVs swayed and bumped back across the corn field. Carl observed from his front porch. He was advised that the trailer was uninhabitable until extensive cleanup by a certified de-con company was completed. That suited him fine. He had no intentions of letting anyone else move onto his place. A man's carefulness got stressed—renters with arrest records, dangerous people on the run, rogues, and now something he'd never heard of, property contamination.

Later that day, with the boys checked in at the detention center, a phone call allowed one of the boys, Louie, who hadn't bolted, to reach his uncle—Carl's brother's brother-in-law. The Circuit Clerk's staff directed the uncle to the County Attorney. It was long after office hours before the contact was made, but the official obligingly came in—after all, the boys' families voted. Bail was granted. Much to the arresting officer's chagrin the boys ate a late supper in the Main Street Diner. "No jail house gonna hold me," Jerald boasted loudly to those in hearing.

The paths chosen oftentimes need to be analyzed and discussed by family and acquaintances. This was the case for the three. Their paths veered from the previous generation. The boys' families were intact. "Me and the woman both worked, provided, you know, and advised. We read to them when they's little fellers, even sent 'em to kindergarten." Earl and Jerald's father was speaking softly, as he shifted his foot back and forth in the dirt, his shoe sole sinking into the soft earth. "We took 'em to church." The two fathers leaning against the barn gate on the twin's father's farm, the glow from their cigarettes punctuating the late spring evening, pondered.

"I reckoned Louie may have taken after his mother's brother. Sometimes blood rules," Louie's dad said, then turned and rested his foot on the lower rung of the gate.

"That high school riffraff may have had a lot to do with this." The twin's dad ground his cigarette under foot and sighed. Finally, after considerable back and forth discussion, he allowed, "The preacher might have it right—any family not affected is just plain blessed. I drunk a little beer and run the roads a right smart in my young days, but this bunch don't seem to want to know nothing or to be nothing."

Louie's dad had been silent for some time. "Times has changed though. Young people are different. They got more time. I worked. By ned, we all had to work. This generation, big part of them, don't even know who their daddy is much less their grandpa. No direction, a road to trouble sure and certain. I'd a let em' lay up in jail a week or so if it'd been left up to me. I hate to say it cause they're mine and Carl's people, always knowing it all, not a'tall like Carl or me, but they shouldn't a bothered in this. Wonder one of 'em weren't right in the middle of the whole mess, making and all. Of course, Carl's sister might not be so innocent. Bet she's been furnishing their tobacco. I told her it wouldn't do, boys over there by theirselves." Louie's dad quieted, removed his handkerchief and wiped his eyes and nose. 'leave 'em alone. They've got to get experience,' that's what she said."

"Well, you can see about the experience now. Some say we might still get them ordered to rehab at the court hearing. Can't be sure though. Half the county's tricks was found in boxes in that fly trap. Sure never thought we'd raise three thieves. Durned if I don't feel like hunting em up and taking a running and go and kicking all three of their hind ends."

Chuckling, the twin's father allowed "That might not be the best plan. All three are pretty good size men." The discussion progressed until well past midnight. Both men made profound declarations followed by long pauses as the next thought of something to add.

Meantime Amanda was swelling with news and needed to get it off her chest. The enforcement team, their paraphernalia, the chase across the field all needed to be reported. After considerable thought and organizing her story, she decided to call Freddie.

"Hello, Freddie, bet you can't guess who this is?"

"Yeah, I think I can."

"Who?"

"Oh, Amanda, we both know who's called. Got any news? What'd Mommy say about sending to git me?"

"Freddie, she ain't saying much toward that. I'm guessing she wants you to stay and get her six hundred dollars' worth. These last few days will be gone before you know it. Yes, I have got some real big news. You know I've been telling you them boys over at the trailer would wind up dead or in jail. Well, know what? I was right. All three of them—Louie, Jerald, and Earl—just got a good washing down and hauled off to the clinker. What ya think about that?"

"Well, I hate it for 'em; Can't be much worse than being in here though. Was they making?"

"Must a been, police put up a mighty show—tents, buckets, spray ever where, a yellow ribbon tied all the way around the place. A big white sign is stuck on the door. Ain't sure what the sign said, couldn't make it out even with binoculars."

"Doused me if I know how they thought old Carl'd put up with that." Freddie's mind reviewed their plight and allowed that he'd thought a right smart of all three of 'em except he knew Amanda slipped over there ever chance. He wasn't sure the twins hadn't been egging her on, showing her their shoulder tattoos and such. Danged if he'd let Mommy talk him into any more such doins. This rehab nonsense was driving him crazy.

Amanda wasn't finished talking about the day's excitement. "I believe that Louie was probably the pappy of all that went on. He's older, you know, and he was always going to do something big—get him a diesel pickup or a four wheeler or some such. I wonder how in the world they expected to get by the law. Stuff they bought at the hardware store and the drug store, Aunt Beck said was both dead give-a-ways, not to mention the awful smell that drifted off toward Carl's. He was in the cornfield back toward the trailer nearly every day. Aunt Beck said it about right," Amanda continued after a chomp or two on her gum, "Sometimes people's got an idee bigger than their brain."

Freddie said, "Bye," and hung up, his mind filled with concern for the boys. He'd meant to remind Amanda to be sure and give Mommy his message and to ask about Freddie, Jr. but forgot both until sometime later. Amanda, in a way, was going to miss the boys. It was fun slipping over, enjoying laughs, pizza, and flirting with them. Earl, the biggest twin was sweet. In fact she wasn't totally sure whether or not he was Freddie, Jr's. daddy. She never raised the issue though. That family wouldn't have acknowledged him or spoke to her for that matter. Freddie'd have to do. Unlike Aunt Beck, who could take men or leave them, Amanda needed one standing by, not so much for financial support. She wasn't exactly sure what it was—pride of ownership maybe. Her mom wasn't well now, of course, but she'd apparently never needed a man either. After Amanda's dad, none had been around. While her mom didn't say much about Freddie, she talked pretty bad about his mom and her earlier comings and goings.

After his phone call from Amanda, Freddie was, for him, pretty stirred up. He even felt a need to talk. That presented two problems, however, the words came hard and someone to talk to even harder. Mr. Keith was still in the building. His evening shift nearly ended, he was completing staff notes and arranging his desk before locking up for the night when Freddie cautiously approached his desk. “Hello, Freddie, what’s on your mind tonight?” The amiable Keith surprised and pleased to see Freddie’s boldness, smiled and waited.

“Hid’dy. The boys got in trouble.”

“Somebody in your wing?” Keith, not being privy to Freddie’s thoughts, began fishing.

“No, the boys back home, over at the trailer:” Freddie was pretty sure he had previously mentioned the group.

“What happened?” Keith quizzed as he drained coffee from his thermos and offered Freddie a cup. The offer was declined. Freddie put first one hand in a pocket, then the other.

Finally, Freddie’s nerve was up, his out-loud talking anxiety down. “Law got ‘em for making. Put ‘em in jail too. Amanda just called and told me.”

“These boys friends of yours, Freddie?”

“No, I just went over there sometimes, usually to get Amanda. I like old man Carl. He gets me to work on his equipment sometimes.”

"Does Amanda live with the boys?" Keith continued his query.

"No, she just slips over there." Freddie looked at the floor and gave this barely audible response.

After a series of gently probing questions, Keith pieced Amanda's story together; then attempted to draw Freddie out even more. "Your being away that day was probably good. Meth is dangerous."

Freddie didn't know though if Carl should have called the police, that is, if he did. He concluded, "I like it a little better here. I'm goin' to finish the thirty days if I can." Laughing, Keith said, "I'm glad you're staying. It likely won't hurt you a bit."

Back in his room, as he dressed for bed, Freddie was thinking about the good talk he'd had with Mr. Keith. Then he reviewed the process he'd go through getting that last bolt out to remove the water pump on Carl's tractor. Somebody had broken the head off and given up, leaving Carl to add water and antifreeze every few work hours. I'd sure love to be going down to the grocery to get me a Pepsi, Freddie thought as he dozed off to sleep.

# CHAPTER 11

## La Pearl Observes

Just off the waiting area, French doors opened into a large room with floor to ceiling windows along one side. A fireplace with built-in shelves on each side adorned the far wall. The shelves featured an array of books, art and craft supplies, puzzles and board games. Eight or ten residents were intent, seriously assembling or creating objects of beauty from Popsicle sticks, leather, paints, even clay. The potter wheel whirled, the clay climbing from a wad toward bowl-hood in the hands of an unlikely looking artist, a former football lineman. Near the far end of the room a table of three sat. Deidra, sat rail straight, arms extended, adjusting her hands and book for proper distance; the other two lounged in various positions of slouch. She was focused on the book, her voice rising and falling, gruff, then soft as demanded by the story line. Though sprawled around the table, the listeners' eyes revealed serious concentration, visualizing scenes far away outside the recreation room. The scenes temporarily papered over the despair that personal reality had produced in each.

La Pearl, the therapy team social worker, sitting in a padded rocker near the fireplace, panned the room, refocusing her sight from the tedious cross stitching in her lap. This one evening a week was a get-acquainted opportunity, a time for hints of possible redirection for lives out of control. Participation in the exercise also gave her personal satisfaction, a time of creativity. As she recently confessed to Dr. Lee, "This is not work. It's relaxing, a time for reflection, and a time to observe, to maybe find the key to the shaping of a new vision. I love it. What I mean, I guess, is that this is as close to a lab as I'll get."

Deidra's reading had led Freddie to join the table. *Huckleberry Finn* proved just the stimulus. Freddie let his mind float with Huckleberry on the great river, ran with him from danger as he sought natural crevices for safety, or fished from the muddy banks. The story filled Freddie's head with scenes of things other than home; scenes beyond his experience, yet that he could connect with. Deidra felt something akin to pride, believing her influence on Freddie might in some way give him a boost, spunk, as her mother might say. During these times when she felt strength, determination, success, Deidra's demeanor changed. She hardly knew herself, the great tattoo the only reminder of another life, the time of loss, emptiness, and degradation. She didn't know when or where that marking on her body happened or exactly when the craving that eventually controlled her mind began. But on this night around the table in rehab she became the teacher, the organizer, a certain leadership blooming and emitting from her. Deidra felt smart, good looking, needed, maybe not brilliant or glamorous. Without her full awareness, her future began to point toward light. With every step, every sentence, every thought, an epiphany was emerging surely to be the new Deidra. Though sure she would never see any of the residents after this period of rehab, still she thought of them as little brothers and sisters needing her guidance. Later when she discussed her care-giving endeavors and connection with the other residents, Thad, the psychologist, reinforced her.

"Deidra, you're a natural. People listen to you. They seem to want to please you, to gain your attention and approval. Keep it up, girl."

Behind her, she decided, were the hazy days of driving through the countryside in an unfamiliar car with men she knew by name only. Such were her vague memories of the Las Vegas trip. A Richmond bar encounter led to Lexington, a horse farm, parties. She could recall in bits the trip being orchestrated by and for players—ball players, salesmen, lawyers—from several states. She found herself among twelve revelers on a charter jet to Nevada. Leading the group was someone, Deidra mentally referred to as the Head, an average sort—height, weight, looks—she thought. His talents included showing others how to have a good time and as one of the lawyers pointed out, how to manipulate politicians and government bureaucrats. Growing up in Eastern Kentucky, some say, insures interpersonal limitations, but this planner/advisor carried no such baggage. At home in the Governor's mansion, in a mountain cabin, or a palace on the Mediterranean, he negotiated the hotels and casinos in Vegas as though they were his. As they entered the casino, he'd encouraged, "Come on boys and girls. Let's show these high rollers how it's done in Kentucky." Money spilled from the group, with the house scooping up thousands, the spenders shrugging, grimacing, before moving on, ever hopeful for the elusive lady's favor at another table, in another room, on the next toss.

In Vegas, the mountaineer Head furnished Deidra's wardrobe. She bought beautiful clothes, dresses with low necklines, each cut far above the knee, clothes suitable for the clubs. She was noticed, appreciated, and admired. She loved it. Beauty and privilege seemed assured. "Walk over near the window and turn around, Sugar. Let me get the full effect." His eyes narrowed, and bouncing quarters in one hand, he examined her head to foot. This was before the tattoo.

After ten days or so, the party burned down. The group gradually began to exchange looks bordering on hostile. Deidra was dumped on return to Lexington, no money, no luggage. Only vague memories remained—

others were lost in the fog of alcohol and cocaine. The Head had all but pushed her from the cab. "You'll be okay. You're no worse off now than when I picked you up. Keep your chin up." This was his encouragement, thanks, or whatever.

Once the lights were out and the facility settled into night-time lockdown, Deidra sat at her small desk. Only her laptop lighted her surroundings. As she thought about the day, about her "students," her need to express something special surged. For the second time since community college, she felt a need to write—something special for the troubled humanity that she knew so well, but felt she had now risen above. She began.

*O Fathers, where are your sons?*
*Their rippling biceps*
*Their chatter that amuses, challenges, and concerns you*
*Where is your joy, pride of success, and future mark*
*O Daughter what have you done, where is the gift*
*Who comforts you now, considers your thoughts*
*A rift that time cannot heal, the whole now in shreds*
*Shreds that dangle, warp, and blow with the wind*
*O Mothers where are you, your touch, your warmth, your daughters*

Deidra read and re-read the writing. She deleted sections, added them again. She paced the area from her desk to the door. Finally, exhausted with the endeavor, she closed, saving the document. Maybe she needed Mr. Keith's eyes and wisdom. Later that night she dreamed, awoke in her dream, knew she was dreaming, but couldn't escape it. She had moved to a city, maybe Lexington. She wasn't sure. The apartment was near downtown, furnished and decorated in eclectic pieces with matching accoutrements which included a lamp, its stand a yellow naked nymph that came on automatically. She could plainly see the entire layout, but she could never reach the address. The bus stop never turned out right. A ride with two strange men, too, left her stranded. She called the real estate rental lady, whose directions were always clear, but never correct.

^^^

First thing after breakfast next morning, Deidra made her way to Mr. Keith's office hoping to present her writing for his critique before the others gathered for group. "Good morning, Deidra." Always ready to accommodate residents, to make them feel comfortable, Keith folded the file he was busy completing and looked at her hoping to be able to read any sign of distress.

"Mr. Keith, I know you're busy preparing for group, but if you have just three minutes. I have written something I'd appreciate your reading."

After reading the document, he complimented her skill and requested that she let him keep the copy for further consideration. At this Deidra decided to tell him about her dream. "Very interesting, Ms. Hammock," was his only reply. Now encumbered with a writing he didn't understand, a dream he dared not analyze, Keith was in a quandary. Hurriedly, before the residents filed into the group room, he made his way to the staff conference room and presented Deidra's dream report and the writing to the three professionals. Dr. Goatee said he didn't put much stock in dreams and thought the writing emerged from a mind wired for action brought on by her recently assumed care-giver role. "Give it no further thought."

Thad (Long hair MMPI) stood, scratched his head, and turned around in front of the table. "I want more time to study it and to examine the literature on dreams." La Pearl had no comment, but did take notes.

# CHAPTER 12

## Examining Riddles

Friday mornings, dedicated to staffing, discussing treatment plans, and screening potential admissions, meant the staff conference room saw robust activity. Today was typical. The librarian pulled records from hanging files and placed them in stacks before each professional. This staffing team examined each, added sticker notes delineating deficiencies. Treatment plans, daily notes, evaluations, and impressions all were parsed for course of treatment and impressions relative to patient progress.

Indicators that pointed to special medical issues were given to Dr. Lee. This, took time, too much time to suit Goatee M.D. His training, his head, his heart of hearts told him that all was 'matter, all chemical', pure and simple. Talk therapy and documentation had its place—more so before the day of the miracle drugs. Nineteen fifties psychotropic medications led the way for his style of practice. Other members of this team weren't even alive when these early medicines came on the scene. His approach: matter is controlled by the new meds which redirect chemical and electrical charges in the brain. People had begun to function on these meds. Hospital admission and length of stay dropped precipitously. "Addiction, even cases not associated with underlying psychiatric disorders, will be the next to fall, probably genome based." The doctor had reported this to the local medical society recently.

Goatee had done some cell research between med school and his psychiatric residency and had adopted his view of illness. The cell contains all there is to man—something he thought but didn't say in most circles. Certain behaviors increased heart rate, affected digestion, elicited laughter. The chemical reaction did the final trick. Long

Hair, he thought, spent considerably too much time chasing behaviors, attempting to find a thought that produced a "tic," for example.

It was the discussions following staffing that excited Keith. Brilliant minds sometimes offered speculations that made absolutely no sense, yet were argued vigorously. Many of the speculations were later to be compromised by emerging facts. Someone might quote St Augustine, Plato, or some such, and raise issues of lasting certitude for Keith's further contemplation.

Today's first interchange opener came from Long Hair MMPI, "Did you see the inaugural address this week?"

"Yes," all three answering at once produced a certain harmony. The psychologist continued, "What do you think the chewing gum meant he was trying to get across?" President, Obama, along with an apparent secret service attendant stood viewing the parade, busily chewing as the camera panned.

"Or his lingering viewing of the crowd as he exited," Keith's breath was short, coming in quick bursts as he hurriedly expressed this before the thought slipped his mind.

"I'm getting out. There is enough political stuff already out there," the social worker gathering her leather satchel, began to rise.

"No. No. I just wanted to examine the phenomena from a psychological viewpoint. Everybody knows that great men construct phrases, make gestures, visit shrines for specific affect, attempting to generate a certain response. It's just that I can't figure these two." The psychologist was doodling as he talked.

"He sure wasn't mimicking the greats—Washington, Jefferson, or Lincoln." Drawing from his high school teaching and his personal interest, Keith was in tune with the discussion as he pulled at his pant leg to straighten the crease.

La Pearl flipped her hair. "Those guys didn't have modern news outlets. You might be surprised what they would have done. Think of Jackson, for goodness sakes."

The psychiatrist, chuckling quietly tapped the table top with a pen and suggested, "I'm guessing chewing was gum for indigestion and he was just looking for a friend during the long gaze."

The social worker, more composed now, "I think he was making a statement: this term is going to be done right for all of us."

"I don't know," the psychologist continued. "I remember the earlier faux-pas during his first term visit with the English Royalty. Chances for such behavior with his Harvard background and staff preparations were nil. I questioned at the time if maybe he was saying, to heck with your pomp."

"You think that same attitude was being replayed after the inaugural speech?" Keith's interest was pricked.

"Possibly the gum chewing said to a large segment of spectators, look I'm one of you. This is just talk and show. The long gaze prior to exit was suggestive of great and wonderful things seen only by him, almost like Moses looking into the promise land." Under his palm Long Hair rolled a ball point pen on the table and concluded, "Actually, I don't have any idea what that was about."

A file clerk from behind a glass in the adjoining chart room, spoke up, "I'm willing to bet gum makers contributed financially to the inaugural or something. There is a payoff somewhere, not likely for the likes of us though."

"It'll be talked about, that's for sure. History professors one hundred years from now, seeking a nugget to prompt memory and discussion will relate the story about the gum-chewing president." Keith suddenly feared this last remark disrespectful. If so, it had risen from some subconscious level. His regard for all U. S. Presidents, including Mr. Obama, was high.

As a basis for his support of the president, MMPI agreed with economists who espoused greater spending and wider deficits. "I think it was Kaletsky, in his book, *Capitalism 4.0,* who argued that government spending, a forthcoming energy boom, and sensible regulations, point to a secure economic future." The psychologist was refocusing the discussion.

"Security, you got it. That's my long sought-after ticket, the only ticket with intrinsic value to each of us. Coupons good at any time, gently pluck from the security tree, exchange for life rewards." The group looked at La Pearl, each questioning her sudden politically charged remarks.

"Listen, financial security, personal and family security, psychological security, all these are man's ultimate goals. That is what the president stands for in the mind of the mass, if he is properly discharging his duties," MMPI followed-up.

Keith interrupted. "Spiritual security, isn't that even more important? Also, I'm not sure what you mean by security. Man has needed security from the government as well as through government involvement throughout history."

"I heard someplace that a politician's vanity is exceeded only by his pride." This remark from Goatee brought smiles to all.

After signing out that same afternoon, Keith left through the side door into the parking lot. To his right were a series of benches, one now occupied by two residents in hot discussion. "That's a lie and you know it." Both men rose, the older man accusing the younger. Keith, altering his course, approached. "How you two doing?" Hoping to diffuse whatever was burning between the two, He wasn't aware that the altercation had been going intermittingly since the previous group session when the leader had required them to "take it outside."

The older man leaned in, his face close to the other's nose, "I can't stand a liar." During the group discussion, the accused had talked of losing three hundred thousand dollars in his divorce settlement, along with other outlandish claims. The senior resident, knowing for certain he couldn't even count to three hundred thousand, had heard enough. The combatants, eyes locked, pressed close. Keith moving as best he could between the two, eased the young man back a step, then looked intently toward the older man's collar. Slowly he raised his right hand and removed a tobacco crumb before straightening, and gently tightening the flowered tie—the veteran's daily attire. At this, the older man's thoughts turned inward, considering his personal appearance rather than the other's outrageous claims. The atmosphere relaxed. All three sat and soon were discussing an array of interests including Viet Nam, often part of the older man's monologue. After several minutes, the younger man admitted that the three hundred thousand was a figure he hoped to collect when his in-laws passed. The three soon dispersed, two to think about themselves, the third to get on with his weekend.

# CHAPTER 13

## New Englander in Middlesboro

The morning plenary session had just begun when Keith entered the conference room and took a seat Ann had saved for him. After greetings, he was surprised to see Al, the pinnacle hiker he'd recently met, sitting directly in front of him. In fact, the huge frame blocked his view of the podium where a man from the Kentucky Department of Mental Health was reading the resume of Dr. Hammer, the noted epidemiologist from the National Institute of Health (NIH). A bit embarrassed at being late, he whispered to Ann that the drive was so beautiful he lost track of time. The bloom and early leaves along the Cumberland River, always a week or so ahead of home, touched his spirit, awakening parts of him dormant from the bleak winter. Always a respite, the spring staff training was held on a mountain top beyond Middlesboro. There Kentucky, Tennessee, and Virginia meet to express a beauty that he'd always found safely intoxicating.

On the drive he had passed through Pineville. Traveling along the floodwall, he had looked over into a city only two-thirds its former self. There sat a new structure where the community mental facility once stood before the great river stormed the city in 1977, pushing the ceiling tiles out, drenching medical records, and halting operations. Rebuilding meant less-city. That had been before his time working at the agency. Today the river meandered lazily, reflecting trees and shrub along its shores.

Dr. Hammer began his talk, billed as part pep and part admonition. His opening remarks, delivered in a New England brogue, sounded foreign in Southeastern

Kentucky, but the talk carried a promise of living up to the billing. "Ladies and gentlemen, I come before you this morning bringing greetings from your NIH, but less than good news. Our nation is crying out: All Hands on Deck! May Day! May Day! Not merely Pan-pan. From the gang-clogged streets of Chicago, from the nation's kidnap capital of Phoenix, from the import cities of Florida, from the beaches of San Diego, from one southeastern Kentucky Valley to the next, from each crossroad throughout the flatlands of Kentucky, the cry, the pleading, is the same. Mom is crying. Dad is in anguish. Where are our beautiful children? Court Rooms are clogged. Jails are full. Schools are floundering. The church is in a quandary. Folk, we have a full blown emergency. Something is askew in our great society. The need to dull the senses, to numb the pain has outstripped our resources, our knowledge, and our will. You who are on the front line see the victims and patch and salve their wounds. Good for you. Thank you. But fellow troopers, we've got to move into and behind the lines. Impetus for this deluge must be better understood and eliminated."

After Dr. Hammer's introduction, considerable talk time was granted his assistants, each presenting recently published research. Long having questioned what the lure creating this pandemic must be, Ann had concluded there were as many issues pushing the desire for illicit drugs as there are those in search of it. She remembered confiding to Dr. Lee years ago, "Work a random group of people eight to ten hours a day offering calisthenics, swimming, distance running, wholesome food, multiple vitamins, all under strict supervision, leave drugs in an unsupervised bathroom, and somebody in that group will partake and convince others of the marvelous benefits. Consider the national sports leagues." Dr. Lee, no less concerned, had responded, "Maybe natural law has evolved, creating a need for institutions beyond those known and accepted by modern sociologists." Ann shook her head—too much thinking, too fast, not healthy. She moved on to thinking about the possible dynamics of her upcoming group—a combination of staff and residents from the various rehab units across the region.

Dr. Hammer and his assistants passed out printed materials listing types of drugs, their prevalence, the national passageway for each, the crippling cost to society, and other pertinent information. The assembly broke into small groupings around a large conference room. Each group, led by a facilitator, was challenged to analyze and assimilate a list of strengths and weakness within their local community. List and discuss what they saw as causes for the growing abuse problem. What were the barriers to prevention and the weaknesses in the social fabric—the community psyche. As the groups were organizing, Ann made her way to Dr. Hammer.

Smiling, Ann introduced herself and complimented Dr. Hammer on his talk. "I understood the urgency, the all hands on deck, the May Day, but why down-play Pan-pan?" She asked this, mostly an effort at pleasantries or for comic relief.

Dr. Hammer looked pleased, a hint of a smile on his face, "Pan-pan, look it up. It'll be a growth experience." Hint, hint, it isn't of English origin, especially not the English you people speak." Ann's smile faded. That was it. She'd be ready for that donkey during the afternoon question and answer session. She hadn't particularly liked his New England brogue. The inflated condescending attitude was totally unbearable.

That evening Keith, Ann, and Al sat together at dinner. As it turned out, Al and Ann were acquaintances, having met in a number of area hospital emergency rooms. His rotation practice at LMU, her emergency room practice in Pineville took them throughout the mountains. Often they traveled together transporting patients. Sometimes they performed temporary fixes at mining disaster sites, four-wheeler and other vehicle accident locations and, too often overdoses. Each respected the other's professional approach—her broad experience, his more recent training in diagnostics and his impressive knowledge and use of the latest in medical equipment.

"Al has decided to stay in the mountains to show us older folk how today's medicine should be practiced. Besides what does Madison County have that we don't? I'm planning on introducing him to some Pine Mountain beauties at next month's festival, maybe I can even wrangle a judging assignment for the pageant. I've got friends in the mountains, you know." Ann's comments were quick, but the tone was light. Her admiration of the mountains and the people came through. Keith was pleased to hear that Al wasn't leaving. Too many good doctors settled near city universities. The mountains offered limited opportunities for professional camaraderie. Gone were the days when a lone practitioner led his community's social and economic life in addition to the practice. Not that the foreign doctors who tended to migrate to the area weren't appreciated, but Keith thought a friendly Kentucky accent was often missed in local practices.

Ann ordered salad, winking at the waiter, "My special salad." Keith requested broiled cat fish, but Al declined to order. "Excuse me; I've got a couple of calls to place. I'll catch you later." Al's excuse was accepted. Keith noted, however, that the great hulk of a man refused bread at each of their two encounters. The motel restaurant meal, always a delight for Keith, tonight was spiced part New Orleans, part Southeast Kentucky style. Ann's salad, equal to filling a peck basket in Keith's estimation, was shades of green, red, purple and yellow topped with bacon crisp, and black walnuts—looked fairly tempting.

Attractive, always moving and thinking at full speed—that described his diner companion. "Keith, what do you think of Al?"

"You're not thinking of marrying him, are you?" Keith hoped his eyes showed him to be kidding, but wasn't sure.

"No, silly, I'm much too old for him. I mean what do you make of him? Single, here in the mountains, wanting to stay, preferring solitude, atypical, don't you think?" She sounded sympathetic, maybe a little concerned, but certainly not gossipy. Ann wasn't the type. That's what he liked about her. She was straight on, honest, kind, reflective—so much more than a pretty smile, a good figure.

"I'm not sure what to make of him. He's friendly, interested in our people obviously. I've just had two brief encounters." The two, enjoying the eating together and comfortable conversation, made it last the better part of two hours. A heaping bowl of blackberry cobbler topped with ice cream completed Ann's evening. She might eat salads religiously, but she felt it gave her the right to indulge in deserts. Keith teased her about it. It gave her energy, she said.

Late that night or early morning Keith was awakened by screams, not screams of panic, but something more Eolithic, something one might expect in a jungle horror movie. It was coming from the hall somewhere beyond his door. Cautiously, he entered the hallway clad in his pajamas and the motel house coat. Two doors down, Al was standing in the hallway, facing the wall, seeing not the wall, but something. Keith thought whatever the visual, it must be truly horrifying given the continuing screams.

"Al, what's wrong?" Getting no response, he hurried to the room and phoned Ann.

Running up the stairs, not even considering waiting for the elevator, Ann arrived momentarily, dressed only in her pajamas. Quickly she shooed the guests, crowded in the hallway, back to their rooms. Standing a safe distance away from Al, Ann began in a soft voice. "Al, this is Ann. You're in Middlesboro, Al. Al, everything is okay, dear. You're safe. Al, this is Ann." Slowly Al's body began to relax. He turned and looked blankly at Ann, then at Keith further down the hall. Ann took his face in both hands and looked intently into his eyes.

"Ann, I didn't know you were here. What are we doing in the hallway?" The speech was halting, but soft. The eyes slowly began to reflect comprehension. Ann asked Keith to call 911 for an ambulance while she maneuvered Al back to his room.

In room 108, Pineville Hospital, Al gazed at the woman whose chair was pulled close, her face too near his. "Al, do you know what happened back at the motel?" Al nodded slightly, then shook his head to indicate no. Ann continued, "You were in the motel hallway dressed only in your shorts. Your outburst frightened all of us. You've experienced this before?" Again, a measured nod, "What

I'm guessing we have here is a classic case of after-contention-reaction."

"PTSD you mean!" Al's eyes narrowed.

Having been careful not to label or diagnose, Ann proceeded. "If tests verify my hypothesis, then we know where to go." She placed her hand gently on his forehead. "Oh, no, not a scalpel known to man enters there." Al responded as he removed her hand.

"Who said anything about opening that big head? You and I are going to do a little re-wiring." Ann smiled.

"You've hung around those therapists too long; consider yourself a psychotherapist now, do you?" Al's countenance continued to darken.

"Let's start from the beginning; I think you're ready. The battle is partially won. You realize something is not right. You have pushed yourself to the extreme, completing medical training, seeing greater vistas outside yourself. That's a big part of the healing. Psychiatry may want to tamper with your wiring through talk, which is fine, but what you and I are going to do is work topside. Thus far your prescription has been excellent: work, focus, serve, learn—things we're put here to do. The only mistake is the use of a second medicine. Feeling terrible is perfectly normal in your situation. Alcohol, your medicine of choice, numbs that. The wrong mix, alcohol with certain other drugs exacerbates the problem." Ann curled her forefinger under his chin slightly lifting his head. Their eyes met, each seriously examining the other. "We're going to fix that. You are not the first physician to fumble his own prescription. What you've got may last a lifetime, but you are going to manage it, much like managing arthritis, allergies and a hundred other maladies we all face. Cherk up! There is already too much ululating for a man with your genius to add more." At this she removed her hand, stood erect and smoothed her skirt. With a mischievous grin, "Watch the RN's. Some have a peculiar sense of duty." The sedative began reaching its destination, Al's eyes were barely open, his mouth, however, spread in a trusting smile, Ann thought, as she turned to leave, pleased with her wittiness, and with the obvious connection between him and her.

# CHAPTER 14

## Old Carl's Social Security

Carl pushed open the front door at the rehab facility. Even at seven a.m. the lobby was accessible. No staff present until eight-thirty, however. Not seeing anybody to inquire about his interest, he sat in a chair against the back wall farthest away from the entry door and fairly close to a door that opened to another room, he guessed. Picking up a *Time* magazine from a table nearby, he began thumbing through the pages. Closer examination of any page, he decided, didn't make any sense to him. Finally a topic of possible interest: "The Government is Headed for Fiscal Cliff." Noting it dealt with government spending, income/expense things, his mind wondered back. He doubted whoever wrote that had ever looked at a cliff. As boys, he and an older brother often sneaked over the hill to the old Collins place hoping to catch sun-grannies out of the creek that ran more than a mile through their bottoms. Just off the path on each side, limestone outcroppings ran parallel to the bottoms. On one occasion his older brother had detoured a hundred yards or so from the path and jumped to reach a grapevine that hung from a large walnut tree. Kicking off, he swung far out over the rock face, a sure enough cliff, maybe fifteen feet above the slope of the hill. The swing broke loose, dumping him down below on his back, luckily between two boulders. "Wonder it hadn't crippled him," Carl had expressed. He knew better than such foolishness, even back then.

Carl was soon interrupted in his thoughts by voices coming through the wall from behind him.

"You know when the computer makes that humming noise, even though no one is using it, I heerd some fellows talking down at the service station. One said it was gathering information, could even gather thoughts from people up to fifty feet away. All this information is sent to a big government-operated outfit."

"I don't believe a word of that. It's against the law. Besides what could the government do with it?" the second voice inquired.

"You just don't know. Could be they are finding out about robbers, drug sales, and probably terrorists".

"Bull."

"Hello, may I help you?" Keith, always early, had entered the lobby and crossed the room to address Carl who was sitting with his legs crossed, his good hat in one hand which he bounced against his leg.

"Well, I don't rightly know. Been told a work-hand of mine is here. I had to drive down to the social security office today and his mom asked me to look in on him while I's down here. Freddie's his name."

"Oh, yes, I know Freddie. You're probably aware by now that we don't officially open until eight-thirty. I'll locate Freddie though and see about a meeting maybe before he eats breakfast. Are you on the visitor list?"

"I can't rightly say. I'm his neighbor. He works for me a little now and then."

"What's your name, sir?"

"Carl Sweet. Jest tell Freddie, Carl's here."

Keith, perceiving a dilemma, moved to the receptionist's desk, produced the list and quickly, against protocol, added Carl's name. Keith had heard the name in discussions with Freddie and, always willing to accommodate, paged Freddie to the visitor's meeting room down the hall. He then led Carl, who was holding a brown paper bag by its twisted top, out of the lobby.

"Carl, I have to ask, what is in the bag?"

"I don't care nary bit to show what's in the poke."

Unrolling his twist at the top, he revealed three pops, some crimp-cut loose tobacco and rolling papers, and an oatmeal cake wrapped in cellophane. Carl understood sending roll your own tobacco. At three or four dollars a pack he didn't see how they expected poor people to afford to smoke. He'd bought Old Gold's for twenty-two cents back of this.

"Carl what are you doing way off down here?" Freddie was all smiles, obviously pleased to see somebody from home, maybe even anticipating a ride back. He sat, then rose and approaching Carl, patted him on the arm. "I had to come down on business. Your mom wanted me to bring you a few things." The two took chairs at a table mid-room, looked one another over, and began asking and answering questions. Soon Carl's voice took on what Freddie knew to be his serious tone. "Freddie, you are a good boy, well, man now. This month down here I hope will do some good, git you away from some of the company around home—the three that's been over in my trailer and Buddy, the boy that drives that Mustang. You know who all I'm talkin' about. Reckon you heerd what happened to the trailer crew. Got a hearing coming up, I'm thinking they'll get some time. Thiefin's up there around two thousand dollars' worth, that plus the drug charges. The judge ain't got much leeway."

"Yeah, I heard. Hate it for 'em."

"Well, they brought it on theirselves. I hate to admit it. One of 'em belongs to my own brother, but they ain't no account. You know, Freddie, you ain't like them boys. I knowed your old daddy. Me and him took out a stand of timber over on Roundstone, must a been fifty years ago now. Just big old boys, didn't know something couldn't be done. Made good on it, too, best I recollect."

Freddie sat silent for some time, "You worked with my dad? Before I was born? He work good?" Freddie eyed Carl who nodded.

Carl leaned both elbows on his knees and turned his face to Freddie. "Yep. I never seed a better man with a Kant hook, big barrel chest, you see, stout as a bull. I'll tell you something else. He was the best at keeping a old diesel running as I ever seed. We picked up a loader that had been left out on a hillside as junk. Got it for nearly nothing. Good thing too. We had nearly nothing. Anyways, your dad'd tackle anythang, Freddie. I'm guessing that's where you got your mechanicin."

Carl suddenly had something entirely different come to mind. He'd planned to let that trailer rust down right there in the field. No way was he paying five or six thousand dollars to clean up that sorry lot's mess. But what if he could convince his niece's husband to help on the project? As a licensed EPA cleanup man, maybe he'd allow somebody to use his equipment and do the job just for the cost of supplies, then sign off on it. "Say, Freddie, thought about what you'll do after this stay?"

"Some." That was as far as Freddie had gotten toward a plan. He knew he could work on diesels. He daydreamed about the tools he'd need, about seeing the smoke stack puff after his tuning. "You say my dad was good at working on diesels?'

"The best. Now that you've got broke away from home, what about coming back and living in my trailer, working a day now and then for me?"

"I heard buildings had to be cleaned up after meth makin,' dangerous to live in. Maybe even against the law."

"I've got a plan for that. You might even brang that gal, Amanda, and her baby." Carl wasn't interested in getting any more closely involved with Amanda than he already was, but an enticement seemed to be in order. Best he could tell, she jumped any time a man beckoned. She appeared to be the kind that could whoop and cavort with the best, but didn't have a lick of sense, probably couldn't even peel potatoes. He really wanted to advise Freddie against her, but he knew better. Get in the middle of people like that, he'd be the one to get straightened out or flattened.

"Carl, I'm gona have to study some on this. I got some idees for when I get released." Rehab to Freddie at this time was merely a sentence to be served.

After some time and bidding goodbyes, Carl left. Freddie went to group with important thoughts centered on diesel mechanics and further discussions on the matter with Mr. Keith. Carl went in search of the Social Security office.

In the downtown business district, Carl stopped twice for directions. "The office is just off Engineer Street" had been one response. Carl admired the name, Engineer, sounded like doing something. Back home the county had renamed ever' durn road – Lady Slipper, Ocean Boulevard, Ivy Lane and so on – some kind of regulation had to do with EMS. Pure foolishness to him; however, he hadn't raised a stink about it. Today though, he was ready to fight. For nearly ten years his social security check had come every month, around the twenty-fifth, and had increased a little each year. For the last two years though there hadn't been a dime's difference, same month-in month-out. He was going to get to the bottom of it.

At the Social Security office Carl was a bit startled by the set-up. Just inside the door sat a big uniformed armed guard. The receptionist was behind a glass window with just a peep hole to speak through. Immediately Carl decided that the fight must already be on, that a lot of people likely hadn't got a raise.

"Your name?" The receptionist didn't look up.

"Carl." This came out at a little higher pitch than normal for Carl.

"Carl what?"

"Carl Sweet."

"Take a number." The speaker nodded to plastic numbers hung on a board beside the window and continued to turn pages in a brochure or magazine. Instead of taking a number, Carl stole out without looking at the guard. This was surely too big a battle for him to get mixed up in.

"Looked to me like the government had already took up arms. You'll hear of a bad fix before this is all over." He reported this to the gathering at the store the following morning.

Harm Jones leaned forward in his chair, his elbows resting on his knees, his fingers touching at the tips, and asked, "Carl, do you think there's gona' be a war?"
"Wouldn't surprise me none."

# CHAPTER 15

## Deidra In Hammockville

Home, where the family grows, laughs, cries, works, and recreates is the veritable stand-in for the original garden. Peace is the norm, frankness is tempered with kindness, and provisions are bestowed joyfully. Tranquility had not existed in the Hammock home for years. Earlier the family hopes centered on an only child, one dressed for a princess life, fed the diet of choice, enrolled in developmentally sound activities. Daughter Deidra had responded with early speech, rewarding snuggles, and adorable performances. Her dark hair, blue-green eyes, bright smile, all signs of health and happiness, created a pride of accomplishment in her mother and father. The parents proudly related her special traits to friends and family members. Such had been *Hammockville* for fifteen plus years. There had been temper tantrums, demands and defiance that, of course, they were sure she'd outgrow. During her second year in high school, the castle moat dried, the drawbridge no longer provided safe refuge. A storm hit the Hammock household, one not prepared for. "It'll pass, just adolescence," her dad often repeated with certainty in his voice. Mom agreed. She wanted to believe it. Mr. Hammock worked for the regional utilities company beginning as a lineman, eventually promoted to a supervisory position offering financial reward, security and some community prestige. His wife was able to stay at home with the little girl to assure proper care and training. This lasted through Deidra's first twelve years. Mrs. Hammock then accepted an executive assistant position working for the CEO of a large lumber operation. Life was orderly. They took expensive vacations, bought a new car every two years, and purchased within reason, anything they wanted.

A change came about, which began to turn the family tranquility into a nightmare. Deidra began demanding freedom, not just from family oversight, but from society norms in general. She wanted to spend too much time with her boyfriend who was rumored to use drugs. Other cronies, roaming the malls, and partying in the parking lots were not choices of the parents. Mom and dad purchased her a new Mazda, hoping that might free her from the less than wholesome companions. Instead, there were bent fenders, traffic tickets and later nights out. Eventually, she totaled the car. Then, she didn't return home. The first time she was gone for three nights. If the parents suspected drugs, neither admitted it to the other or to anyone. Nightly they patrolled the teenage haunts determined to bring her home and end the delinquent behavior.

Nearly six months into the erratic conduct, Mr. Hammock located Deidra lying asleep (he prayed) along the highway four miles from town. Her resting place was an embankment visible to passing cars. At the hospital, the attending physician explained how lucky she was. She was very near death. After her stomach was pumped and she spent two days in ICU, she was moved to a room for a few more days of inpatient care. She sneaked away AMA after the first night in the private room.

"I'm not going to subsidize this suicidal behavior or become co-dependent or whatever the clinicians call it. She is on her own." Dad made the pronouncement.

"You can't mean that. She's seventeen years old. Out of control maybe, but she is our daughter." Her mother was distraught. "Maybe we should ask our pastor to try an intervention," she continued, doubting that a solution lay within reach.

"Look, we don't have a daughter anymore. We have an addict who once was our child. She no longer cares for us, for herself, for anyone else. The only hope we have or she has is that some way a capture can be accomplished. The demon holding her hostage is powerful, greater than life itself. I'm thinking taking legal action might be all that's left." He had never dealt with legal authorities except for her traffic violations—tickets, and accidents.

"Surely, you aren't considering having her locked up with those awful people or committed as insane," her mother's voice shrill, her upraised hands shook.

"Look, we're going to lose her. I'm talking death. Something drastic is required. She's been hospitalized near death, destroyed a car, stolen over five thousand dollars from our accounts. I'm sure her boyfriend took my weed eater. This is drug addiction, clear and simple. It is beyond us. We don't have the solution." Two days later, Mr. Hammock approached the county attorney with a proposal. "I'm willing to file an affidavit, or whatever it takes, declaring that my daughter is a danger to herself and others and that she has stolen over five thousand dollars from us."

"Mr. Hammock, are you sure you want to do this?" The county attorney asked the question, the seriousness, the consequences, weighty issues.

"Of course, I don't want to do this. What else is there? She is going to die." Mr. Hammock's voice broke. The official subsequently signed a warrant for Deidra's arrest, the charge, a danger to herself and others. Several days passed before officers located her and then not as a direct result of their search. A motel manager's tip unknowingly disclosed her location. He had been concerned after two men left without their female companion who hadn't appeared that whole day. Concerned, he had finally entered the room and found her sleeping. Unable to awaken her, he'd made the call.

Ten days later the drug court judge called Deidra's case, heard police testimony, and questioned Deidra and her parents. Eventually he asked if they considered long term rehabilitation a sensible alternative to jail. The stealing charge would be dropped. Both parents nodded assent; any more answer was inaudible. The judge directed an assistant to help with arrangements. While Deidra remained in jail, the assistant made calls, met with the parents together, then separately. After two days, a facilities listing was reviewed. Mrs. Hammock requested, "Could we possible get a placement in Kentucky so we can visit regularly?"

"I strongly discourage the frequent visitation. The farther away she is placed, the less likely her assortment of friends will intervene." The court worker was firm. Mrs. Hammock turned to her husband seeking assurance in the matter.

Mr. Hammock spoke up finally, "I was stationed in San Diego. The climate is perfect. She can't get much farther from these jerks here. Is there a placement available in that area?"

"I'll be glad to look into it, sir." The worker obviously understood Mrs. Hammock's reluctance to give Deidra over to unknown people in a distant location. She smiled as she patted the mother's hand.

Mr. Hammock again spoke up. "How do we know how much it's going to cost?" The assistant agreed to make the call regarding the location and for particulars, and if the Hammocks agreed, to arrange travel and registration.

"Of course, the parents probably should go along to insure check-in." She said this knowing the referral might not be reliable on that front. Two days later the family was on their way, carrying a certified check in the amount of thirty-one thousand dollars, the cost of one month's treatment. Deidra responded in one word sentences throughout the plane ride, her thin hands folded in her lap, her eyes averted.

Mrs. Hammock stood at her kitchen sink completing last minute tasks. The window above the sink looked out on the swing set, out of use for years, the seats catching the breeze, rising and falling; the sand box no longer cluttered with shovels and buckets, now featured flowers; the dog house, no longer home for the dachshund. Everything in view was there possibly awaiting grandchildren that might never come. The last thought, too selfish maybe, her thinking quickly returned to the disturbing present. "Will I ever see my daughter again?" She said though no one was present to hear. Her thoughts meant more than just will I ever see Deidra again. The true meaning was, will I ever see the real Deidra again, the one I love, the one I cherish beyond life itself. Her whole body hurt as she pondered this dilemma the family faced.

On the return flight from California, the Hammocks held hands for a great part of the trip. Her nose and eyes red, his head turned, eyes to the window viewing the nothingness at thousands of feet above the high mountain range, the prairie, the city lights and the meanderings of the great river—a dividing line between them and their daughter.

“Thirty days will pass in no time. After all, we’ve spent many days not knowing her whereabouts.” Mr. Hammock spoke as thought escaped his consciousness. The only question that he had was, can they really help her?

“Do you think it will help? The treatment, I mean.” Mrs. Hammock’s misgivings were rooted in experience, an experience that she believed no mother should have to face. Losing one’s property, being shunned by one’s friends, these combined fell far short of the loss she was feeling. In her mind, only death itself surpassed this family catastrophe.

“We’ve done the best we know. Prayer, that’s all that’s left.” Mr. Hammock felt the rising guilt. Reaching back into his memory to conjure an answer, he thought of his personal parental shortcomings. Had he spent too much time at work, indulged her too much, laughed when he should have counseled? “What’s wrong with me, my family, our community, the nation?” Knowing he couldn’t answer any of his own questions, and that his wife couldn’t either, he put his arm around his mate and pulled her close.

The parents spent ten anxious days after returning from San Diego. Then the pining ended. The Hammocks learned that Deidra had been seen in one of the fast food restaurants in town. She was in the company of old friends, laughing as she proudly proclaimed, “I escaped from California—I’m going to be my own overseer.” The thirty day treatment had ended after a week, the money wasted. Deidra’s downward spiral resumed.

# CHAPTER 16

## Beck's Family Business

Fifty years earlier, before Aunt Beck operated her business at the old home place, her dad as patriarch trafficked, also illegally. His MO was much different. Drug use had not mushroomed in rural Kentucky, but moonshine late in his day was becoming passé. Bootleg whiskey in a dry country was equal to milk, bread, or gasoline—to many an absolute necessity. Not only were the one hundred proofs important, there was something about having one's own supplier. Buyers referred to them as their bootlegger, as they might say, my barber. Traveling through an adjoining wet county a customer often passed legal outlets, then once home, drive several miles to his supplier to buy the least expensive half pint available at twice the price.

Not all the profit accrued to the seller, however. A middleman much like Beck's controller got a cut. He fronted the purchase, assured legal cover, and took half the profits. This arrangement didn't suit the retailer, but operators who didn't comply were soon forced out. With no cover in the court house, officers raided and served papers. Beck's dad managed to sell a little moonshine along with the "red", as locals referred to the bourbon. These locally distilled spirits were neither controlled nor condoned by the financier who often had community respect, large landholdings and bank stock. These earlier controllers had important contacts and their shady side wasn't widely known. Their participation, same as the bootlegger's extra sales, was on the sly. Womenfolk and the children had no hand in Beck's dad's business, except now and then when her father was away, Beck's mom allowed well- known customers to enter a back room, fill their own bottle from a gallon jar and leave the money on a table. She always said,

“Being a church- going person, I don’t handle no liquor.” Other times that same customer might experience a sense of kinship or brotherhood as he and Beck’s dad strolled off from the house, supposedly to look over a shoulder high tobacco crop. Then stepping a few feet into one of the rows and plucking a jar from between the plants, they’d pass it one to the other. Swallowing the powerful liquid produced red faces, a prolonged “whew,” followed by warmth spreading across their shoulders. The two bonded in thought and deed. As the hiding place had to be rotated, an encounter often moved, maybe to the barn, the bootlegger kicking around in the hay to produce the miracle medicine, the elixir of mirth. Time spent sitting on upturned buckets, or on a stall door sill, presented opportunity to share concerns, interests, and plans. This neighborhood “bartender” and his patron knew each other’s lore for generations.

One of Beck’s father’s favorite stories involved a term he spent in the Atlanta Federal Prison for selling untaxed liquor. “Treated me the best, fed me hot dogs this long,” measuring with his hand their length on his forearm; the report given with a glint in his eye. “I cleaned up the head-mans’ office ever’ night. He’d always leave a half glass of good red for me. If the old woman dies first, I hope to go right back there.”

Overall Beck’s generation witnessed little change—same house, same family, only the specifics differed. Beck passed pills to her “peddlers” (couriers as she referred to them) who sold the meds in parking lots and along the county roadways. Others she sold directly, greeting her customers at the door, collecting their cash and re-locking. Security and safety were always a concern. Her regional controller had arranged for motion lights, loud blasts mimicking gun shots on demand, and even a communication system, its lights blinking visibly from the doorway and connected to objects unknown. Customers were made aware of the safety measures and were cautious. Beck's house was heated with kerosene heaters in the front two rooms. Both these rooms opened to the front porch. In the large room to the rear, a wood-burning stove fed smoke into the old fire place chimney and warmed the remainder of the house. In summer, fans and open windows sufficed for air conditioning. Home cooking smells never greeted visitors. The kitchen, where Beck and her sister alternated cooking duties, mostly opening cans and preparing greasy combinations which were supplemented by Wendys or McDonald's specialties, was off limits to her customers. After one such meal of pork and beans, macaroni and cheese, and sliced ham, and while Amanda washed dishes, Beck reminisced aloud about the day's business. "The imagination of these people amazes me," referring to a middle aged couple who had left the house just before supper. "Doctor said they had to get a drug test before he'd renew their prescription, to see they weren't using something else. Well, they's selling most of the doctor's pills, taking the rest and usin' their meth makings, so no way was they gonna pass any test. So he says he got him a 'whisser', whatever that is, passed his mother's clean urine for the test though it. Looked like it come right out of his you know what. And listen to this, his wife had a condom on her body. Don't ask me where, filled with her sister-in-law's clean urine—durned if they both didn't pass.

"I got half of each of their prescriptions for sixty dollars. That's thirty times forty dollars for me. They got half theirselves. Good business, huh?" Sis rolled her eyes at Amanda. "The big man with his smart Florida connections, don't know a thing about it neither." At that Beck slapped her ample thigh and guffawed hysterically, stood, pulled her skirt down in the back and proceeded to assist Amanda by drying dishes. Her monthly doctor calendar was filled with familiar names along with their Dr. appointment-dates. Her local suppliers came by the legal drugs under false pretense and delivered them to Beck for her distribution at street prices.

In earlier days Beck had attended worship services with her mother and considered herself religious, maybe not certain of her salvation, but satisfied. She had been taught there that low-life bootleggers in time would find that their sleaze money was not the ticket to the real life. In the end, it would burn just like everything else. Eventually though, she heard a different part of the sermon, a part she could hold on to.

Part of that sermon became her mantra: *"Digging in the earth, men today find evidence of earliest people making and using beer and wine, anything to dull their minds, to blur their surroundings, to make them happy. They had to and we have to zone out, as the young folks say. They couldn't and we can't face life. This is true today and all the way back to the beginning. It's just the same—people have always thought themselves smarter than their maker, capable of making a real life. It's a part of our nature. We can't stand ourselves."* Beck tuned out. She'd heard enough. People were going to use whether she was involved or not.

Somebody's gonna benefit, why not old Beck? This thought filled her. Fears and doubts were vanquished. Conscience assuaged, her thoughts had turned to development of the specially marked calendar and other clandestine efforts as insurance against half-rations and destitution. No matter her path's course, the dangerous turns, the violence just out of sight, she had weighed her alternatives and followed the historic family trace.

Out-maneuvering her controller, she used extended family members and those they recommended. These special people made monthly doctor visits for prescriptions while exhibiting carefully staged or sometimes real pain. Her people used to visit physicians in surrounding towns to get scripts from each, but the computer crimped that practice. Pharmacists began cross checking each script to prevent multiples. Beck smiled inwardly when she thought how the process now yielded fewer pills, but remained profitable. Her co-conspirators, their office visits tracked by Beck's calendar, turned over the product and profited. Retailed, the merchandise yielded considerable cash which Beck carefully counted and stored in metal containers which were encased in cedar box-vaults and buried in a crawl space under the house. No definite plans for using these gains had evolved, maybe a condo in Florida someday or a faraway cruise were sometimes in her daydreams. Mostly her dreams were confined to accumulating, storing, and maintaining. "You'uns is ever last one dependent on Ol' Beck," she'd often proclaim to Sis or Amanda.

# CHAPTER 17

## Deidra Reports and all most Shocks the Counselor

Thursday morning group, always underway by nine a.m., usually proved interesting, but difficult for Keith. The nineteen residents, divided among three treatment staff members, brought with them baggage from fractured lives, back roads experiences that were unspeakable in polite company, scars none too subtle. Often disagreements sprang up among residents, arising from shared life experiences or from stories disbelieved or jealousies over opportunities squandered or enjoyed and so forth. Keith generally guided, but let residents' concerns and episodes be laid out for all to examine. One resident's report sometimes helped cancel concerns for what another considered a dark secret.

This morning, Deidra, in one of her more relaxed rehab moods, held the group's attention. "I left home, for the most part, at sixteen. My daddy hadn't abused me. Mother adored, smothered, and adorned me—no yard sale stuff in my wardrobe. Both my parents had jobs at the time, so money was not a big concern. School was both fun and boring. I liked English, did well enough in science and math, but I hated the rigid scheduling. Be there five days a week, eight to three thirty, attend gym, chapel, stay late for Pep Club, Key club, Beta Club, a lot of stupid stuff. At home mother picked up, cleaned, cooked, and managed the house without my help. Dad did all the yard and garden work. I was doing okay until tenth grade. This big senior hunk of a football player began hanging around, talking, talking, talking. First thing you know he talked me into following him out behind the stadium bleachers. Don't blush, Mr. Keith, I won't tell it all." They all laughed including Keith who shook his head. Group members were seldom shy about specifics, even if they had a notion that repeating them was inappropriate or that they represented something private, immoral, or illegal. "I'm going to skip a lot," Deidra continued. "Let me just report that life quickly became ugly. I've been uncomfortable and felt unworthy. This has gone on for years. Jail was the worst." She paused and waved her hand before her face, "Too confining to suit my taste."

At this, Keith's group members laughed, one leaning to the next to report a personal experience, or to elaborate on the meaning of taste. "First lock-up at seventeen, the women were crammed into a space designed for half that number." Deidra cleared her throat, uncrossed her legs and pushed her sweater sleeves up. "After a few days and on a dry drunk, as some of you like to say, I was holding forth on this and that when a two hundred pound babe slapped me to the floor. Well, I didn't exactly hit the floor. My head first bumped on the edge of a metal table. It took several to restrain her. I bled all over the place. The jailer hauled me off to hospital emergency which cost the jail eight hundred dollars. The jailer wasn't pleased as you might guess. His jail paid the hospital bill. But you didn't need to know that, did you? Anyway, jail time ended and so-called good times came back around. Mom and Dad were tracking me like a couple of sleuths, one motel to another, day job to day job." Deidra repositioned herself in her chair placing her hands on each side of the seat and leaning forward. Then pushing her hair behind her ear she continued. "This might give some idea how my life progressed."

"Then after a third or fourth sentencing, I don't remember which, the jail contracted with community do-gooders for us to do work, cleaning up parks and such. My supervisor on one of the days took another girl and me barhopping. We all got falling-down drunk and they fired the supervisor and extended our jail term by thirty days." She looked around for reactions. All members appeared focused, interested because it tracked their personal experiences or because she was a good story teller, she wasn't sure which. "That was before I got the idea that warmer climes might help. A friend I made in jail and I rode a Greyhound to Florida to pick tomatoes." She smiled. "We slept in the fields along with fellow workers, bathed in a pond and ate the fruit of the land, all the time taking whatever drugs we could afford—except I never took meth. I knew better than that. The teeth, the sores, the baggy clothes, I'd seen all that. Took LSD once, scared me to death." She paused and looked down. "So it was generally easy to get oxy, heroin, cocaine, and various pain pills. I'm not sure, but I think it was during this timeframe that I got this." She gestured with four fingers brushing across the tattoo on her bosom. Freddie stared. He thought the cat smiled—at him.

"Late in the picking season, Florida got unbearably hot. I got sick from acidosis or something, sick of the dirt, sick of the pickers, and wanted to get back to more civilized living. I began hitchhiking back to Kentucky." Deidra looked at Keith to see if maybe she'd gone on too long. Getting no negative response, she continued. "Remember, I'm giving an abbreviated account, leaving out sleeping under a thin sheet of plastic in a Florida rain with a sharp stick for protection. Believe me, a weapon was needed and I can tell you, 'thumbing' is no fun either. By the time I got back, I felt like I'd walked most of the way. Mom and Dad captured me after a few days. I say captured. Actually, I think I wanted them to rescue me. Once home, I spent the better part of a month in bed. Mom carried my meals, and Dad looked sad. He attempted advice, trying hard not to explode. That ended too. As soon as my energy returned, so did I—first down to Wendys, then joining with old friends, to old haunts, to old habits. Goodbye, Mom and Dad, so long healthy food and a bed all to myself. I needed something, an antidote you might say, for loneliness. Home life in general was a bore, a zero, you know what I mean?"

"Wait a minute. What happened to the friend who went to Florida with you?" It was the cold girl, her hands tucked between her legs.

"She was in handcuffs the last time I saw her." Deidra gave her a look designed to cut further questioning.

"Were you ever afraid," Mr. Keith, out of character for him, interrupted?

"Any fears came from details I don't care to discuss." She shook her head, obviously clearing her mind of something the group was not to hear. "There were always jerks, of course. After the return home and leaving again, I moved in with a couple of guys, I don't remember their names, in rent-subsidized housing about fifteen or so miles from Mom and Dad. The apartment building was fairly new, attractive with rolling beautifully landscaped lawns. It should have been a good place, but the fellow next door overhauled a car engine in his kitchen, the couple on the other side tried to dress out a cow in their living room. You get the picture." Deidra crossed her legs, her skirt riding up several inches above the knee. "One of my roommates bullied two of the neighborhood boys. I say neighborhood, actually they lived in an old school bus some distance down the road from our complex. He talked them into making meth in an abandoned van on their property. He purchased the makings in surrounding towns using their ID's when necessary. The boys were nineteen or twenty and neither read *Aristotle,* if you know what I mean.

Our bully used his cut from their labor to pay rent, buy food and gas, as well as the cocaine necessary to get us through the day."

"All right, Deidra, it seems that you have perspective as to where you've been and hopefully where you are now," Keith interjected, certain that the report could continue indefinitely. At this point his confidence usually waned, not sure which way to lead the discussion. "Anybody wish to comment on Deidra's presentation?"

"Was you scared?" Freddie spoke first determined to get a better answer to Keith's earlier query.

"Yes, she was scared, you numbskull," a heavy-set woman in her early twenties got involved. She waved her notepad in front of her face, shooing the ignorance from about her person.

"Let's try to remember what we promised, no name calling," Keith, a bit discombobulated now.

"What on earth were you thinking, going to Florida to work in the fields?" the same female followed her previous comment.

"She wasn't thinking. Period. She was on a tare." a third voice stated. The owner of the voice sat with his rump slid slightly forward, his head raised as though looking somewhere above the group.

"Actually, I was thinking about staying warm, a little money for dope, getting far from home, revising my reality, hiding." She sat silent for a moment. "Oh, the truth is I don't know." Deidra raised her eyes from the notepad and looked around the room. Her last statement gave Keith an uneasy feeling, a thought that she was briefly disconnected, viewing something from one of her previous experiences.

"Let's wrap this session up. We'll hear from someone else next round." With this Keith began shuffling his papers readying to leave. The patients, eager to leave, past ready to smoke and move around, quickly left the room. Near the exit door, he noticed Deidra leaning against the wall next to the framed emergency exit plan. He could tell she was crying, but trying to hide it. He walked slowly over. "Deidra, can I help?"

"Mr. Keith, nobody can help me." She looked at him and fumbled in her bag for a tissue, not finding one, she wiped her face with the palm of her had. "I've wasted so much." She paused. "People in my wake, good people that is, I've trampled." She took a deep breath and turned her head to stare out the window. "I'm worse than the prodigal son."

"You can't be worse than him. You don't have a jealous brother," Keith was attempting to interject a little levity, though he wasn't sure that was appropriate. "I'm told that these feelings represent the beginning of healing, Deidra. I could say things like I know, I've been there, been dried out, had to move in with my mother. That probably sounds empty, but it's true."

"Have you been on bottom, had to be dried out, have you taken advantage of whoever cared enough to get in your path?" Deidra looked away. "Nobody even comes close to my sorry behavior, Mr. Keith. You have no idea. Any change is already too late."

"Meet me for lunch. I'd like for the social worker to join us." Keith knew that La Pearl listened and gave appropriate responses at these times, followed by hugs. Hugging wasn't his talent. Rehabilitation, to Keith, was a combination of efforts. Mostly though he knew it involved among other things a change of environment, a re-focusing away from the drug, and grasping a set of tools for maintenance. He considered the twelve-step program to be the most likely tool since it had worked for him, so far. The three ate lunch from the cafeteria in an adjoining room and talked. La Pearl periodically reached over to put her hand over Deidra's. Eventually a plan evolved.

"We're going to the mall shopping tomorrow evening." La Pearl was holding Deidra's hand as she spoke. Keith, can you take Deidra to the workout room today and work out an exercise program with the physical trainer?"

Keith nodded and then turned to look at Deidra, "Deidra, think you might lead a training discussion on the twelve-step plan with residents on Monday?"

"I don't know. I'll try."

Having devised a plan, the two leaders left the luncheon somewhat hopeful. The resident departed a bit unsteady on her feet, reserved, her affect flat—in the eyes of the social worker.

The following morning a patient from the women's wing approached Keith to report. "She refuses to get out of bed."

"Who?" Keith's mind raced, considering who among the group might have gotten drugs, or was suffering from withdrawal.

"Deidra."

"Why?" Keith hardly believed the message.

"She didn't offer no excuse." The messenger shrugged and moved off to the breakfast room.

When Keith approached Deidra, she sleepily responded, "I'm not well," and kept her face toward the wall.

Keith and the social worker failed to agree on reasons for the lay-in on their follow-up. "Non-specified illness" was entered into her chart, and Keith made his way to the psychiatrist's office.

"I've got one for you, Doc." With that, Keith explained the episode with Deidra the day before and then presented the morning dilemma. "Do you think maybe she suffers from bipolar disorder, Doc?"

"Keith, I hesitate to label. We need to schedule a full assessment, a psychological evaluation, a good physical and go from there. As you know, many addicts do have underlying problems, sometimes to the level of dual diagnosis. This is a possibility in Deidra's case. Certainly much of her behavior suggests a reason for self-medication. The self-medication often masks the root cause."

"Doc, sometimes I feel that this is all in vain." Keith was sinking, questioning the efficacy of rehab, of intervention with people like Deidra.

"What's in vain?" Dr. Lee had never seen Keith waver in his commitment to patients.

"You know, these people are crazy on drugs, crazy without drugs. Maybe we ought to just let them alone." Keith wasn't sure he believed this, but sometimes doubt overwhelmed him.

"Well, I'll tell you, Keith, many of them have troubled psyches, their pain and misery has led to a search for relief, that's true." Dr. Lee was searching for the proper response to Keith's doubts.

"Maybe we should just prescribe and monitor—on the street corner even." Keith was aware that most addicts were going to get their dose anyway.

"What about the high school student in pain for a broken ankle, for example, who seeks relief, relief that leads to addiction." Maybe this might stir Keith in a healthier direction. Dr. Lee was floundering. "You remember we've tried methadone on the street corner. In fact I was involved in a case that included an entire family." Dr. Lee sat back in his chair and looked away, out the window across from his desk. "There were parents, children, in-laws, the whole shebang." He chuckled at this. "Every one of them was on assistance of some sort—food stamps, Medicaid, disability, you name it." Keith shuffled his feet and straightened in his chair. He wasn't sure where the story was going and he had patients waiting, but out of respect for the doctor, he said nothing. "Along with several staff members," the doctor smiled as he continued, "I was ordered to Louisville to meet with DEA officials. We were taken through two locked doors and dressed down unmercifully." The smile progressed to laughter. "I felt, I think, like the man who had been beaten with a rubber hose by the time the DEA officer completed his harangue."

"What in the world was going on?" Keith could hold back no longer.

"We had been cited for taking the same route each day to pick up the methadone, placing staff in danger. The truth is the bank building where the drugs were secured was in sight of our clinic. There seemed to be no alternate route."

"So what did you do?" Keith briefly forgot his patients.

"We complied as best we could. That's not the point though. It came a year later. The father who seemed to control the family was arrested for gun-running, selling the methadone and other drugs. Officers found over four hundred thousand cash dollars in their search of his property. We finally concluded that DEA officers had been tracking our patient. Knowing the danger our staff might be in, but without compromising the case, they had dressed us down. We were to take special precautions.

Keith, what I'm saying is, we probably have no choice but to continue and be happy with the twenty-five to thirty percent success rate. Care givers and educators throughout the system always have doubts just as you're feeling. Think about the nurse in a nursing home, working with a patient who has been comatose for years, the teacher in a failing school working with children who are disinterested, even dangerous, the social worker seeking foster care for children who are essentially lost in the system, the judge considering child custody with two unworthy parents contending. We may have to wait until some whiz in a west coast lab or in the north east peels back the cell, finding the lock and the key to these brain issues. So far the keys found have unlocked mysteries only to reveal others locked just as securely."

"Thanks, Doc. I appreciate your listening and your thoughtful response. I've got to get back to the group." Keith left the meeting wondering what hidden message the doctor had passed along to him, hidden, that is, from his initial hearing. Maybe he had debunked any idea of legalizing the use of more substances, and wholesale prescribing. All care givers have their own set of unsolvable issues, he decided.

Psychiatry to Keith had a mythical quality, the ability to be so down to earth, yet scientific beyond his comprehension. Today the doctor was no longer M.D. Goatee. He suddenly, and not for the first time either, became a matchless personage, one capable of seeing through the walls in patient's lives. Coffee shop rumors often portrayed certain doctors as labeling everybody presented to them as neurotic, borderline personality, or some other popular disorder, but not this man. He examined, re-checked, consulted, diagnosed, treated and got results. His patients got the best. This last statement, a compliment made about the doctor by Ann some eleven years ago. Keith had no doubt but that the two, Dr. Ann and Dr. Lee, had saved his life. He required no ongoing medication. He felt blessed. This same outcome he hoped for Deidra.

# CHAPTER 18

## Our Best and Only Doctor Is Out Of Control

When the officer noted a car over an embankment, no accompanying skid marks and no apparent second vehicle, he approached the scene wondering why. He traveled this road to and from work daily, always observant. As the duly elected constable for his district, an unpaid elected position, he had respect for the oath of office and a commitment to preserve the peace and protect the citizenry *(much like Barney Fife)*. This required more vigilance than the average passing driver might demonstrate. Closer inspection of the stalled vehicle wasn't easy. The auto was over the shoulder but still aligned parallel with the rural highway and leaning precariously toward the deep drainage ditch. Opening the front door on the upper side, then holding it back with his body, the constable observed a male, age fifty or sixty in white shirt tie, and his suit coat lying across the back of the passenger seat. The man with neatly trimmed goatee was dead or unconscious, but had no obvious signs of injury. Failing to get a response and noting that no one else was inside, he did a broader visual. Two liquor bottles lay on the floor of the passenger side. The back seat was even more interesting. There lay two matching colt revolvers much like those seen in western movies. Under the two guns was a sheet of white paper with names typed in four columns of five each. The heading: *People Who Need to be Shot*.

"Nurse, I've got a man out here unconscious and I'm afraid to take him to jail. Could Doc take a look at him reckon?" Doc Jones took care of his few patients from birth to death and sometimes visited the jail on request. The constable was comfortable calling his office under the circumstances. His prisoner was still out. Also, the only other medical team in town required patients to take a number, to sit for hours, and then to answer questions they'd just as soon not answer. The constable had vowed never to darken that door and hadn't, except the one time. A sore toe had cost him a day's work.

"Doc, can you take a look at someone? It's a jail request." The nurse squinted, and seemed to honk the request through her nose as she bent around the half-open office door.

"Send him in." Doc Jones was just about to take his afternoon nap and wasn't particularly pleased about the interruption. His practice for over forty years had been limited to the county, most of which was within the Daniel Boone National Forest. The county seat, population twelve hundred, and its only incorporated town suited his nature. Both the doctor and the county populace appeared to be mostly at rest.

"He's not in here." Nurse McNab's lower lip protruded more than common. Doc had been a little too direct in saying, "Send him in." Being past the marriageable age in her mind, she was a woman who blamed men for not seeing and respecting her better qualities. The constable had heard men around the jail, who thought her to be too curt, refer to her as old "soup lip." Of course, being a government man, a representative of the court, he'd never refer to a lady in that manner.

"Where is he, at the jail?" Now Doc was not particularly interested in a trip over to the jail and his voice showed it.

"He's out at the curb. The constable has him in his car."

Seeing the doctor was sure enough out of sorts, the nurse became pouty, casting her stare at a forty-five degree angle at the floor between her and the doctor.
"I guess there is a good reason he's out in the car?" he grunted.

"Can't wake him."

"Oh. That's different." Doc Jones grabbed his scope and made for the door.

After the preliminaries, the constable telling in great detail about the find and the probing, listening, and curling the eyelids back the doctor backed away from his stance, half in, half out of the vehicle. He straightened his shirt tail. "Constable, you've got yourself a drunk man here, belongs in jail."

At the county detention facility, Dr. Lee slowly awakened. Officers processed evidence and completed documents charging him with DUI. They were puzzling over what to do with the revolver and note. Questioning the Doctor's business in town and hearing mentioned the community mental health center, the deputy asked Dr. Lee if he knew or worked with the counselor over there, "Keith, I think is his name." Keith, whom he'd talked to several times when delivering court referrals to the rehab unit.

"As a matter of fact, I do and we're very good friends." Dr. Lee slurred his words and leaned his head forward nearly touching his knee.

Keith had previously been involved in similar incidents in other counties with Goatee M.D., and when called readily agreed to join the melee. Goatee, M. D. again needed an advocate. The last incident had involved Dr. Lee's attempt to enter I-75 on horseback via the Williamsburg exit ramp. Alcohol was involved in that case also.

On arrival, Keith observed the offender handcuffed to a metal table in the lockup, his clothes askew, his head bowed low. The psychiatrist, known to all acquaintances as gentle, mannerly, thoughtful, and never violent or belligerent was an unlikely candidate to be in such a scrape. Keith and the doctor's family had seen this other side though. They knew that once a month or so, the doctor stockpiled enough liquor for three or four days of total inebriation. This usually took place at home involving only family; however, now and again the spree began after his Friday clinic in one of the rural outpatient facilities—thus today's escapade.

At home the doctor was mild mannered and attentive. He even carved an entire wild-west cowboy and Indian scene of balsam for the children's play. He did the dinner dishes and delivered quiet responses to any inquiry. What might be considered his wildest habit involved horses, which he loved and understood much as he understood his patients. His favorite summer weekend outings involved riding and demonstrating at the summer rodeo events throughout the area.

Educated in New York, Dr. Lee had gone on to become board certified in psychiatry. A second marriage, which he and his wife considered successful for over fifteen years, was amiable, except the binge now and then. Though disconcerting, his wife chose to overlook these lapses. They often laughed and reckoned that any marital competition had been depleted with previous mates. No political arguments, vacation destination conflicts, nothing emerged that seriously riled either.

Keith knew the court personnel throughout the catchment area as he often interceded on behalf of rehab patients and these officers knew and respected him. He knew Dr. Lee's case might necessitate more verve than he could muster though. To begin defusing the situation he found Dr. Lee in, he introduced him to the detention team as the medical officer down at the community mental health outpatient clinic and described his typical work day including his regional rehab duties.

"Yeah, my granny goes down there for her nerves," noted the jailer. A deputy sheriff spoke up revealing that his brother was a patient at the clinic. Others joined in, each agreeing what a good thing it was to have in the community. The sheriff utilized the agency to help in mental commitment cases. The jailer said he often took inmates there for their meds. Rapport established, Keith introduced a new facet.

"You fellows know that your circuit clerk serves on our governing board." He didn't mention that the county attorney also served and that he despised Dr. Lee over a child placement hearing. Dr. Lee had recommended that the family stay intact against the attorney's recommendation. Nevertheless, mentioning the circuit clerk, the enforcement officers' major court liaison and asset, reinforced their previous good service comments which ultimately accrued to Doc. "I realize, that Doc was found drunk, his car disabled, with two guns visible, along with this strange note. The guns and the note, I can explain. Although they're firearms, these guns are merely decorations worn for his hobby-riding in our local summer rodeos.

"Also, the names listed as needing to be shot are all staff members serving various clinics across the region each of whom will swear they are dear friends of Doc's. He will tell you the same about them. You might have heard someone in our area express that a person "ought to be shot" if they dump trash along the roadway or pull in front of them in traffic. Have any of you ever heard such?" Not waiting for an answer, Keith moved on. "For instance, Doc deals with people like me every day, staff trained to a level, but unprepared to deal with deep-seated emotional problems or serious brain disorders. We make stupid recommendations to Doc and, at times, to patients. He takes it on himself to teach us how to help those that the community has often given up on. The twenty names on this paper are staff people who need Doc's attention. He meant no more than you or I mean when we say in an off-handed, inappropriate way that someone should be shot. He merely meant to address stupidity, as he sees it. These staff people have been observed committing clinical errors that he felt strongly about."

By this time, most of the officers were focusing on the good that the Doc was doing for their people. "Keith, what do you reckon we can do to help matters?" The constable *(Fife Like)* was now hating that he had raised such a ruckus.

"I don't rightly know, but Doc wasn't operating the car when you found him. Those of us who have observed his driving will testify that he never travels at more than twenty or thirty miles per hour when he is drinking, that he always takes less traveled routes, and that he has never been involved in a serious automobile accident. As to the list of names, you could call them. Ask them what kind of friend he is. It'd be a great favor to your circuit clerk, to the patients down at the clinic and to me if you'd just forget this ever happened."

"Just let him go?" the sheriff spoke up rather sharply Keith thought.

"Gonna raise a right smart of a stink taking this all the way through court." The constable really didn't wish to be called away from his work to testify in court against what was probably a good man, a good man for the community. He certainly didn't relish being questioned by a defense attorney, probably made a fool of. Somber-faced officers nodded in the affirmative. The sheriff, depositing a sheaf of papers in a waste basket, began gathering Goatee M.D.'s paraphernalia in preparation for his release. Keith phoned a local garage to make arrangements for delivery of the doctor's staff car.

Dr. Lee didn't show up for his outpatient or rehab duties until Wednesday of the following week, taking two vacation days to recuperate. Keith, frustrated with the inconvenience for staff and patients made a bold decision. He, La Pearl, and Long Hair MMPI would confront the doctor. On that Wednesday the day of his arrival, the three converged on him in his office. Keith opened, "Doc, we're concerned about you and troubled for the patients. We've discussed last Friday's escapade and decided to deal with it at this lowest level, sheltering you from executive action. I have dealt with local authorities in three counties now intervening for your intolerable, self-destructive behavior. We think it's time that you faced the issue and got help."

"I know my actions aren't acceptable. I must do better." The doctor speaking in his usual calm manner looked neither at Keith nor the other two. Under similar circumstances, others might try to explain or to declare the encounter an unauthorized kangaroo court, carried out by staff members who had no authority in the matter. Dr. Lee made no excuses.

"Doctor Lee, maybe an explosion from time to time is what you need to get out whatever it is. You treat each of us as though we're fragile merchandise. I suspect this passivity carries over in all areas of your life. Better still, try striking a golf ball, slapping a handball, something with passion, but harmless." MMPI was aware that Dr. Lee knew more about his recommended approach than he ever would and felt a little silly advising him.

"I know what you are saying." Dr. Lee was lightly tapping his cigarette lighter on the edge of the desk.

La Pearl interjected, "Doc Lee, we love you. All of us need you. We're scared, fearing for your health, a terrible accident, personnel action by the executive staff. Taking a social drink is one thing, but periods of total drunkenness, blackouts. That's beyond the pale."

"You are all three absolutely correct. This frank discussion is appreciated. I have patients waiting." The doctor shook hands all around as he rose to leave.

"Doc, don't call me or have anyone else call me if this happens again. No way am I continuing to enable your destructive actions." Keith knew the encounter was serious at least for the three instigators. At the door, Doc looked directly at him for the first time, "I understand. Thanks." Later, Keith mentally re-examined the entire confrontation and wondered if the doctor's final look reflected acceptance, self-pity, introspection, or total rejection. Actually Dr. Lee was just being himself. Short answers, no confrontation was his style.

Dr. Lee understood the gravity of the situation, the danger he posed to others, the frustration of co-workers, and the grief he must be causing his wife. He enjoyed the work and recognized that the agency's corporate image was at risk of being compromised. The executive staff might be forced to take action. Something, he knew, had to be done. Maybe he needed a behavioral substitution to relieve his internal turmoil or rest his mind. He needed to change. Instead of re-reading Freud, talking to a minister, or MMPI, he decided to take matters in hand. After careful consideration he decided to buy a metal detector. This might occupy his mind, get him outside more, and allow him to ride one of his horses to possible treasure sites. Not interested in finding class rings or nickels and dimes, he'd study forested riding areas for possibilities. Relics of yesteryear pricked his interest. Finally he settled on *Wildcat Battlefield*, a site deep in the National Forest where he had ridden many times. A serious Civil War battle had been fought there in 1861. He had read on the internet that it was the first engagement of regular troops in Kentucky. Zollicoffer, CSA pitted against Garrard, leading the Union forces and in an area isolated until recently, a probable spot for relics.

Purchasing the detector and finding several spent bullets and a piece of an old rifle on his first field test, brought on a new obsession. Friday afternoon would no longer be devoted to drink. Rain, snow, heat nor cold were to interfere with the search. If the weather was uncooperative, a trip to the library, a search of the internet was to fill his hours. Eventually, he'd join a local *Civil War Round Table* discussion group, travel with other relic hunters, and maybe contribute articles to the archives of the local historical society. In both work and play, he'd live a more healthy existence. It felt right.

# CHAPTER 19

## Amanda Runs Away

"Where is that little ignoramus? I'm going to pinch her head off. Should have on her first day in this world of torment and shame, which heaven knows she's just adding to." Beck was tromping through the house muttering, the floor boards giving under foot, the few whatnots bouncing on shelves. She was looking for Amanda. Aunt Beck's voice was not louder than usual, but severe, severe enough to make Amanda's palms sweat. Even the officers later that morning wouldn't do that.

It had begun early with Aunt Beck demanding that she leave her bed immediately and see to her baby. "He's been crying for nigh on twenty minutes!" Needs a dry garment probably; food wouldn't hurt him neither. Ten or twelve hours is a while for a little feller to wait."

Amanda had given up nursing the baby after the second week, so feeding required more than taking him to her breast for "natures finest"—as the hospital nurses had admonished her to do.

"It hasn't been ten or twelve hours! Let me tell you, I was up twice last night, at one and at four-thirty feeding him and I'm tired. Freddie, Jr. gets good care, I'll have you know." Noting her aunt's slur, she was more direct than common. Her eyes flashed as she responded, eyes that old Carl described as "yeller," referring to her as "that cat-eyed gal of Sis's."

"Don't get smart with me, you little half-raised mommy," Aunt Beck continued. "As soon as you get him cleaned and fed, run off down to Walmart and get that list of things I gave you yesterday. Don't forget to take the WIC voucher. It'll cover most of his order. I ain't made of money, you know, or do you? And get your mom and me some pretzels and a carton of Mountain Dew." Aunt Beck scratched first under one breast then the other.

Amanda added an ample supply of lipstick, pressed her lips together before the dresser mirror, and left the room.

On arrival at the store, Amanda moved first to the jewelry display, not the one with the three dollar necklaces and rings. She preferred looking at the better stuff. At Amanda's request, the woman managing the display looked a bit askance, but opened the secure case and removed a set of earrings, the ones with two small diamonds. What Amanda was interested in was down-counter a couple of feet—a gold bracelet with two brightly colored jewels and priced at one hundred sixty-nine dollars. Amanda turned first one way then another, flipped her hair and inserted the earrings. Then she moved in front of the small mirror mounted down the case just over the bracelet. As the clerk bent to adjust some merchandise, Amanda leaned over and stuck her right hand over the glass top and into the case. All the while she was bending and peering into the mirror, her head turned just so, to better admire the earrings. After a quick swipe, she inserted the bracelet behind the waistband of her jeans, jeans tight enough to prevent any slippage.

"Thank you, ma'am," using her sweetest voice. She then passed the earrings back to the clerk. "I'll tell my boyfriend I would like to have these for my birthday," she said. The clerk did not respond and Amanda moved on to the baby food and diaper aisle.

Smooth move, Amanda, she was thinking, plastic bags wagging from each hand as she exited the store. Just outside the sliding glass, however, that thought dissolved. A female associate wearing her name tag stepped into Amanda's path. Two male security guards leaned close on her right and left. "Miss, please remove the bracelet from your waistband and hand it to the associate." The guard to her right was speaking.

"I have no idea what is going on here!" Amanda screeched. "You three bullies trying to frame me for something? I ain't done nothing! I just come down here to give you some business and git my baby something to eat." Her tone revealed nothing but hurt. Her eyes vacant showing an inner concern for baby, maybe. Her shoulders drooped to express helplessness. Had the video camera not been so exact, the three likely would have slunk off declaring it a case of mistaken identity.

"Miss, please hand me the bracelet. We have a clear video of your theft." Amanda said nothing, obviously considering her options. "Otherwise the police will be called. You may be aware that their searches are more thorough, taking a look at more than just your waist-band." She pointed. "Look just across the parking lot. See that police cruiser over at the McDonald's window? How long do you think before you're downtown removing your shirt? So hand it over, now." The female came across strong. An invisible cord was slowly being tightened around her neck. At least that is how Amanda felt. She'd heard about strip searches. They didn't have to get more specific.

"Okay! Here, take the thing! I got no use for it anyway." Amanda squared her shoulders, looked the associate directly in the eye and stepped close as she passed the bracelet into the lady's hand. One of the guards had moved a few steps away and was talking on his radio by this time. Soon two city police officers had Amanda in handcuffs and seated in the cruiser. One officer accompanied the employees back into the store to get more information and do a further review of the video. The officer with Amanda offered a cigarette or mint. She shook her head. Sobbing, her voice breaking, Amanda asked him to call Aunt Beck. Even in her brokenness, even cuffed in the back seat, him under the wheel in front, she noted a slight tightening across the officer's shoulders at the mention of Beck. But he complied.

Hardly had Amanda got seated in the anteroom off the lobby of the police station when Aunt Beck strode in, her huge frame blocking most of the light as she moved through the door. There are times to be defiant, times to question authority, times to yell foul. Aunt Beck knew and ably utilized all such tactics. This wasn't such a time. Before entering the anteroom and before the tirade about Amanda's ignorance, she addressed the officers: "Good morning, officers. I hate it about this mix-up. The girl ain't been just right since the baby came. You know about some women getting all tore up, doing unordinary thangs, not knowing their people, thangs like that. Well, this poor girl," with that Aunt Beck's voice became a low whisper. "I don't know how long we can keep her. Bless her little heart. She's got no daddy, no husband. Her mother is sick. I'm about all she's got and you all know that ain't much. By this time the recording officer had the necessary papers completed and Amanda was released into Aunt Beck's custody with a court date to be set later. The girl, shrunken with the circumstance, followed a few steps behind to the old car. "Did you git your thangs? The baby needs milk and I'm dying for a Mountain Dew".

"Yes, I got the things." Amanda asked, "Freddie, Jr. alright?"

"What in the world was you thinking, little lady? Don't you know they've got enough pictures of you just entering that store to paper your room with? If your mother was able to take care of your baby, I'd a let them keep you. Maybe you'd learn something. I'll swear I was smarter than to pull such a trick when I was nine years old."

Amanda held her tongue. Her thoughts were a different matter and they were racing first one in front, then another. Finally she settled on a plan. Mom and Auntie, they'd just have to get along. Inside the house Amanda made her way back to the kitchen to deposit the baby stuff as Aunt Beck updated her mother, emphasizing stupidity several times too many, according to Amanda's count. Dropping the bags on the table, she passed through the kitchen door to the outside, letting it close quietly. From the yard, she "lit a shuck", as Aunt Beck liked to say, for the twin's and Carl's nephew's home. No longer in sight, as the trailer had been, their new home was still within jogging distance.

"Hid'dy, boys. How ya been?" Amanda hadn't been with the boys since the trailer bust and hardly since Freddie, Jr. All three looked a little gaunt, she reckoned. Their clothes were dirty and reeked of chemical smells she knew were meth ingredients. Aunt Beck didn't put up with nastiness, so the dirty clothes and acrid smells were not something she appreciated. "Boys we're going to have to clean up a little around here if I stay."

"Barely got in the door, already started bossing." Carl's nephew, Louie, spoke first.

"How do you know we'll let you stay," whined Jerald, the smaller twin.

"Wait up, men. Let's not get too far out ahead here." Turning to Amanda, "What about your baby?" If the baby-care issue cleared, the larger twin, Earl, was seeing potential. He and Amanda had been powerfully close. It had been a long time and she was fitting her jeans really good today. The pink of her cheek, the sheen in her hair, the whiteness of her teeth, the tightness of her shirt, these he took in at first look, even though it would have been impossible for him to express just what he saw. The picture expressed itself in a feeling, no, a notion akin to one generated by hot cocoa, or lemonade in season, or maybe, for some, hot coffee on a brisk fall morning. Earl had a strong urge, an urge bordering on wild no holds barred desire. He skipped to the latter, never capable of conjuring or at least stating, underlying thoughts.

Losing the girl was no big deal to Beck. Besides she'd known within a few hours her whereabouts. But after a few days, Amanda's mother broke down under the strain of trying to care for little Freddie and Beck had a business to run. The sisters concluded that the other grandma must step up. "That sorry Freddie has some responsibility here and his mother too, Beck allowed."

So Beck loaded the baby in the old Impala and transported him the short distance along with supplies to last only a few days. "You're going to have to help out a little. His mommy is gone.  My sister is wore out and you know how busy I am." Placing the baby carrier on the kitchen table, Aunt Beck exited without an answer. At first Freddie's mom was delighted, as women sometimes are whose babies are grown. The rocking, hugging, kissing, delivering a bottle, dressing in cute gowns, next to playing baby dolls is just about the finest experience possible in this life. But Freddie's mom, a frail little woman who didn't remember how hard it was to care for a baby, soon ran down. After the diapers, formula, and other supplies ran out and with no way to get these necessities, she called Carl for help.

"Why, yes, I don't care nary bit to go get that baby a few tricks. What's he need?" he'd readily responded. Ever the obliging neighbor, Carl delivered a week's supply for baby Freddie's needs. "Baby is a pretty little helpless thang, ain't he? You might ought to call that rehab center and tell his daddy you've got to have some help." Carl spoke even softer than usual in the baby's presence.

After Carl left the house, Grandma Byrd, placed the call. "Freddie, this is your mommy. You're going to have to come home. Amanda has run off and that outfit has dropped her baby on me. You know, Honey, I'm not able to take care of no baby." Freddie heard the request. He wanted desperately to come home, but Mr. Keith had just that day begun the process that he hoped would insure the diesel repair training that he so desperately wanted.

"Mommy, it's a bad time for me to leave here. I've nearly got my thirty days in and it looks like I might git to stay longer for some trainin'." Freddie could neither let his mommy down nor Mr. Keith, not to mention Amanda's baby. "Can I call you back in the mornin'?" This was going to require some studying on his part. His head low, his hands clasped behind his back, he strolled to Keith's office after the call.

"Mr. Keith, I'm in a bind. You know I've told you about Mommy and about Amanda and her baby." At this point he choked. No words formed in his head or came from his mouth. His hands sweated. His face flushed, and he shifted from first one foot to the other.

"Yes, Freddie. I remember. What's going on?" Keith had become familiar with Freddie's communication patterns. He nodded the young man to a chair, got up and poured him a cup of water, and sat a distance away from him on the edge of his desk.

"I have to go home." Freddie's words more a sputter than a coherent statement.

"Go home? What for?" Keith's words were delivered much calmer and quieter than he felt. Much of his day had been spent trying to get an extended stay approved. The hurdle of pre-admittance exams for the training program, no small task, was still to be resolved. Keith identified something about Freddie, but he didn't have the vocabulary to adequately express what he was feeling. The young man's wiring had been affected, maybe serious early abuse. Anyway, Freddie often couldn't respond to direct questions. This carried over to written responses, creating a testing nightmare. After several starts and stops, Keith finally understood the problem—his mother needed help caring for Amanda's baby.

"I'd like to come back though." Freddie was no longer just choked-up, tears came which he quickly wiped away with the palms of his hands.

"This is against protocol. Let me look into it with administration. How about we talk tomorrow morning?" Keith was almost as distraught as his patient. A lost cause ten days ago had just today become a possible win. The young man immersed in a lifetime of poverty, ignorance, drugs, and general privation was on the threshold of escape. At least that was Keith's hope.

The same afternoon, after calling Freddie, the grandmother tiptoed around the house for some time during the baby's nap. But as mothers and grandmothers are prone to do, she opened his door a crack so as not to wake him. She leaned her ear close listening for movement or breathing sounds. Her household had no monitor. Hearing nothing, she pushed the door ajar enough to peer inside. Still hearing nothing, she moved into and across the room where the baby was sleeping in a large cardboard box. His breath was coming in short puffs, his face flushed, and his forehead too hot. Alarmed, she walked across the room then back to the sleeping infant. Usually these things took care of themselves. Nature is a wonderful healer. But what if special care was needed, maybe even a doctor. The troubling thoughts kept building one after the other. She decided to act, but having no car, and no one to send out presented obstacles.

"Carl, I hate to bother you again, but this baby is sick and I don't know what I am going to do. You know yourself a baby can be fine one minute, then burning up sick the next. He might get better just as quick as he got sick. I just don't know." The anguish in her voice was clear. The ability to assess need, the desire to fix the hurt, the uncertainty all touched the old man.

"You hold on. I'll come over and we'll talk about it." Carl had heard of Home Health, the Health Department, special services for families, but he'd had no experience with these services and didn't exactly know who did what. On his way over, he decided if the situation was serious, he'd call the County Court Clerk. She'd know what to do. She collected the taxes on his old truck, notified him when his license plates needed renewed, and provided the necessary decal. Smart woman, she was. Inside the house, with the distraught grandmother, the baby hot and crying and drawing short breaths, Carl thought he recognized an emergency.

"Hello, yes, ma-am, this is Carl Sweet from out on the pike." His call to the clerk gleaned a recommendation.

"Mr. Carl, I'm always glad to hear from you." She treated him nice. "Sounds to me like the baby needs to be taken to the hospital emergency room or maybe you might call the Health Department for help." He settled on the Health Department. Too many reports of big hospital bills made him shy of the other. The Grandma continued to rock, and wipe the baby with wet towels.

"Visiting a sick baby at home is not a common health department practice, especially without a doctor order," an RN from the department informed Carl of this during the phone discussion.

"Tell you what I'm studying about doing. I'm gonna call the county judge-executive and ask him what you can and cannot do." She agreed to stop by rather than have a big hullabaloo. Carl explained the complications. He also presented a very serious diagnosis based on a calf he'd just lost to pneumonia. The nurse, recognizing the possibilities and finding out the mother was unaccounted for, took precaution and notified social services. The health nurse and the social worker arrived at the same time. After several questions, a survey of the household, consideration of the two caregivers, judgment was reached to remove Freddie, Jr. from the home, his safety in question. "I don't know what I'm to do," Grandma Byrd expressed this as she wrung her hands.

"You gonna have to have some advice." Carl left the house devastated. Poor little thing, absent mother, no father, one sick grandma, and one near helpless; "It's a sight what two idiots can produce." This Carl spoke aloud to himself all the while thinking about how cute the little fellow was. Perfectly normal to his way of thinking, little round face, bald head, but what was to become of him?

# CHAPTER 20

## Al awakens to New Treatment, New Goals

Al awoke to bright sunlight streaming warm and agreeable through his bedroom window. Usually he was out of bed, showered and drinking coffee by five a.m. The stark white room, the hospital bed with the tray and the drip to his right; it was a minute before he realized where he lay. He had only a second to consider this before the door opened swiftly and a slight woman in white coat with stethoscope dangling, computer clasped to her bosom with one hand, glided bedside.

"Hello, Dr. Soldier Boy. It's about time you woke up. There're patients to see and records to update." All the time she was unfolding the computer on the table. Ann, the female intruder, knew he was to wake up this morning, and not before. After punching in considerable information, according to Al's calculation, "Here is your schedule for Saturday: clinic in Knoxville, however, not to see patients but to attend a weekly PTSD group, followed by twice a month intensive therapy sessions. This is a golf reservation for Friday afternoons at Middlesboro and this is for Sunday afternoon house boat and bass-boat rental on Lake Cumberland." A sheath of papers accumulated on his chest as Ann identified each.

"Hold! What are you talking about? What time is it?" his voice a little gruff as he attempted to wrest control from this wound-up, self-directed woman.

"You should be asking what day it is, Doctor Soldier Boy. You've been hibernating here for over thirty-six hours. During this stretch I've been on the phone with experts from here to Houston, to Baltimore, Washington and New York, not to mention reviewing every reputable computer website available on the topic of PTSD. You, my friend, are in the arena with the bull and take it by the horns you will."

"For such a lightweight, you punch hard and fast with a long reach. This will require some processing." Al had to admit that he felt relaxed and rested, a feeling not recently experienced. Her bedside manner, though a little too sweet for Al's comfort, would have impressed Dr. Kildare, maybe even Ben Casey, M.D.

"Don't try to bamboozle me, Al. Your mind processed this before the final period. There is some very good news. The SCANS indicate that your brain is perfectly normal. So I intend for you to act perfectly normal, even though you saw things in the military that humans should never have to view." Ann fingered her stethoscope. "Listen, people probably have been experiencing this ailment you've got since the first rock fight down at the watering hole tenably somewhere in North Africa. My theory is that our ancestors imposed this man-made PTSD ailment on one another. Then passed the contributing behavior down to us and we must live with it. I'm going to show you how."

"I'm not sure how much of you I can take." Even as he spoke, Al realized that this bigger than life personality had words he needed to hear and was determined to somehow infuse them into his being.

"Now, Al, don't worry. You'll see very little of me, except to monitor your meds, check your schedule, and kick you back into line from time to time. Most of our encounters will be via email, or telephone." Ann liked the guy, his kindness, his quick mind, his dedication to her mountain people, his service attitude truly a community treasure. Besides, she felt sorry for him, sorry for the sick state the world continued to demand. Fights over power, oil, and religion; fighting, mankind's historical trademark down through the centuries, had even become a tool for measuring history. A demand that the best, and fittest must sacrifice, die, or be maimed and turned loose back into the societal stream. This had befallen him.

"You're free to go, Doctor, a regenerated man." Ann was smiling as she left the room, her high heels clicking on the terrazzo.

Al turned through the pages she'd left, his new life in print placed on his chest, not by Hercules, but by Diana herself. Ann had left without even a goodbye, none of that touchy, feely, huggy stuff for that lady. He felt safe under her counsel, direction, or imprisonment, not certain which, but, one or all—rewards for the skirmish. Life was going to get better. He was prepared to get up and pursue the apparent lifelong fight strategy. The attending nurse came in with prescriptions, release papers, and a hospital packet, his reparation, he assumed. Outside the hospital, Al walked along old U.S. 25, which runs north to Corbin, south to Middlesboro. Redbud, just losing its bloom, dogwood filling its place, Pineville along the Cumberland offered unequaled beauty and fresh air. These recognitions, a product of rest, thankfulness for the care of a good doctor, for life, he wasn't sure just what. He was filled as he made his way toward the old court house square where he planned to sit on a bench under the canopy of tall greening trees and think.

As he approached the court square, a loud speaker was blaring, a crowd gathered, the speaker, one hand high in the air proclaiming the gospel of Jesus Christ welcomed him. Not what he'd planned, but the shade was good and the metal chairs accommodating. He joined the crowd and listened:

*"My friends, it's Sunday and you've gathered here to worship the almighty, to learn the truth about where you came from, where you are going, who you are. Note the person next to you. Only elements from the original clay molded by design, I tell you. Once the DNA expressing itself in that man was in a perfect state, in the garden; that wasn't enough to satisfy him or us though—no troubles, no hardship, no pain. More was demanded. Pride of self required that we know more, that we be like the Maker himself, thus the casting out, the lost garden, thus the fall, thus the separation from our Father. This separation is fulfilling itself to date with the high rate of poverty, fatherless homes, alcohol and other drug abuse, crime, unemployment, abused children, unbalanced budgets, environmental pollution, greed, war, hate, distrust. Are you seeing these things presently right here in this town, this county, this nation; recognize any of this as truth? Now, let me tell you something. There is better news. In His time God came to the fallen garden. Yes, He came himself to reveal what the first among us once saw with their own eyes. He came to tell us he loved us still. We are taught that all have sinned and come short; that belief in the eternal, belief in the saving grace through Jesus grants anyone/everyone eternal life. Belief that loving God with all our being, loving our brother as ourselves is also parcel to the abundant life while here. This is accompanied by security, peace and joy. Read it for yourselves friends. It's all printed right there in the four gospels. Change direction for yourself, your family, your community, your nation. All mankind believes something. Work it out for yourself. You'll be satisfied. No excuses...*

At this interval Al slipped from his chair and began the trek back to the hospital parking lot where his automobile had been left by some member of the entourage that delivered him to the hospital. What the preacher reported, he'd seen in man's actions leading to poverty, to war, to misery as well as happiness. The message, familiar since childhood—man has problems relating to his Spiritual Father and to his brother. Al's reading had included a review of various religions. He agreed with C. S. Lewis who wrote that grace and the Christian belief system made more sense to him. The after med-school promise to assist in healing Al held just as strongly today as on that day back at the university. He had always felt this went a long way toward loving others, but healing the human beyond the cellular, that might just be his new commitment. Such acts surely spoke to a great portion of the minister's proclamations he'd just heard. To truly fulfill the brotherly love command, he decided he must learn to treat ancillary problems, those not responsive to prescriptions—food, shelter, education. Too many of his patients presented themselves hungry and unaware of environmental dangers.

Ann's prescription that he stay busy, that he accept the one-day-at-a-time sobriety philosophy, and that he take care of himself physically, he would try to practice concurrent with his new holistic service approach. Any preaching, he'd leave to the clergy.

That evening back in Harrogate, alone in his bed, no attendants coming and going, his mind turned again to service, not just professional service, but service that considered woman his sister, man his brother. First he knew he needed an anchor—a rural health clinic supported with special federal/state dollars that provided for expanded medical care with physician assistants, serving a large catchment area. A family practice serving significant numbers and including basic needs such as shelter, food, and clothing coupled with preventive health training, emergency care, outpatient, and inpatient treatment all were in his vision.

First thing Monday he'd make calls to the Health Commissioner in Kentucky and his counterpart in Tennessee, present the outline and seek recommendations. He wasn't particular which state, however, the mountain location was a must and not negotiable. Second, co-ordination was necessary involving ministerial associations and service clubs. Much of the work had to be performed by volunteers. At this Al closed his eyes—satisfied and ready for sleep. Tomorrow he'd start the process.

"Hello, Roger, this is Al." Roger was serving as Commissioner of Health for Kentucky. Al hoped he could guide him to the money necessary for his incubating plan for service.

"Al, how are you doing? Last I heard you were behind a big gun in Iraq." The two had been friends since undergraduate school at the University.

"Well, the guns are behind me now. I'm great, and you?"

Not waiting for an answer, Al moved on to his business. After explaining his emerging plan, he phrased the questions. "Where do I begin? Is there technical assistance? Is there money available for such a project?"

"Tell you the truth, Al I can assist very little in this. The regulations, the coordination necessary among the various agencies, it's beyond me. However, I can provide contact information and assign a department planner to provide some assistance. You're going to be surprised how many times you'll be expected to answer the same question. I'm told that the new health care legislation unfolding over the next couple of years has already generated upwards of fifteen thousand pages of regulations. We think med school was difficult. Imagine digesting all of that."

"Roger, you don't know how I appreciate your assistance. If duties ever bring you to Southeastern Kentucky, I'd love to take you to Pine Mountain State Park for a good meal, maybe a round of golf." Agreeing they should get together, Al made his second call. This time to Nashville to discuss the same issue with Kentucky's counterpart, also a physician acquaintance he had met on rounds in Knoxville. The questions were the same, the answers were very similar. The challenge was to be amplified with each subsequent contact. Ann had indicated that he needed a full plate at all times. This was beginning to look like a platter.

# CHAPTER 21

## Beck Takes On the Courts

"Hello. No!" Beck had just finished her last cup of coffee for the morning. There was a pause while she listened. "Surely not!" Ending the phone conversation with Freddie's mother as soon as possible, Beck dropped the receiver a little hard, bouncing it out of the cradle. Afterwards she banged doors louder than common and stomped through the house slamming items in place. She wasn't too fond of Amanda's baby, especially since she footed most of the bill for raising it and its mother didn't have a lick of sense. However, the baby belonged to them and nobody took anything from old Beck. She put on her better dress, grabbed her purse and drove away, forgetting to change from her house shoes. If the old Impala's energy had been sufficient, screaming tires would have echoed across the neighborhood. At the county attorney's office Beck's car slid a little in the turn and stopped just short of the front door. "J. B., what's going on here?" Her face drawn, her entire body puffed up, Beck presented as a formidable foe.

"Hello, Beck. Actually I'm trying to make out this note my wife left earlier. What can I do for you?" If he knew the reason for Beck's visit, he wasn't letting on.

"J. B, you and that bunch of yahoos down at social services or family and children services or whatever it's called, took my baby." Beck knew J. B. He'd keep his prints off any such action, but, by heck, the blame went directly to the head man in her mind.

"Slow down now, Beck. I didn't even know you had a baby." He smiled. "Why are you in such a huff?"

Details regarding the removal and placement of Amanda's baby had been handled by an assistant. J. B. counted votes before signing any such documents; however, he knew the broad details. The old lady didn't have the best name. Everyone knew her family had been bootleggers for generations, but she had the uncanny ability to deliver several hundred votes in any countywide election, enough to tip the count for or against a candidate whether that candidate was still breathing or not.

"You know I ain't got no baby!" The thought struck her funny, even though she didn't let on. Some of the puffiness dissipated. "I want you to get that baby back where it belongs!"

"Now, Beck, you know my authority goes just so far. This is out of my purview. You'll have to see the judge." This, J. B. hoped, would at least get her out of his office.

"Purview! Purview my foot!" The puffiness returned. She knew a run-a-round when she heard it. Mealy mouths afraid to make open decisions galled her.

"I'm shooting straight with you, Beck. Here, I'll call the judge for you and get an appointment in his chambers." J. B. hit speed dial, listened briefly then began to talk—the phone on speaker. "Judge, I've got one of our fine supporters here in my office with a family problem, needs to talk to you pretty bad."

"What's the deal, J. B.? I'm right busy." Judge Corn knew when J. B. mentioned supporter, he meant someone to be "sugared" if possible. "Send 'em on down. Who is it, by the way?"

" Beck, from out on the old pike. You'll know her. Thanks, Judge, see you at lunch." Relieved, J. B. turned to Beck for affirmation, but none came. "Anything else I can do?"

"Yes, you can tell me who has that baby." Beck was rising to leave pulling at her dress and scooting a foot back into a house slipper.

"I honestly don't know who has the baby. Some foster care family, I suppose." He wasn't about to turn her loose on some unsuspecting family.

"Soon as I see the Judge, I'm calling you and I want that name. We're talking about a baby here, not some hound you legal connivers sent to the pound." Beck closed the door a little extra hard as she left. Halfway to the court house, Beck realized she still wore her house shoes, but it didn't generate enough concern for her to return home and change. She was on a mission.

"Come in, Beck. Good to see you. Haven't had the privilege since the election two years ago." Beck had delivered the largest cash contribution made in his last campaign along with two hundred plus names with assigned amounts, thus solving any legal cap issues regarding cash contributions.

"Judge, I hate to bother you, but my niece is going through some trouble. Her baby, poor little thang, has been taken away and placed out of the family. I was under the impression that children in these cases were to be placed with close kin, that is, if they're the responsible type. You know I fit the guidelines, aunt and all." Her tone changed as she began painting the social workers. "The brilliant wax-legged and toenail polished state workers, who aren't even elected, just know-it-all's, took our baby without even consulting me. I want you to get that baby back for me. Oh, and I can give details about the little mother's problems if you wish." Beck now took a much calmer, reasoned approach with this black-robed official. She wasn't sure just how far his power extended or how much a few hundred votes influenced his opinions. Rumors went around that his decisions oftentimes favored younger women with pleadings. She knew her trade limitations, however.

"Beck, you'll have to appear before the court. I'm not certain of the outcome, but rest assured, the word of a fine woman like you carries weight with me." The judge, fearing to get too committed on this without more information, hoped the answer sufficed. Out in the hallway Beck stirred in her purse for her cell phone. Unfortunate for those nearby, she tended to think the smaller the phone the louder she had to talk to be heard.

"J. B., this is Beck again. The judge says I'll have to go to court. That means you'll prosecute don't it." Beck was actually calling to get the name of the foster care parents. She had a plan. There wasn't a family alive that didn't have issues and she'd find theirs.

"Beck, this won't exactly be a trial, just a hearing." J. B. wanted to get loose from this and soon. Beck was not the kind to accept no for an answer. Legal implications be hanged.

"You know what I called for. I want to know who has my baby." Going around the barn for an answer wasn't her way. She drove straight through the alleyway.

"Percy family, live just off the pike, out past your place. Turn right about the third driveway. Their name will be on the mail box. You know I'm out on a slick spot here. That's all the information you're going to get." J. B. was tired and busy. It was about lunch time and his voice revealed this or something, Beck wasn't exactly sure. No matter, his usual smooth talk had little influence on her anyway.

On her way home Beck paid a call on her beautician. Not one to waste money, a comb out, a perm and a little highlight once or twice a year met her beauty needs. This was a business call. "Come in, Beck, I haven't seen you in days. You're looking good as usual." The operator came around the chair and hugged her, which was unnecessary in Beck's mind. She was one of Beck's most most profitable couriers. But the operator's nature was to make each visitor feel like her very favorite one.

"I need a little information." Beck knew if it happened, somebody visiting the salon told it, to be repeated more than once by the beautician. "Are you acquainted with the Percy family out off the pike past me? They keep foster children. I need to know any dirt."

"I've heard of them. Funny you should ask. Somebody was just recently in here talking about them. Let me think who that was. " The operator knew better than to hold back on Beck.

"What about the dirt?" Beck was in a hurry. She didn't want a long report about how the old man laid out all night coon hunting while one of the neighboring gents slunk around the old man's back door or some such. She was interested in child care.

"What kind of dirt?" The proprietor recognized the urgency.

"Anything about watching over the children placed there." Beck narrowed the discussion.

"Oh, yes I remember. There was a numbskull in here a few months back, brought his mother in to get her hair colored—pinkish—right smart looking too. He was laughing and telling about how they managed a toddler they had some time back. He said they wired a section of one room with some kind of a battery, gave the little kid a shock if it tried to leave from the area. Is that the kind of thing you're interested in?"

"That'll do." Beck gathered her purse and moved out the door without further comment.

The following Friday, Beck settled on a bench in the courtroom. Across the aisle sat the Percy family and two young women, state workers, she allowed. All stood at the direction of a court officer until the judge took his seat. The judge asked who was speaking for whom and Beck stood. "Judge, I don't know much about how this operates, but I've got some information you need to know before we get too far along."

"Ah, yes Ms. Beck, please approach the bench."

"What bench? Your Honor." Beck's face flushed. Pointing in front of him and down, the judge directed her to come forward. "What is it, Ms. Beck?"

"Judge, those short-skirted chuckleheads working for the state placed my baby in danger and I think he should be immediately removed for his personal safety." Words were coming fast even for Beck, implying urgency.

"What sort of danger, Ma'am?" Everything was out of order, but the judge moved on.

"Judge, I have three notarized affidavits here proving improper care and probably abuse perpetrated by this family against their charges." The circuit clerk, another special friend who had added the document's notary seal, had advised her to say "perpetrated" and "charges." After reading the materials, the judge called the workers to the bench, repeated the allegations and asked if they had investigated the two homes—Percy's and Beck's. It was established that they had investigated one, but not the other. He asked if there were problems with the Percy home and why they hadn't considered Beck's for the placement. The worker in platform heels responded that they had not known of Beck's interest and that there had never been deficiencies in Percy investigations.

"No deficiencies! Do you call electrifying the play area like an invisible dog fence good child care?" Beck wondered who had recommended these two for their jobs.

"I'm sorry, but the state will need to respond to these allegations and, under the circumstances, investigate Beck's home for immediate placement of the baby. Should Beck's household be found unfit, another foster placement must be found today." Beck speculated that it being Friday, and likely her nails day, high heels probably wouldn't find any problem with the Beck placement.

"Does this mean I get my baby back, Judge?" Beck thought she knew the answer to the question, but wanted to hear it from him.

"I'm guessing you will, Ms. Beck." The judge wanted this issue to go away as soon as possible. The older he got, the quicker election time seemed to come around.

# CHAPTER 22

## Thad's Introduction

Thad was sitting in his swivel chair looking out across his desk over top a cup of stale coffee, several medical records, and a week's accumulation of papers. The view beyond the widow, mostly leafless trees revealing the crags and washes on the far hill, was vaguely visible in the late afternoon gloom. Snow was beginning to fall from the oppressive cloud cover. He was thinking about his boyhood in Grand Rapids, about ice skating, the theatre—things that he missed. Not that Southeastern Kentucky had not offered a rewarding several years, it had been challenging, educational and interesting. The dynamics among the treatment team had provided growth beyond expectation.

On that first day in Kentucky, Thad had arrived at the community mental health executive offices a few minutes early, just in time in fact to observe the receptionist picking up the phone and answering, "Hello, mental health center, can I hep ye?" Obviously a great cultural divide existed between his university back in Michigan and this. After the phone call, he had gotten full attention from the greeter, who offered coffee and a donut. The best he could understand, she explained that he was to be interviewed by the executive interview team at eight-thirty.

To fill the void and maybe to practice his ear, Thad inquired of the lady, "Ma'am just down at the service station, I asked the attendant to check the motor oil in my car. He said, 'I don't care to.' Then asked that I pull the hood and he checked my oil."

She squinted, concentrating on his statement. "Good for him. Sometimes these people don't take kindly to long hair, not that it bothers me." She quickly averted her eyes when she realized that Thad was now squinting back.

Without realizing it, Thad tossed his head, the long hair bouncing over the collar of his coat. "No, I mean, yes, it was nice of him to assist, but that is not what puzzled me. I don't care to, is negative, essentially meaning no. Yet he did it."

"Hmm, that is strange, I guess." With that she turned and began looking through a file drawer, apparently ready to end the conversation. Thad took up yesterday's *New York Times* from a nearby table, a bit surprised to find it in the office with a lady who talked like no one he'd ever heard before. He'd read southern novels, knew about southern dialects, but wasn't prepared for what he had been hearing.

"Morning, Thad, isn't it? Come in and meet the crew. Don't worry. They'll not hurt you." Thad followed. Turning to those in the office, "Folks, this is our new clinical psychologist recruit. Put on your best front and remember this fellow can read you." The smiling CEO communicated slightly better than the receptionist. He introduced Thad to five suited individuals representing various programs offered by the center. Questions relating to family, school, and interests allowed him to relax. He was glad they didn't ask why he applied for the position. It was strictly for the money. The Appalachian region's difficulty in recruiting professionals pushed the pay scale much higher than those closer to universities. After six years of training and the accumulated college loans, he was financially pressed and disappointed to discover something he should have investigated beforehand. Master level clinical psychologists didn't earn all that much.

One of the older interviewers' final comments surprised him. "You know, he said, "long hair on a man bothers some people. Heck, I say you make him cut it off and whatever brought it on will come out some other way—long fingernails or something." At that the team members all laughed, but not in a heart-felt, meaningful way, Thad thought.

Outside the interview office, Arthur, the older man took Thad's arm, leaned in close, and announced that he was having a fox hunt over at his place that evening. "Would you like to come, meet some staff, eat good home cooking, and hear the most beautiful music known to mankind?" Relieved that he likely was being seriously considered, Thad acquiesced, took down directions, and left not knowing that the music mentioned referred to dogs barking and the hunter's horn.

Later at the motel, his home for a few days, that is if he was hired, Thad asked the clerk what people did at a fox hunt. "That depends. Some of the old timers build up a good fire, gather around it, argue over whose dog is out front, eat beans, and drink whiskey. Some of these new fellows are more sophisticated. They have judges and such."

"Do they ride horses?" Thad had seen the pictures of beautiful horses gliding over fences, riders in fancy habits, hounds running with noses close to the ground.

"I doubt you'll see that kind of hunting around here. Mostly it's about drinking, enjoying the outdoors, that kind of thing." Thad was getting a mental picture. Surely with other staff present he'd be safe.

The route to the fox hunt proved a bit daunting—blacktop, gravel, dirt, a gate, blocked by a pickup with two fellows inside. "Park over off the tracks. We'll take you on back to the hunt." The voice coming from one of the occupants sounded normal. It continued once he was in the truck. "Greetings, I'm Elmer. We're glad you're here, Thad."

Thad smiled a thin nervous smile and shook Elmer's extended hand realizing that this was apparently another outsider. "Thank you. I'm excited." His body language spoke of something else, however. Maybe fear, Elmer thought.

Elmer continued, "Don't let the talk, that is the dialect, scare you. These fellows are for real. They've recruited some of the finest clinicians I've met anywhere and have plans to revolutionize care-giving in the region. They've gathered enough master and doctor level staff to start a university—psychologists, psychiatrists, speech therapists, you name it."

Elmer as a Ph. D. psychologist, who worked on a regional basis over several programs, was present specifically to assess Thad's worthiness for employment. "You might have already guessed I'm not from this area of the country either." He explained on the ride how local staff members often assigned nicknames to professionals, his being Rorschach. "Out of respect they seldom call you by the assigned nickname."

"What do you mean?"

"Usually they just address the therapist as doc, ma'am, sir or mister. Don't be offended. These people are in awe of your training, never having worked with mental health professionals, and they make special efforts to satisfy."

"It's different, but interesting." Thad wasn't spooked yet.

"Just listen until familiarity with the mores lets you find safe ground. Nuances will be read as carefully as your analyst did back in grad school. Try not to offend. By the way I overheard some referring to you as Long Hair MMPI." Thad grimaced a little, but said nothing. When they arrived, the group was gathered around a hay wagon loaded not with hay but with food prepared by master cooks whose attention to texture, aroma, spice, and mixture peculiar to the region insured an eating pleasure. That is, if you liked veggies well-cooked, ham smoke cured, and pies piled high with slightly browned meringue.

"Come around, Thad. Make yourself acquainted, get a plate, and eat, eat a-plenty! We don't want anybody going hungry here!" The host, well into his second plate, sat a couple inches from a half gallon-jar of moonshine and seemed pleased that Thad was there.

A few yards beyond the wagon, a string of fifteen or so white, black and tan dogs were tied on a line hanging between two scrub oaks. Some lunged against their collars as though eager for the hunt while others lay licking their paws or scratching. On a rise maybe a quarter mile away stood a huge black barn used for tobacco curing, Thad was told. Limestone outcroppings decorated the high ground with dogwoods lacing the timbered draws. A more scenic spot Thad thought he had never encountered. To date his taste and experience had lent itself to urban settings with their beautiful museums and tall buildings. So he was impressed, but not overly.

After dinner the participants separated generally by interest groups—local staff and therapists, social workers—as the dogs were turned loose. Sniffing, grunting, a few already barking, the dogs tore around and over the hill. The hunters heard no more of them for the entire evening, leaving Thad to wonder about the overall objective.

Arthur, as the host, passed the huge jug and told stories funny to the teller. La Pearl sometimes sighed loudly as the host's jokes seldom met political correctness standards. Elmer (Rorschach) twisted his shoe toe in the dirt, shook his head, and grinned. The host's world view and community outlook had been formed prior to the nineteen fifties, and forever out of step with current rules.

The fourth pass of the jar gave Thad power, courage he hadn't felt since dorm room discussions. He cleared his throat and proclaimed he had a joke. Silence indicated proceed and proceed he did. The content and punch line now long forgotten, but one fact stayed with him. His joke fell flat. People chuckled a little then drifted from the group. No one slapped him on the back. University humor didn't play well here. Around midnight the party dispersed, some to their cars parked near the host's house, Thad to the pasture gate—the evening's talk of the local poisonous vipers producing lively, high steps on his part.

Late that night, early morning actually, as he prepared to retire, Thad was listening to a favorite pod cast. Suddenly it dawned on him what was so unsettling about his new surroundings. He was essentially in a scene of the popular movie, *Thunder Road,* cast in the Southeast. The moonshine, the dialect matched. All that was missing so far was a U. S. Marshall chasing a dangerous, uncouth mountaineer. This new position, if he got it, was sure to produce interesting patients. He had never owned or even shot a gun, but the necessity of having one crossed his mind. He wasn't sure if it was the moonshine, the night spent on the hillside supposedly listening to the hounds, or Arthur's wild tales that led his mind to such depths. Things looked better the following morning as he strolled down the street looking to eat breakfast. Not knowing which way to walk or what to expect regarding food, he stopped another walker to inquire. "Where is a good place to eat?" His question simple, he expected a simple answer.

"Are ya a Democrat or Republican?" inquired the man, revealing that two front teeth were missing.

Somewhat dumbfounded, Thad responded that he was registered as an independent back home.

"Well, then, sir, I don't rightly know. If you was a Republican, I'd recommend the drug store on the west corner down on the courthouse square. On the other hand, Democrats take their meals on the east side of the court house in the drug store with the big glass front. I guess you'll have to decide for yourself."

Sometime later another inquiry somewhat clarified the issue. He was told that political discussion was taken seriously. Locals had secrets that were to be kept in-house so to speak.

Thad chose neither drug store, but a small diner just off the square. The meal itself proved nearly as baffling as the man's restaurant recommendation. It came with grits, which he had never tasted. The biscuits were covered in gravy and contained bits of sausage, he thought. Everything floated in grease. This was not his regular breakfast—a bagel and coffee most days.

# CHAPTER 23

## Escaping With Bouncy Leggs

On the morning of her fourth day retreat—to room, to bed—Deidra rose early, showered, dressed, stripped the sheets and prepared to re-enter the world of rehab. Making her way to Dr. Lee's office, she signed for an appointment to see him after the breakfast hour. As she entered the cafeteria, her demeanor was neither muted or vibrant—rather neutral Keith thought. Something was different though; her blouse was buttoned, hiding the tattoo.

After breakfast, a little reluctant, but determined, she entered Dr. Lee's office. "Good morning, Deidra. Feeling better this morning?" Dr. Lee's seemingly heart-felt greeting always comforted. This morning, his gentle probing soon brought on a measured smile. She was ready for help. Anything to reduce the pressure she felt—pressure to produce, pressure to explode, to run, to use.

"Dr. Lee, I think I'm ready. I need your help to escape these spirits in my mind." Referring to the fears, compulsions, whatever it was controlling her behavior as spirits seemed as good as any descriptive term.

"Tell me about these spirits." Dr. Lee was encouraging her to open up.

"They drove me from high school, followed me from one man to the next, destroyed my work, and now they are so overpowering, I know my life is threatened."

"Threatened how?" Dr. Lee asked, probing now for any dangerous-to-self-thoughts.

"Threatened, not for the first time by any means, but this time the threat has no counterbalance. My forty-one years has meant nothing—no family, no body of work, no real friends, no wealth to attest that I've passed through." It was as if her brain chemistry had suddenly changed. If a life light existed, she desired its warmth, its brilliance.

"I see. Good, good." Dr. Lee's pat answer when he agreed with a statement was two goods. "What have you in mind?"

"I was hoping you'd tell me." Deidra was a little put off by Dr. Lee's question.

"Deidra, you realize that medicine is much more than a magic pill. What you suffer can be partially controlled by medication which I can prescribe, but healing requires strengthening positive personal behavior, taking small deliberate steps toward sobriety, associating with gentler personalities, absorbing from them traits of calmness. Often when training horses, we pair a high-strung animal alongside a less-spirited one. You'd be surprised the difference in highs and lows one observes in the nervous animal."

"Dr. Lee, surely you aren't comparing me to a nervous horse, my behavior merely spirited, my thoughts bent toward being easily spooked." Deidra thought she knew what the doctor was advocating—better company if she was to change behavior. She also remembered how he loved horses.

"You might do well to come down to the stables some Saturday morning, get a feel for the calm versus nervous animal and the effects one has on the other." The doctor's training and personal demons were both at work as he reviewed a plan.

"I might just do that." Deidra became a little excited, a little scared as she'd never mounted anything other than a pony on a lead and then accompanied by her parents.

"I'd like you to meet with Keith, tell him of our discussion, and request his assistance in planning your attack, O.K?"

Dr. Lee was certain that Keith's thorough approach in such matters would involve full treatment team consultation and result in a concise treatment plan for the patient.

After speaking with Dr. Lee, Deidra's mood, though contemplative, was not too high, but definitely not low enough to go back to bed either. Keith noted that her behavior in the group sessions was appropriate. While preparing for dinner that evening, she was interrupted by a summons to the lobby. A visitor, someone from her past, Bouncy Leggs, the patient who had stormed out of group and walked away from the center on her group's first day greeted her, smiling, smelling of Old Spice and wearing a gold bracelet.

"How about going out to dinner with me?" With no hesitation, Deidra gathered her purse under one arm, said, "Sure" and followed him to his car. She gave no thought to signing out, to asking permission. Just grab the opportunity and act.

"How about we go to Cracker Barrel?" The man's voice soft, his face smiling, a bit too soft, a bit too smiley.

Deidra should have registered danger, but she didn't. He passed the turn into the restaurant and drove on toward the country.

"I thought we were going to eat." Deidra began to be just a little concerned at this point. Men who said one thing and did another were not uncommon in her experience.

"Na, maybe a little preparation first might improve our appetite." The main road behind them now, he pulled the car on-to an abandoned lane, turned off the ignition killing the lights, and produced a packet from the console. "Hold out your hand." Complying, Deidra received a number of pills he shook from the container. "Enjoy." With that Bouncy Leggs swallowed, she didn't know how many. Deidra raised her hand to her mouth pretending to swallow the pills, but held them to be dropped into the door pocket to her right.

"I've been to Chicago, Detroit, and Arizona since I left you guys at the crazy house. Look at this." Leggs turned on the overhead light, opened the console between them and produced a huge roll of bills. I've made more money since you saw me than all three of your healers there at the crazy house have made in six months."

"Where else you been?" Deidra was remembering Las Vegas and other trips she'd made and was speaking of the cities he'd seen.

"Woman, I've been north, south, east, and west; got a bundle to prove it too."

"Ever have second thoughts about leaving rehab?"

"Are you kidding? And miss the good times?" Bouncy Leggs lit a cigarette with the car lighter. The glow made him look more sinister than she'd noticed before.

Of course, his move came soon. Deidra dodged the first attempted kiss. "Listen," she stalled, " I haven't eaten since lunch. My body is telling me, first things first. A bite to eat, then we both can enjoy a good frolic."

Not in the best mood, Bouncy Leggs reversed the car and sped along the main road, but again passed Cracker Barrel. Instead, he motored downtown and parked in front of a diner. Its feature, a ham and egg sandwich, grilled along with hamburgers and other culinary, its taste compromised.

"Sit here," Leggs virtually pushed her down into a booth occupied by two men who looked much the same as he did, naked arms with veins standing out, hair over their collars, cell phone attached to their belts, expensive slim fitting jeans, and cowboy boots. Suddenly an inner voice, maybe Dr. Lee's, came to Deidra that these were not the horses she needed to be paired with.

"Excuse me." After ordering, she rose and moved toward the bathroom down the hall past the kitchen. Instead of going inside the toilet, she exited the back door nearby and began running down an alley, slowing only at the street. In the next block, a taxi stand sign blinked. Welcome, welcome, she thought as she ran toward it.

"Can you take me out to the rehab center?" Deidra didn't know yet how to explain her absence or if re-entry was possible. The cabbie set his meter and drove away, past the restaurant where she could see the three men through the window, still unaware of her escape. She took a deep breath. Relief warmed her. Back at the center, she walked briskly down the hall that led to her room.

Barely getting into her pajamas before the knock, Deidra was suddenly facing the night nurse, carrying a food tray, a compassionate soul.

"Honey, you missed dinner." She placed the tray on the table in front of the window.

At the kind gesture, Deidra broke down, crying. "What is wrong with me? Why do I follow a fool's path so quickly? What will become of me?"

The nurse, guessing, probably correctly, why she'd left, hugged her gently, "Now, now, Honey women have needs just the same as men."

"No, you don't understand. I walked away with a man I'd seen for a few minutes only one time." Her voice was barely audible. Truly questioning her sanity, she slumped against the nurse, who seated her and presented the food in hopes of halting the melt down.

"We're going to give this a good forgetting. You are here, safe, and I hope, clean." She patted Deidra's arm. The frequent drug tests would bear this out one way or the other. As a practitioner, she knew better than to believe any report given by an addict. The nurse sat close to Deidra as she recounted the entire story from Bouncy Leggs denouncing the group through the taxi ride. The nurse's hope that she hadn't used would be confirmed within a couple of days.

The following morning Deidra made her way to Mr. Keith's office. "Come in, Deidra," Deidra smiled a weak smile and sat in the chair nearest Keith's desk. "Dr. Lee tells me you wish to start a new slate, to plan for a life. I'm happy for you." Keith got up from his chair and moved to the window, his eyes focused on something far off. "Not everybody knows this, but I'm on the same road, one day at a time for eleven years now. He turned back. Let's get started." Deidra was relieved at his kindness and encouraged by his confession. Keith produced a journal and asked her to begin with first a statement relative to sobriety, not a lifetime of sobriety but one day only, followed by a list of worthwhile daily activities. The assignment lasted a better part of two hours, Deidra writing, Keith advising, recommending re-writes for clarity:

PLEASE, JUST ENOUGH STRENGTH TO STAY SOBER FOR THE NEXT TWENTY-FOUR HOURS

A. GRANT ME THE ABILITY AND OPPORTUNITY TO PAIR UP WITH PRODUCTIVE, WHOLESOME PEOPLE AT ALL TIMES

1. To be of assistance to those less fortunate who might have similar burdens
2. To work with my doctor to insure proper medication for stability
3. To visit local school classrooms offering young people encouragement that they might escape the trap
4. To get a job to support myself and help others…

She focused and worked seriously, the list lengthening. Keith helped her pare it to ten items, each demanding a lifetime of practice. It was a start. The cold, lonely, rootless feeling, the abused body, the shrunken spirit required more than a list. The path ahead she intuitively knew would be steep and winding. For the first time in years, after reading over the finished product, she silently prayed, admitting where she was and requesting divine intervention, maybe because the treatment steps recommended it or maybe because of Mother's teaching.

At the conclusion of the morning session, Keith surprised Deidra with a request: "My AA group is scheduled to meet with an incoming class at the community technical college to discuss the pitfalls surrounding addiction. I'd like you to join and talk about your experiences."

"I'll try," was her only reply, but she was grateful for the opportunity.

^^^

The evening before, after she had escaped from the men, Bouncy Leggs finally got concerned about Deidra's lengthy absence. He knew of cases where sober addicts over-dosed, their re-introduction intake overpowered their system. Making his way to the bathroom and knocking loudly, he called her name. No answer prompted entrance and revealed no Deidra. He'd been snookered by a stupid woman. The friends in the booth, recognizing his dark mood, remained quiet, except one asked, "Anything wrong?"

"No, no. Let's get out of here. She's blown us off. You can bet I'll find her. No heifer takes my stuff and walks away from me without some kind of payback." Bouncy Leggs assigned each man to circle the building while he drove several passes block to block for a three block radius. Finally, resigned that she'd disappeared, he loaded his detectives and sped out of town. A late night parley had been scheduled in Lexington. Bouncy Leggs was eager to meet a Detroit contingent and get straight a few knotty issues. Business had been good and expansion was planned if the dumb cluck delivered and extended him sufficient credit. He was thinking everything through during the drive.

At the Lexington rendezvous, Bouncy was directed to ride in the Detroit car with the contact. Two Detroit accomplices rode in Bouncy Leggs's car with Legg's two Kentucky companions. One of the Detroit men drove and seemed to know where they were going. The three Kentuckians, divided between the two cars were too cool to ask. The route retraced their trip as far as southern Madison County. There the two cars turned south and east and progressed into the Daniel Boone Forest where they stopped. Leggs was kept in his car while his two friends were questioned and cajoled.

"You're the two that's been dealing the Chicago stuff. Weakened down, passed off as Detroit excellent. That gives us a bad name, you know." The more aggressive of the two Detroit men made the accusation. Bouncy's friends were surprised, caught with no prepared answers.

"No. You've got us mixed up with someone else." He turned to his buddy. "Tell them. We only deal through Bouncy." Bouncy was hearing snatches of the conversation from his position in the other car, but couldn't join in their defense.

"You stay out of this." His driver held Bouncy's shirt collar tight.

"My sales were off sixty percent last month. My buyers were yelling about poor quality stuff." The speaker ordered Leggs's companions out of their car as Leggs watched from his. "Kneel, scum, you don't double deal with Detroit." The two Detroit men wrestled both men to the ground and the one with the gun shot each in the back of the head.

Bouncy witnessed the shooting, but barely. The driver had encouraged him to try some of his stuff as they traveled and by this time he was groggy, in and out of consciousness. The driver no longer held him by the collar. Enough of his senses were working though to realize the seriousness of the situation. He flung his door open and left the car only to fall face down after a couple of staggering steps. He began crawling on all fours as fast as he could into the briars and saplings growing beside the forestry road. His driver soon caught up and Bouncy too was murdered, a knife wound to the throat and extending to the back of the neck. Not killed instantly, Bouncy had time to ponder. "The heifer got away." Of course, no one knows for sure what his last thoughts were and the investigators speculated about his and his assailant's final moves.

Deidra and Bouncy Legg's acquaintances around home had no idea what happened after the three left town. It would be nearly a year before newspapers recounted events transpiring that night in the dark forest. A burned-out automobile covered by limbs and bushes was found in a ditch. The final view for the three had been the dark and foreboding forest—normally so beautiful and enticing for those seeking respite. The vehicle with its charred human remains inside the trunk had served as their year-long grave.

The preacher recruited by the funeral home staff spoke long and loud, lauding sober living, condemning drunkenness, and warning all within hearing: "life is but a vapor, repent." The funeral director, the grave diggers, and the few family members heard the remarks repeated at each grave site. Observers shook their heads, each in his or her particular way, and with saddened demeanors viewed the casket, repeated "such a waste" or "so sad," then walked away taking short steps, considering. Bouncy's father, Phillip, went home and shined his shoes. His mother poured a glass of wine.

Down at the grocery, after reading the news report of the three's demise, Carl mused: "Poor devils. Won't be spreadin' their pison no more." But he knew that another three had already filled the void. Leggs's group at rehab was long gone, but the report of his murder circulated among the group currently in session. To what avail, Keith wondered. There was much more to Bouncy's life.

# CHAPTER 24

## The Party

Saturdays, very special to Linda, alias La Pearl, were a time for organizing, cleaning house, and calling her mother. Phone calls often lasted the better part of an hour, Linda discussing work, and her mother reviewing the family as they attempted to maintain ties from two states away. The daughter had migrated to Southeastern Kentucky, a location visited during childhood vacations and once with a church group doing mission work. Social work was natural for her and the subsequent college training easy.

Accompanying her father, as he had served food to the homeless, further ignited her special desire to serve. The spring sun, the song birds, the warm breeze combined to support her mood. “Hello, Thad. Thought you, Keith, and Dr. Lee might like to come over for burgers this afternoon.” Such phone calls were often placed by her. She had assumed the role as social organizer for the team. Team members coming from big city environs and oftentimes directly from university found the slow and easy life a bit stifling. Many left the area because of the isolation unless these social contacts got established early on.

“I’m not sure, maybe. It depends on my batch.” Thad’s home brewery was obviously operating. “If the operation concludes in time, can I bring you a few bottles?”

“Certainly, that’d be nice.” Linda had heard that new brew often gave imbibers a stomach issue, but was willing to chance it. I’m sure we can squirrel it away before Doc sees it.” Linda began thinking about the doctor’s drinking issues. Only a few years before they had always made sure Dr. Lee had plenty of beer or other alcoholic drinks at these events. Otherwise, Saturdays would have been out for him. Keith, already reformed even in those days, had always attended and whooped it up just as the others, his drink no stronger than lemonade. His assumed task was to manage the grill. Linda felt at ease with the three men as she would have with three children or three church ladies. Her conversation matched her far ranging interests; her knowledge was respected by all—the men treated her as one of the guys. This treatment wasn't tied to looks. Linda's straw colored hair was usually in a long pony tail that bounced as she walked, her brown eyes flashed mischief or intelligence as the occasion demanded and caught the eye of many a suitor.

As Linda dragged out the cooler and set up the grill, she reflected on an earlier occasion with the empty homebrew beer bottles covering the table, the group had moved their chairs near a bed of pink blooming peonies. Discussion had focused on specific cases or issues that each considered interesting. "Doc, I've been wondering if this area has more addiction, more inbreeding, more chronic health issues, and more violence than most any place in the nation—per capita that is." Thad had a need to understand his adopted community, to take specific cases, to relate them to the culture and history they had discussed.

"That's a good question. Overall the agency serves about fifteen thousand patients yearly. Out of a catchment area of around two hundred fifty thousand, that number is probably comparable with other parts of the country." Dr. Lee had arrived several drinks ahead of the group, but early on he had held up well.

"I understand that. But we aren't the only practice in town. I look at the full jails, the waiting list for rehab.

I'm not convinced." Thad had intended someday to gather statistics on the problem, maybe publish something in the psychology journal on the topic.

"I don't know where you get the inbred idea. We're probably healthier on that front than some of your cities." Keith always took offence at this insinuation. "People in the mountains are more likely than most to know their lineage for two hundred years and distant cousins might be more likely to marry. That doesn't mean they are inbred." He laughed and reported that his people might be considered pure bred, however."

"Don't get riled again, Keith. It's just a question. I have no supporting data." Thad had done enough testing and counseling to suspect the accuracy of part of his hypothesis, and not only that, the literature had suggested such for years.

"My opinion regarding addiction is that it's much larger, the etiology somewhere deep in our culture." Linda stood to move her chair into better shade. "At times it shows itself, I think, because of society's actions, like the policy accompanying Medicaid back in the sixties." No one responded and she continued. "The health coverage for marginal families adversely affected those whose income was not high enough to survive, but too high for the benefit. To qualify, the father was edged out of the home, becoming so-called 'sundown fathers', which led to broken families, poverty, and out of wedlock children. This spun broken communities and the accompanying drug and alcohol epidemic." Linda's social consciousness was not limited to specific patients.

"Ahh, you might be right. Society provides the hotbed for many of our ills." Dr. Lee's speech had become a little slurred as he arose and walked a bit unsteadily across the lawn. The group deep in discussion took no note when he drifted over into the next yard, entered the pool gate and stumbled headlong into the ten foot section. The splash alarmed Keith, who jumped and ran to his rescue. It took all three to pull him out, the difficulty of the job surprising them and causing them a little concern for their own safety. The party was over. Keith, wet and annoyed, loaded the dripping doctor into his car and took him home, all the time wondering how to explain the soggy delivery to Doc's wife.

"Mrs. Lee, I'm so sorry to come into your home, drenched as we are." Keith had no words to mitigate the situation. "Doc tripped and fell into the pool."

"It's okay, Keith. Don't worry about it." Keith knew she'd seen Doc delivered in worse condition and he said nothing else other than, "I'm sorry," again before leaving.

Thad meantime had gathered his bottles, good for another batch, assisted Linda in clearing the table and cleaning the grill, and left. Keith returned shortly and stayed to assist in straightening the kitchen, his wet clothes clinging and uncomfortable, Linda thought. He wanted to discuss group dynamics as it related to the current rehab residents. Sometimes his group discussions devolved, he thought, into meaningless banter and bordered on serious conflict—the let's take it outside kind. "Linda, do you have a specific agenda for each session? I mean is there an outline you develop each morning?" His question, meant to help him learn how to draw the group back to useful dialogue when mayhem threatened, sounded silly to him even as the words came out.

"Why don't you sit in with Thad or me during an afternoon session? Then we'll discuss the event afterwards. I'm not saying we're any better at this than you, but we can learn from one another."

"Thanks, Linda. Sometimes I'm uncertain even to the point of wondering if what I'm doing is harming rather than helping."

"Nonsense, you're an excellent counselor." Linda knew his sensitivity about his clinical training. She also knew that his concern and natural leadership ability, and not his professional training, carried his sessions to successful conclusions.

On the way home from Linda's party that evening, Keith thought about that afternoon years ago and the pool episode, his concern about his clinical skills, and about how skillfully Linda had calmed his anxiety resulting from the issue. He had loved that earlier day's open-ended discussions, but he had felt sorrow for Dr. Lee.

At that time Keith had been sober for several years, but he still maintained a strong memory of the misery associated with addiction and what Dr. Lee was going through.

Today's get-together had been so much different. No alcohol for Dr. Lee. He brought a box of hand-forged tools, an old axe or two, parts of guns, belt buckles, and buttons from the grey and the blue armies of the nineteenth century and various other items rescued from their burial places. He'd read a paper depicting actual events that happened on the historical Wilderness Trail which wound its way through their catchment area. His artifacts brought to life the westward migration so important to the development of the nation and how it played out right where they drove, walked and lived.

Neither Linda, Keith, nor Thad was ever bored by Doc's new found interests. Each article had a story. Regarding the military items, he knew where each army stood when the relics had been dropped, who was leading, the significance of the battle attached to each. If the artifact was a hand-forged tool, he knew whose homestead it came from, the family's place in history, their contribution to their community. He had become an encyclopedia on Southeastern Kentucky. Local historians sought his advice when an issue stumped them. As a history buff, his enthusiasm for knowing everything there was to know about a topic ran nearly as deep as his desire to know medicine.

Old house sites deep in the Daniel Boone National Forests had become haunts for Dr. Lee. On horseback rides with the local saddle club, he noted flowers blooming where no people lived, rotted stumps of a long abandoned orchard, or a mound, the remains of an old chimney. In the vicinity of these, he spent hours listening to the purr of his metal detector, waiting for the sharp beep that indicated a find. He might never find the sack of gold coins, but then he wasn't looking for them. Diversion, peace, information, these were the rewards he desired.

His wife responded to her close friend who questioned his frequent absences, and whether she worried about him being in the forest alone.

"I think embedded with his desire to help people is the need to know their heritage, to bring their forefathers alive. Also, he may be convinced that knowing what came before helps us to see trends and better prepare for what's to come. I applaud him. I help him organize and categorize every find. I prepare his papers, and if I didn't have to travel by horseback, I'd be right out there with him." The wife had left much unsaid. She felt that the energy from such a mind as the doctor's required broad vistas to prevent being cramped.

# CHAPTER 25

## The Lobbyists

Elmer (alias Rorschach) arose early on this particular Friday, a day set aside for a trip to the capital city of Frankfort, the seat of power, the clearinghouse for patronage to insure southeastern Kentucky against raiding parties from Louisville, western Kentucky and other parts of the state. The state government had a way of taxing eastern coal with a codicil tying portions of the extraction tax to the counties of origin, then transferring the money to fund improvement projects far out of the region. Even though he knew nothing of these matters, the executive staff had honored Elmer with the nomination. Specifically, he was to keep Arthur, the old fox hunter, on task. The visit to Frankfort, designed for currying goodwill, would touch sources of revenue, purveyors of favors, and personages steeped in public relations. Left on his own, Arthur was known to trade favors that might, or might not fit with agency goals. That is, if the favor traded assisted a special interest of his, and he had many, the agency suffered in the compromise.

The entrance to Arthur's place with its curving drive lined by old walnut, sycamore, and maple trees, the trimmed pastures beyond, bordered by a clear mountain stream fed by cold limestone springs caused Elmer to question why Arthur at his age continued his fast paced work. Today's events, no doubt, would explain.

"Hello, Arthur. Your place looks mighty pretty this morning." Elmer was trying to express himself more like a southeastern Kentuckian, Arthur thought.

"Hey, Doc, drive around behind the barn, I want to show you something before we leave." Arthur always addressed Elmer as Doc, respecting his special training. Driving through grass sparkling with morning dew, Elmer could see the cattle herd in the distance. A team of sorrel horses and a matched mule were penned near the barn. Behind the barn was maybe a hundred sheep. A fierce ram strolled from one female to the next, smelling each. "Now did you ever see such a sight? Ain't he got it made—all that possible loving and mighty little competition; check out his business end." Psychological terms entered Elmer's mind. Laughing and slapping his leg, Arthur advised, "We'd better get started. I've got to see a man about a dog." Elmer, having no idea what the latter meant, turned the car in the general direction of the capital.

"Doc, see that old home-site over there?" Arthur pointed off to the right. They were a mile or so from Arthur's place. "Use to be a barn back there in the walnut grove. When I was a boy, my brother and I were fishing the creek just over past the walnut trees. I heard this great commotion and, naturally as a ten year old, I wanted to investigate. Well, we eased up toward the barn and in a pen on the far side from us there was an awful carrying on. People were apparently having fun. We entered the barn and peeped through a crack. There were three grown boys staggering around in the pen and two young women. The women had horse bridles on, the reins wrapped so as to keep the bridles stable. One of the men had a western saddle tied to his back. Several others were seated on a log near the far fence. Every one of them was near naked. Wonder what the poor horse thought when he had to take that bit with woman slobber all over it? They don't spit, you know."

"Women don't spit?" Elmer had lost the thread in the monologue.

"No, you ignoramus, horses, they slobber.  We didn't tell Mammy and Pappy about what we saw. In fact we weren't sure ourselves what we saw."

By this time Elmer was uncomfortable. He was unsure where the story was going or whether or not it had any validity. He had experience with urban myths. Maybe this was developing into a rural version. Arthur wasn't finished: "Doc, do you think seeing that might have affected me?"

"I'm not certain. Something interesting surely made you what you are. I feel safe in saying that."

"Ho, Doc, what are you saying?"

"Arthur, you realize it takes a lot of polishing to make a fine diamond." Arthur interpreted this to mean the psychologist was either pleased or impressed. Had Linda been present, her feeling might not have been so kind. She considered Arthur crude. Nearly everything coming from his tongue was politically incorrect and disgusting in her estimation.

During the drive Arthur told many stories of conquests and jokes which he considered hilarious. The jokes were told in alphabetical order under specific headings, including Irish and farmer. Elmer smiled, sometimes laughing and Arthur was pleased. The two drove into Frankfort along the broad capital streets and eventually entered the capitol building. Near the cafeteria Arthur greeted a well-dressed, serious-looking gentleman, held his arm and leaned close saying something Elmer didn't hear. Then louder, "Mr. Secretary, we're going to need some of that coal severance money to expand the rehab beds down home. Don't forget to put in a good word for us."

"Now Arthur, you know the local boys, the judges and mayors, make that decision." The secretary was not curt, but direct.

"I know who makes the decision, but I know who the big man is, who they listen to." With that Arthur gently patted the man's back and moved on. "That was the state Secretary for Local Government—little man, big job. I've heard he calls me old whistle britches to some of our judges, but we can make him come around when the time comes. Let's go on down and see the Behavioral Health Commissioner."

They walked the winding halls until at last they were seated in the commissioner's waiting room. Along the way, Arthur introduced Elmer to the State Auditor, promised her a mess of greasy beans next trip and recommended that she review the use of certain Eastern Kentucky emergency funds. Might be some available for counseling services.

"Good morning, Gentlemen. Come in." The secretary led them into an office painted dark blue, nearly navy, furnished with a semicircular walnut desk and gold lamps. It hardly looked like a business office. The Commissioner, a psychiatrist noted for cleaning up and emptying out the old state mental hospitals, was not the usual back-slapping Kentucky political appointee. "How may I be of service to you two gentlemen this morning?" Arthur, ever attuned to nuances, introduced Elmer as Dr. Elmer and mentioned his research on deinstitutionalization of the mentally ill and the developmentally handicapped, not revealing that the paper was his dissertation and or that it was done several states away. This interested the commissioner, however, who went into a long discourse on Sweden's program.

When conversation allowed, Arthur interjected, "Commissioner we're poor down home and you've done a wonderful work setting up the funnel to catch federal money for us, but right now we've reached a plateau. Rehab beds for addiction are filled with long waiting lists, the jails are full, and as you know, provide no treatment. I don't know if you are aware of it, but our program is nationally accredited. The first one in the nation, I'm told. These agency boys down home take service serious. Any help you can be, rest assured you'll not be embarrassed." The Commissioner nodded and smiled and glanced at Elmer. "That's the Joint Accreditation Commission for health care?" Elmer nodded. "Yes, I noted a staff report to that affect. Congratulations."

After some small talk and comments about the governor's upcoming budget battle and how Arthur would take care of his representatives, the discussion wound down. "We thank you for your time, Commissioner. Come down sometime. We'd like to show you around." Arthur was moving out the door. He turned to Elmer, "Let's step around to the Executive Assistant's office. That's where the real greasing is needed." They walked three doors down and entered another office just as the man Arthur wanted to see came out of his inner office.

"Hello, Arthur, get in here and tell me something, you old scoundrel. How ya' been?"

Bumping him up a notch administratively, Arthur addressed this physically huge man with a personality to match as Commissioner, introduced Elmer, and began the greasing. "I've got something at home you're going to want. He stands sixteen hands at the withers, his tail and mane white as snow, otherwise sorrel, and he's a walking fool." Elmer had absolutely no idea what Arthur was talking about, but further talk revealed it to be a mule, the one he'd seen penned behind Arthur's barn earlier. The mule was purchased in Tennessee specifically for this officer and paid for in full by Arthur.

The special gift grew out of a late night drinking bout involving Arthur and other staff from their agency and the state department staff following an agency compliance review. The state official, boasting of his farm near Lexington, had mentioned his need of a good mule for decoration. He, too, was from the mountains, but deeper in.

"We're counting on you to help us a little with the big man down the hall," Arthur said. After several loud stories, and much laughter, the men patted each other, congratulated each other on various campaigns they had participated in. The visitors departed demeanors jovial all around.

The next stop was in the Education Department where Arthur felt even more at home, his background having been in the field of education, and the state school superintendents having previously been elected officials. Arthur and the department had ties going back for years. The Deputy Superintendent, into whose office they had stepped, had been around long enough to provide major assists in cut-throat Kentucky politics, especially for governors, legislators, and superintendents. "Arthur, what brings you to Frankfort, besides money, I mean." Both men smiled, shook hands, and Arthur introduced Elmer, again emphasizing doctor.

"Mr. Superintendent," Arthur boomed, again 'smoozing' by upgrading his official title, "We're drowning down home; you probably know better than us, the drugs are killing us. We need education money to get the word out to the little children to try and curb this epidemic."

"I know Arthur, but you realize that the local boards control access to the classrooms and money for any ancillary programs." The Deputy fidgeted a little, Elmer thought. Arthur had struck something.

"I know you're constitutionally limited, but a big man has a long reach." The deputy looked pleased, puffed even. "By the way, I've got a pretty solid commitment from three of the local county judge-executives down home that they're all for naming the new regional technical school for you." The Deputy now beamed.

"Oh, Arthur, what little I had to do with that location was strictly for the young people."

"Yeah, yeah, I know, but your influence showed up, and we're all grateful." Arthur affectionately clasped the Deputy's hand and moved toward the door after a few stories and a joke.

Out in the hall, Arthur stepping proudly, all but doing a little dance, addressed the younger man; "Danged good day, Elmer." Arthur was visibly pleased while Elmer failed to see much future benefits accruing from the visits. On the way out of town Elmer was directed into a parking lot alongside a bar and grill, Arthur's favorite Frankfort watering hole which also featured thick, juicy grilled steaks. The food was to his liking and the liquor was plentiful. Also, Arthur loved to talk trash with a rowdy waitress who matched him advance for advance, to depths never before witnessed by Elmer in a restaurant setting. Food orders completed and several drinks down, Arthur undertook Elmer's education in Kentucky politics. "Son, Kentucky is dragging up the hind-end in everything from fat people to diabetes, as you know. Poor devils in our area line up every four years, vote wrong, and wonder why they're always sucking hind tit." Elmer did know. His study of the area census data revealed high smoking rates, hot cancer zones and educational deficiencies. "Our people live a particularly hard-scrabble life, especially since the Civil War. Before that Kentucky was in the forefront in agriculture and politics and economy. Those of us in Appalachia reaped the benefits same as the rest. We had Henry Clay, you know, and were major players in every national election for decades. After the war the situation changed. Leaders recognized that they had to get matters back under control."

"What do you mean under control? What changed?" Elmer needed clarification, more specifics. Arthur rambled on explaining that the state fell under the domination of a one-party system, and that to maintain position, only friends were rewarded. This system, he said, prevailed until fairly recent years. If you backed the wrong horse in the primary, during my day, it was back to Ohio for work at least until the next election.

In those days we didn't have two parties. We had factions in one party. If you were in with the winning faction, you got the state job. State work was about all the jobs we had in our area through the 1950's. *Jim Crow Laws* throughout the south were also part of this emergent post-Civil War system to maintain power."
Arthur turned in his chair. "Hey, Greasy Tit, we're thirsting over here." Arthur's outburst startled Elmer. The remark was loud enough to carry across the room.

"I hear you, Old Flabby Butt." The waitress accustomed to such, answered just as loudly.

"I'll make you think old flabby butt. Ever hear the one about the old buck?" Arthur's voice louder this time.

"Yes, the last time you were in and I don't want to hear it again. I'm busy." As she responded, she placed drinks on a tray.

"Where was I? Oh, yes, about the system supported by patronage. Do you know I controlled the patronage jobs in my county on and off for a period during the last years of the *New Deal*? I say on and off because sometimes I misjudged a primary candidate. Only time it's been worth much since the *New Deal* was during Johnson's so-called *Great Society*. Then it fell apart because of the Appalachian Volunteers, VISTA workers, they called them, coming down and meddling." Arthur grimaced at the last. "You know I always wanted to fox hunt on his Texas ranch. Never did though."

Elmer thought Arthur had begun to drift and asked, "What ranch?" just to keep him talking until the food came. "Johnson's ranch, that's right. Remember he wanted to get back there so he could piss off the front porch." Arthur laughed and hit the table with his open hand. Drink glasses tipped, water splashed, and Elmer dodged. By now the waitress was beside the fox hunter, an arm lazily draped across his shoulder and gazing into his eyes. "I apologize. I got a little carried away, talking about pissing off the front porch." Arthur winked at the waitress as he said this.

"I'll bet you do that, too. I'm holding this next drink until you boys eat a bite. We don't need any serious accidents." Knowing their orders were next up, she moved back to the counter. Arthur was quiet only a second until he thought of an appropriate joke to share.

Not much can be reported about the remainder of the afternoon. Arthur napped on the way home. Elmer focused as best he could on the highway. At Arthur's house they were greeted from the front porch by his wife, a sophisticated older lady, too sophisticated for Arthur, in Elmer's opinion. "Here you are, coming in drunk again. What's going to become of you, old as you are! Surely a little common sense should be showing by now."

As Arthur staggered onto the porch assisted by his wife, he shouted over his shoulder, "Remember, Doc, always take a load home with you." Again Elmer was puzzled. Anyway he turned over the day's events in his mind for logical examination but meanings evaded him—most of the conversation little more than gibberish. Nevertheless it was memorable and somewhat enjoyable. Arthur had obviously been encouraged by something that transpired in their meetings. Maybe a special handshake, a wink or some such had passed between the communicators that he had missed.

Neither man knew that this would be their one and only trip to the capitol together. Even on this date Elmer's resume` was being vetted in Georgia for a CEO position with a sister agency. He'd be gone within thirty days. For the second time in his career, Arthur was to retire to his farm the next month for health reasons.

# CHAPTER 26

## The Board Meeting—A Conflict of Interest

"Confidentiality is the question, not to mention exploitation." Thad's face was a little red, at least for him. No one ever saw him lose the neutral demeanor generally cultivated in his profession. The team was considering an administrative request that four or five patients attend a governing board meeting and present a personal rehab picture. Thad's concern was the possibility of compromising patient confidentiality. In his estimation, the administration was merely exploiting patients by show-casing them to the community for public relations purposes.

"We ask these same patients to attend AA meeting and there to lay out their life. Even a better example is presentations they make before school groups. I hardly see any difference." Linda spoke matter of fact, no emotions showing. Keith said nothing, leaving the decision to professionals to present their arguments whose legal liability might be an issue.

"There is a chance those chosen to report will benefit much more than the administration or the board. One of our responsibilities seems to me, includes introduction or re-introduction of our patients back into society." Dr. Lee thumbed through a brochure as he talked.

"Protecting confidentiality and preventing exploitation are important, but this possibly falls short of indictment in those areas. After all, actions of the board may well determine the availability of so called bread and butter for both patients and staff." Dr. Lee had chosen his words carefully, hoping to salve Thad's concerns.

"Okay, I'll go along so long as the patients aren't identified by surname or home-town." Thad had softened.

The four staff, now somewhat in agreement, reviewed the nineteen patients and narrowed the field to six, divided equally male and female. Freddie was ruled out, Thad arguing that his communication skills and fear of groups in general might be too much. Deidra was accepted and so reviews continued until the six were chosen. The group was given alphabetical letters instead of names. The staff read the bios.
A—thirty year old male… former football star from Mississippi State, tall lean except a pouch where ten years earlier ripples existed…family intact… in his words: "addiction began after the cheering stopped, cocaine use primarily, sell some, use some"…three years college…employed four years as medical supply salesman…referred by primary care physician… financial assets includes house and sizeable 401 account.

B—twenty-two year old male, unemployed since boyhood, son and grandson of alcoholics…no known community attachments other than addicts and pushers since grade school…never married, two children by different women, completed sixth grade…referred to rehab from hospital emergency room—no assets reported

C—forty one year old female, good family background, likely dual diagnosis—mental illness and addiction… estranged from parents…limited employment background, GED plus two years college… sentenced to rehab by court—no assets reported

D—sixty-one year old male… real estate developer with major projects in three southeastern states… no reported addiction in family… began drinking forty years ago, added pills in his fifties… three grown children, estranged from family… high school graduate, self-taught engineer…self-referred—two to four million dollars in assets reported

E—eighteen year old female from single-parent family… mother addicted, high school education, patient began using in high school… no work history…no recent contact with mother… sentenced to rehab by the court—no assets reported

F—forty-eight year old female… both parents addicted…no family connections… sexually abused beginning sometime before age eight… mother of three all put out for adoption...sporadic employment as waitress, and hotel maid…addicted from her early teens—no assets reported

After reaching a consensus on the six participants, Keith was to carry out the notification to proper administration officials, get residents' agreement that they would participate, and provide support in their preparations. The board meeting—catered food, financial and staff reports—was successful in Keith's mind, and certainly the response of board members confirmed the positive effect of using patient personal stories. Each addict's talk was followed by hearty applause. Members gathered around the patients at the end, the men extending handshakes, most of the older women hugged long, their wet eyes shining. Keith wasn't privy to this information, but most board members left the building filled, believing their volunteer time to be well spent. Many, though encouraged, were uneasy also, wondering what would eventually happen to those who had spoken, and considering how many others were out there untreated. Some board members had first-hand knowledge of family drug problems and heart-wrenching stories of lives out of control. A few, however, doubted the wisdom of spending tax money on these "bums."

One had employed an addict for nine years. He broke over, and left him in a lurch; the worth of the nine years left unmeasured. As they left the meeting, this same employer cornered another board member from a neighboring county. "I worked a dried-out drunkard as a salesman, led the sales force seven out of the nine years I employed him. One day he walked out, went on a spree, and hasn't been sober since." He wrinkled his face and virtually spit out, "You can't trust a drunk."

The man listening to this tirade looked at the sidewalk. His experience had been similar in that he too had hired an addicted person. The employee had been dried out innumerable times and gone through a rehab program four times. Not wishing to alienate his friend, he merely said, "I had one, too, who performed admirably for several years until his death. Contributed considerable wealth to the company, as did yours, I presume?" At this, the first speaker cleared his throat, but said nothing. They shook hands and bid one another good night.

# CHAPTER 27

## Freddie Gets a Ride

Mommy's phone call with home news had left Freddie in a quandary; then, came a second call, the news still worse. Frantic this time, his mother reported on the baby being snatched by the state and that she'd asked Carl to come down to rehab and get him. Mr. Keith's approval or not, he saw no alternative but to leave. Meantime, Carl's plan to deliver him home fell through. He got down in his back and the trip suddenly became out of the question, but he was still able to instigate a plan. He'd called his nephew, against his better judgment.

"Say, Louie, could you come over here and git my old truck and go down to that rehab place and git Freddie. His mommy's having a fit. You likely heard about Amanda's baby."

The nephew, the same one living with the twins and sometimes Amanda, knew the situation and agreed, glad to have a vehicle at his disposal, glad for a chance to get out of town and glad to leave Amanda and her aggravating vacillations between flirting with first one then the other and moaning about Aunt Beck.

A fourth person was in the house with them today, however, which altered the dynamics—Buddy Mustang. Buddy insisted on going along to the rehab center. He had business with the man Louie was to deliver home.

It was dark when Louie and Buddy arrived for Freddie. Their journey had been hindered as they stopped and supplemented their morning dosage of meth with a substantial number of pills. Freddie was watching at the front door, all the time glancing down the hall, fearing Mr. Keith might appear. His things in a plastic bag caught up under his arm, he virtually lunged for the truck on its arrival and was inside before realizing it wasn't Carl driving and that a second person occupied the seat beside Louie. When his eyes adjusted to the darkness and he recognized Buddy, he considered jumping from the vehicle. By then the truck was leaving the parking lot, wheels spinning and jostling the three. He held on to the dash and looked straight ahead, not knowing whether to say, hello, or what. A few miles down the road, Louie turned in a direction he was sure wasn't toward home. The highway sign said, KY 80 west.

"We're taking you on a short-cut, Boy." Buddy snickered, and Louie punched him and laughed as though they had a special secret between them. "Freddie, I been thinking about the four hundred you owe me. You know, Buddy always collects." With that he unfolded a knife, barely visible in the dim light of the dash. Freddie could see well enough to recognize the curved end of the blade. Pretending to clean his nails Buddy continued, "Thought any about how you're going to meet your obligation?"

"Yeah, I got a job to do for Carl. You can have that money."

"Carl ain't never paid nobody four hundred dollars for a job. Better think again." With this Buddy shifted for room, removed something from his pocket, dumped several pills in his knife hand, and ingested them, holding the knife close to Freddie's face in the move. Freddie was scared, but could think of nothing to do but wait for whatever was coming and it might be coming soon. Louie suddenly turned right into a graveled lot without slowing down. The truck slid sideways throwing gravels against a darkened trailer boasting a beauty shop sign. He drove around to the rear. "See that air conditioning unit over there." Buddy was pointing with the knife and addressing Freddie. "Reach there in back and get the tools. Go over and deliver us some wealth." By wealth Freddie knew he meant the saleable copper from the unit. "Don't try to run either." Following this threatening comment, he touched the knife blade to Freddie's cheek. The knife scared him, but no worse than attacking the unit. He'd heard of people getting electrocuted tearing in for the copper. He left the truck and walked slowly to the unit. He easily lifted the cover. Further intrusion baffled him. Cut the wires? Being uncertain whether it had a ground, unable to see inside the trailer to determine if there was a breaker and noting the wire running through the wall was in conduit, he was shaking, not just his hands, either. The big knife, the hot wire, some choice he thought, but he plowed on, his heart and mind racing. In minutes his apt hands had the copper and he was running back to the truck.

"Good boy. That should cover about twenty-five dollars of your debt. Maybe I ought to just apply that to interest though." The successful heist didn't seem to moderate Buddy's sinister attitude. Soon they were back on the road, to where, Freddie didn't know. Buddy continued to show the knife, pretending to whet it on his pant leg or to pick his teeth. Carl's nephew had been quiet since leaving the trailer, the drugs wearing off or fearful what Buddy would do next. Freddie didn't know which. After several miles, Louie turned right onto an unpaved road and suggested stopping for a bathroom break and more of what he called "refreshments." Approved by Buddy, this plan led them onto a smaller unused drive, then to a dirt track and deeper into the Daniel Boone Forest, the location known only to the other two. Freddie had no idea where they were; just that it was isolated, quite.

"Move, let me out." Buddy was pushing him hard against the door. Outside, Louie moved quickly away from the vehicle and deeper into the woods. Meanwhile, Buddy pushed and tripped Freddie causing him to fall hard on his face. Buddy instantly straddled his back. Penning his arms with his knees, Buddy grabbed both hands full of hair and began slamming the debtor's head into the dirt; shale and gravel cut Freddie's lips. His nose and mouth filled. He couldn't even cry out. Buddy rubbed his face back and forth against the rough dirt and gravel until he tired. He then got up and moved toward the woods to relieve himself. Freddie, barely conscious raised to his hands and knees, spat dirt, shale, and gravels before getting his breath through his mouth. It would take several tries to clear his nostrils. By the time he got his first breath, he was running into the woods in a direction opposite the others. Though never a fast runner, this time he was loping faster than he ever imagined possible, anywhere away from the painful death which was sure to come. Running, slowing, stopping, listening, this sequence lasted for what seemed hours. At last, totally exhausted, his face bloody and nose still dripping blood, his shirt front wet with bloody dirt, he fell against a large tree and collapsed at its base.

Back at the truck, high and angry, the boys searched a broad semi-circle around the truck cursing and calling Freddie, threatening what they'd do if he didn't show himself. Freddie, over the next hill, was not to be located. He might be limited in some ways, but he was a survivor. The two drove on toward home, Buddy cursing and beating the dash of Carl's old truck.

Freddie awoke before full light. Scared now, not of the two men, but what might be lurking in the deep woods, and for good reason. His first visual was a bobcat looking straight into his eyes from some thirty feet away. To his right, he could hear saplings being knocked about by something unseen. His moving to get up and find a stick or something for protection spooked the cat and it disappeared in great bounces. The noise off to his side turned out to be a harmless doe and her twins. Safe, for the moment, his mind turned to other pressing matters. Where was he? His terrible thirst and hunger were next in line behind his fear. He looked in the four directions trying to decide which way to go. Definitely he didn't want to go back. Buddy might still be lurking. Scattered leaves leading to the tree indicated the way he didn't want to go. The lay of the hills sloped in what he thought to be a northeasterly direction. The sun wasn't showing, but the growing light suggested he was right. So he determined to follow the slope thinking it might lead to water, maybe a creek or river with people close by. All day he walked, stumbling, trying to keep his eye on the highest peak beyond the slope and to the east. At dusk, he ambled into a copse of willow surrounding a gurgling spring, clear and cool where it pooled against a smooth flat rook. Falling to his knees and drinking his fill, he sat back to think.

"Hey, Boy, what're you doing here?" Startled, he turned, expecting to see Buddy, but instead two men dressed in camouflage were glaring at his distorted, bloody face, torn shirt.

"I don't exactly know," was all that Freddie could get out. Shaking and breathing deeply in and out several times, he continued, "I'm lost, Sir. I mean Sirs. I don't even know where I am." The limited responses lasted several minutes until the men determined him harmless, sure enough lost, and introduced themselves.

The bearded one said, “I’m Three-Fifty-Seven and this here is Rocket Launcher.” Freddie knew that wasn’t their names, but better judgment told him not to let on. “You help us out in the morning, we’ll feed you and see you back to civilization.” Freddie had no better idea and happily agreed. He wasn’t sure to what, however. After a dinner consisting of Vienna sausage, crackers and a fruit bar, the three made themselves as comfortable as possible. Freddie slept in short naps for most of the night. “This root is killing my back.” “That durn frog just keeps croaking.” “Wish I had a blanket. I’m scared stiff of a copperhead crawling close to get warm.” These gripes and others came up every time Freddie dozed off.

Early morning found them stomping around, working out the soreness. Rocket Launcher looked hard at Freddie. “You ever use a mattock?”

“Yeah, heped Carl dig a septic tank hole once.” Freddie briefly thought they might be thinking of a grave. He soon gave this thought up as more questions arose about his experience with a weed hook and axe. Something unbeknown to him was going on, but he figured it required a little more revelation. The three shared some beef jerky, an apple, and water for breakfast. Freddie drank the water, but had to awkwardly suck or lick the other. His lips were sore and swollen, several teeth were loose. Revived and fed, the two began cleaning the area of any trash, not that they were that environmentally conscious. Others might suspect the real reason for trash being in the area. Many a project had been pilfered because of sloppy site work.

“We’d better move.” Three-Fifty-Seven led the two of them around huge boulders nearby and began moving sapling brush that hid two well loaded four-wheelers carrying more than Freddie thought possible. The rear tray

of one was piled high with pallets of small green plants. These Freddie guessed to be marijuana. The other had a five gallon bucket stuffed with tools for planting, a sack of fertilizer and various other items wrapped in black plastic. "You follow us, Boy. This'll take a while." Freddie followed leaning slightly forward, his head aching and his face raw and burning, scabs forming.
Rocket Launcher stopped to review a topographical map and announced: "We're about right here," pointing with his forefinger at the sheet. "We need to move around the hill to that spot." He gestured in front and slightly up the hill. "The morning sun will be hitting better there." On site, Freddie was given the mattock and directed to begin clearing a spot approximately fifty feet square, no matter that he was painfully sore. Three-Fifty-Seven removed a set of posthole diggers, attached folding handles and walked off through the cedars. Rocket Launcher followed with a double hand-full of plants, a bucket with loose fertilizer hanging on one arm. Freddie, hidden from any path by thick blackberry, wild rose-bush briars, and young cedar, could not be seen from fifteen feet away in any direction. By noon, sweat poured and stung his facial injuries. His eyes watered as he dug and pulled. The site was showing promise, he thought. The two captors, or rescuers, he didn't know for sure which, finally returned, tossed him a bottle of water and began spreading moth balls and chips in six inch grids across the field. He was directed to add a small spoonful of fertilizer to each grid. The three punched small holes and placed the plants, careful not to break the stems as they packed earth around each. "If we can keep the thieves out, we're talking half a million here." Rocket Launcher was thinking big.

The task completed, Freddie was directed to stay by the four-wheelers, well out of sight of the field. He wasn't out of hearing though. "We'll set the charge on each corner. Cut you a stake and stretch this wire."

"We gonna use a snake?"

"You can if you want to. I'm not about to. Thought I'd have to change my shorts a minute ago when a dead stick hit me on the ankle. Wish you hadn't mentioned the darn things. I shiver even being out here." The voice, recognizable as Rocket Launcher, continued, telling of several snake encounters, finally asking: "Should we do it?"

Three-fifty-seven responded: "Tie the snake in, you mean?"

"No, I'm talking about getting rid of the other snake." Freddie heard all this discussion from a short distance away, only bushes separating them. Except he didn't get Rocket Launcher's answer and he wasn't sure what to make of that. Limping, slightly stooped, rubbing their backs after the exercise, the two forest farmers moved to the four wheelers. "Get on behind me, Boy. We're going to get you started toward home—my beef jerky has worn off. The old lady will look mighty fine tonight." Rocket Launcher chuckled. After forty-five or so minutes, the two four-wheelers, one ridden double, were stopped at a fork in the track.

"You follow that right leg about half a mile. You'll come to old U. S. 25. Go left there. That'll take you right home, maybe fifteen or twenty miles." Freddie dismounted the three-wheeler and looked in the direction Rocket Launcher pointed.

"Say, Boy", Rocket Launcher leaned in close. "You got any family?" His fierce eyes caused Freddie to look down, then sideways.

"I got Mommy." Freddie's voice broke a little as he said this.

"Anybody else?"

"Amanda and her baby. Well, they ain't exactly family. Well, they may be." Freddie felt something bad coming. All this time Launcher was writing these names on a piece of paper torn from the topographical map.
"Hold out your arm." Launcher drew his huge hunting knife from the sheath at his side, and quickly drew blood on Freddie's forearm rubbed it on the paper, which he stuffed in his shirt pocket. "That represents a blood oath as insurance that you can keep a secret. You know what secret I'm referring to?" Freddie nodded. "If this crop gets destroyed or stolen, we'll hunt your folks and kill every last one of them. I'll skin you. Understand? You ever seen headless bodies floating in the river? "

"I ain't sayin' nothin' to nobody."

"Swear it." Launcher extended his hand. Freddie accepted it and they shook, but instead of releasing, Launcher began to squeeze so hard that Freddie's knees buckled and he leaned far back away from the man, all the time fearing the bones in his hand were being broken.
"I swear." Freddie finally got this out and, freed from the fearsome grip, fell to the ground. The man explained that the blood on the paper represented a blood oath, a deposit so to speak. "If we have to look you up, we'll get the rest. Get the picture?"

Freddie was relieved to get off the vehicle and to be sent away. He couldn't worry about probabilities. He trudged along the dirt road wondering if he'd ever get home to Mommy. He really wanted a pop. It was late afternoon when he reached the blacktop. Feeling more secure and believing that the men had told him the truth, he began the march homeward passing the US 25 sign. His bedraggled look may have frightened drivers along the route. No one stopped. He sat down beside the road. He got up and walked. Late that night or early morning the lights of the all-night food mart and gas station at the edge of town came into view. Freddie stayed in the shadows as best possible until he saw through the window that the night clerk was the only person inside.

"Mommy, this is Freddie."

"Where in the world are you?" Nothing had been heard as to his whereabouts for almost three days. Carl had notified her that the nephew was bringing him home, but he had heard nothing from Freddie either.

"Mommy, I can't tell you everthing over the phone. This feller here at the station is letting me call. I'm coming around the back way to Carl's barn. I want you to slip down there and bring me something to eat. And Mommy, bring some medicine too. I'm skint all over. And bring a shirt. Mommy, don't you let on to a soul about where I am, not even Carl."

The last mile around to Carl's barn was nearly that, Freddie's last. He was exhausted, dehydrated and starving. He may have resembled Ulysses in his beggar outfit returning from his great odyssey, except no way could he have strung the bow for Amanda. In fact, he gave her no thought and it may have been just as well. Likely more needy than Penelope, she'd sought out and moved in with her suitors and showed no longing for Freddie. Nevertheless, he'd seen at least two of the one-eyed monsters.

Inside Carl's barn, he sat on an upside down bucket with elbows on his knees, his chin in hands, dazed until his mother startled him by touching his forehead with antiseptic gauze. "I swear, Freddie, you look mighty crippled up." However, the little light given off by her old flashlight and further investigation relieved her concern about him being crippled. She was soon forced to leave as Freddie refused answer further questions. He ate the fried potatoes she'd brought and moved to the end of the driveway to sleep between two round bales of hay. Sleep didn't come as circumstances might have suggested, however. A gnawing sound nearby haunted him for some time. The barn was nearly as frightening as the deep woods had been.

During Freddie's ordeal, Carl had been busy, hot on the trail of his truck and Louie. The bad back and no transportation prevented his moving about, so he used the phone. He kept the wires hot as he contacted everybody that came to mind. Beck had barked at him when he asked her about the boys.

"When you see that worthless Freddie, tell him I'm expecting a little help raising his youngun." A call finally came to him from a deputy sheriff who had traced the license plate from the old truck to him. The news was not good. His truck had been hauled to the Chevron station in town. Its twisted condition prevented towing. The nephew was all right, but in jail. Buddy had been flown on to Lexington in serious condition. The driver had dropped a wheel off the road and the speeding old truck was wrapped against a tree. The nephew was thrown out, but Buddy had to be extricated by an emergency crew with their *Jaws of Life* apparatus.

"I hate it. It's my fault, I guess, sending that boy off like that." This statement somewhat baffled the deputy. He thought the old man should have been upset about the truck.

# CHAPTER 28

## *City Hosts Beck's Sales Meeting*

Beck had just put Freddie Jr. down for his nap and sat at the kitchen table in a contemplative mood. Something wasn't right. Two weeks running sales had been off, at least collections had been. She was going to get to the bottom of it. That silly Amanda hadn't helped any. Leaving her to care for the infant had occupied too much of Beck's time and concentration.

No matter, she hadn't been too busy to notice the declining income and now it had to be addressed. Freddie's mom, now miraculously recovered once the baby left her house, must step up and help a little. She'd have to come and assist Beck's sister, the baby's other grandma, for at least one day for this situation to be addressed.

Beck slammed her hand flat on the table and rose to check on the baby. As she paced from kitchen to bedroom, coffee in one hand and cardboard fan in the other, a plan evolved, one she'd never before used. She decided all the couriers had to be called together for a good dressing down. She'd have the meeting in the seldom used city/county community room, a bare room inside a metal building, a feeble community development effort.

She would charge each one for lunch ordered from the Colonel. A casual observer might question the brashness of holding a meeting on city property to discuss a slump in illegal drug sales. Beck had an idea. She congratulated herself on the brilliant scheme forming in her mind and held back a smile as she pondered the details. The cover, *Bingo*, lent itself to Beck's bellowing numbers over a microphone with slightly veiled threats regarding getting off their butts and selling, selling the goods, collecting, collecting the cash, and delivering, delivering satisfactorily for and to the *woman*. The bedeviled group needed to get it straight. They were not working for the *man*. Big Beck was the boss. They'd squirm.

Satisfied she'd thought through the problem all the way to a solution, she began phoning. Pride had taken a firm hold on Beck.

The community room next door to city hall and the police department accommodated upwards of one hundred. Beck needed tables and chairs for about thirty. She needed a stool and lectern beside the microphone. The city clerk and maintenance supervisor, glad to assist in a fund raiser for victims of fires and other disasters (as Beck billed the meeting), even added a fresh bouquet of flowers on each table. Beck loved the idea of hiding in plain sight. It appealed to her sense of personal pride. It proved she was smart, smarter than the Mayor even. The players filed in, afraid not to respond to Beck's invitation—retirees, a beautician, and so on. Only two or three looked out of place—gold chains about their necks, men with diamonds—but city hall saw all kinds and nobody noticed. Cards were ten dollars each, contributions to the needy never questioned. Today Beck represented the needy, needed diapers, in fact.

Beck called out the numbers until squares were filled. She recognized winners and issued a certificate at the front table along with whispered threats and admonishments, looking and sounding her sternest. Between cards, she proclaimed to the group, "You people ain't making no money. I'm not pleased." The game lasted a little over three hours. Faces didn't reflect the usual relaxed demeanor associated with friendly competition though. The message seemed to be getting through.

As the players left the building, nobody noticed the rental car across and down the street. Unknown to Beck, two federal agents were following a drug trail from Florida to the area. Specifically, they were tailing one of the unsuspecting bingo players known to them because of several set-up purchases. Something strange was going on. Their suspect was an unlikely candidate to be attending a downtown social event in mid-day. She had changed her behavior. She never left her salon in the middle of the day, in the middle of the work week. The agents filmed the entire group as they left the building. Sometimes even city hall was involved in the business and they weren't taking chances.

Being careful not to get too far out on such a sensitive issue, the lead agent phoned his supervisor. "Full throttle ahead with a full investigation, no matter where it leads" was the order. "If city officials are involved, arrest them too." Carefully crafted questions around town and cautious investigations of all the bingo players led to more questions. Some were surviving rather well on their known sources of income. Others were reported by neighbors to have considerable traffic, visitors making only brief stops. Days later, buys were set up, including one from Beck—just good police work practiced since prohibition days at least—before warrants were secured for each of the bingo players. City hall was no longer suspected.

The night of the raid, a great howl could have been heard throughout the community had Beck been outside on a nearby hilltop. Her door burst open after a brief but hard knock. Four officers with search warrants in hand rummaged throughout the house as one cornered Beck. The baby cried. Beck's sister cried too. Drugs were found behind a splash board in the front room and inside the kitchen stove casing. Her cash escaped the search. The crawl space under the kitchen porch was occupied by a dog and various cats, so no sign of human entry was noticeable. Her trap was accessed by pushing the money through a PVC pipe behind the bathroom commode. The pipe coupled to one running through the ceiling and looked to be part of the sewage ventilation system. The loose coupling allowed the top pipe to be slid upward exposing the opening. Money slid down into one of the trunks. The pipe was tightly sealed at the hole through the cedar, and through the trunk top. When the trunk got too full, the pipe clogged, and a new trunk was attached.

But Beck was caught. She was mad and a little scared. "What do you think they're going to do to a seventy-two year old woman?" The officer didn't answer her inquiry. He wasn't sure if she was feeling sorry for herself because of possible prison time or announcing her bargaining power. Amanda was hauled in from the twins' place to care for the baby. Beck was escorted to jail. Whispered threats were passed from cell to cell where her couriers were housed.

Within hours Beck was released and huddled with her attorney. He had also arranged with another legal practice for the release of all the couriers. Her attorney, known throughout the region as the man to get when serious matters came up, didn't even have to shed his pajamas to make a good day's wage. Business people and public officials clamored to pay monthly retainers just to keep him from accepting a case against them should the occasion arise. Of course, he laid aside the silk lounge wear, donned shoes that were not run down at the heel, gold cuff links, and imported ties. He drove around in a

Porsche or a huge Lincoln, ate in gourmet establishments out of town. He liked to explain to clients that he could take a case and win either side depending which side retained his services and paid the hefty fee. Much to Beck's chagrin, her case required fifty thousand dollars in cash up front, another thirty-five thousand if an appeal was required. Her very nature was to haggle over price and win, but not this time.

Beck was immediately hospitalized after settling with her attorney. Some said it was a stroke, others her heart. Doctors at the medical facility didn't exactly specify. Notes in her chart indicated she was unresponsive, had to be fed by drip and later by hand by the attendant nurse. In a lucid moment, she whispered, asking that her sister be summoned. Once alone with the sister, Beck came alive, somewhat frightening the sister and began whispering orders to prevent passersby from hearing.

"Get me a sandwich and some fries and a Mountain Dew from Wendy's. Call all the couriers. A list is hidden inside the old dial phone up in the attic. Tell them that a body can't tell, Beck may come out of this. They'll get the message. Make arrangements to stay in the room with me as long as I'm here." Beck wiped her forehead with the corner of the bed sheet. "And request a transfer to the nursing home just as soon as possible. Tell them it's a money thing. Staff there can keep me comfortable as well as they can here. Oh, and when you bring the food, put your chair against the door so nobody can get in. If someone tries, tell them you're praying and sitting there so as not to disturb me and put all the food packaging in your purse." The sister, a bit overwhelmed with all the directions, was counting off on her fingers, as Beck talked. "Also, have that sorry Freddie or somebody tune up the old car. Check the hoses and belts, too." Beck screwed up her face as she spoke of Freddie.

For the next two weeks, the sister traveled into and out of the hospital, servicing Beck's requests. Once when a nurse leaned her ear to the door to listen for any patient disturbance and heard a voice, she opened it and peeped in. Immediately, the sister began praying out loud, punctuating her statements with "amen" or "that's right." The nurse shook her head and moved on down the hall. This same ruse was adapted at the nursing home once the move was accomplished. The sister, who at home had been hardly able to speak decisively on anything, had requested a room at the end of a hall farthest away from the nurse station and stayed with Beck day and night. The two were seldom disturbed, except for meds and food.

Beck felt she had to stay in shape. She couldn't lie in bed until the trial. She'd atrophy. Three or four times a day, the sister dutifully placed her chair against the door and sat there blocking entry. Beck couldn't touch her toes, but she bent as far as possible for as many times as possible. She shadow boxed, her feet planted wide. She held her hands high above her head as she ran in place. She spread her legs stretching the tendons, lay on her back and kicked her feet high in the air, her voluminous legs preventing much more than a knee high kick. She lay on the floor and walked her feet up the wall to get the blood to her brain. Her sister was never comfortable when all this was going on. Beck was big. The sight wasn't exactly pretty, maybe not even healthy.

After the months of this faked illness, court day presented a picture. Carl, limping slowly, innocent to any organized ruse, wheeled Beck to the front of the courtroom. She slumped forward in the chair, her head down, a string of drool hanging lip to bosom. She couldn't speak even if she was capable of thinking speakable words—this reported by an accompanying nurse from the home.

Words a-plenty had been spoken for weeks before her trial, however. Officers in the courthouse were regaled, "Poor thing, just lying there. Can't say a word. Probably can't see either," they say. "Old Carl" they continued, "remembers when she was a girl. Her and her mammy went to church ever week. Her daddy and his daddy weren't no account; can't hold that against her though—didn't have much of a chance. Taking care of her ailing sister and that baby; she's had her hands full... Ain't saying what she was doing was right, but she ain't all bad, poor old thing."

The message carried by friends of Beck had earlier moved like a vapor across the entire town, spread to the surrounding crossroads, and snaked through the hollows like a breeze that touched everyone. No possible juror escaped its mitigating effect.

Declared a pauper, an attorney was appointed for Beck by the court, coincidentally from the same law firm as the attorney who secured her release and planned the fifty thousand dollar defense.

The defense had requested a meeting with the prosecution prior to the trial. "You know a conviction isn't going to mean much here. The state gets a medical bill, the defendant doesn't know whether she is in jail, a hospital, or a nursing home. Where's the justice, the logic?"

The prosecutor agreed to give it some thought. Both huddled at the bench with the judge on trial date. Of course, poor Beck couldn't offer any defense.

Six months or so after the arrest, the court records would reveal that Beck was let off for time served—that being two weeks in the hospital and five months in the nursing home. She was to continue to be under court supervision and pay a ten thousand dollar fine. The court supervision was not extended to out of state nursing facilities once the trial was over, however. The couriers got from one to five years and fines somewhat less than Beck's. Most were probated early.

If neighbors had been observing, they would have seen Beck and her sister pull away from the house during the early morning hours on the day following her sentencing. Attached to the old Impala was a U-Haul trailer. They would have been surprised to see that Beck was driving, hauling her ailing sister—to where, these neighbors would not have known. Of course, no one had seen her scratching around under the house beforehand. Her last words to Amanda; "Get them men tested. One of the sorry things will have to help raise your youngun. I'm leaving a few dollars in yonder on the dresser to get you by for a few months, that is, if you got enough sense to take care of it."

The regional controller, the person or persons who arranged the Florida connection was never mentioned in court or named by anybody in the community. Amanda, short a baby-sitter, moved her few things back into her grandpa's old house along with baby Freddie Jr. The twins and Carl's nephew were doing time in the county detention center, presumably a year for the meth charges. Buddy Mustang, released after six months in medical rehabilitation, was spending his days down at Buddy's Variety Store, housed in a building previously used as an automotive fuel and service outlet. It contained an assortment of former yard sale items and dump pickings.

Managing from a wheel chair, legally acquiring pain killing prescription drugs for his own use and selling a few along that he acquired other ways, Buddy was making do. Old Carl was coaching Freddie.

In letters to Amada, her mother gave updates. She and Beck were in Sarasota, Florida, not in a condo, however. Beck didn't like the contract (she did relent and move into one in later years). Neither were they on the beach, but several streets away. Instinctively, Beck knew better than build a house on the sand or too close to the ocean. They did walk, she said, to the beach nearly every day. They'd enjoyed digging clams. Beck was considering taking on a man, the right kind, of course. Amanda's mother was doing much better in the warmer climate.

# CHAPTER 29

## Renfro Valley, With Ann, Keith, and Al

Saturday mornings were always an active time for Ann. Her emergency duty didn't begin until midnight and the day was hers, hers to spend with friends, usually Al and Keith. Today Al was driving the three to Renfro Valley for breakfast in the Old Lodge Restaurant with its limestone rock floor, log walls, and dark chestnut paneling. Keith was pleased to be picked up along the way. These mornings allowed Ann to assess progress or regression in the two in their quest for sobriety, all the while discussing issues ranging from therapy to international affairs. Renfro Valley, a little out of their normal range, required an early start.

In route, before picking up Keith, Ann noted Al was more contemplative than usual. "What's got the big man so quiet this morning?"

"I don't know. Incremental progress, it's just not happening." Thinking that he was probably referring to his *Rural Health Clinic* plans, she refrained from interjecting, hoping he'd continue. "Ann, you know life is just too complicated. Everywhere I turn somebody seems to raise barriers to my clinic proposal. Both state health officers, Kentucky and Tennessee, thought the idea excellent and provided contact information. I call, get a pre-recorded request to give the first three letters of the person's name I'm trying to contact, which I don't know, then voice mail. If I do reach someone they speak language that means nothing to me. I'm at a dead end."

Laughing, Ann announced, "What you need is an expert who speaks bureaucrat to sort through the tangle."

"You may be right. But I have met with some fellows who are organizing a visiting medical team to serve in Haiti for six months…some foundation funding it. Maybe something like that'd get it out of my system." Partially miffed and borderline horrified, Ann asked, "Give up your plan for our mountain people?" Her concern also was that he was slipping away from her intervention, her guidance.

"Not exactly give it up. Just get some practice in a broad service spectrum. Surely the needs in Haiti provide that opportunity."

"Al, you know I'm for you, whatever course you follow." Ann was suddenly shaken. Losing the weekly contact with her charge was part of it, but chancing Al's loss of direction was more troubling. "I'll tell you what. Let me make a couple of calls. There is an organization in Northern Kentucky that specializes in threading the red tape maze for practices. They work in several states and their expertise ranges from *Rural Health Clinics to Urgent care"*.

"Leave it to you to have a ready-made plan." Al was perking up, or as Ann liked to say, *cherking* up. The cell phone, computer and FAX, coupled with an expert team might bring his plan to fruition even as he did the Haiti service. It might take six months to get all the paperwork done and the approval.

At the restaurant, the three enjoyed country ham and the trimmings. Ann mentioned regretting its being too late in the season to experience the red bud bloom. "It was prettiest here about three weeks ago." Talk skipped from first one topic to another but finally settle on books of current interest. Tolstoy's *The Death of Ivan Ilych* just read by Al had been much too depressing. Ann decided that book might have contributed to his downcast look earlier. "The death of the old man was about as vivid as Wolfe's account of Brother Ben, both downers for me," she said.

Keith's favorite this month, Follett's *Winter of the World* had suited his notion for relaxing reading. The author's weaving actual historical events into an interesting novel always hooked him, since his college major had been history.

Ann's comments, far afield from the others, reported reading mainly scientific journals. Of special interest recently, an article in *Cell Biology*, "In Vetro Studies of Actin Filament and Network Dynamics," the discussion of which caused Keith to look closer at his food while Al's questioning delved deeper into the cell. A priori work, knowledge which eventually proved why and how a medicine worked intrigued both Ann and Al. To read about the workings inside a cell and deeper still, inside a protein within—its growth, its skeleton, its discarding of waste, made her field come alive. This coming alive invigorated her much the same as that day in sophomore biology when her high school teacher introduced the microscope and the huge world that expanded out from the small speck in focus.

Very soon, noting what she perceived to be Keith's discomfort with the in-depth cell discussion, Ann changed her topic. "I also read a most interesting report this week on trauma." Thinking she was going to delve into lost limbs, blood, and crushed skulls, both men pushed back in their chairs, glancing at one another; after all the breakfast wasn't over. Ann continued. "Have any of you reviewed the ACE study?"

"Never heard of it," Al was quick to respond.

Shifting her position and placing both hands on the table, Ann proceeded. "ACE stands for Adverse Childhood Experiences—trauma, if you will—such as physical, sexual, psychological abuse, bullying, war. Researchers found that chronic diseases may be caused decades later by experiencing extreme childhood trauma, especially if they are subjected to four or more."

"So, where are you going with this?" Al wanted to move on. Keith had heard something that pricked his interest, however.

"Well, it turns out that trauma affects the autonomic nervous system (ANS)." Ann looked at Al as if to say, you know what that means.

"And?" Al was harassing Ann in mostly a kidding way. Again, Keith was thinking of a patient and wanted to know more.

"And," Ann lifted her head and made a dramatic hand gesture over her food, then continued. "In PTSD that chronically aroused ANS causes the body to react as though under threat. The flight or fright mechanism gets screwed up after prolonged trauma. The same thing happens in children. It affects their IQ, increases school failure and delinquency."

"Wow, does this mean substance abuse may be related to childhood trauma?" Keith seemed intrigued.

"According to this study yes. And, the DeBellis study revealed the actual physical changes brought about in the brain due to trauma."

"Are you treating me?" Al, again half-kidding, leaned in close to Ann as she continued. "I don't know much about this, but for some time, I've known intuitively that something happens in patient's lives that later plays out in their behavior. I think of Freddie, for instance, and his communication problem." Keith decided that he might begin asking what happened questions as opposed to what's wrong when interviewing patients.

Fearing that Al might be feeling some discomfort with the discussion as it related to PTSD, Ann again changed the subject. "What plans are you two making for this spring?"

Al talked of Haiti. Ann laid out her plans for updating emergency care in Williamsburg, and Keith focused on rehab. His current group, he said, was completing their thirty days the next week. All but two had successfully completed the treatment and five had applied for and were accepted into the ninety-day program. He was encouraged. Twenty new patients had already been screened for the next session. He'd introduce the next round with his usual talk about the war on drugs. Someone would compare it to the earlier thirty-years-war in Europe—at least in duration—and again declare this one to be lost, as someone else questioned strategy.

Keith's concern that he'd lost two of the current group, one of whom was Freddie, might prove partially unfounded. Unbeknown to him, the frightened survivor was again on the move, with old Carl now cheering him on.

As the trio exited to the parking lot, they were stopped and greeted by another rehab staffer, Dr. Lee. Ann could see his horse trailer across the parking lot. It moved almost imperceptibly as the horse stamped flies or shook himself.

"Hey, Doc, what brings you to Renfro Valley this bright spring morning?" Ann was always glad to see the doctor. Seeing him sober on a Saturday was a double treat.

"I'm on a hunt in the area; a treasure trove really. Did you ever hear of Salt Petre?"The group moved slowly across the parking area to a stone wall where all four leaned or sat.

"I heard about it as a boy. World War II vets claimed the army gave it to them to keep down the sex urge". Al laughed as he told this.

Lee continued: "Not too far from here the Salt Petre was mined in huge quantities for use in the War of 1812 primarily. Hundreds of people worked the caves where it's found. I've been privileged to view some of the primitive works. It's a complicated chemical process, but the technology is rather simple. Mostly it's a matter of leeching. The whole area is strewn with artifacts dating from the 1790's, some even from the indigenous peoples here before the European. I enjoy riding the old trace that Daniel Boone followed when he came into Kentucky."

Realizing Doc's need for lengthy talks when illuminating his new found obsession, Ann interjected, "Doc, the country ham is wonderful here. I'm sure you'll be glad you came. Give my regards to the family."

"All right... But you should make plans to go with me sometime. If you are hesitant about horseback travel, we'll explore on foot."

Keith spoke up, the only one of the three who might actually enjoy such a jaunt. "We may just plan to do that."

# CHAPTER 30

## A Secret Place

After hiding in Carl's barn overnight and a big part of the following day, Freddie was discovered. Carl was checking the hay for eggs often hidden by hens preparing to hatch new families. Carl, crawling around a huge roll of hay, concentrating on his search, was startled by what suddenly confronted him.

"Ho, you've skeered the daylights out of me! Why Freddie, that's you! What in tar-nation has happened? Your face looks like it's been run through my corn sheller and why are you hiding down here in the barn?"

"Yeah, it's me. Hate I scared you." Freddie hardly knew where to start, his words not yet organized sufficient to unravel recent events. "I come home."

"I can see that. I sent for you, you know." He paused. "I found what was left of my truck and got word about the worthless two that come to fetch you. None of us had the slightest idee what had happened to you, afeerd maybe we'd hear of you bein' in the hands of a mortician or some such."

"Well, I ain't dead, don't reckon." He almost grinned as he reported on the trip home, Freddie's mind kept going back to Buddy. "What word did you get about Louie and Buddy?" Carl reported the two's circumstances. Freddie sort of hated to hear about the wreck, but was relieved, too. At least they wouldn't be running him anyways soon. He could go see Mommy and get a pop and something to eat.

Carl had removed his old felt hat and was scratching the side of his head, all the time looking off into the distance, out the driveway, over the surrounding hay field. He had broached the subject with Freddie earlier about his living in the trailer. Now the thoughts were expanding.

"Freddie, you know how I ain't had a machine breakdown that you couldn't fix, at a right smart savings at that." Carl went on, first reiterating his like for Freddie's dad, how they'd made a dang good team. From that, he branched out to discuss getting by, that is, making an honest dollar, paying your own way, being somebody, not turning out like the twins, his nephew, or Buddy." Uh-huh was all Freddie said, but he did nod his head though.

"Freddie, you talked earlier about getting you some training, becoming a diesel mechanic. I been studying some on that. Son, I think you ought to do it. Go back down to that rehab place. Tell the man about what a fix you've been in. See if he'll help you. By jacks, get yourself some training, Son. I'll jine in and help you when you git back; we'll be like two coons in a rossen ear patch." Carl was smiling, pleased at having Freddie around.

"I don't know, Carl. I slipped off you know, just had a little better than a week to go. He may not want to fool with me no more. I'll talk it over with Mommy though." As Freddie was saying this his mind was drifting to the blue shirt with his name over the pocket, to lots of diesel engines backed up awaiting his attention, to people requesting that he do this or that rather than ordering him around.

"You study about it. Tell you what I'm aiming to do is git you a bus ticket back down there. Fact is, I'll git you one there and back. That way you won't be stuck again." Carl was getting more animated, more generous. "Maybe I'll even git you a new outfit to wear, from down at the Walmart." This sounded good. But Freddie's response was anything but exuberant. At times like this, he must be careful. He'd been conditioned from early childhood that when things were looking good, something bad was coming.

At the close of his and Carl's discussion, Freddie walked home, his mind full of conflicting thoughts. Mr. Keith probably was not going to welcome him back. Carl might be planning to get him in trouble. He wanted to see Mommy.

After quizzing Freddie about his trip home, Mommy fried bologna, made gravy, and opened a large Mountain Dew. "Freddie, this is the longest I've been by myself since you was born." She sat at the table and watched him eat. Freddie told her about his trip home. Both cried a little. He talked about the training, then about Carl's proposal. "You'd come back home, wouldn't you, that is, after you got trained."

"Yeah, expect I would."

^^^

Tuesday morning Freddie walked shyly into Mr. Keith's office with his return home ticket in his pocket as Carl had promised. His new black jeans swished as he walked. "Freddie, what's happened to you?" Keith had been disappointed by his departure. But seeing the scabs on his face and his contrite look softened Keith.

"Mr. Keith, I wanted to come back." Freddie revealed the scary experiences of the last few days, and emphasized how much he wanted to work on diesel engines.

"Freddie, I'm not sure you can come back. Walking away from the center is not taken lightly by the administration, as you probably have already guessed. The treatment team will likely speak up for you though. Wait here in my office."

With that, Keith made his way first to Dr. Lee's office and briefly explained the situation. Thad was invited to sit in and the three agreed to go in tandem and plead Freddie's case before the administrator. Persuasion, natural to some, had the added dimension of intelligence and training among the trio. Freddie was re-admitted. Keith immediately set in motion application for his admission to the technical school training program. A hitch soon manifested itself though. Freddie's weak reading and communication skills formed an overlay to his natural mechanical ability. Such were his limitations that school officials rejected his application, agreeing among themselves that Keith was letting his emotions cloud reality. Freddie was hurting. The plan was beyond his grasp. But the treatment team, confident of his potential, was not to be outdone.

As Thad passed Keith in the hall the afternoon after learning of Freddie's situation, he stopped him. "Keith, I've thought about Freddie all morning. Maybe there is a solution. Let's step into my office and talk." Thad sat at his desk and pointed to a chair for Keith. "Caterpillar has a tremendous business here in town serving the mining companies throughout the mountains. Do you remember that fellow, Ratliff, referred from over there, a member of their sales force at the time? He has since been promoted to manager in charge of all their service. He frequently expresses his thanks to the rehab center in his AA talks across the region, gives us credit for his success." Keith smiled, knowing that he had a little something to do with the man's success. "I'm thinking maybe a call to him might be a good idea, in Freddie's behalf, that is." Thad, tenacious in all matters he considered important, was on Freddie's case. After lunch hour phone tag, he finally made contact, but was told that the company didn't have any openings. But Thad pushed on. Agreement was finally reached that Freddie could serve a month long unpaid internship in the local shop and then there would be an assessment.

The first day at the shop Freddie was called, "Boy," by one of the mechanics and told to sweep the floor. Nobody expected the day's outcome. When the buzzer sounded announcing quitting time, mechanics, foreman, and the general manager were strolling out of a building cleanly swept, all grease removed—some of which was previously thought to be part of the concrete. Tool benches were cleaned and organized for efficiency. This didn't cause a big hubbub, but Caterpillar employees took note. The following morning workers arrived to find Freddie aptly cleaning the fuel injectors on a D-eight dozer. After inspecting his work, the general manager announced, "Get that man a uniform and give him some work." The uniform didn't have his name over the pocket, but Freddie stepped pretty high, Keith thought, as he gathered his tray and utensils that evening at dinner.

---

Freddie's metamorphosis came in a steady stream over the next few months. His work always completed timely, was never rejected by the customer. Within ninety days, his shirt sported his name over the pocket. He received a check each Friday for a thirty hour week. He'd have gladly worked sixty for the same money, but labor laws prevented him doing so. He laughed when the men joked him about girls. Nobody called him "Boy." He was formally introduced to customers. The shop foreman marveled at his natural ability to handle tools and his diagnostic skills. He wrote letters home to Mommy and to Carl. He called Amanda, who begged him to come see little Freddie. She was happy to hear he had money.

After six months, he was ready to go home. On arrival, Mommy said she'd needed him awfully bad, Amanda demanded a blood test. Carl held to his earlier commitment. His barn sported a boxed room for parts and tools. A potbellied stove was added. The central alleyway now had florescent lighting and a chain hoist in the center. Sheets of Styrofoam insulation sealed its entire length. A dry toilet, built a few years ago for farm laborers, served as the bathroom. A roughly painted sign on the barn front announced: *FREDDIE & CARL'S EXPERT REPAIRS*. Not that Carl participated in the work or the proceeds, but it gave credence. Carl was respected. He assumed the role of protector shooing away any loafers suspected of drug use. He put both Amanda and Freddie's Mommy on allowances. He kept account of hours worked on each project and parts supplied, the parts procured at cost through an auto parts dealer friend. What the dealer didn't carry, he ordered. A listing of hours worked and bills for parts were delivered to his nephew, a brother to Louie. This kinsman had done well—a successful CPA who managed accounts for county businesses and who loved and respected Carl. When he wasn't shuffling around at the aforementioned tasks, Carl sat in a cane bottom chair leaned against the side of the building, moving with the summer shade or inside the building near the potbellied stove during inclement weather. Freddie often said to Carl, "I like it." And Carl often laughed.

# CHAPTER 31

## Deidra's Coming Out

"Deidra, I've got some good news and some not-so-good news for you." Dr. Lee, fearing that he might spook the woman, was progressing carefully, realizing that she likely would hear and process only a portion of what he was about to tell her. "I think you are suffering from, that is concurrent with your addiction, a chemical imbalance in your brain."

"Are you saying I'm crazy, Doctor?" Deidra quickly shifted into a defensive mode and began twisting her hands in her lap beneath the table. Her mind rushed from one episode to another that made her fear such a diagnosis might be correct.

"No. No. You are anything but crazy. The imbalance does create serious mood swings which I'm sure you are aware of. We all have them. Yours are a bit more precipitous than the average."

"So does that mean I'm doomed to failure no matter how hard I try or what I try?" She was beginning to feel even sorrier for herself. Recently she hadn't felt as though she could conqueror the world, but not so bad she wanted to stay in bed for days either. Yet lacking the secure feeling associated with self-sufficiency, she felt what she was most familiar with, panic and edginess. Was that part of the definition of crazy? Deidra didn't know. Her eyes, the twitch near her mouth, the trembling lip, gave the doctor a possible view into her thoughts.

"Listen carefully. One thing you must understand is this: some of the most successful people on earth suffer the same disorder as you." Dr. Lee was thinking of executives, teachers, clergy that he had treated over the years. For a minute Deidra felt that the doctor had left her, left the room and was living in a different time, interviewing another patient.

"Then why am I not successful?" Deidra knew that for forty-one years her life hadn't amounted to much and was beginning to wonder if this so-called mind-fixer could make any difference for her.

"The divergence between you and the successful individual is personal health management." At this, Dr. Lee retrieved a brochure from his desk file and began quoting from it: "Bipolar is a lifelong disorder. There are milder and more extreme cases. I believe yours is mild. The brain's chemical imbalance brings about manic highs and depressive lows. These can be managed—education, medication, therapy are the keys."

"You're telling me I can be successful or somebody at least functional?" Deidra's voice rose as she leaned forward in her chair, hope now building and replacing the doubt.

"Good. Good. You're getting it. Yes, you can lead a productive, balanced life with proper treatment." Dr. Lee was now thinking about her episodes of despair, degradation, running and using. He knew her trace would be winding and steep. But the balanced life to be achieved and maintained through medication and the other two elements—education and therapy—was certainly probable.

"Dr. Lee, what do you want me to do?" Deidra took a small notebook from her purse and prepared to write.

"We're going to do three things." Dr. Lee leaned forward and clasped his fingers together. "First, the meds you are currently taking need to build up in your body to a certain level for maximum benefit. So they are one of the musts. Second, Thad will provide literature for you to read on managing the mood swings. That's part of the educational component. Third, Thad or Linda will meet with you every Friday to talk—the therapy. Simple isn't it?" Dr. Lee knew it was anything but simple, but he believed it was doable.

"What about you? Am I not to see you also?" Deidra had confidence in the other two, but Dr. Lee, for now, represented the real expertise in her mind. What he'd just said made such sense.

"Yes, indeed. We'll meet once monthly. That is if everything is going well. We'll meet monthly for a meds check." Dr. Lee turned to her chart, making note of the visit. "Oh, and don't forget the standing invitation to visit the horses on Saturdays." Deidra wanted to hug him, to express gratitude for the hope that she suddenly had and which had so long eluded her. He didn't hug patients, but she knew his feelings and gathered her things for exit. His receptionist gave her an appointment card to see Thad that afternoon. Back in her room she reminisced about her stay at rehab, about getting to join the extended-stay group, about possible work and training. Then thoughts turned toward home, to her parents. They would want to know about all that was happening. She made her way to the lobby phone and dialed.

^^^

"Come in, Deidra. Sit down. I need to get a few things together." Thad, always thorough, was gathering written materials for Deidra to read and then discuss at their next session. "I've reviewed Dr. Lee's report. I'm sure you are pleased with the prognosis."

Turning his attention to the handouts, "This is one of my old college texts. I've marked relevant chapters. These are two brochures produced by pharmaceutical companies with information. And this is a great paper presented at the National Psychology Convention this past spring." Smiling, he said, "All you need to know about bipolar disorder. If you will read these, we can discuss and clarify their content at our next session."

Most people might have been overwhelmed by so much information, but not Deidra; this represented a challenge, something to occupy her busy mind which she was certain had shrunk—addicts don't present many intellectual challenges.

"Now, I want you to go next door and talk with Linda. She has news of interest." Thanking Thad, Deidra took the materials and left for Linda's office.

Linda looked up and smiled when Deidra appeared in her office doorway. "Deidra, I'm glad you could come by. Events move pretty fast in the advanced rehab program. We already have a work placement." Linda tapped her writing pen on her chin. "By the way, it was your first choice, I think, the Sheltered Workshop. You are to report tomorrow morning at eight sharp." A lot was happening and Deidra was trying to process it all. Therapy sessions, meds check, educational meetings, NA/AA meetings, work; boredom was unlikely. She smoothed her blouse and shifted her purse to the other shoulder and smiled.

The workshop functioned as a factory; however, employee makeup differed. Addiction and various other disabilities, including mental illness and developmental delays plagued almost all the workers. Contracts awarded by the U. S. Military and other governmental entities supplemented local orders. Gill Fuller, the president, a short man whose belt created a roll above and below it, greeted Deidra. He offered refreshments and a chair. He charged right into the interview. "What do you as a potential executive assistant have to offer us, Ms. Hammock?"

"I can make you look good." Deidra looked the executive directly in the eye. She already knew the tact she was to take.

"Make me look good? I beg your pardon, but that may be quite a challenge." He smiled at this and pushed back in his chair, his white socks showing, stopping short of his pants leg to reveal hair on the fat calf.

Deidra had already looked around enough to see areas of need. "For example, the note on your desk begins as a memo but has a friendly letter ending—not appropriate. Lines four and seven have typos. In line four, two letters are reversed in the word referral; line seven has three spaces rather than one between accepted and delivery." She was reading the letter from across the desk and upside down in her vision.

"Ahem, do you make it a habit to read the boss's mail?" But he was impressed as he leaned forward to confirm her discovery.

"Only if it is my job to do so, In this case, my objective was not to intrude on your privacy, but to demonstrate how you can be made to look better. Also, I'd have the maintenance crew clean the glass in the front door

and re-hang the sign on your office door. It's off center."
The interview progressed. The interviewer alternated between being intrigued and scared, but finally decided to chance her.

Once on staff, Deidra's goal matched perfectly with her first interview answer. She began with Gill. His shirts, the fitted style, neither fit, nor were they stylish. The front puckered between buttons. The tail, too short rode out of his pants. He was advised to purchase at least five shirts with wide yokes, and in dark colors. To accent the new image, his pants, too, needed updating. Pleated khakis with a slip waist expansion eliminated the roll above and below the midsection. The white socks had to go, substituting dark mid-calf style. The re-invention didn't come without several squabbles. L. L. Bean and J Peterman catalogues were reviewed. A discussion was held with his wife. Deidra won. Next she tackled the governing board. During her first board meeting, questions regarding travel costs, utility expenditures, and whose work was being done were issues that consumed the entire meeting. It was impossible to take minutes. No real business seemed to surface.
The next assembly would be different. She initiated the agenda, with the president's approval, of course. The first item introduced a *professional staff* report. This consisted of two foremen introducing workers from three different departments —making a military water bag, putting a new cover on a jeep seat, and assembling a newly repaired vacuum cleaner. Board members watched and circulated among the demonstrations asking questions as they moved along. The finance report and other business items passed with what Deidra considered reasonable discussion. As the members filed from the facility at the end of the meeting, Deidra overheard several comments.

"I didn't know little Willie Whitcomb could do anything." Willie had peeped out his parent's backdoor at this board member, a neighbor, as she had gardened for the past few years. No words had ever been exchanged between the two.

"I thought Brad was dead. Hadn't heard a word about him in years...He stayed high what time I knew him...broke his mom and dad, you know." This member shook her grey head and clucked. Deidra was certain the board members' remarks represented connection, an understanding of why they met each month. She also thought Gill strutted a little on his way out.

Deidra reported all this and more to Thad, Linda, and Dr. Lee. All were pleased for her. Thad needed confirmation from the president as to her overall conduct. This conformed with agency policy as it related to treatment. The president, effusive in his praise, quelled any concerns: "Remarkable woman; wish I had forty like her." He examined his fingernails and then his shirt cuffs as he spoke

# CHAPTER 32

## Riders Up

"Whoa!" Deidra's feet were out of the stirrups. The horse was bolting to the right while she was leaning much too far left. The next lunge and she was unseated, landing hard on the ground and losing her wind momentarily. Recovering her breath, the pain and nausea confirmed that she was hurt. A huge knot was visible on her left forearm. Dr. Lee reached her first and pronounced the arm broken. The day had begun on such a high. The May sun was warm, the birds were flitting and singing. The old barn warming in the sun, creaked, emitted rank smells peculiar to horses and inviting. Riders wanted to examine the animals, the leather, the alfalfa and oats. Simply arriving at the barn fulfilled a horse-lover's need for escape. Grooming, riding, and feeding were extras that later led to long discussions and questions, things to think about between visits.

Deidra had been coached on mounting the horse, which was then led around the long barn several times. Dr. Lee's teenage grandson held the lead and coached her.

After several starts and stops, mounts and dismounts, Deidra declared her readiness to venture out on her own. Never having ridden without assistance, Deidra offered him little direction. The horse sensing the lack of control, wandered first to one succulent clump of new spring grass then to another, his head down more than up. Saliva covered his lips, grass was rolled forward then back in his attempt to chew around the steel in his mouth. This lasted the better part of an hour, horse and rider moving in zigzag maneuvers across the field beyond the barn. At the far edge of the field, saplings, briars and other growth, chocking a drainage ditch created a perfect animal and bird habitat. It happened that the horse and two wild tom turkeys met on this site. Deidra was in the saddle lazily attempting to guide. Turkeys aren't easily spooked by farm animals; however, today proved otherwise. The turkeys rose with thunderous flapping. The horse's back first lowered giving the rider the impression of squatting. Then he bolted at a right angle. Even the calmest, gentlest horse, one which has eaten from the handler's palm, one that might have laid his head over his owner's shoulder, has fright parameters. He may lick a roaring gocart as the driver stops to chat, walk close to a running chain saw, or stroll casually among a pack of barking, nipping dogs. Somewhere there is a limit. He breaks away from that self-control instilled by the trainer. Deidra's horse relapsed. Instinct prevailed. It did what horses do. It knotted up and then ran.

Dr. Lee looked into her eyes, bent low his ear to her chest. He listened to her heart and felt the pulse at her wrist. The latter caused Deidra to wince and moan in pain. Then he attended the lump on her forearm. After contriving a makeshift sling with a halter rope, he transported the patient to the hospital emergency room. Doc's grandson and several riders gathered in the hospital awaiting news and, as they waited, told stories of incidents of other horse and rider injuries. An older rider related a story about a one-eyed quarter horse that fell over a steep incline as riders stopped for lunch among the big trees in the national forest. The horse turned over and over to rest finally against a huge poplar. His rider, holding on to bushes, finally reached him, called on him to get up and both struggled back up the embankment. Only the saddle was damaged. Other stories were gorier—a horse rearing and falling back on the rider, the saddle horn causing internal injuries. Deidra's wound, it turned out, was less serious requiring only a cast from the elbow to the wrist. Deidra revealed to the emergency room nurse, "I have totaled an automobile, hitch-hiked from Florida, and abused drugs on the very rim of hell with the devil himself, but never before had a broken bone."

The emergency over and Dr. Lee back at the barn, he directed Deidra's horse into a circular corral. He took a light nylon rope and swung it in the air around his head much like a lariat. Without striking the horse, he encouraged it to circle the enclosure on a clockwise run and then counter clockwise, allowing the horse to stop after each. At each stop, the Dr. stood still with the rope at his feet, as the horse approached him and laid its head on his shoulder. These maneuvers he had learned viewing tapes of *The Horse Whisperer*. It helped the horse to recognize him as friend and boss with no harm done to either. If Deidra was so minded, it would be safe to remount as soon as her arm allowed. Next time, he'd lead the horse from his mount until she gained confidence and natural control. Doc knew both the joy of riding and the danger involved. Twelve hundred pounds of animal bred to jump, buck, and run was not to be taken for granted.

# CHAPTER 33

## The Confession in Dr. Ann's Emergency Room

"Doctor, I'm an addict." Deidra blurted this as Ann entered the examining room. She was embarrassed to be in the presence of a beautiful woman who also happened to be a noted physician.

"I know. Goatee M.D. briefed me." At this, both women looked at one another and giggled. Deidra wondered where this doctor had heard the nickname given the psychiatrist and passed along from group to group as they moved through rehab. None ever dared address him as such. Finally controlling her laughter, Ann related that she had known Dr. Lee many years and that, in fact, she had worked part-time with him for three years. It was during that tenure she'd picked up considerable psychiatric experience. Her duties were limited to doing physicals for the psychiatrists. Doing med checks, questioning patients, and observing therapists naturally pricked her interest. Through study and experience, she had become quite adept. This Deidra learned later from mutual acquaintances. "Don't worry, Ms. Hammock. You will not be prescribed Percocet or anything else contraindicative. Guess what, I took an oath a long while ago to do no harm, at least I think that or something similar, was in the oath."

Deidra was smitten, drawn to this woman's power, her intellect. They had connected. "Doctor, I wish you were on my treatment team." Deidra felt a little embarrassed making such a statement to someone she'd known less than fifteen minutes. Ann was working at a nearby table making arrangements for a cast.

"My dear, I am on your treatment team and plan to repair that arm this very instant." Ann knew or at least suspected what the woman meant. She knew a lot about her circumstances, ability, and prognosis, relative to her addiction and disorder—not the broken arm. Each woman felt a kinship in this early relationship, but for the moment, neither chose to say more.

That evening Gill, Deidra's boss, got word of Deidra's accident. His first concern was for himself. How would he do without her? He immediately felt guilt for lack of concern for Deidra and called rehab for a first-hand-report. Discovering that full recovery was expected and that she could return to work on Monday, he sighed and sat down to his usual after- dinner cup of strong, hot coffee, the two adjectives always emphasized when he ordered out. Deidra had truly changed his world. Employees now asked for his opinion, governing board members often congratulated him on shop progress. His wife complimented his new emphasis on wardrobe. From parking lot to air filters, the property was clean and orderly. All this and more—he was on a diet, losing weight and thankful for the adjustable khakis. "The woman has power," he often said this aloud even though no one was present to question or respond.

Monday, Deidra was back at her desk, but something was different. It wasn't the cast either. The boss noticed her speech was different. Looking close as he'd been taught in working with addicts, he suspected her eyes were dilated. Thinking it must be the pain medicine, he went about the morning business until he realized that Dr. Lee would never have prescribed a narcotic. He went to her desk and finding her away, opened her catch-all drawer and saw the medicine bottle. The label indicated antibiotics, but the pills didn't resemble any antibiotics he'd ever taken.

Rather than confront her and risk being wrong and sure enough causing a problem, he called the rehab facility. The only staff available was Keith.

"Say, Keith, could you come over here a minute?"

"Do you mean now? I'm scheduled to meet with a resident any minute." Keith's days, always filled, left little time for unplanned out-of-facility consults.

"It's Deidra." The boss had to say no more.

"I'll be right there." President Gill was in his office, having said nothing to Deidra, who was wandering aimlessly around the shop, stopping at work stations to make boisterous comments. No one was laughing. All knew this behavior was out of character. Keith examined the pill bottle, identified the medication as Percocet, and motioned for Deidra to come in. "Deidra, it's obvious you aren't yourself today. Have you been taking these?" He showed her the pill bottle.

"You've pilfered my desk! How dare you!" Turning to her boss, she added, "And you! I saw that bottle in there when I came in this morning." She knew trouble was coming. Thinking as fast as the medicine allowed, she had attempted a quick defense.

After the encounter, and with Keith and Deidra gone from the premises, the president called his wife. "Honey, the most horrendous thing has happened. I'm not sure I can go on." Thinking he must be contemplating suicide, the wife became frantic.

"Now, Darling, hold on just a minute. What has happened?" Thinking the worst, maybe one of the children had died or his mother, she hardly knew where to begin to unravel this partial report.

"Oh, Honey, They took her away." He couldn't bring himself to admit that Deidra's dilemma was an employment rule infraction of her own making.

"Took who away?" This surely wasn't a family emergency reference. He was talking too loud, then too low. She thought, he's crying, I do believe. Finally he got the message through. She understood. Neither his nor any family member's life was in danger. "You'll just have to get another assistant, Honey. That shouldn't be too difficult."

# CHAPTER 34

## The Florida Sunshine

Many times a big woman doesn't look attractive in skimpy swim wear. This is especially true if, like Beck, she is over seventy, not in control of her weight and has varicose veins. Beck had been thinking for some time that she needed a man for her old days and actively began the search along the white sandy beaches. Her original intent was to find an old, white, conservative, Republican who drove something like a late model Mercury Marquis. The Republican or Democrat part didn't make any difference except she'd heard somewhere that Republicans had more money. Realizing such a man likely favored more conservative women, she wore a modest house-dress over the neon green two-piece bathing suit, figuring she could always let it fall open at the right time.

Having created no obvious interest during the first few soirees, she added a spectacular diamond on her right hand. It was glass, of course, but she knew no one could tell if she flashed it appropriately. This resulted in one beach stroll encounter, which was followed by ice tea at the beach bar and a request that she drive the suitor home. His driver license, she learned, had been "called." Beck considered it a bust.

Not all was wasted though. Beck's sister hooked up with a gentleman in the beach parking lot after one of their strolls. He followed them home, drank their coffee, ate their oranges and, Beck thought, made himself too much at home. Besides, he drove a Toyota Tacoma pickup and bragged about the gas mileage and the fact that it had two hundred and fifty thousand miles on the odometer. Beck had had enough of such talk. She wasn't impressed. The sister's health, on the other hand, improved with each visit. "You gonna wind around and lose your benefits the way you're carrying on," Beck often admonished, but it failed to stall the progress.

Four months after their meeting, the two loaded into the little truck, their sparse belonging piled in the back, and headed to Arizona. The boyfriend had convinced Beck's sister that the desert air would strengthen them both. They'd get by on his social security check if her disability check petered out. Beck and Sis had never been separated since girlhood. Both cried. "Who's gonna keep check on your girl, your grandbaby, and help me around the house?" The sister heard, but she didn't hear.

It was about this time that Beck remembered she'd never before needed a man and decided to re-evaluate her priorities. "Who wants to wash dirty underwear and sweep ashes from around an old codger's chair?" she was heard asking the neighbor who replaced her sister on the daily beach walks.

"Yeah, and clean his filth off the commode seat?" The neighbor had buried three husbands and Beck realized she spoke the truth. A substitute for matrimony, therefore, became a priority. Always the one to come with a tight workable plan, Beck began to ponder. Finally she decided to call old Carl. He'd always managed to get by. Besides she wanted to get an unbiased account of Amanda and the baby's activities and circumstances.

"Carl, you know who this is? Don't say my name out loud over the phone." Beck explained that she was calling to get the news about you-know-who and who, as well as about what was going on around.

"Well B—I mean, ma-am, things are going right fine. The boy and me, well, we're making do. You might have heard about the repair shop we've opened." Carl made it sound as though he and Freddie were working side by-side tearing into the big engines. Beck knew better than that. He'd never even changed a plough point in his life. He'd made a living though, was considered a good farmer by neighbors, and managed to always turn a profit on trades. These things Beck respected. She had confidence in any advice he might give.

"Say, Carl, I'm considering my options. I've been thinking about how to make a little money, stay busy, that sort of thing—thought you might have some recommendations." Beck didn't want to come right out and ask how she could turn an honest dollar.

"Well, I'll tell you, Beck, err, I mean ma'am. Trading is where the money is. I've made money on everything from mules to farm equipment and land down through the years." Carl could have gone on except Beck stopped him.

"How would an old woman get started?" She had some ideas, but chose to hear from someone who had been successful.

"Git you something to trade on; most any artickle has worth to somebody. There in Florida, I'd think about fishing tackle, boats, thangs like that."

By now Beck's mind was clicking. She might even invest in real estate.

"Thanks, Carl." She was about to hang up, then thought of Amanda and her baby. "Do you see anything of Amanda?"

“Yes, indeedy, her and the baby stop here at the shop nearly ever day. Freddie put her together an old car, you know, Pontiac, I think. What paint is left on it is red. It could just as well be a Cadillac as far as she is concerned. First thing she done was paint a sign on the back glass. *Town girls slip and slide, country girls grip and ride.* Freddie don’t know for sure what it means, but thinks it mighty funny.” Carl was in his comfort zone gossiping with Beck.

Beck laughed her booming laugh at this little story. Then she sobered. “Is that sorry Freddie helping any with the youngun?” Beck knew that welfare barely provided for a baby’s nourishment.

“B—err, ma’am, you’d be proud. That boy gives her more money ever week than she’d get if he was paying child support.” Laughing, he continued, “Gets visiting rights a couple of times a week, whatever that means. He stayed with her all the time for a while. Got tired of it, I reckon. Of course, I’m a-gin such actions myself. Can’t tell these young people nary thing though; liable to be another baby there, I’m afeerd. But long as they keep them twins and that thieving nephew of mine in jail, maybe thangs’ll work out though.”

“Carl, I’m gonna have to hang up. My phone minutes are about gone. Don’t mention to anybody that I called.” She chuckled. “Take care that you don’t get crippled up lifting and pulling at them big motors.” Beck’s cell phone, one of those given out to the needy, was handy. She giggled and called it the presidential phone. Fact is, she requested a red one. The program didn’t have a color selection, however.

Carl weaved his way through equipment, motors, and parts to Freddie's work space. "You know old Beck won't do, but I sort-a like to talk to her." Freddie didn't respond. Carl's talking hindered him.

After the conversation, Beck's business plan began to evolve and then congeal. She'd organize a two pronged business. First, she knew from discussions that many snow birds, as the locals referred to them, came to Florida, leaving family and lifelong nests seeking the warmer climes only to become dissatisfied and move back home within months. They sold everything through the classifieds. She'd buy these quick-sale items. Just down the road was a large outdoor flea market. She'd sell there.

Over the next few months this evolved into purchasing automobiles, trucks, travel trailers, and boats along with the what-not items suitable for a flea market table. The larger items requiring bills of sale, she transferred directly from the owner to purchaser, keeping the cash transactions free from government tracking. Those that didn't move quickly, she frequently sent to Carl and Freddie to sell back in Kentucky. Bored retirees she hired often used a *tow dollie* to deliver pickup trucks and the like for a small sum, plus gas and fast food money. She arranged their overnight lodging herself to keep costs down. The legal transfers were made directly to Carl and Freddie.

Rumors suggested that Buddy Mustang's extra meds came packed in some of the transport. This was never substantiated. People talked just the same. The business turned a profit. Beck was busy and pleased.

Sis called some months after moving to Arizona. Her paramour had proved less than satisfactory. He rode out on an old horse from their canyon shack nearly every day. Going prospecting, he said. The sister never saw any nuggets, maybe a pottery shard or broken flint he claimed was a knife blade. More often than not, he returned with a couple of Indians from the reservation—all three drunk.

She wanted to return to Florida. Beck made her suffer as much as possible with stinging remarks about how foolish the move had been, but in the end, she sent the sister bus fare for the trip back. "They all think old Beck's made of money," she said this to a neighbor as she reported the sister's imminent return.

On her return, the sister was added to the business staff for room and board in lieu of pay. The arrangement, satisfactory to both, allowed expansion. Beck bought while the sister tended the flea market table. Profits rose. The hard work finally began to take its toll on Beck, lifting boxes, tugging at lawn equipment. She awoke with her legs aching and sharp pains in her knees and shoulders, sometimes so serious she had to be helped from bed to chair where she'd sit for an hour or so before sure enough stirring. It was during one of these sitting spells that her thoughts turned to her mortality. This serious consideration in turn led to her joining the community church in town and to closing out the business.

Soon she was standing during worship service, her arms upraised, her body swaying to the music. She was right at home, same as she'd been all those years ago when she and her mother were church-goers. She even chaired a committee that did interventions with addicts and organized drug educational programs. Nobody knew her heart, but outwardly Beck had come full circle; however, so long as she was breathing, those back in Kentucky who knew her well would watch and wonder.

# CHAPTER 35

## And One More Makes Three

"Hello, Doctor." Ann answered her door after peeping through the glass. She was surprised to see Deidra. The encounter in the emergency room had been their last. Keith had relayed the message to her, however, regarding Deidra's episode in the workshop. He had been attempting to identify the source of the Percocet. He knew it hadn't come from Ann, but wanted to discuss possibilities, maybe a lapse in hospital protocol. His investigation eventually led to a new arrival in rehab that had, she thought, befriended Deidra with pain killers the night the cast was put on. Both the new arrival and Deidra had been dropped from the program in accordance with administrative regulations. No matter that the treatment team tried persuasively to preserve Deidra's status, the rule was firm. No addict under any circumstances who knowingly abused drugs on the premise could remain on the job. Subsequently Keith had arranged for her to stay a couple of days with him and his mother.

"Deidra, it's so nice to see you again." Ann, never one to be caught without appropriate words no matter the circumstance, hardly knew how to deal with this sudden encounter. "What brings you to Pineville?"

"Dr. Ann, I'm so sorry." Deidra's hands were shaking. Tears were welling in her eyes—which Ann noted looked normal. At least she didn't suspect that Deidra was high. "I let Mr. Keith down, the rehab down. I really thought this treatment with Dr. Lee and Mr. Keith might be it for me. I don't know for sure why I'm here apologizing to you, but you were so thoughtful and kind there in the emergency room when you fixed my arm, but now my actions may have put you under suspicion."

"Sit down, Deidra. Let me get us some tea and then let's talk. You do drink tea?" A slight nod from the visitor sent Ann was off to the kitchen. Deidra looked around the room and through the arched doorway into the next. Each room was decorated comfortably, with very few, what Deidra considered trinkets, ceramics and such. On one wall were built-in bookcases which held more books than she'd seen except in school and public libraries. An entire section was dedicated to medical and scientific research journals, another to medical texts, old and new. She began to realize why she considered this woman special on first contact. In this room, she was certain, was enough information to substantiate a world view to match most any scholar's notion in science, history, international affairs, economics, math and physics.

"Now, do you want sugar or milk?" Ann asked noting the woman's interest in her books.

"No, thank you, just plain tea. You have a lovely place."

"Thank you. It's comfortable." Ann smiled at Deidra and they sat together, each leaning forward and sipping tea.  Now, Deidra, let's get down to business. What can I do for you today?"

"Dr. Ann, I'm a whore, an addict, and I'm probably crazy."

"Hold on. Next you're probably going to say you smoke also." Ann was smiling as she said this and both broke into laughter, loud and extended considering the situation. The wall was down. "Deidra, do you know what a whore is? In earlier biblical times, the term sometimes referred to an idolater. Now are you an idolater?" Deidra looked confused. Ann bowed forward looking her directly in the eye and continued, "I think not. Today a whore is one who sells herself for money. Are you selling yourself? No, you have been gainfully employed while trying to maintain sobriety." Deidra took a sip of tea and looked down at her hands. "As to crazy, my evaluation of you indicates sane, non-psychotic behavior, no danger to self or others."

"Let's examine this issue." Ann took a notepad from a side table and began to sketch, drawing cells and labeling each. With a red pen she drew other cells. Molecules were drawn out and labeled some representing medications. Electrical impulses were designated by lines. "I'm sure Dr. Lee explained the chemical issues in your brain. Here they are on paper." Pointing first to one drawing then another, she explained how the medication molecule affected changes necessary to control certain confusing brain activity. "Deidra when you become super active, out of control, impulses flaring," Ann pointed to the sketches for emphasis and better explanation of what was happening. "Your self-medicating, experimenting so to speak, is an attempt to control that activity. Sometimes it works temporarily. When you fall from the high, the manic state, to the unbearable depressed state, you take something else, hoping your spirits will raise again. In the final analysis these medicines fail, but you keep trying. You eventually begin to crave. I've given you an over-simplified explanation of your so-called craziness, but I think you get the message."

"Doctor, I understand what you have said. But why do I keep repeating the same old destructive behavior?"

"You may never answer that question, at least to you satisfaction. Personally, I don't think you have to.

What you do need is scientifically proven treatment that controls this function." Ann again pointed to the drawings. "Controlling the brain malfunctions will allow you to achieve a level of behavior acceptable in polite society, a level comfortable enough to live with. So *cherk up.*"

Ann looked intently at Deidra, not harshly, or questioning, but commanding. Deidra didn't feel under her spell or control. She did feel a certain power. Whether it was her understanding of Ann's sketched information and that understanding equaled power or something mysteriously imparted to her by the doctor's strong will, she didn't know. She had witnessed something similar long ago in grade school. An out of control sixth grade child, totally unmanageable, had responded to a certain teacher aide. The aide merely took his hand. A calm and gentle child walked with her into the school building. Minutes before he had kicked the principal's shins and torn the buttons off his teacher's blouse. The aide had no special training. She probably had no idea what the gift was that transformed the lad. Anyway, Dr. Ann had something; maybe that calm horse thing that Dr. Lee told her about. So much for that, however, a calm horse had left her with a broken arm.

"So, what are you going to do?" The doctor's question broke her train of thought and took her by surprise. She was equally surprised by her answer: "I'm going to *cherk up*, get a job, a place to live, take my medicine, continue to see Dr. Lee and you, if you allow me to." Ann nodded her head, smiled, and walked to the telephone and hit speed dial.

"Keith, this is Ann. No, sorry, I'm not coming to see you and your mother. I need a phone number, Al's. Yes, Al's cell phone. I've mislaid my work phone. No, I'm not thinking about courting him." She smiled at Keith's kidding. "He's going to help me with Deidra Hammock. I'll tell you all about it later."

She bent to write the number. "Okay, take care." Deidra had no idea what was happening, but Ann got the number because she hung up and immediately began dialing again. "Hello, Al, this is Ann. Yes, Pineville emergency Ann. Now listen, I've got a deal for you… A deal… something you'll be interested in. The company in Northern Kentucky that's to put together the *clinic plan* for you, they're going to need a local contact. I have the person… Heck, yes, she'll work independently… Smart? What are you talking about? She's smart and fast as the hornet that hit you in the forehead last time you threw a rock at its nest—traced the trajectory of that missile instantly, remember?" Al recalled telling Ann and Keith the hornet story. "This woman can, Skype, email, whatever, between you and the company, keep things moving while you're off in Haiti doing good. I'll let her live here with me until you leave; then she can house-sit for you during your absence. We'll get together later this week so you can interview her and work out the details."

Turning to Deidra and without clarifying Al's response, "I'm taking you on. That's what you wanted, isn't it?"

# CHAPTER 36

## The Present Speaks

"What in the sam hill were you people thinking, Keith? You've cost my workshop, our work workshop, excuse me, a million dollars. Hell, it may be ten or twelve million. That woman knows more than you, Goatee, and everybody else here in the rehab center. Now, you've put her back on the street. Be damned if I can understand it."

"Here, have some coffee." Gill, the sheltered workshop president had never before visited his office, but they talked often. A bit of a slob, Keith had thought in the past, however not recently. He had always been the *let it happen captain* type, never raising his voice, and certainly never given to crude speech. Keith wasn't sure whether to go into counseling mode or to try and respond to his questions and less than subtle statements.

"Deidra broke the cardinal rule here in rehab. She used. We can't help someone high on alcohol or other drugs." A personal situation kept coming to Keith's mind. His one slip-up during divorce proceeding after returning from the Gulf War—that was before this eleven year dry run. One week-long, in the bed with a bottle, had cost him his first job after returning home. Turned out, he hadn't accumulated any vacation time and had no operating cash. He had worked a few days in a local car wash earning barely enough to eat. The dirty, infested sleeping room, he paid for by selling some of his Kuwaiti souvenirs. His fall had been hard. It is possible someone could have flagged him, helped save his job, and prevented his long slide into more misery and degradation—maybe not. These memories should have faded after all the years, but they hadn't. They influenced him every day as he intervened in the lives of floundering patients. The memories of a happy marriage, which failed miserably after his service tour, they all lingered. Was there something more he could have done for Deidra? He had so hoped that she'd make it.

"I have a friend in Pineville. She called last night. Your executive assistant, Deidra, is staying a few days with her." Keith saw no reason to keep this from the president.

"Do you think she'd mind if I contacted her, talked to Deidra?" Gill's voice was much stronger now. His face showed signs of his embarrassment for earlier comments, as well as signs of relief. He had a lead. Hope was building. These people at rehab had no idea the pickle he was in. The Chamber of Commerce had listed his workshop among the city's top five businesses, one of which was to receive the county's *Business of the Year* award. For a non-profit enterprise employing the handicapped, this was absolutely unheard of. Business leaders believed in profits, not government handouts. These same leaders were about to honor his establishment. It seemed only a short time before that his governing board had considered closing the doors, another failed government sponsored enterprise finished. He needed help. He needed it quickly. He knew of no one he could turn to except the executive assistant who had pulled him and his organization out of the proverbial fire.

The next evening Gill, the workshop president, was in Pineville knocking on Ann's door. "Boss, what are you doing here? You look terrible." Pulling the president into the front room, Deidra was unbuttoning and re-buttoning his shirt in mid-section, correcting their order. "Where is your shirt with the wide yoke and your khaki trousers?"

"Sorry, Deidra, things have not been going well." By this time Ann had entered the room.

"Dr. Ann, this is Gill Fuller, the president of the sheltered workshop where I was working before my," she stopped, and looked at the floor, "misstep." Turning to the visitor, "This is Dr. Ann. I'm staying with her for a few days."

"Deidra, you've got to help me." The president was shaking his head as he said this.

"You know I can't be there to check your wardrobe each morning." Deidra knew he was talking about operations, but hardly knew how to respond. "Besides, I have a job."

"No, that can't be." He knew coming back to work was impossible for her as the workshop operated under the same regulations as the rehab center. He had no idea how she could help, but he also had confidence in her ability to figure it out. "Is it possible for you to write down a plan for me to follow?"

"Of course, she can." Ann entered the conversation with the same confidence, Deidra thought, a mother might express in behalf of an overachieving daughter being asked to speak at the school Beta Club banquet.

"Deidra is doing consulting work for the *DAA Consultants, LLC, firm* over in Harrogate, Tennessee. This will fit nicely. Being one of the A's in the firm name, I'm sure I can speak for the entire group." Ann was fairly sure of her ability to convince Al of the importance of an LLC designation and that Deidra was the woman for the job. She or Deidra could easily download the form necessary to establish the company Ann had just dreamed up. It had to be signed and filed in the Clerk's office in either Kentucky or Tennessee.

Deidra was flabbergasted. Only Dr. Ann, she thought. Nobody had mentioned a consulting firm for Al's work. Of course, using the computer and phone and adding the workshop duties was doable, maybe even a good fit—considering Al's time requirements.

"I'll tell you what boss, keep your computer on. The regulations, plans, and advice will be coming. Also, we'll Skype. I want to see your outfit each morning."

"Oh, thank you, Deidra, and thank you, Dr. Ann. This is good news. My life is saved. And, Deidra, I think we can pay you up to seventy-five dollars an hour. That's what we paid the accountant for our management audit, remember? Although we'll need to put a cap on the hours per week, you understand." Deidra nodded and looked at Ann, raising her eyebrows as if to say, wow!

"By the way, Boss, Keith phoned to apprise us of your visit. He also mentioned your language in his office; now that is out of character. Let's hear no more such reports." All were laughing now, Gill especially. No one raised his spirits like Deidra even when she was scolding him.

After the president's departure, Ann gave Deidra that penetrating look. "Deidra my position is not particularly safe here. In my professional opinion though, the busier you keep yourself, the larger the task, the better you'll function. What do you think?" Keith, whose judgment she never questioned, had profusely reported details about Deidra's turning the workshop around in the short time she had worked there. So these instantaneous decisions weren't made without some foundation.

"You might be right," Deidra replied. "At least I won't be bored. I can see that." The next few days were not without problems for Deidra. She had doubts, doubts about her ability to co-ordinate Al's pending enterprise, doubts about staying sober, and above all, doubts about her sanity. Three times she called Dr. Lee, but got him only once. "Give the medicine a few days. You'll see results very soon. The two times Dr. Lee wasn't available, she reached Thad. Instead of telling what was wrong with her, he grunted encouragement each time she faltered in describing what she was feeling. The phone discussion lasted over an hour each time. After hanging up, she always felt better. Finally, after four days of being anxious and uncertain, she began writing the operations manual for the sheltered workshop. Even after beginning the project, there were times, she told Ann, "When I want to throw the computer across the room, run, and scream."

Giving her that penetrating look, Ann said quietly, "You will not though, will you?"

The question became a statement to Deidra, or a command that seemed to become her very own. "No, I will not, not today."

# CHAPTER 37

## Carl's Breaking Bad

"Hello, Amanda, honey, is that you? Don't say my name out over the telephone. Just say, yes, if you know who this is." Beck didn't know exactly what, but she still feared something back in Kentucky. Likely the brutal way her door was broken and the swarm of officers who had pillaged and pilfered throughout her wonderful old home before subduing her under threat. Those times that she and her sister sat late into the night remembering old times, the raid story grew in certain specifics, shrank in others. It's known that certain *Appalachian Tales* from Kentucky's past and the more recent *Walking Dead* TV series frighten even the brave. Beck's leaving Kentucky stories, growing incrementally with each retelling, similarly scared the big woman all over again. Rumors back home had Beck maintaining her trade from the sandy beaches of Florida. This too, might account for her fear. The truth may never be known, but her friends knew that Beck feared to be identified when calling home.

"I'm so lonesome down here I'm about to die, Honey. You probably heard about that foolish trick your mother pulled—going off to Arizona. Of course, she's back now, but mopes around the house like an old sick hen. Pining for that old man, I reckon. I swear sometimes I wonder if she's sure enough my sister."

"I'm so glad you called. Little Freddie Jr. took a step yesterday. He has out-growed that outfit you sent. Reckon you might send him a few things? I ain't had a thing new since you left. Freddie is helping some with diapers, milk, things like that; pays the electric bill too."

"Listen, Honey, I've got a thing or two on my mind. I want you to get that baby's sorry daddy to bring you down here for a few days. Don't come thinking you're gonna stay though. I ain't made of money, you know." Beck had a desire to see the niece and her baby, but more importantly, she wanted news. News of local events, who was marrying who, who was managing the selling, who was tied up in the courts. Topping all that was what were people saying about her. She readily acknowledged that poor little Amanda didn't have a lick of sense, but she was a pretty good hand at gathering and repeating the news.

"You know I ain't got the money for a trip." Amanda seized on the opportunity to raise a little cash, maybe enough to get her a new ring. She had been sort of thinking about a tattoo also, maybe something romantic like a butterfly high on her right breast. Some of the tops she'd seen at K-Mart accented those. Those girls who went for lizards, spider webs and the like, she did not understand. A rose on her ankle was her second choice.

"I'm gonna send you a few dollars, enough for gas and a bite to eat coming and going. Don't run off to the store and waste it neither. Call me when you get the money, and we'll settle on the date." Immediately after hanging up, Beck began fretting about wasting the money. Sentimentality had never plagued her, but now her thoughts ranged from snowball bushes, to Easter lilies, even to old Carl. The thought that she might be slipping had begun to haunt her.

^^^

Freddie was not having the best morning. Attacking the rear end on a bucket loader, he was stumped as to getting the bolts loose. Such equipment, often used in hostile environments, might go twenty years without needing a breakdown like he was attempting today. The parts seemed to grow together. He'd skinned his knuckles when an open-ended wrench slipped; he'd hammered the handle end off his best ratchet. Now as he stood studying the problem, Carl's often stated admonition came to him: *the Lord gives wisdom to those who ask.* Right then he believed that was what he needed, but he got interrupted by Carl's hollering him to the telephone. Had he known what was coming, he'd have held back a minute and offered up the prayer.

"Freddie, can you run over here a minute?" Amanda's voice didn't sound like she was in distress, or needed money, or diapers. In fact, it sounded right sweet. Hmm, he usually initiated these calls.

"I'm pretty busy. Guess I could though." The visit offered a surprise well outside the parameters of his desires. Amanda wanted him to take off a week and take her to visit her mother and Aunt Beck. Pity filled Freddie as Amanda recounted that the old folks hadn't seen little Freddie since he was in the cradle, that he didn't even know that grandma. "Amanda, your old car ain't fit for such a trip." "Now, Freddie, we know you can keep any old clunker running. That's no excuse."

"I don't know how to get to Florida." This did present a problem, for neither did Amanda. She had been there with Beck, but spent her time napping and chattering, paying no attention to routes. Freddie had never been farther than Harlan County when he helped deliver a piece of equipment for Caterpillar and again with the rehab group.

"Old Carl knows how to go. Ask him if he'll go with us." Freddie was trapped.

Carl's first response was, "That's the foolishish thang I ever heerd of." On the other, hand he'd sort of like to see the old women and he had never seen the ocean. Before responding though, Carl leaned his chair against a barn pillar in the workshop, hooked his heel in the bottom rung, and crossed his legs. "I've knowed Beck since she was a gal. Course I'm a couple or so years older. You and me both know she is trifling, a liar, and a rogue, but I can't hep but sort a like her. Fact is, we're a little kin through the Boltons." Chuckling, he continued, "One time, we was just children, ten or twelve, I guess, and we'd clumb up in a mulberry tree out behind her daddy's barn—eating berries. That was after we swum in the creek that morning. Actually she swum. I didn't have nothin' to swim in. I looked up, and there she was naked right down to her belly-button, and up to it, too. Plagued me to death; didn't bother her a lick. Anyway from up in that mulberry tree, we had a good view of the barn, crib and other outbuildings as well as the wagon road leading back to them. Mind you, I weren't supposed to be there. Mammy and Pappy didn't want me around no liquor business. Directly, here come a wagon, pulled by two good mules. Feller driving had on bib overalls, a jump jacket, and knee-high gum boots. Don't know what kept him from burning up. He hollered Beck's daddy out. "Guess you want this corn in the crib, don't you," he said this big and loud.

" 'Where else would you put corn?' This was not said in a mad way or a pleasing way either. The driver pulled the wagon through between the two drying rooms. He begun shoveling with a big scoop, I guess eighteen inches wide. Didn't take him long to get down to the floor of the wagon. I noticed the floor wasn't but about three ears deep. That left fifteen or so inches of bed underneath and unaccounted for. Both men began to remove the boards revealing wadded coffee sacks, fertilizer bags, old rags and so forth. Under these was row after row of half gallon jars, protected from breakage by the stuffing. The jars were full. We could tell cause Beck's old daddy picked one up, shook it good. 'Look at that bead,' he said, then tasted of it.

The delivery man was right proud of his commodity. Both men 'ventually bent down to ground level at the bottom of and below the crib storage area on our right, one man at each end. They each reached around, slid a hand through a crack and unhooked something behind the panel. I know they unhooked it cause I heard the metal strike wood as the hook was turned loose. Then they slid the entire panel out along the alleyway toward the back of the crib. It looked like the panel was three or four boards high, serving as underpinning for the crib. The secret hidin' place opened, and they carefully stowed the jars. I'm guessing they's forty or fifty gallon."

'This'll have to do you a while,' the delivery man said. 'Old Hoskins has been out on his hoss two or three times now, riding for his exercise, he says. I know better.' Hoskins was the constable in his district, you see."

Carl looked at Freddie to be sure he had his attention. Freddie seemed to be listening, but you could never tell for sure. "You may know some of Hoskins' people. The Ledfords and Smiths over on the creek are his kin."

"Um hum." Freddie felt he needed to get back to work. He took up the air wrench and attacked the bolt. When he finished the job and shut the wrench off, Carl started up again, shifting topics.

“You know the handiest tool ever made?” Not waiting for an answer, he continued, “The hoe.”

“The hoe?” Freddie never challenged Carl, but this needed further clarification.

“Yes, sir, a man can stand purt nigh straight up and do his work; takes a bad strain off his back.”

“I guess so.” Freddie was examining the thread on the bolt.

“Another thang, the double shovel happened to be a lot of help.”

“Never heard of one,” Freddie was preparing to attack the next bolt with the air gun.

“Guess not. You’re a town boy; never got learnt much.” Carl suddenly remembered that the double shovel went out of use before Freddie’s time. “It’s a two pointed plow, cleans out the balk.”

“Hmm, I’s raised in sight of where you’se raised.” The use of town boy as a negative didn’t sit just right with Freddie.

“That’s the truth, but town had moved out here by your time. I can remember when they weren’t two houses and a barn or two from here to the court house.” Freddie started the air gun. Carl just talked louder when Freddie hammered, but this thing was too much. He sat back and continued thinking about old times, not necessarily the good old days, just old times.

The next day, after having slept on it, Carl agreed to go to Florida. Freddie was to check the old car out and the voyage of exploration was to take place within the next few days. For the four, the trip was not equivalent to the first moon voyage or Columbus's journey of exploration, but pretty close. Carl was going to study their route in consort with the manager down at the service station. Amanda was to gather things necessary for the baby. Freddie raced the engine, drove around the block, applied the brakes going uphill and down to confirm the car's worthiness. He determined that replacing the oil and air filters and adding a second used tire for an extra spare to be sufficient preparedness.

Carl's lengthy questioning of the station manager and anyone else available gave him a vague knowledge of the route, sufficient to get them underway at least. Jellico Mountain, just over the Tennessee border, provided the first obstacle. The old Pontiac developed a loud grinding noise and they made several starts and stops, finally stopping at a service station where Freddie had to change out a front wheel bearing. Otherwise the old car proved most satisfactory. Carl napped scrunched in the back among the baby seat, a pile of diapers, and toys. Amanda chattered on and on about Freddie Jr., or about getting a tattoo, or the next stop for fast food. Freddie concentrated on the road, grunted acknowledgement to her comments, and speculated on how long eight hundred and fifty miles were and how many hours until journey's end. His awareness didn't allow his thinking about the Ponce de Leon visit in search of the fountain of youth or the Spanish rule of yesteryear. Neither was more foreign to him than his imagination regarding what was to come. He dreaded the alligators which some of the shop visitors warned about, but he sort of wanted to see one too. Sharks were something else. He had no desire to see them. Aunt Beck's tongue was another thing that bothered him. She always pointed out, in various ways and sometimes without coming right out and saying it, how dumb Amanda was and how sorry he was. Finally settling on the fact that it was to last only a week and that he'd get to see the ocean, he moved on to daydreams and to fixes for equipment breakdowns.

After eighteen hours on the road, which included several bathroom breaks and considerable driving around Sarasota looking for Beck and her sister's house, the weary travelers disembarked. "You're looking good, Carl." Minutes later just out of his hearing, Beck declared to her sister, "Did you look at Carl? Poor old thang, he's breaking something awful, ain't he?"

Early the next morning, Carl and Freddie talked Beck into walking them over to get a look at the ocean. Beck didn't bother to explain the Gulf of Mexico part with them. She'd never get it across. "Beck, I never thought I'd see the day, you and me walking right beside this big water. The sound reminds me a right smart of the spring tides back home when I was a boy. The water roared out of the hill behind our old home place."

Beck explained the clam digging. "Just scratch around in the sand and get your supper." Freddie allowed how he might be able to get by here. During the course of the morning, Carl got afraid of the crabs. He had seen something like that on TV that was powerfully dangerous. Whereas, Freddie was freaked by what he thought to be a dangerous shark swimming in the surf. Neither man ventured over to the beach after the first full day. Nevertheless, a week ocean-side has a way of slipping away—one day driving each way, one day on the beach, and four catching up on the news. Beck's sister had very little to add during their long gossip sessions. Beck said she was still broke down over the old man out in Arizona. She did spend considerable time caring for the baby while Freddie, Amanda and her aunt perused the tourist shops. Beck bought the baby an alligator bath toy and Amanda an ankle bracelet to match her own. They told stories, they sighed when appropriate, and they belly laughed when tickled.

When the company was saying their farewells, Carl thought he saw a tear well in old Beck's eye and thought of the old saying that *a tear from that eye would pizen a rattle snake* and he was glad a full- fledged tear didn't materialize to roll from her cheek and create havoc. The sister, he thought, just looked sad and maybe a little worried. Amanda hugged and patted the women. They patted back, but didn't hug that much. Each tickled little Freddie Jr. under his chin and they were off, cramped among baby things, a bag of sand dollars, and a small pail of sea shells that Beck would be for them to take back to remember the trip by.

Several tiring hours later, with Amanda at the wheel, the trip was dramatically interrupted. They weren't far south of Valdosta, Georgia. Carl and Freddie were asleep when the baby dropped his toy alligator onto the floorboard of the car and began screaming. Amanda reached back over the seat trying to retrieve the toy and swerved over into the next lane causing another car to leave the road for several yards. No real harm was done, except a traffic safety officer failed to see the harmlessness of the act. He was on the entrance ramp with a clear view.

The stop, likely to pass as no big deal, turned more serious. Amanda's driver license had expired. After asking where they had been and where they were going, the officer decided the occupants might be high or transporting and decided to make a limited search.

"Hey, what's this?" The officer was feeling under the front seat. Duct-taped between the springs were several packages. He removed these, determined they were likely illicit prescription drugs and examined the seat on the driver's side. There, too, he found packages. Each was filled with pills of suspicious size and markings. Of course, all denied any knowledge. Whether the search was legal or not, no one asked, or knew to ask. The drugs definitely were not. It was alleged that the car belonged to Freddie.

What the officer didn't know was that the car had been sold for scrap and that there was no title or traceable record. Carl, his country gentlemanly manner touching the officer, convinced him to let Amanda and the baby go on home. Carl had the appropriate license and would drive. Freddie was to go to jail. Freddie had seen *Cool Hand Luke,* and *Down From the Mountain.* He didn't know if the chain gangs portrayed in those pictures were still operative, but he wasn't about to find out.

Before he could be handcuffed, he jumped the guardrail and tumbled over an embankment, then darted across a narrow bottom to a creek. Scared and not thinking things through before plunging in, he found himself in a deep hole of water somewhat over his head. Unable to swim, he was ready to give up, to be drowned.

By the second time he broke the surface, his mouth spewing water, he was expecting death. The whole of his life did not pass before his eyes, however. What did catch his eye was a fallen tree, its trunk embedded in the bank, and angling under water in his direction. Kicking, splashing, spewing, he managed to grip a tree limb submerged a few inches below the surface and begin pulling himself toward the creek's edge. He heard the officer say, "Man on the run; bring the dogs." Another voice answered, "Copy, over and out." He assumed the remainder of this conversation had taken place while he was under water, walking the muddy bottom of this unnamed creek. Not only were the dogs coming, he was pulling himself along the downed tree toward the creek bank on the side where the officer stood by the car fifty or so yards away.

Carl and Amanda were released and told to go, something an experienced officer would never have done. But the officer had his hands full trying to retrieve the escapee. By this time the rookie officer, who ordinarily served as dispatch for the local sheriff's office, had blundered more than once. He failed to get Amanda's name or address. Carl's driver's license was checked, but address and specifics were not recorded. He felt both exhilaration and concern about the search. He'd found drugs, but was it a legal seizure?

Meantime Freddie had no alternative but to move closer to the officer if he was to survive. He kicked and pulled along the tree limb to trunk to bank, pulled himself up, gained footing and began running downstream along the creek's edge. Seventy-five or so yards along he spotted a shoal, rocks showing the width of the stream. Plowing ahead, he slipped, jumped and managed to reach the other bank. Not knowing how long it would take the other officers to arrive with the tracking dogs, he ran on.

For the second time in less than a year he was running, this time through a narrow strip of woodland that lay parallel to the creek, running not for his life, but for freedom. He had no idea where he was, only that he had to get through a part of Georgia and across Tennessee. He could tell by the sun that it was getting very late in the day and that he was traveling north, hopefully toward home.

Finally, his legs giving out, he collapsed against an embankment at the edge of an open field and rested. Dusk had surrounded him when next he was aware. A dog was barking and not too far away, he judged. Scrambling up the bank, his head first appearing over it then his body, too late he recognized that a skunk, its head down, tail up had him in its sights. He got the full spray. Realizing there is not much else a skunk can do to a full grown man, he ran directly over it. The smell was suffocating with no let up the farther he ran. A thought came to him: dogs likely didn't like skunk smell much better than he did. Perhaps the hounds would purposely lose his trail or the trail be masked by the smell. He never knew for sure, but he ran late into the night, through row-crop fields and pasture land, falling into drainage ditches, straining to use what little moon-light was available. He never heard the dogs again.

At last, crossing a fence into an open field he began to relax a bit, to feel a little safe. Growing up in rural southeastern Kentucky, most people experienced the thrill of riding or at least knowing the horse. Not Freddie. The fence he had just crossed was boundary for a bay gelding with white blaze and one white stocking, unseen as yet by Freddie. He was a lonely horse with no pasture mate of any kind. He looked on any intrusion into his domain as an opportunity to get acquainted and play.

Freddie first noted something amiss when thundering hooves came galloping across the meadow, the horse sliding to a stop just inches from him. Immediately the horse wheeled and ran away traveling in a great circle only to come back at full gallop, tail in the air. It was very nearly a scene from the *Ghost Riders in the Sky* song, sparks flying from their horses' hooves, a song which Freddie was fond of. Not knowing what to do, he began jumping, waving his arms and yelling; "Whoa! Go away!" As part of his game, the horse veered just missing him and at a barely safe distance, kicked his heels and rump high in the air. At mid circle, the horse stopped and snorted loudly. Freddie decided this would be the final charge and began running toward the far fence. Reaching his destination before the horse resumed play, he leaped high as he could and struck a board at the top of the woven wire. A big part of his chest was over. He wallowed on across. He had visualized either his drown or hoof-beaten body during these past hours. His heart beat faster just thinking about it. After running, walking, sleeping in that order, he stumbled on to a blacktop road mid-morning the following day. It appeared to be running a little north, a little west in his estimation.

"What on earth? I believe we have a skunk in here," the petite lady managing the mission clothing outlet declared. Freddie had stumbled into the little crossroads community along the blacktop and found the mission. Visitors moved to the other side of the room as he searched the shelves for clothing. Gathering an outfit, he asked the price, but the lady forfeited, instead suggesting he go along outside. At a service station food mart across the street, he purchased a large can of tomato juice. The attendant said, "Buddy it may take more than one can," as he held the door open encouraging him to leave.

Waiting until an occupant exited the bathroom at the side of the building, he had crept close enough to catch the door before it closed. He understood that no way was the attendant going to extend the skunk-man a key. In the bathroom, the door locked, the skunk-man undressed and rubbed and poured the tomato juice head to toe. The juice application was simple; getting it off was the problem. The sink didn't lend itself to body rinse so he splashed water from the faucet as best he could. When he left the bathroom, his old clothes in the waste can, tomato juice and water covered the floor and most of the walls. The room not clean and never inviting, was now virtually uninhabitable. Too late the attendant caught on. Freddie was gone.

^^^

Carl was worried about Freddie as if he were his own boy. He called Beck to see if she had heard anything. He didn't dare call the Georgia authorities. "Hello. Beck, You heerd any thang of Freddie?" After a detailed accounting of events since leaving her house and confirmation that she knew nothing of Freddie's whereabouts, Carl made a decision. "Beck, did you hide them drugs in our car?"

"Now Carl, you know better than to ask me that. I never double-crossed a friend in my life. Even if I was still in the business, you know any such poor hiding as that was not my way." Some people one knows intuitively not to trust. Beck was one of those people. Carl read people like he read the land, read his livestock, read a trader appraising his goods. He might not be capable of naming or explaining this gift, but he knew he had it. Contrary to logic, Beck was innocent in his opinion. Later he called her again to apologize for his suspicions. She had gone to the store and Amanda's mother answered. When he hung up he wasn't at all sure about Sis's innocence in the matter. Maybe Beck was better at lying, and Sis wasn't as capable, or could Sis have acted alone?

^^^

The trip home likely would have been much more difficult for anybody but a *survivor.*

Freddie smelled a little better, but home was still a long way off. How far away he was from the deputy and jail he wasn't sure. By midday he was on the outskirts of Valdosta, the interstate in sight. Knowing he couldn't walk or hitchhike along the interstate, he settled on a bench inside the Love Truck Stop just off the entrance ramp. He hoped for a ride offer from some generous soul, but wasn't sure how to get it. A driver for Walmart happened to be discussing a truck problem he was having with the manager within Freddie's hearing. "I've got a bad hydraulic leak on my trailer lift. You got anybody here who might be willing to take a look at it?"

"I'm sorry, sir, our only mechanic is out on a road call. You might call over to Good Year. Sometimes they send a man out."

"Thanks." The man walked past Freddie looking disappointed. Walmart trucks move on a tight schedule. He had a deadline to make connections at the distribution center in London, Kentucky. Of course, Freddie wasn't privy to this information, but he summoned enough courage to approach the man.

"Sir, I might can fix your hydraulics." The man looked askance at the beggar, skunk-man.

"Oh, yeah, what makes you think so?" Freddie took considerable time, the man thought, to organize his words. "I got a garage." That established, and with no alternative close at hand, the driver led his find, the perfect picture of a real-life *swamp man*, to the rig. The burst hose was quickly removed, the leaking section cut away, and with the manager's permission Freddie used Love's shop press to add new couplings. The pleased driver was ready to motor toward London, Kentucky carrying his new passenger riding shotgun. Freddie was thankful and asleep after a few miles. He awoke at the truck scales near the Kentucky/Tennessee line. He worked out his itinerary in his mind. Get close as possible to the rehab center, have the driver let him out, walk the remaining leg, and ask Mr. Keith to deliver him home.

^^^

"Freddie! How nice to see you! What brings you in today?" Keith was busy writing in a folder. He thought Freddie looked a bit frazzled and tired. He began to think he smelled a faint skunk odor.

"I wanna git home." Freddie's full answer to the question must wait to be delivered on the way home.

"Do you want me to drive you home?" Keith was busy, but an hour or so out of his afternoon wasn't that much. The request came from a former client who he understood had done okay and who appeared to be in distress.

As Keith stopped the car in front of Freddie and Carl's shop barn, Freddie noticed a newer model pickup truck parked near the entrance. Carl was sitting on his bucket and a youngish man was leaning against the open barn door. Freddie thought about running, but noting the Kentucky dealer tag on the F150 diesel, he decided to chance joining the two. Carl shook hands with Keith, thanked him and invited him to sit a spell. Keith declined, saying he had to get back. Freddie moved toward the two men, his head held high, his chin jutting. A casual observer might have thought he was trying to impersonate a military drill sergeant. Actually, it was much more important than that. He was returning as the man who had out-foxed the *Hound of the Baskerville.* Not only that, he had faced a charging *War Horse,* then proceeded to outrun it. Unlike *Don Quixote* who was confused about the damsel in distress, Freddie sent his damsel home while he remained to settle the score of the ages. Freddie didn't exactly have these thoughts. His demeanor merely indicated that he might have.

"Freddie! Freddie! I'll be dogged! I was sure you was in jail in Georgia. Son of a gun." Old Carl was so glad to see the younger man that he almost hugged him. Instead he gripped his arm and sat back down on the bucket to continue the conversation. "Mister, if'n I paid such money as that for something, I'd want to live in it, raise corn on it, or sell a heap of goods out of it." The man was trying to sell Carl the F150 truck to replace the old 1979 Ford that the boys had wrecked on the night of Freddie's one-sided altercation. "Hadn't been for that rogue nephew of mine, I wouldn't even be in the market."

"Mr. Carl, this isn't 1979. The market has changed. This truck is only four years old. It's a diesel, four-wheel-drive, with tilt and cruise, and a CD player. Nineteen thousand is a good price. Look here at the blue book on that baby."

"Hold it just a minute. I ain't even sure what all you're talking about, but I'm sure of one thang, I don't need 'em."

Freddie moved on into the shop, leaving the men to haggle. He wanted to see that everything was in order.

Later that evening, Carl brought him up-to-date on the Georgia mess. The sheriff's office had little to go on except the license plate which could be traced. Fact is though, the old car had been sold for salvage. Freddie had attached the plate from that wreck on to another wreck. When the appropriated plate was followed up on, it turned out the owner lived over in Lincoln County, but had been in Afghanistan for several months. This the Georgia official learned by phone from the sheriff in Lincoln County, the plate's previous owner's home county. Freddie, the survivor stood tall and free once again.

# CHAPTER 38

## Twin Maturity

"Move to the back, boys. Let these men in, new recruits." The deputy jailer laughed as he said the last. The twins were anything but recruits. They were being stabled by the state, compliments of the grand jury. Subject to the upcoming trial, they might be county-fed for some time. Earl, the larger twin, whispered to Jerald, "Which one you think you'll have to whup first?"

"I ain't picked him out yet." The boys were nervous, and though neither would admit it, they were also scared. Their circle of friends had just as many tattoos, big arms, and missing teeth as anyone in the huge holding cell. If necessary, they'd likely hold their footing. This section of the jail held forty-five prisoners mostly for drug-related charges, if you included theft under the influence as drug related. Thin mattresses were stacked in the hall just outside. Apparently there weren't enough bed accommodations.

Jerald pointed this out to Earl. "Which one of these buggers you gonna bed with?" His twin snickered at Jerald's remark.

"I'd hate for Dad to see this," Earl responded. "That little tad of meth sure brought on a tangle of inconvenience. Unk' and Mom may not be able to solve this. It'll take more than a statement and a signature." The twins knew their mother and uncle had anteed-up several times before, but those cases weren't this serious. Cash bonds hadn't been required.

"I kind of like this jumpsuit. The color orange don't suit me much though." Jerald was trying to joke and think about something besides his dad.

"Listen up, boys. Hank here will give you the protocol." With that the jailer shook his keys, attached now to his belt by a leather strap, then waddled off down the hall, his consumption of jailhouse macaroni and cheese showing.

Hank began his tutelage, "You men are new. You might note we run a clean house here." Sure enough the overcrowding had no adverse effect on order and cleanliness. "You'll be assigned certain duties. Bathroom duty goes to the new neighbors." A chuckle in his voice was accompanied by an assortment of snickers from the inmates standing close by. "We eat at seven, eleven-thirty, and five-thirty. Snacks between are your responsibility. The deputy will deliver them on request, and, of course, cash up front. Any questions so far?"

"Yeah, do we ever get to stretch?" Earl brashly posed this, really meaning is there an exercise room or walking track.

"I'll get to that," Hank continued, "You can visit the library anytime during the day." The room contained seating for ten, books for a few more, and two laptops without internet access. That didn't matter much to Earl and Jerald or most any of the inmates whose time and interest for study and learning had passed. Most of them considered one smart or not smart and made no connection between study and knowing. Others, who might have been scholars in earlier years, were now slow at comprehending, their minds racing wildly or dulled, preventing concentration.

^^^

"Come over here and sit down a minute, Boy." Earl looked at the man sitting at the table. He had faced down bullies, even bullies with big biceps. This guy didn't look all that tough.

"What do you want?" The two were the only ones in the weight room.

"I want to arm wrestle you."

"Sure." Not knowing what was coming, Earl saw no alternative. He also thought that just maybe he could win. He had worked out daily since lock-up, bench pressing nearly two hundred pounds earlier that day. What he didn't know was that his opponent had bench pressed over three hundred pounds daily for years.

"Left or right? It makes no difference to me." "Right, if you don't care." Earl began to have second thoughts as the man took his hand, and he had opportunity to see the bicep a little closer.

"Count of three. You count."

"One, two, three." Earl dragged the count out as long as possible before throwing every ounce of his strength into his right arm. His hand and forearm were slammed hard against the table top. His opponent stood over him, reached and got a handful of his shirt front, lifted him from his chair, and stuck him to the wall behind the table, pressing his body against Earl so he was unable to kick or to move either arm. After what seemed a very long time, the man spoke.

"My name is Joe. They call me Big Joe or Mr. Big Joe, if I wish." With that the man loosed Earl and he staggered against the table. "Now what I've demonstrated to you, little brother, is just how tough you are. Got the message?"

Earl nodded, but didn't attempt to speak. "I know your name is Earl, but I'll be calling you Little Brother. Listen up and I'll explain things. You see, I've got a group here. We meet every Monday evening down in the library." Big Joe's voice got much softer, almost as though another man was inside him doing the talking. "The boys and I study the good book, the Holy Bible. I'd like you to join us. See if you like it. It'll do you good. I'm here from the state pen, farmed out so to speak. My time has been hard and long and it's not near over. Your time will probably be much shorter, but it'll seem long. Anyway, four years ago I became a changed man. Christ entered my life, and from that wonderful day, I've worked to pass his message along to the likes of you—a prison ministry, you might say." Relieved, but flabbergasted, Earl, still gasping, responded, "Sure, I'll give it a try."

"Listen to this," Big Joe began his teaching by quoting from a small pamphlet produced from his pocket.

^^^

Jail time for Earl and Jerald took different paths—Earl to preaching, Jerald to more of the same, only more sophisticated, ranging across the continent and south to Central America. As best he remembered, it began in the exercise yard. "What ya got in your pockets, Boy?" Jerald was stretched over a bench crosswise the back cutting into his spine as his head dangled toward the ground. A man held him by his hair while a second one twisted his arm.

"Got a credit or debit card? Momma gonna send you any money?" The two men both larger than Jerald dragged him from the bench pressed him into a near squat against the fence, blocking any surveillance.

"Hear, hear, Boys. What's going on here?" Grabbing each in turn, a third man freed Jerald. "Move along you two. Is this any way to treat a new neighbor?" Turning to Jerald, the man extended his hand, "I'm Iron Man. Sorry about your trouble. Some of the boys don't understand the welcome wagon concept. New arrivals sometimes need a little assist. You know what I mean?"

"Yes Sir. But why'd you help me?" Jerald, thinking of the man's safety for interfering, was considering the possible consequences for the intervention.

"I told you, Son, my name is Iron Man. Think about it." At this Iron Man smiled, not an almost laughing kind of smile, but a knowing smile that Jerald couldn't interpret. Then he spat on the ground. "I been watching you and your brother. There is a good chance I can be of further assistance."

"Like how?" Jerald had heard about jail-house ruffians, about the cons, about the rapists. Which one was Iron Man? "You gonna protect me, us?"

"No, no, no, I'm talking dough."

"Pushing? Inside? I don't think so." No way was Jerald going to involve himself or his brother either, in business sure to extend their stay.

"I'm talking about outside stuff. You'll be joining an outside work detail within thirty days or so. Wonderful experience, picking up crap along the roadside... You'll be proud. The community'll be proud. Life will be better for ever body." He grinned and looked away. Iron could have been making humor or being cynical. Jerald didn't speculate.

"How do you know I'll be on the roadside cleanup?"

"I'm Iron Man. That's how I know." Again he smiled the smile—supposedly clarifying any mystery. "Listen now. I've got a proposition for you. Once your detail is on the road, the deputy will grant certain rewards. For example, to enter a service station or country store for refreshments, that is, if you have money. Have you got any money?"

"No. Remember, I just lost it. My new neighbors took it. My brother might let me have a couple of dollars though."

"Okay, if you approach the deputy in a 'yes, sir' sort of way, he'll likely allow you to use the phone where you stop for refreshments. I'm going to give you a local number to call. No matter who answers, ask for Toad."

"Toad, what kind of name is that?"

"It's the same kind of name as Iron Man; that's an important point to always remember. Anyhow, that's no concern of yours." A man's name means something. Jerald's dad had always emphasized that. But he was speaking of name relative to action; Fred's a drunk, Ben's a good mechanic kind of meaning. Later that day, Jerald continued to ponder what the Iron Man/Toad names really meant. The only thing coming to mind: strong and croak made him smile, until he thought about it some more.

^^^

"Keep your bags off the ground. You'll tear holes in the plastic. Somebody will have to follow you. We'll be picking up paper and cans only to re-pick them up until dooms day." The deputy was somewhat ill-natured, Jerald thought. He'd already jumped on the whole crew because someone had placed a bag in the lane of traffic which had gotten scattered all over the highway. This might not be the day to ask for phone privileges.

By noon, the inmates were working in harmony. Trash bags were properly tied and placed a safe distance from the traffic along a five mile stretch of the state road—a bag every one hundred or so feet. Retrieving the cans and paper and pieces of old tires, a hub cap now and then, wasn't bad. The aluminum cans were prized. At the end of the day, the inmates were allowed to sell these at a recycling business and share in the proceeds. What Jerald hated was the road kill. If a possum had sun dried, it wasn't bad, but a recent kill, one swelled to bursting, its stench sickening, that was different.

"Hey, you environmentalists, what's the ruckus about?" Two men in the lead were in heated dispute. The deputy was leaving his air-conditioned perch to investigate. "Pick your end up, stupid." The two had come upon a deer carcass.

"Watch out who you're calling stupid. I ain't touching that stinking thing. I ain't stupid neither."

"Now, boys, remember where you are, out here in this beautiful sunshine. Better still, remember where you'd be if not here. Get you two or three plastic bags and make a body bag. How do you think the coroner deals with the dead he finds along the highway?" The deputy was hot and wanted to return to the truck.

"Sure, we'll put it in the back of the truck. It'll be stink, pull up, stink, pull up for the rest of the day. We'll be the lucky smellers." The two worked at the project, one holding his nose with one hand and poking, shoving, lifting with the other. They placed the so-called body bag in the truck as near the driver as possible.

Once the men had washed up, and grabbed their sandwiches from the truck cab, the deputy led them into the service station single file to buy drinks. He stood near the cash register carefully watching his charges to see that each picked up only what he intended to pay for and then paid. At the register, Jerald ask for and got permission to place his phone call.

"Hello. Let me speak to Toad?"

"Speaking, what do you want?" Jerald shifted his weight to the other foot. The voice was not all that pleasant, and he was uncomfortable. He really didn't know the reason for the call, but Iron Man had been insistent.

"Iron Man told me to call."

"Your name Jerald?"

"Yes, sir."

"I may have an opportunity for you. Interested?"

"I'll talk it over with you." Jerald suspected that he knew what the opportunity was, but was hesitant to say over the phone.

"It's in your line of work, good pay too." Toad had connections from Southeastern Kentucky to Nogales, Mexico. He needed men—tested, trainable men.

"You know I'm pretty tied up right now." Jerald knew no better way to express his position other than maybe say, "Buddy I'm in jail."

"I know. I've made allowances for that. Just give your forwarding address to I.M. I'll find you."

^^^

"I can't breathe." Jerald was on his hands and knees, dragging a heavy duffle bag by a strop over his shoulder.

"Gringo!" The voiced word hardly out, when the bag Jerald was dragging was knocked hard against him, pressing him flat on the ground, in the dust, face first. Coughing and sputtering, Jerald got back onto his hands and knees. If I get out of here and get my five hundred dollars, I'll see that Indian's head float. This was Jerald's first thought as he again began the crawl. He's too sorry to learn English, looks like he's been fed on green fruit—wormy and sour. Jerald moved forward a foot or so, dragging the bag. The supplier had said the cocaine and weed weighed sixty-five pounds. It felt like two hundred. Jerald turned his thoughts from the despised Mexican. He had seen the tunnels used by smugglers portrayed on TV—electric lights, room to roll carts on tracks, carefully designed walls with calculated ceiling supports, and ventilation. This one had no such amenities with barely a crawl space, dust sifting from the top, flimsy plywood and a limited number of spindly pine studs for support. A fan at each end provided virtually no air. He was told it was five hundred feet from the Mexican side to the U. S. His lungs, knees, hands, and shoulder spoke of miles, not feet. Jerald's jail term and encounter with Iron Man all those years ago were a mere visit to *Baskin Robbins* compared with this.

Surviving the tunnel had begun to consume Jerald. His mind played and replayed his bitter thoughts. This is my last trip to Nogales and that Mexican who shoved me. It'll be his last too, that is if I make it alive. Jerald had never killed or had anyone killed, and if he made it across or under the border, he knew he'd likely forget the Mexican. The supplier who furnished the infernal guide introduced him, called him Amigo. The rude savage hadn't had enough sense to shake hands. He just grunted. Gringo was the only word he pronounced that sounded familiar to Jerald. Mostly he just pointed or roughly shoved Jerald in the direction he was to go. Probably hadn't been out of the jungle before. These angry rumblings allowed Jerald to crawl a foot, then drag—struggling for a breath of air with each move, hot beyond burning, vacillating between his survival thoughts and seeing headless bloated bodies floating in a contaminated river.

^^^

The TV camera panned the applauding audience and settled on the central figure sitting behind an ornate desk of oriental design, colored bright yellow with green floral scenes painted across the front. The man behind the desk, Reverend Earl Sizemore, sat back in his chair, smiling, a hand raised in greeting for the studio and TV audiences. His suit, black and shiny, was accented by a bright chartreuse handkerchief folded into the breast pocket. This item matched his open collared silk shirt. Several years in these plush surroundings being idolized by a mass of people had let Earl erase his memories of trailer living and jail.

"Friends, friends, friends, let me first thank you for the generous donations that make this weekly broadcast possible. Without your love gifts, I could not be here with this special message of L O V E! " The word love was dragged out for emphasis. "For those of you here for the first time or who haven't viewed the show before, I want to introduce Sister Billie Jean, my lovely wife and yes, to thank her too. She is a full partner in this endeavor." Billie Jean stood and bowed low, first to Reverend Earl, then to the studio audience, and finally the TV viewers, her too-black hair falling across both shoulders in the performance. Her eyelids fluttered revealing enhanced lashes. The sweep of her hand in the beauty pageant wave showed the bright red nails, much too long for preparing scripts or much work of any kind. She blew a kiss to all. Diamonds on her fingers sparkled in the bright studio light, sparkled just as she and the reverend, too, sparkled in their own way.

"Members of the audience, viewers out there across America, Billie Jean and I have traveled a long hard road to get here. The lane was often muddy, boulders blocked us, sleet and rain hindered us. Men lacking faith held us back. But let me tell you something, love prevailed!" The audience burst into applause. "There is power in love! Where two are truly bound together as Sister Billie Jean and I are, the bond multiplies the strength! It is so much greater than just the separate use of each person's power. The world cannot prevail against it! Sister Billie, give us a few words, would you, Honey?"

Looking at the camera, dabbing her eyes, lowering her head, her shoulders shaking, Billie finally attempted speech. "My darling, what you just said touched me so." Sister Billie wiped her nose with a silk hanky, too chocked up to go on.

"Now, now, Sweetheart, just relax a minute." The camera focused on Reverend Earl. Rising from his desk, he moved to Sister Billie's side. "She loves you folk so much." At that the audience again broke out in applause, the praise team raised their voices in song.

"I'm okay." Sister Billie rose from her chair to stand by her husband, taking his hand and raising it high above their heads. She spoke above the singing and clapping. "Just now I was overcome, thinking about the hurdles we've bumped over, how you dear people, out of pure love, now make it possible for this our special man here to carry on." She swept his hand toward the audience. "Now that I've got my senses back, let me remind you that this program costs a great deal. Without your help, we cannot even be here next week. Please, please, please take the information scrolling on the bottom of your screen and contact us. As you'll note, money can be sent by check, money order, credit or debit card, or if you prefer, you can contribute on-line." Turning to her husband, "Reverend Earl, get back to your desk and preach to us." She blew him another kiss as she backed away and mouthed, "love-you."

After what he thought was a successful delivery of the word to the hungry, needy world, Earl walked to his car, whistling the tune *Just a Walking in the Rain.* Sister Billie's feet hurt, so he was bringing the car to the front entrance. From fifty feet away, he noticed a man leaning against the front door of his Escalade. "People don't respect anything."

Earl mumbled, to himself. The following thought wasn't much better. This 'cat' probably wants a handout. He surely knows by the auto—I take in, don't hand out. What if he is planning to do harm, one of those anti-everything, rabble rousers who doesn't like my message? Or possibly he plans to mug me.

"How may I help you, sir?' Earl squared his shoulders and put on his best smile. The man was clean, but not overly. He wore a coat with un-matched trousers, and a tie frayed in the knot, likely from consignment or Good Will.

"I'm here to help you, Earl."

No one, not even Sister Billie, had called him Earl in years. "Ahem, I beg your pardon. What is it you think I need?" Something about the shabbily dressed man sparked a spot in Earl's mind, like a smell that conjures memories of a boyhood toy or a view in a strange land reminiscent of something previously experienced. That was as far as he could go in identifying the stranger or solving whatever else was creeping around in his mind. The shoulder length hair, the full beard lying on his chest offered no hint. "Earl, you need a reminder, a course changer, a priority review." The man knew that Earl had no idea with whom he was exchanging words and he intended to remain unidentified as the discussion continued.

"Well, friend, let's have it. What do you know that I don't or that I have forgotten?" Earl was more relaxed now. The man apparently meant no physical harm. He, too, leaned, against the car, close to the man, indulging this strange person who felt a need to give advice, no matter the person, the topic, or the circumstance. The man beside him, his arms folded in front of his abdomen surely must be such a man.

"Earl, you've left your first love. The lane you're in bends toward the created, not the creator. Let's arm wrestle, Little Brother."

^^^

"I can't believe it." Carl spoke to no one in particular as his morning group gathered around the unheated stove at the store. He had seen on the news the evening before that the famous Atlanta preacher, Earl Sizemore, had been accused of mismanagement, tax evasion, and lavish living on funds solicited from religious followers.

"You might have expected it though. Remember how he was around here as a boy." Robert scratched under his felt hat as he spoke. "He probably ain't no different from the other'n. I heerd he's living up in a fancy hotel over in Owensboro or somers. Untelling how he's gettin' his money. What's his name?"

"Jerald, they's twins, Earl and Jerald. Had a good daddy," Carl continued. "I had mighty high hopes for Earl once he started preaching." Carl dropped the local newspaper from his lap and adjusted his straddle. "He was a preaching machine. I seed him down at Willow Grove git down on the floor by the pulpit, hold the mike with one hand, thump the floor with the other, and scream for the congregation to let loose. Lot of them did too. Some tore their shirt buttons off, pulled their hair, shouted, got up and jumped around. He got action!"

“I recollect he brought a lot of the drug people into the fold.” Robert, the same man who asked the twin’s name, spoke up again.

“You’re right. I had forgot that. He sent people out after them, called them ‘mobile ministers.’ Baptized more people than all the preachers put together around here.” Carl looked off toward the back of the store, his eyes not focused on anything in particular. “I had a mighty high opinion of the boy, at that time.”

A third man, Elmo, uncrossed his legs and began. “Them two’ll likely wind up about like they started when they’s living on you, Carl. They’ll be eternally chasing mammon. Ain’t a nickel’s worth of difference between ‘em to my way of calcalating.”

“Maybe, but I think Earl’s a good man at heart. He just got careless with his money-counting.” Carl could not dismiss Earl’s good work because of a money mix-up. “You watch and see. The giverment’ll give him trouble now.”

Tommy, a lean-faced man, sat slightly out of the circle, his usual place. As he readied to speak, he leaned forward, elbows on his knees, palms up to rise and fall with each word spoken. His adams apple moved up and down, but much faster than his hands. “I heerd they got no use for church or preachers, nohow.”

“Reckon what he’ll do if this sure enough blows up on him?” Someone from behind the stove asked.

“Don’t rightly know, Elmo interjected. “He might come back here and wash houses or something like that. He never did work. I doubt he knows how." The talk continued around the circle of men.

Talking more than any of the group had heard him during all their morning sessions combined, Tommy continued. "Betcha one thang, that high-heeled, slick-legged wife won't be coming back here." Several men nodded assent to this prediction.

"Ah, law. It's a hard world, men; hard to know what to thank." Carl made this comment, as he rose, gathered his newspaper and jar of Sanborn coffee and moved out of and away from the circle. "Better go. Freddie'll be looking fer me."

## CHAPTER 39

## **Old Carl's Kin**

"Get away! Out of the road, you bum." The driver had stopped on the I-75 exit ramp. A man in his forties who could easily pass for sixty-five stood near his lane holding a piece of cardboard, Penciled on the board were the words: "Hungry. Need help to get home." The words were hardly legible, the cardboard stained and torn on the ends. The man wore a moth-eaten toboggan, a worn and faded army coat, plaid wool pants with frayed cuffs, and tennis shoes, a gap between the sole and the top near his little toe area.

"You tight b…" Louie stopped short of finishing the final word. Something he didn't need was an altercation with some tight-fisted, know-it-all. He probably attended church, too, he thought. Raising a hundred bucks a day was no easy task. He had to have a few more than that if he ate.

"I thank you, Ma'am." The lady in a SUV slowed and handed Louie a five dollar bill.

"Bless you, Mister. Good luck." Now that was a churchy spirit. His own spirits lifted, Louie turned to face the next vehicle. The face he presented showed the wear of lots more than his forty-four years. His teeth were gone, his hair long over his coat collar and matted, his eyes dull. Old Carl's aging nephew, the one who was with the twins when they were raided for making meth, the one who wrecked Carl's truck, is no longer a boy, no longer making, and no longer in the old neighborhood. Every day the same, only the location and the jobs change. "Turning cardboard" as he and his friends referred to it, had been profitable enough for over a month. Before that he had walked the residential section of whatever town he happened to be in, seeking work—actually it was money he sought.

^^^

“Need me to clean your gutters, Mister?”

“Not today, I guess.” The elderly gentleman eyed Louie, not like he was trying to identify him so much as to determine if he might identify with him. Louie caught the look.

“Mister, I’m from down in Laurel County and don’t know anybody here. I hate to unburden on you, but I’m hurting. My wife is down here in the hospital having a baby. I have no work, and we have no diapers, baby formula, or anything else for a little one. Just a one day job, that’s all I’m asking for.”

“Laurel County man, you say.” The possible employer had traveled in his work and knew people in most of the surrounding counties. “Ever know any Beckams over there?”

“Heard of ‘em. Old man Beckam operated a feed mill as I remember.”

“That’s right, R. L. Beckam. I used to call on him when I was on the road. Small world isn’t it? How much did you say you’d charge to clean the gutters?”

“You want them washed as well as cleaned out?”

“Yes.”

"Downspouts, too?" Louie was working the old gentlemen, separating the job into parts, so as to charge for each part.

"Yes, the works." The man thought, what the heck? The guy needs work and is willing to work to help his infant and wife. Having the 'willy' to work went a long way in his opinion.

"I can do the entire job for a hundred and twenty-five. You furnish the ladder and supplies." The prospective employer thought the price a little steep, but he hadn't had any ladder work done for some time. Maybe the figure was reasonable.

"Okay, it's a deal. When can you start?"

"There is a problem, Mister. I'll have to do the work tomorrow. I'm scheduled to be back at the hospital this afternoon to sign a lot of papers."

"That could be a problem, but not an insurmountable one. My wife will just have to go it alone. We shop on Tuesdays, you see. I guess tomorrow is as good as today. What time can I expect you?"

"Is seven too early?" Louie knew these old guys got up early and respected that in others.

"No. No, seven is fine. My kind of man... Got a job to do, get up, and get at it early."

The next part was the hardest. Louie groped for just the right words. "Mister there's just one other thing. I hate to bring it up, but I have to. Is there a way you could pay me for half the job today? The hospital is requiring a fifty dollar deposit. I know that ain't your problem."

"Whoa, that's a little out of the ordinary, isn't it?"

"It may be. The lady at the desk said I had to pay fifty dollars is all I know."

"No. I'm referring to paying you up front for work not yet done."

"Yes, sir, I guess it is." Louie turned, his shoulders drooping and took a step or two to leave.

"Say you know R. L. Becham, do you?"

"Not really. My family knows all the Bechams though." Louie knew he had the man just where he wanted him. The man counted out two twenties and a ten and apologized for not having enough cash on hand to pay the full half of the hundred and twenty-five. The next sunrise found Louie in another town, another neighborhood, plotting strategy.

^^^

Twenty or so years earlier, the lane had already taken a dangerous turn for Louie. "Uncle Carl, why'd you stay here?" Louie and Carl were out in Carl's side yard in the shade of a June apple tree. Carl was peeling one of the yellow fruits, the peel coming off so thin Louie thought he could see through it. This was a short time after the twins' and Louie's release from jail, the meth and burglary charges and convictions finally paid for in full. He was glad, but not thankful that Uncle Carl was letting him stay a few days. Louie thought Carl might even be persuaded to buy him a car. This had gone through his mind more than once, so he was on his best behavior, acting interested in his uncle.

"Well, sir, I tried a move and didn't like it. My Uncle Josh talked me into going to Ohio back a number of years ago. I's about sixteen, I guess. He said he'd git me a job and he did. I worked about three months, made good money, too, but I's homesick. Never said nary thang about it though. One weekend my uncle was coming down to see about his place, the one right here where we're setting and I come with him. He had two or three other riders. I don't remember just who."

"Did he come back a lot?" Louie was wondering if he attempted to farm from that distance.

" 'Bout ever weekend for several years. It's hard to get this place off your mind. Anyway, that weekend, middle of June, leaves out, boys fishing, Mammy's garden-stuff in, and Pap's tobacco crop about ready to lay by. I thought it had to be the prettiest place this side of that beautiful home to come."

"Wasn't Ohio pretty? What town was you in?"

"Dayton." Carl paused and took out a twist of tobacco. "Yeah, it was right pretty, Miami River flows right through it, but the buildings was too close. It smothered me. I tell you, Son, when we hit town, here at home, it must have been eleven or twelve a Friday night, there's a sight I never hoped to see. You know the light on the Main Street down there by the courthouse." Carl gestured with his thumb in the direction of the courthouse. "By Ned, when I left there was a stop sign there on the corner, but it had been replaced with the yeller flashing light that's still there, too."

"That surprise you, did it?" Louie sat back off his haunches onto his rump in the grass, under the apple tree, in the shade. He inwardly smiled as he kept Uncle talking, winning his confidence.

"Dang right, it did. Never had been a traffic light in town. I'll tell you something else. The state had laid new blacktop and added a turning lane. It might have been Eisenhower's road program doing the work. I don't know." Carl took his hat off and ran his fingers through his thinning hair.

"Things had changed in a short time," He continued. Louie often thought about how nothing ever changed around there.

"That's what capped it fer me. I decided that if home was going to change, I's gonna watch it."

"Did you have any girl-friends in Ohio?" Girls were something Louie liked to discuss, be it Amanda, or any one of several who hung out down at Wendy's.

"Na, I's too busy working. I tell you something else, Ohio gals weren't as purty as ourn. These mountain gals, they make a show." After a pause, he added, "that is, them that ain't course like the Friedmont women over on the Creek."

Carl grimaced as he thought of the Friedmonts. Louie showed a sly grin. "Ever think about marrying?" "Oh, I could a married two or three times, I guess." Carl also smiled. He straightened in the chair. He'd never been one to take the initiative as far as women were concerned.

Trading cows was one thing, but courting was something else altogether. Two girls came to Carl's mind, one of the Stigalls and the youngest Pike gal.

Louie thought he noticed a slight flush on Carl's face, and decided this might get good. "How come you didn't?"

"Ay, never found one that suited me just to a tee. Some couldn't think about nothing but indoor plumbing, going to the store, or high heeled shoes. Others couldn't cook a thang." Carl cut a slice from an apple quarter and handed it to Louie, holding it between his knife blade and his thumb, then stuck the blade through the core at his feet and left it there.

Neither Carl's relationships to women, nor his relationship to place were easily explained. They were just part of him—women conjuring awe; place bringing comfort and security. These relationships had no known beginning and couldn't be aligned with a logical principle. Carl missed out on the woman relationship, but place continued to satisfy him—the bales of hay, the garden spot, the graying barn, the distant hills to rest his eyes on hiding something that he meant to look about some time.

^^^

The years after Louie gave up on Carl buying him a car had not been smooth:

"Hey, Mister, get up." The officer approached the park bench and began shaking the man sprawled there, wrapped in plastic. Not getting a response, he pounded the man with the palm of his hand, not too hard, but certainly sufficient awaken a heavy sleeper. "Wake up, Mister!"

Louie roused and began unrolling himself from the plastic. “What’s the problem, Officer?” Squinting, he asked, “You are a police officer, ain’t you?”

“You can’t sleep here, Buddy. City ordinance prohibits it.” The man had the look of someone who hadn’t been accustomed to anything much better. Louie rose from the bench, folded his plastic, picked up his cardboard mattress and stumbled off down the sidewalk.

“Hey, Mister, you can sleep down at the precinct, if you like.” An overnight holding cell was empty. The officer dreaded the ride, the warm car, the smell that was sure to penetrate his clothes and the auto upholstery, but he had pity on the man. He was obviously in poor health, cold and likely hungry.

“Sure, I’d like that.” Louie knew the bed meant a cell, thin mattress, and a locked door. It also meant donuts and coffee the next morning. Most precincts had those items—brought in by secretarial staff or officers who rose early enough to stop by their favorite coffee shop. That would hold him until the baker or grocer dropped something edible out the back door.

“Say, Buddy, could you lend me a buck?” After coffee and donuts on the front steps of the precinct, Louie made his way through mid-town working the early morning walkers on their way to work.

“Look, Man, if I had money to give to such as you, do you think I’d be out this early, going to work?” Sidestepping to keep from passing too close, the walker passed on.

“Yeah, yeah, I know you got bills to pay.” Louie mouthed these almost in a whisper. Breathing was hard.

His energy sapped even before the day really began. People, buildings, autos all were a blur.

"They told me over at the health department that my sugar was out of control. I went in to see about my eyes. They hardly looked at them." Louie was sitting on a low wall that ran along in front of the church where the volunteers had fed him and thirty or so like him.

"Sugar, you say? What about it?" The man sitting on the wall right next to him, who had also dined in the church, stopped talking to himself long enough to respond to Louie.

"They take blood, test it, and tell you if your sugar is out of whack. Mine, they said, was averaging over five hundred. I guess that is high enough for them to say it's out of control."

"They got your blood?" The man's eyes were open wide, wild looking. He got off the wall and hurriedly walked away leaving Louie by himself, to his thoughts, thoughts that included where he might spend the night and whether he had energy enough to get there. Even in his mind, Louie didn't go back home. He didn't think about old friends, about jobs he'd had, encounters with others like him, or the drugs that paralyzed his reasoning. His thoughts ranged to the next meal, a place to sleep, and the police. Looking first one way, then the other he, too, left the wall and stumbled, he hoped, toward the next hand-out, the next meal. His main fear was falling into the grasp of someone needlessly violent.

The lady on the bench in front of the library next to Louie was singing loudly what she called opera. Her black dress, once a garment for evenings out, was spotted, stained by months-old food droppings. Her hat was adorned by half a feather, one chosen from under the pigeon roost located somewhere over the library doorway.

Louie removed his right shoe and what was left of a sock.

"My toe feels funny."

The lady glanced over at the foot and its blackened toe, but continued to sing. In exactly the same singing voice, loudness, pitch and all, she queried, "Dirt or rot?" She was busy trying out for an important part and didn't have time for further discussion. The imagined judges were walking by, some shaking their heads, none of whom wanted a closer encounter with either of the two.

"Lady, I merely said my toe don't feel right." Louie spoke much louder this time. He didn't appreciate judgmental people, especially someone who thought she was singing for an opera try out in front of the public library.

In her same sing-song voice, she said, "I heard what you said. Now cover that nasty thing up or I shall call the stage manager."

Louie shifted his perch, put his sock on and replaced the shoe. "Oh, boy, I can't take more of this!"

"Adios, Dirty man." The lady then announced what she said was the opera's final love scene and continued to sing.

By the time Louie made it around behind the grocery, darkness was close. Once there he peered into a trash can, but finding nothing he cared to sample, moved on to the large bin. He moved a crate in front of it, and climbed on where he could look over the lip at the contents. A perfectly good looking grapefruit, he thought, was lying to the rear of the huge smelly container. He leaned forward, pushing and pulling until lying half in half out, the prize was within reach. As he reached, however, darkness became absolute. It was not the natural phenomenon associated with night. It was from within. Louie suddenly saw nothing, heard nothing, felt nothing.

"What's that?" Sergeant Clemons was speaking to his partner.

"What's what? I don't see anything." The partner was surveying the rear of the store. All doors and windows appeared closed. No one was around.

"There, hanging out of that trash bin." What the partner finally saw, he likened in his mind to the teenage prank where two dummy feet and legs stick out from the trunk of their automobile. The two men, making their nightly check around businesses in their precinct stopped the car and walked cautiously to the bin.

"It's a person!" Clemons announced, his voice a little more animated than usual.

"It doesn't appear to be trying to get in or out either," the partner noted.

"You get the legs. I'll get on the crate and hold his underarms to prevent his falling. I assume it to be a him." Once Louie was retrieved from the dumpster and placed on the concrete beside it, the partner checked for pulse as he dialed 911.

“This may be difficult. He doesn’t seem to have any identification on him.”

The sergeant straightened, shaking his head. He backed away a couple of steps before letting go his nose.

The ambulance roared around the corner of the building, diesel smoke puffing from the exhaust, red lights flashing, and siren blasting. The emergency team quickly had Louie loaded on a stretcher and placed in the vehicle. As the driver pulled away, the EMT was listening, his stethoscope pressed to the man’s chest. The officers didn’t know whether Louie was dead or alive. The emergency team didn’t say.

## CHAPTER 40

### Amanda Takes a Turn for the Worse

"Get up, slut. Your big rear end is showing." The man had felt differently about the rear end only minutes before. The woman, whose name he didn't know, didn't respond. She was bleeding from her nose, her lips were bruised and swollen, a gash over the brow had begun to ooze, and her bra strap was broken. "You ain't hurt that bad. Quit playing possum on me." With that, he gave Amanda a kick in the ribs. The man, having adjusted his belt and putting on his shirt leaving it unbuttoned, turned and left the room, actually a boxed-in shed in an alleyway off Main Street.

^^^

Amanda's last trip south all those years ago had not been planned or easy.

"Hey, Auntie, guess what?"

Beck didn't know what and didn't care to guess. Amanda probably needed money.

"What is it, Amanda?" Beck seldom welcomed calls from her niece.

"Me and Freddie, Jr. are coming to see you."

"Sure enough? When?"

"Right now, we're in, Sarasota. I's just calling to see if you and Mommy was home."

“Yeah, we’re home. Come on.” Even though she consented, Beck was dreading their arrival. Ten year old Freddie, Jr. would be into ever thing on the place, go through her drawers, misplace her hedge trimmers, and whatever else he took a notion to play with. Amanda never noticed and Beck couldn’t be everywhere all the time watching him. At least she’d have a few minutes to hide stuff. She and Freddie had been down a couple of times in years past. On their last visit, the little brat broke her best Scottie dog, one left over from her flea market days. Amanda hadn’t really planned a trip to Florida. It just happened.

“Let’s take a trip,” Louie had said. At the time he was doing pretty good, plenty bad enough, but not as bad as he had been nor as bad as he would finally be.”

“Where to?” Amanda was high. The two had romped and frolicked on the creek bank since early morning.

Louie had come strolling in to her house that morning and announced “I’ve come to make your day.”

“I bet you have.” She knew Louie wasn’t talking about her day, his maybe. “How you plan to make my day? Umm what’s that I smell?”

“I’m taking you to the creek, just like old times.” Each gave the other a knowing look before Amanda began gathering towels and a blanket. It had been years since she, Louie and the twins had run the roads together.

Amanda was thinking, as she hurried through the house and advised Freddie, Jr. not to leave the house or yard, that she had missed Louie. He looked ragged, but not a lot different. His round head still fit tight, close to his shoulders. His blue eyes were still pretty.

^^^

Somewhere near Chattanooga, Louie suggested they stop at a rest area. His morning fix and the smoking were wearing off and Amanda was sleepy. She'd been driving the old car all morning. Freddie, Jr., asleep in the backseat, his baseball glove still on his hand was resting on his cheek, mostly hiding his face from her view in the mirror.

"I'm gonna take a walk while you all rest," Louie said as he climbed from the front seat. Amanda quickly fell asleep.

"Mommy, I'm hungry."

Amanda, still sleeping, heard words, but failed to get the message. Freddie, Jr. was peeking over the seat.

"What'd you say? Where's Louie." Amanda awoke confused, not sure just how long she'd slept or where she was. She looked around the rest area and wondered what time it was.

"I said I'm hungry. I ain't seen Louie since I woke up." Freddie was using his petted voice, a whine actually.

"Okay, Honey. Let me get you something from the vending machine." Rummaging in her purse she found it empty of coin or bill. Slowly it began to occur to her that they were miles from home, hungry, with a quarter tank of gas and no money.

"Freddie, reckon he's gone?" Some people were just not dependable, even during the good times.

"I don't know. Don't see him nowhere." Freddie, Jr. craned his neck, looking past the vending machines, then up and down the main road, now taking on the little man attitude on seeing his mother's concerned expression.

"Well, this is a good fix!"

Amanda decided to wait around for an hour. If Louie wasn't back, she'd have to figure a little on what to do. After nearly an hour, Amanda made a decision. She'd go to Aunt Beck and Mommy's. But how was she to get there with no money and no gas? The condition of the old car wasn't a consideration.

She decided, I'll do what Aunt Beck'd do. "Honey, just hold on a little while. We'll get us something to eat. Do you need to pee before we start?"

Once they started, Amanda wanted to keep moving. It was getting late in the day and where she planned to go might close early.

"No. I'm hungry though." Freddie, Jr. was back in his petted mode.

"Hid'dy, I'm Amanda and this here is my boy Freddie, Jr." The church secretary looked up from her computer screen and smiled. Luck was with Amanda. The most gigantic church she'd ever seen was located just off the exit ramp, and she aimed to tap it for funds.

"How may I help you and your son, Amanda?"

The secretary had seen too many transients, being so close to the interstate. These two fit the profile.

"Ma'am we're trying to get to Florida to see about my sick momma, but we've run out of money. I's wondering if your church might help. I've got nobody else to turn to and my little boy is hungry."

Freddie Jr. didn't look like he'd missed too many meals, but he chimed in. "Ma'am, I don't remember when I eat last." Freddie's lower lip stuck out and quivered as he spoke. Amanda had sounded pitiful when she said "sick mommy."

"I'll need to call Pastor. Please be seated. This shouldn't take but a jiffy."

Into the phone Amanda heard the lady say: "Pastor, we have a mother-son couple needing financial assistance. Do you wish to see them?"

Of course, Pastor did. He controlled the cash box under all circumstances.
The transients were ushered into the plush surrounding of the pastor's office. Preparing a good sermon came easier with wide screen TV, aquarium, velvet drapes, and gold desk ornaments. A lady in a long flowing skirt, her hair done up in a bun, stepped quietly out a side entrance to the study as the two took seats in front of Pastor. Amanda looked the man over.

She squinted, considered again and asked, "Earl, is that you?"

It was the Pastor's turn to squint and examine. "Well, yes, that's my name."

"Don't you know who I am?" Forgetting that it had taken some time for her to recognize him, she was a bit put off. But she knew she'd taken the right exit. He'd have money.

"I know from the face that I'm supposed to know you. Help me out a little."

It had been nearly ten years. Amanda's hair no longer had the blue streak in it. She was heavier. Her face wasn't as crisp.

"I'm Amanda, Earl, for heaven sakes!" Earl had changed too, and wearing a dark suit, silk shirt with gold cuff links, he didn't resemble the Earl who had traipsed around the trailer in his shorts. He even talked different, she thought; however, she'd know that dimple and those fingers anywhere.

"Amanda! Well, I'll be. And this is little Freddie?" He stood up, shocked.

"I ain't little." Freddie resented the comment.

"No, son, I didn't mean you are little now. You were just a baby last time I saw you." Pastor Earl's demeanor changed somewhat. He wasn't one hundred per cent sure just whose little Freddie really was. After all he, Louie, and Freddie had all spent a great deal of time with Amanda. A planned shake-down came to his mind.

Thinking he'd just as well get on with it, he asked, "Amanda, what in the world brings you to Tennessee?"

"Me and Louie and Freddie, Jr. was just out running around. Louie disappeared." She looked down and twisted her bracelet. Left us at a rest stop... Don't know where he went or what he was thinking leaving us stranded like that. I ain't got a dime and we want to go see Mommy and Aunt Beck"

"Louie." Earl paused and tapped his desk with a pen. "I hadn't thought of that dude in years. How is he doing?"

Actually, he was hoping that Louie didn't know about him being in this area. He definitely might try shaking him for spending money.

"Same old Louie. About as dependable as a feral cat, in my opinion," as Amanda said this she was questioning her judgment in running off with him. Never one to resist any show of affection, no matter how casual, she'd only now begun to question her actions.

"That doesn't surprise me. Say you're going to see the folks? They still in Florida?" Earl's spirits were rising. Apparently this was just a chance encounter.

"Yeah, I figure it's just as close to Florida as it is back home."

Earl smiled and nodded his head. He hesitated to ask how much money she wanted, but knew it would be more than it would have been had he been a stranger.

"So Earl, what's been happening with you besides becoming a big- time preacher? Are you married? Got any children?"

"Well, I'm not a big-time preacher, just pastor of this needy flock."

Earl was being modest. He knew he was big-time. His three thousand member congregation, few of whom were financially needy, confirmed this opinion. This pastoral call was the last before Earl's even bigger operation to come in Georgia. "Yes, I'm married to Sister Madge. She was just leaving when you came in. I wish I had recognized you and introduced you. You'd love her."

It, of course, was untrue. The less Sister Madge knew of his Southeastern Kentucky background the better. She was a hard, demanding woman intent on making something of him with her well-honed financial talents. That she had done, too, but not nearly the something he was to become.

A woman was out there in the not too distant future to fulfill that dream—Sister Billy Jean. Unknown to him, Billie Jean had heard him on the radio and attended a service to see him in action.

"No, Amanda, we haven't been blessed with children, yet."

^^^

Amanda's acquaintances over the years from Kentucky to Florida to Tennessee were seldom gentle. Amanda's short-time, brutal friend made his way from the shed to his old truck, his ladders hanging from bed racks; empty paint cans, their various colored dried spills showing. His shirt still unbuttoned partially revealed a tattoo. A passing observer might have guessed it to be a pirate head, but Amanda, who had been in a better position to view it, later declared it to be a likeness of Satan. The tough looked solemn, but held his head high as one looking across town or county. His expression, no contriteness showing and revealing no guilt over past deeds, thumped his right fist into his other palm as one who had just been mistreated might. All this time, he was thinking over and over, dirty whore bitch.

Amanda rolled over, got on all fours, and pulled herself up by the bed post. The bed was the only furniture in the room which was illuminated by a single overhead light bulb. "What's Sam going to say," she mumbled. She used the corner of the bed throw to wipe the blood from her face, put on a skimpy uniform—mini-skirt, heels, and see through blouse—and left.

Back in the room, a rent by hour, day, or week affair that she shared with Sam, Amanda washed her wounds and fell into bed.

Observing Amanda in bed on his return, Sam was confused. "What are you doing back?"

He had sent her on rounds earlier. They ordinarily lasted until early evening.

"I'm hurt."

"What do you mean hurt?"

Not having looked at Amanda, Sam was unaware of the swelling, the forming scabs, or the cut over her eye. She never got out of sorts with him. So the hurt part didn't register.

Sam moved to the bed looking down at her. "What in the world happened?"

"He whupped me."

"Who whipped you?"

"I don't know. You told me never to ask names." Amanda was crying now.

"Did you get the money?" Sam was going to be really mad if the bum had stiffed her, him.

"Yes, I got the money first, like you always told me to. It's there on the table." Sam managed the money. Amanda got her keep and a little spending change and drugs.

"What did you say to him?" Sam needed to know the exchange for future reference.

"I didn't say nothing. He just did his business, got up, put his britches on, and grabbed me by the hair and starting in beating me." It didn't register to Amanda that Sam had said nothing about her wounds or asked if she needed anything.

"Did you notice what he was driving?" He thought her answer might help him find the man whose actions were sure to cost him money. Amanda was in no shape to send out again.

"Yeah, I think he was driving an old Chevy pick-up with ladders, and paint buckets. It had paint spots and overspray all over it. I think it was black," Amanda said without raising her head from the bed.

"You'll have to lie in a few days. Nobody will want to fool with you looking like that. Freda can double up."

Sam picked up the money from the table, put it in his jeans pocket and turned to the door. His jeans had a hole near the back pocket showing a black undergarment, the cuff was worn through at the heel, the ragged part dragging along the tile floor as he left.

When Amanda awoke the next morning, her face swollen and her ribs sore, she realized that Sam's few things were gone. On the table lay a ten dollar bill and a receipt showing the room rent had been paid for another week.

^^^

"Please to wake up, Missy." The man addressing the woman was obviously not a Knoxville native by his talk. He was, however, someone with a background where down and out, hardship, and brokenness were understood. The woman lay on her side, her mini skirt pushed up showing her panties, a broken elastic sticking out away from her leg. Her camouflage shirt was pulled tight across her shoulders, a purse serving as her pillow.

"What?" Amanda roused, but barely.

"No sleep." The man had cleaned around her bench bed and now had to move on to other sections of the bus station. He had let her sleep the entire time it took him to clean the area even though it was against policy. The incoming clerk was likely to call the police.

Amanda weaved as she crossed the hard tiled floor to the door, her-high heels clacking, the noise bouncing back from the high ceiling. The heels showed wear, the plastic covering gone from each an inch or so above where they hit the floor.

"Spare a buck, Buddy?" Amanda accosted a man she passed. There had been few so late at night. A car passed filled with teenage boys.

"Hey, whore woman. How many times you been down tonight?" One of the boys yelled this then turning to the others who were laughing, said, "Old bitch must be sixty years old."

As Amanda walked, her thoughts concentrated on the next step. Freddie, Jr., Mommy, Aunt Beck, Freddie were all back there somewhere but didn't surface. She vaguely heard music. George Jones was singing *Choices* when she entered the all-night diner and pool hall. A man and woman were on the floor, moving as to dance. A couple sat on stools at the counter, another, his head down asleep beside them. Amanda slid heavily into a booth nearest the doorway.

"Mind if I sit, Honey." The lady who had entered the diner behind Amanda was dressed much the same as she, but she appeared younger. She sat without getting a reply. "You sick, Sugar?"

"I don't reckon." Amanda struggled to get this out.

"You look flushed like you're sick, " the woman insisted.

"No. The health nurse give me shots yesterday," Amanda said although she wasn't sure when the health authorities had caught up with her and given the treatments.

"Aren't you afraid of passing something on?" The woman continued to probe.

"No. One of them give it to me." Again Amanda's voice was weak, her tone flat. The woman slipped from her seat and moved to another part of the diner. On the booth in Amanda's line of sight a taped napkin was labeled with: "Call Skip for a good time" and a phone number. Amanda's head lolled over the back of her seat and she passed out for the third time in as many hours.

The male dancer loudly joined George, "*I'm living and dying by the choices I make*."

Knoxville had been a stop among many for Amanda over nearly a decade, a decade, that is, since leaving Freddie, Jr. with Aunt Beck and her Mommy. It would be her last.

^^^

"You're gona' have to get out and git a job. I ain't keeping you up, raising your youngen, and cleaning up after youens." Aunt Beck had puffed around the house for over a month now. Before that she had been civil enough to Amanda and her son, but six months was beginning to look like a move-in.

"I's out all morning walking, asking, and looking, then walking some more. I'm wore out." Amanda knew Aunt Beck's patience was wearing thin with their visit.

"Who'd you ask fer a job, the opera house?" Amanda had just been singing a medley of her favorite country songs, including John Connely's *Rose Colored Glasses.*

"No one. I went to Walmart, then to Wendy's and to Krogers." Amanda hadn't got past the check-out at any of the stops. She asked at the register if they had any openings and in each case was given the same answer: "You'll need to check with the office." Just as well, she thought, "They'd a wanted a drug screen." Mommy had given her a few dollars the day before to buy Freddie an outfit. It barely covered the pot she bought on the corner closest to home.

"You ain't got enough to git home on. I'm furnishing that boy's sorry daddy a place to stay back in Kentucky and you're gonna have to get out of here. I ain't made of money, you know." Aunt Beck was beginning to warm up. That discussion had happened just before supper.

After breakfast next morning, as Amanda left, her expression was serious, Aunt Beck thought. Maybe she is sure enough going to try and get work. That was the last time Aunt Beck, Mommy, or Freddie, Jr. saw her.

Beck called Carl after several weeks and no Amanda; these phone inquiries to Carl reported no sign of her in Kentucky. Beck had had enough.

^^^

"Hello. Yeah, this is Freddie." Beck was on the other end, a phone call that Freddie always dreaded; he'd hoped it was Amanda. Freddie had missed Amanda, but it was a sidling kind of miss. That is, it didn't just head-on knock him down. Early on, when they first moved in together, Carl had had to intervene, making him cancel her credit card and hide his checkbook. While Carl wasn't the type to make anybody do anything, he did have considerable persuasive powers, especially with Freddie. Amanda kept poor house and couldn't cook worth a dime. Freddie did nearly everything that was done for Freddie, Jr.

"Freddie, you gonna hafta get your sorry hind-end down here and get yer boy. His granny and me just ain't able to take care of him. Besides, he's your responsibility."

"Well, I guess he is—mine and Amanda's."

"Well, she ain't here." In the months since Amanda left with Louie, Freddie had heard from her only a time or two and then only through phone calls between Beck and Carl, and that before she dropped from their sight too.

CHAPTER 41

## Freddie and Buddy

Several weeks after Amanda's funeral and after Beck and Sis had returned to Florida, the repairmen's work rhythm resumed—Carl, Freddie, and Jr., that is. On this Monday morning Freddie arrived at the shop at just good day-light to build the fire and organize the day as was his routine. On this morning, however, a van was parked virtually against the entry.

"Freddie boy, come here." Even though he couldn't see the speaker or the driver, he recognized Buddy's voice and his vehicle. Buddy's attempt at sounding pleasant failed.

"What do you want?" Freddie asked as he moved close to the passenger window.

"I've got a business plan for you." Buddy nodded and smiled as he addressed Freddie. "Been thinking how hard you and Jr. work and how I could improve the cash flow around here, make life a little easier for you and the boy, you might say."

"I got a business plan." But Freddie's fear was rising. Just because Buddy was wheel-chair bound and at the moment latched to the floorboard of the van didn't preclude him from being dangerous.

"I know you got a business plan, but look at you operating out of a barn that is not even yours, greasy all the time, no vacation days. Son, you deserve better."

Freddie stammered, "This suits me."

"Let me put it another way. The Florida connection has taken me on, replacing whoever replaced old Beck, providing I can organize the couriers."

"I'm not interested." With that Freddie began unlocking the shop door, hoping he could scoot through with the van pulled so close.

"Listen, Hoss, talk's over. You are going to be one of my couriers."

"What makes you so sure?" Freddie's lip was trembling. His hand was shaking so hard the key missed the keyhole.

"Don't stand away from me. Come back around here where I can see your eyes."

Freddie did as he was told.

"Now listen. I'm going to say this once. Either you line up or something mysterious, bloody and frightening will happen, first to you, then to Jr., and finally to old Carl. You realize I can get it done too, right?" With that Buddy pushed a package into Freddie's coat pocket. "This'll get you started. See you Friday. You know how the business works. Go singing." After those words, Buddy patted Freddie's shoulder, then turning to his driver, ordered, "Get rolling. We've got people to see, arrangements to make."

Freddie didn't attempt the lock after Buddy left. Instead he walked around the barn past a John Deere backhoe, a Caterpillar Dozier, a tractor with a bush hog attached, each representing a job that needed to be started, today. He saw none of these. His legs felt numb, his steps short and feeble. The second time around the building, he stopped at his truck and leaned against the grill. It was too early yet for Jr. or Carl's arrival, still he looked first toward home, then in the direction of Carl's house before turning and leaning his head on the hood of the truck. He then began crying uncontrollably. I can't. I just can't. This thought kept going through his mind as he fought for control and for some idea as what to do. When the tears finally stopped, Freddie reached for the package Buddy had stuffed into his coat. Ripping it open, spilling several of the pills on the ground, he clasped two and swallowed them down. All this was done almost mechanically, giving the act no conscious thought.

Later that day as Carl walked over to the shop, he stooped to pull a dried horseweed beside the path near the back of the barn. When he looked up a red fox kit was peeping through a wide crack from the barn, the section not partitioned off for the shop.

"You little rascal, you know you're safe here, don't you? Well, I reckon you are. Ain't a fowl on the place now and I sort of like the looks of you."

That encounter was short-lived before he knew that Freddie was absent. It wasn't time for Jr. to be there, so he began trying to locate Freddie, first calling his home and getting the report from Jr. that Freddie had left for work earlier. Carl then called the store to see if he'd stopped there. Harm broke from the group around the stove and answered the ring as the proprietor was busy filling an order. "You seen anythang of Freddie?"

"Yeah, he was in here early this morning. Didn't say a word to nobody. Just got a pop and left. I don't recollect him even looking at any of us. Course I can understand that. We ain't much to look at." Harm laughed at his joke, and looked around to see if any of the other loafers considered it funny.

"Harm, if you see or hear tell of him, could you call me here at the shop?"

Without saying good-bye, Carl replaced the receiver and scratched his head under his hat band. Meantime Freddie was driving aimlessly along the country roads nearly two counties away and thinking. He couldn't let Jr. or Carl get hurt. His long ago experience with Buddy's violence was still fresh in his memory, as if it had happened only yesterday. No way was he going to endanger Jr. or Carl. If he was out of the way maybe Buddy would move on to someone else. Thus a plan began to emerge. Freddie drove several more miles, not knowing or caring exactly where he was or his destination.

Mommy's dead. I never knew my Daddy. Nobody can help. Buddy will kill us all. The shop will close. Amanda is gone. The twins wouldn't be no help. Earl's just a preacher. Jerald's gone. Louie wouldn't help if he could. Buddy needs to die. For some reason, Freddie's mind began running to boyhood years. He never thought of Mr. Keith, Deidra, Doc Lee, or Thad. In his desperation only one alternative made sense. It took hold, rushing through his entire being and congealing somewhere short of reason. The pills may have been fuel for such thought; however, circumstances were doing the driving.

Just ahead the road took a steep turn to the left. The straight between Freddie and the turn stretched five hundred yards or so and he could make out the tree line which defined the turn. He pressed the accelerator hard against the floor, gripped the wheel with one hand, unfastened his seat belt with the other, and sped directly into the trees, head-on toward a huge poplar. Inches before impact, the right front tire struck a limestone boulder large enough to turn the vehicle slightly. This threw Freddie hard against the door. On impact his body was flung from the truck and he lay quiet among the dried leaves.

Possibly ten minutes, possibly an hour, a day, Freddie wasn't sure, passed before he regained consciousness. The trees along the road looked so tall, so strong, their few leaves still hanging on so vibrant in the breeze; even the cattle grazing with purpose beyond the roadway expressed time, place, strength. These were miraculously there within his view and he noticed.

Alternatives to death that he'd been unable to conjure up earlier were now plentiful. I might call the sheriff. Carl probably can figure something. Me and Jr. can disappear. Freddie's lifelong standby won out in the end. He'd run.

The farmer mending fence on the far side of the pasture, home to the cattle herd Freddie was observing, heard the impact and rode his tractor around to offer assistance.

"No, I ain't hurt, just skint a little here and there."

"From the looks of your truck, you're a lucky boy. I'm glad for you."

The farmer reminded Freddie of Carl—his kindness, his desire to assist, his bib overalls and gum boots, his brimmed felt hat, his referring to Freddie as a boy.

"Where am I?"

Freddie remembered he needed to move.

"Well, Sir, if you go right yon-way about two miles you'll be in East Bernstadt." The man pointed in the direction Freddie had been traveling. "From there it's maybe five miles on to London."

"Thanks."

Freddie headed out toward the blacktop and started to walk away.

"Wait, son. It's just as easy for me to travel around the road home as to go back through the field. You can ride on the fender."

Freddie wasn't all that steady. His head hurt and he had to hold tight with both hands to maintain balance on tractor, but the ride reduced nearly a mile from his walk.

"What about your truck? Want me to call somebody when I get to the house?"

"No, thanks. I'll send somebody out from town," Freddie said, but his plan didn't include doing anything about the vehicle. Once he reached London late in the afternoon, and after dumping the remainder of Buddy's pills into a ditch line, he made his way to the bus station, purchased a ticket and made a brief call to Jr.

"Our money is in the bottom of the old tackle box, behind that old trunk. It's pushed back between two studs in the attic wall, on the right as you enter. Bring it, and meet me in Florida. Don't tell nobody you're leaving, not even Carl. Leave now."

Jr. didn't get to say anything but, hello. The silent phone left him baffled, but he knew Freddie's ways and hurried home to the attic, He was on his way within the hour, the old truck's tires singing on I-75, the well-tuned motor purring—he thought. Intuitively, he realized that he and his dad were going to Aunt Beck, the why continued to nag him, and why they weren't traveling together was unclear.

^^^

It had been a week and Carl hadn't heard a word from the two Freddies. He was sitting close to the phone in the shop, his cane leaned against the styrofoam wall. Both his hands were busy, knife in one, a cedar stick in the other when the door was flung open. Buddy in his power chair rolled in bouncing on the uneven floor, his driver close behind.

"Where is Freddie, Old man?" Buddy made no attempt at pleasantries.

"I don't rightly know." Carl spoke sharp, at least for him, as he folded his knife, dropped the stick, and brushed shavings from his lap. "Wish'd I did."

"Don't toy with me. Where is your ward?"

"My what?"

"You heard me! You ain't deaf," Buddy said, grabbing a hammer from the bench nearby.

Carl, detecting the danger, stood and attempted to back away, but was caught by his chair. Buddy swung hard striking the old man in his mid-section. Carl slumped to the floor. Buddy spat, looked at the crumpled body, and turned toward the exit.

That was early in the morning. Harm and some of the men from down at the store, as usual, came by later in the day to discuss the mystery surrounding Freddie and Jr's disappearance.

"I found him right there." Harm told the EMS driver as he pointed to a spot near the phone.

"Thought he was dead, a stroke maybe."

The EMS attendant thought that he was very near death as they loaded Carl onto a stretcher. At the hospital, doctors soon discovered Carl's injury and knew that it was from a powerful blow. Dr. Madden called the sheriff. "Some kind of a blunt circular implement was used to strike Carl in the stomach area. It stuck his belt. It likely blunted the force of the blow and saved his life. What quality the life will be if he survives, I'm not sure. The surgeons are working on him now."

Dr. Madden returned to his work. The sheriff brought in the state police. Even the county attorney appeared at the scene. An attack on a man of Carl's status, his gentle nature, and his age caused an outrage throughout the community.

Down at the store Harm declared that, "They ought to draw and quarter the devil that did that to Carl. You know what the scriptures say about people like Carl. *Rise up before the hoary head and honor the old man."* Others nodded solemnly.

A careful review of the crime scene including the parameter of the barn yielded a picture that didn't take long to interpret. The pills Freddie accidently dropped beside the barn, the wheelchair tracks leading into the work area, the van tracts in front of the premises, and the hammer on the floor provided solid clues pointing to a drug-related incident. Nobody suspected Carl of being involved in the trade. That left the two Freddies. They, too, were unlikely suspects.

"I'm thinking we ought to question Buddy Mustang. Rumors are always circulating about his business dealings," the county attorney said to the assembled investigators.

By the time the sheriff and his deputy reached Buddy's junk shop several hours after the attack, Buddy's rage had subsided and he was thinking much clearer.

"We've got to get away from here," he had said to his driver sometime before the authorities arrived. They were well on their way to Memphis when authorities entered the open but unmanned store.

^^^

"Oh, Sis, look who has come to see us two old women!" Beck had rolled her chair to the door, responding to the ring. She had one hand over her mouth. With the other she clasped Jr's arm. "Let me look at you." By this time Sis had rolled near. She began clapping her hands and laughing, more of a squeal than a laugh as she reached for Jr.

"Come over here and let me look at you, Jr. I never thought I'd ever see you again." Sis wiped her nose on her sleeve and leaned forward for a better view.

“Jr., what in the world has brung you to Florida.” Beck asked in a way that caused Freddie, Jr. to think she might be thinking he was in her old business.

“I don’t know for sure, Aunt Beck. Daddy called and said to meet him here. You heard anything from him?”

“Why no. How come you two didn’t come together?”

“I don’t know. He just said to meet him in Florida. Called me on the phone...”

“That sorry thang. It’ll be a wonder if he ever gits here.”

Beck turned her chair and moved toward the den, beckoning Jr. to follow and to sit on a chair between the two women.

Early the following morning, the phone rang and when Beck answered, Freddie’s voice came through. “Hid’dy, I’m here”

“Come on in.”

Beck was a little perplexed as to why he would call.

“I can’t find youens.”

“Where are you now?”

“I don’t know. I’m in Sarasota though.”

“Look around you and see if you can see a street sign.”

Freddie thought Beck spoke in a way that implied, "you dummy."

"Wait a minute. I have to put the phone down so I can look."

After some time Freddie returned, he said, "It's B something V I S T A," Freddie spelled.

"Go back and git me the spelling of the first word, and look on the buildings. See if they's a number."

After another silence, Freddie spoke, "It's Buena, I think. The number on this building is eight hundred and twelve."

"Stay put. Jr,'ll come and git you.

^^^

Carl was in surgery until late afternoon. Nurses were running in and out. Doctors were consulting outside the door, then re-entering, as the friends from the store waited. It was nearly five that afternoon when a team of three surgeons entered the waiting room. "Your friend is going to make it. The surgery was complex, its success questioned several times, in fact. His age was a factor, but he is tough." The speaker held up his hand, turned and left the room. The others followed. What the doctor didn't say was that Carl's spleen was seriously damaged and that a large section of his gut was removed, requiring a colostomy.

"Them boys looked mighty wore down, didn't they." Harm addressed the group. The old friends each expressing agreement, rose, shook hands all around, patted one another, turned their heads aside to hide their eyes, and shuffled from the room grousing as they left, "Don't seem possible this could happen to Carl!"

"Ah law, we don't none know what we'll have to face, yet."

"Can't see what's come over the young people."

"Dogged if I know what's gonna be done"

It was three days before Carl woke up, that is, enough to express awareness of those around him. He grasped the bed rail, pulled the sheet up under his chin, looked frantically around the room and quizzed the nurse, "Where am I?" The words which were attempted several times, came in a whisper, so the nurse had to lean close to understand.

"You're in the hospital, Mr. Carl. Just relax. We're taking care of you."

"Where's Freddie?" Carl turned his head left to right as though looking for the man.

"Freddie?"

"Yeah, Freddie Bird, my partner?"

"Oh, you mean the man who disappeared with his son."

"What do you mean disappeared?" The nurse, recognizing that Carl was getting more agitated from this line of talk altered her earlier response.

"I mean he is out of town. Authorities seem to think he'll be back in contact any time now."

Hearing this, Carl seemed to relax and was soon snoring.

Aunt Beck meantime had called her contacts back home and learned of the violence against Carl and continued her calls until she got the details regarding his condition. Freddie and Jr. were sitting at the breakfast table studying automotive repair manuals when she rolled into the room, bumping the table with her chair. Her face red, her wild eyes flashing, she slammed her fist on the table, raising substantial alarm for the two men. "I wish that rotten ass was right here." She extended one hand out beside her chair to indicate where. Then she made a circle with her hands, her thumbs nearly together and clinched them as though squeezing something.

"Who, Aunt Beck? What are you talking about?" Jr. got his voice first.

"That rotten, cowardly, scum, Buddy Mustang. Hell's waiting for such as him." After several questions Beck related the story that unfolded after the two Freddie's had left town, that Carl had been severely hurt by Buddy, that Freddie was briefly considered a suspect, and that Carl had recovered enough to clear matters.

"Is Carl okay?" Freddie finally asked.

"He's alive, still in the hospital in ICU, probably will be confined to a nursing home bed when they can move him." After those words, Freddie got up and walked slowly out the back door. The walk continued for some time.

I caused it. If I hadn't run off, Carl would be all right. Buddy Mustang ought to die. These thoughts reverberated through Freddie's mind.

It was dusk before Jr. found Freddie sitting on a bench along the boardwalk out over the marsh eyes red, and blotches on his face. Jr. considered him to be the worst out of sorts he'd ever witnessed a man.

"Dad, Aunt Beck wants us to come and fix supper." Freddie said nothing, but got up and followed Jr.

"Now, Freddie, what's done is done. You didn't cause Carl's problem. Buddy did. You couldn't have prevented if you'd been there." Beck said, working on Freddie.

"He'd a hit me, not Carl."

"You don't know that. Buddy is unpredictable, except we know he always picks on the weaker party. Listen to me, Jr. has got that car detailing job at Ford and you have a responsibility to help him learn the manuals so he can git on in the garage and me and Sis have to have you here, clear headed."

Beck looked at the floor and scooted her house shoe on the tile.

"Fact is, you're the best nursemaid, care-taker or whatever you call it in the state of Florida."

Beck rolled off toward her bedroom.

^^^

Buddy Mustang, talking with a man through the window of his van in a parking lot somewhere in Memphis, got a disturbing report.

"Uh-uh, no, no, no. You can't unload that stuff here, no way."

Buddy was intent on selling the drug inventory that his controller had fronted back in Kentucky.

"Word is out, man. The governor with all his power wouldn't even touch that stuff, even for evidence against you or me. You, Slick, are a man outside, sort of like a man without a country, know what I mean? If I were you, I'd go deep, hide good and long."

Buddy's driver hearing the discussion made a decision right there in the parking lot. He'd try to save himself. He'd call the Kentucky authorities. Buddy's mind was running along the same line. After considering his plight, Buddy took the initiative and made the suggestion that they turn themselves in and hope for leniency in the courts. At least they might escape the frightening retribution sure to come from the controller. Some things were worse than prison. They had the dope. To finance an escape from the authorities, they had to dispose of it. With the officials surely getting closer, there was no time to establish the financial contacts necessary to satisfy the controller. Buddy's mind was cluttered with the problems represented by each alternative.

On the trip home, Buddy rested with his head slumped forward, not asleep, but not his usual talkative self. He turned his head, looked outside the window, but he didn't see the countryside. He said something.

"What?" Buddy's driver hadn't been able to make out what he'd said.

Louder, Buddy began. "I've had considerable time to observe and think since being in this wheel chair."

"I know. I've been right with you since you got out of the hospital."

The driver set his turn signal to turn as he neared the exit to the Louie B. Nunn Parkway East.

"I watched a spider, tiny little fellow, almost transparent, not black or brown like you usually see. Making a web outside my window that first day home from the hospital? It slid down to where the bottom tie ended, then swung out a little farther from the window. He or she puffed up a huge bag, huge that is, in relation to his size, and climbed back along this strand. Again he tied on and repeated the move. Think about how many webs they make that amount to no more than the spit or whatever they use."

After setting the cruise control, the driver glanced over at Buddy. "Don't you wonder where the little bugger gets all that spit?" The driver was still pondering the spider story.

Buddy shifted his weight in the wheelchair locked tight to the floor of the van and didn't respond.

^^^

"Hello, Beck. This is Carl. Bet you weren't 'specting a call from me."

Three weeks after the attack, Carl got transferred to the local nursing home. He was bedfast, in need of continuous nursing care, his voice weak, but there was nothing wrong with his thinking or talking. One to four of his friends from down at the store took breakfast with him each morning.

"Carl! Honey, it's so good to hear from you. I've called most ever body I could think of trying to find out about you and here you are calling me! Halleluiah! My prayers are answered."

Carl had never been called Honey by Beck nor heard her speak so religiously, but nothing she'd ever done surprised him much.

"Beck, I's needing to hear from Freddie and the boy. My nephew, you know the one that's a CPA, and keeps our records, had word that they were with you and Sis. How are they?"

"Good. They're doing good. Jr.'s studying to be a Ford mechanic. Right now he's got part-time work detailing the dealers' used car trade-ins. Freddie's helping him learn the manuals. Course you know Freddie can't read much, but he understands the drawing, I reckon."

"What about old Freddie? How's he?"

"Carl, me and Sis was just talking this morning. Freddie is the best cook, housekeeper, nurse, and caregiver—I think that's what you call it—in the state of Florida."

At first Carl thought he misunderstood and he asked Beck to, "Come over that one more time." Then he began laughing and couldn't quit. He placed his hand over the mouthpiece to keep Beck from hearing and lay looking at the silenced *Andy Griffin Show* on the TV above the bed. When he finally got his breath, he said, "You don't say? Caregiver is he?" Carl again had to cover the mouthpiece. Never in twenty-five or so years had he heard Beck refer to Freddie in any way except to say, "That sorry Freddie." This new found love tickled him. He thought of Amanda and wished she could have heard the report.

Early the next morning Carl's viewing of FOX NEWS was interrupted when the door of his room swung wide.

"Hid'dy Carl, bet you didn't expect us this early, did you?" Tommy, the first to enter, spoke first. Harm followed Tommy, frowning because Tommy who always sat in back down at the store had suddenly crowded in front of him.

"Hid'dy, boys you are a little earlier than common. Don't matter though." Pointing toward the TV, "Ain't no news on that gentleman worth repeatin' nohow."

Carl clicked the remote, silencing the chatter. What's got you two out ahead of the others this morning?" Carl already knew the why, but he wanted to let matters develop as Harm had planned.

"We went to the sale." Tommy's adams-apple bumped up and down as he said this. His hands, palms up, rose and fell with each word. Harm again frowned, shook his head, and moved a chair closer to Carl's bed, virtually blocking Tommy's vision in hopes of gaining control of the report that he'd worked on all morning, in his mind that is. "Carl, it was a sight to see. You know the field between the barn and the road into your place, the one where your Pap used to raise his cane patch. Well, it was chock full of pickup trucks, cars, even the Amish had buggies parked along the fence."

"You don't say!"

Carl knew all about the sale. His nephew, the keeper of his and Freddie's records, had reported the previous evening. Again, he decided to keep quiet and let the report play out. The place had to be sold while he was still able to settle his affairs and make a suitable will, insuring a fair distribution. Nobody was available to farm the land after him.

"Uh huh, a big crowd," Tommy bent around Harm to interject this comment.

"Them boys know how to have a sale." Harm was referring to the auctioneers. I bet there was a hundred chairs lined up out behind the barn under a big tent. The tent reminded me of the one they set up down by the court house, that time the circus come through, must a-been back in forty-nine or fifty. Anyhow, the auctioneer started talking real kind, sorta like a quiet preacher, explaining how he was going to sell this part, then that part, then another part and how anybody could bid, even put the whole three hundred acres together if they wanted to."

Tommy, overcome with his information, jumped to his feet and stood beside Harm, saying, "That auctioneer slapped his hands together and went to pacing back and forth. Four or five work hands he brought with him went to running through the crowd hollering, 'how much you give', and slapping their hands."

Tommy looked around at Harm. Apparently spent, he sat down.

Harm continued his reporting, "The main man said, 'Today is the day. Don't miss out. You may never have another chance to buy prime acres as we're selling for Mr. Sweet today. As you know, he's in the nursing home over there and has charged us with selling this tillable piece of real estate. We want to get the maximum money for our client and you want a bargain. Then he went into the dangest sing-song you ever heerd. I couldn't understand a word of it."

Harm continued, "It brought over a million dollars! Elmo punched me before the auctioneers got started, pointed out a feller on the front row and said, 'He come to buy this place, told somebody it didn't matter to him how high it went.' I didn't know him, but somebody said he'd bought several tracts around."

Carl looked down along the bed over his feet pointed up toward the ceiling, "Heh, heh, I's just thanking. Pap told me he paid eighty-five hundred for the place. Wonder what he'd say about the sale. I already knowed what it brought. My nephew come by last night and told me."

"Well, why in the shoot heck fire did you let us go on so?" Tommy was again leaning around Harm to speak, his eyebrows raised, his jaw set. Harm just grinned. Carl clicked on the TV in search of their favorite morning program—*Gun Smoke.*

Soon after the visit, Carl's nephew, the CPA, had carved on Carl's stone:

---

*HAPPY ARE THOSE WHO LONG TO BE JUST AND GOOD, FOR THEY SHALL BE COMPLETELY SATISFIED,*

Jesus Christ our Lord and Savior

*EPILOGUE*

A message for rehab:

By Deidra Hammock

Who is to interpret the signs for the unwilling or the ill-prepared? Will it be parents, preachers, or teachers? I am one among millions of weakened souls. Assigned names have been used over and over—Deidra, Freddie, Buddy, Keith, and Al along with millions more—from Maine to Washington, from California to Florida. These are repeated in a hundred tongues along the world's routes, within the boundaries of as many countries; our numbers increasing with each new tongue.

Wars fought on my behalf have shed precious blood and drained the wealth. Strategy has failed. As battles rage, some legal and organized, others haphazard gangland style, my babies bleed and are buried. Friends disappear. Rapid-fire guns have been introduced, but often into the wrong hands.

I am one of the weakened souls. I realize that I've traveled in the wrong lane in my life's travels. Often failing to note the roadside sign: *Lane Ends,* and thus required to ride the rough shoulder, the outcome questionable. My only solution: to carry on in the absence of light, to seek smoother surfaces, to dodge dangerous barriers. Find a safe re-entrance ramp.

*But at last I have hope!*

Rehab has been both enlightening and quieting. Lifelines dangling all around previously went unnoticed, not attractive enough, I suppose. Here in rehab, education, therapy, NA/AA, the wisdom of professionals, each attached to me, safety hooks you might say, clutching me, guiding me safely through emotional storms, or brain storms, I don't know which.

My goal is sobriety. I think that it comes from within. Getting it out is *hard work*. Tiring, I need to be continually

nourished by *The Higher Power,* this often manifested through others who care.
*Old me says,*
Oh, but to get high and take no note of life's traffic around me
*Or the perils near lane's end*
*Oh, but not to have to, says the new*
On to the light—red, green, or yellow
Once more to be on the hard surface, in an open lane
Only to be my own driver, even for a day, I pray

*And that that day be today, forever*

---

*A copy of this message to rehab is clipped inside Deidra Hammock's medical file at the rehab center. It represents her last testament before leaving. Again, we are not sure if it is her writing or something she has adapted. Keith* continues *to use it in group discussions.*

# ABOUT THE AUTHOR

email: mullinsrol@gmail.com

Roland D. Mullins, born in 1940, lives in Mt. Vernon. Rockcastle County, Kentucky, the county divided almost equally between the foothills of Appalachia on the east, and the gently rolling hills west to the Bluegrass. His experience and interests include family life, church work, health care, education, politics, and farming in that order.

Made in the USA
Lexington, KY
26 January 2017